Whispers
and
Dreams

Martha Fouts

Toni,
I hope you love this story!
Martha
Fouts

DEDICATION

For my mom and dad, Gary and Paula, two people who've lived their lives listening to whispers and following dreams.

ACKNOWLEDGEMENTS

I have been blessed with a wealth of family, friends, and fellow writers who've encouraged and helped me to complete this book that's so dear to my heart. I want to thank Robin Patchen for editing a large portion of this novel. Her insight and advice was invaluable to this structure of this story. I also want to thank my proofreader, Susan Cofer Fell. Thank you so much for your close reading, Susan – finding all of those irritating little errors! I also want to thank the Oklahoma City Christian Fiction Writers (OCFW) chapter. I know I couldn't have done this without the education and friendships I have received in that group. Special thanks to my beta readers, Staci Deering, Lisa Loeffelholz, Krystal Dillon, and Sherri Kelley – you ladies rock! Thanks also to the amazing people in Discovery Church of Yukon, Oklahoma for their prayers and support for all of my crazy dreams. I love Discovering Destinies in Christ with you! Thanks to my precious sons, Kale, Keaton, and Karter. Thanks for understanding that your mom is a little weird and makes up stories. I love you guys. And lastly, a big thank you to my husband, Kevin Fouts. You are my constant encourager and support. I know that I am truly blessed to have you as my husband. I love you.

Part One: Whispers
Chapter One

The only thing she worried about was the dog. She'd loosened the bulbs on the porch, so they wouldn't shine if someone flipped the switch. She'd hidden the keys to his truck in the silverware drawer in the kitchen, a place where they obviously didn't go, and where he would probably find them tomorrow, but not tonight. But she couldn't conceive a way to keep the dog quiet.

She'd already taken their clothes and few belongings to the room above Tess's diner, where she and the baby would hide until he calmed down. She'd arranged for Tess to come and pick them both up at 1:30. Sometimes he stayed up late, drinking and partying with filthy trash who only hung around as long as the drugs did, but he was always in bed by midnight. He was thirty-one now and seemed to be slowing down a little bit.

But he was still mean.

He wouldn't even care that she and the baby left, not really. He wouldn't even come looking for them after they were gone, she was sure of it. With Sierra dead, he often complained that her mother and the baby were nuisances to have around the house, two extra mouths to feed. An old woman and a useless baby girl.

But Ida was glad she was here. She was glad that Sierra had called her just before she died. Who would take care of the baby if she weren't here? Him? No. He wouldn't go to the store for formula and bottles and diapers. He wouldn't change diapers. It was terrible that Sierra died, of course, but God had his hand on this little baby. She was sure of it.

"Like baby Moses," She looked down at the precious dark haired, dark skinned bundle in her arms. She kissed her sleeping granddaughter on the forehead and said, "God has His hand on you, child."

The baby opened her bright blue eyes and looked at Ida.

"Oh, shh, shh!" She shouldn't have kissed her or said anything. The baby might make noise.

The six month old gave her a smile.

Ida looked out the window again. No sign of Tess.

"Oh Lord, please don't let the dog start barking when Tess gets here," she prayed.

She saw headlights coming down the street. The car pulled into the driveway. It was Tess's minivan.

Ida silently moved across the living room to the front door. She opened it and stepped out on the long porch. She looked down one side of the big porch and then the other side, but didn't see the ugly dog. Thank the Lord.

She ran down the porch steps to Tess's minivan. Tess jumped out and slid the side door open. She had a car seat already in place in the back of the van.

"Here, give her to me, and I'll buckle her in."

"Bless you, Tess," said Ida as she handed her grandchild to the woman.

"Don't mention it, Ida." The big woman looked down at the baby. "Hey doll, are you comfy in your basket of bulrushes?"

The baby cooed a soft reply.

Tess climbed into the front seat and pulled the seatbelt across her big frame. She put the minivan in reverse and pulled on to the street. They drove a couple of blocks to the diner on Main Street that she and her husband, Phil owned. They pulled into the alley behind the diner and Phil was waiting at the back door.

Ida got the baby out of the car seat and they went upstairs. Tess and Phil had already unpacked and set up a small bed, a crib, and a swing.

"Sorry it's so small. We didn't know if the baby liked

swings or not. Our kids always liked them when they were little, so we got her one." Phil said.

Ida was speechless. She hugged Tess and Phil. The baby had fallen asleep during the short ride, so she put her in her new crib. She laid her on her back and pulled the soft blanket Tess had put in the crib over her legs.

Ida smoothed down the sleeping angel's black hair. "There, you like your new bed, princess?"

She turned to Tess and Phil. "I think we'll be fine. He'll be mad for a few days, but he'll get over it soon. My only regret is that I couldn't take the boy."

"We can get him, too. There's plenty of room for him here," said Phil.

Ida shook her head. "No, the boy is his pride and joy. He doesn't hurt him. He would never let him leave."

"Well, we'd better go and let you all get some rest. Phil is going to sleep downstairs. He has a cot in the kitchen. He also has a gun."

Ida nodded. How she hoped he wouldn't need it.

"Thank you so much. You have no idea how much this means to me."

Phil reached over and gave Ida a hug. "It's our pleasure. It's what the Lord would have us to do . . . ah, I don't think I even know your name."

"I'm Ida, and this is my grandbaby, Whisper."

*****

From my spot at the back of the line in the foyer I can see through the rectangular windows in the back doors of the sanctuary. The candle lighters, my eleven year old twin cousins, are making tiny flames appear in perfect unison on opposite sides of the stage, as my friend Theresa sings the ballad that has been special to Brian and me since high school.

My dad squeezes my hand. I look up at him, and he

gives me a smile. He looks perfect in his black tuxedo and clean-shaven face. I look down at my bouquet of fuchsia tulips and pale pink roses, fresh cut and tied together at the stems with a wide silver satin ribbon. It's perfect.

The doors open. Lisa steps into the sanctuary and walks down the aisle, and the wedding coordinator and her assistant silently close the doors behind her as the music swells at the precise time Lisa makes it to the stage. Perfect.

The doors open again. Now it's time for Krystal to clutch her rose and tulip bouquet and step inside. When she takes the first step inside the sanctuary, I feel it.

It's like a tightening in the center of my chest and a breath on my forearms at the same time.

No, no, no, no, no.

Krystal is halfway down the aisle and the sensation in the center of my chest tightens even more. I can see Brian through the window. He looks perfect today. He played golf yesterday with his groomsmen, and the day in the sun brought out the highlights in his hair and bronzed his skin perfectly.

The hairs on my arm stand up as Krystal makes it to her spot on the steps. I thought I could go through it without feeling this. I thought I could just ignore it and it would go away.

Only one more bridesmaid – Staci.

I swallow and look at my dad again. He tilts his head in a question. Then he grabs my shoulders and wrinkles my veil when he sees the tears.

Staci turns around and looks at me. I shake my head. She puts her hand to her mouth and nods.

*****

August is usually my favorite month. Here it is, ten o'clock at night and it's still over ninety degrees. I trail my fingers in the water as I lay on the inflatable raft in my parents' pool. I admire my perfect French manicure, as the water slips between my fingers, remember that I did not get married at two o'clock this afternoon, and grab the flowerpot I've been holding in my lap. I sit up and vomit in it – again. The flowerpot is almost full – again. I'll have to go clean it out – again.

I must get my mind off of this. I did it. No sense re-examining the situation, or worrying if I did the right thing. I did it – the thing I have wanted to do for at least two years. Seriously, two years? Did I really let it rock on so long? Why didn't I do it sooner?

I'm embarrassed to admit the truth. I was afraid of ending up alone.

At twenty-two years old, I was afraid if I broke up with Brian, I would never find anyone else, and I'd wind up like my mom's friend Barb, who is in her fifties and lives all alone. Unless you counted her two little dogs. She dresses those dumb dogs like kids. She works all day as a civil engineer, comes home at six o'clock, lets her dogs out of their crate, feeds them, takes them for a walk, eats dinner, and then watches TV and plays games on her computer all night. And I was afraid if I broke up with Brian, I'd end up just like Barb. Honestly, I'm still afraid of it. I know it's ridiculous because I'm so young. I should have broken it off the minute I felt The Whisper.

The Whisper is what I started calling the feeling I had. I guess I felt that if I named it, I could deal with it. You know, kind of like identifying the problem. But, even though I named it, I still didn't know how to deal with it, and it will not go away.

I didn't always feel The Whisper. I certainly didn't feel it on my first date with him, but that was back in high school, and that football game was so loud, maybe The Whisper wasn't loud enough. When we went to prom our senior year, he told me he loved me the first time, and I said those huge words back. I truly meant them. I did love him.

When we went to college together I didn't hear it either. But, maybe we were just too busy to hear it. When he asked me to marry him, all I could hear was wedding bells, and all I could see was wedding dresses, gift registries, engagement pictures, and that perfect diamond ring.

The Whisper started the end of our sophomore year in college. It followed me like a black cloud through my junior year, senior year, student teaching, and wedding planning. A few months ago my brother told me that he hadn't heard me laugh in years. Michael's comment has been reverberating ever since.

I swallow more of my stomach acid. Must think of something else. Anything else. I can't throw up again. I hate throwing up. I look around my parents' backyard, trying to find something else to focus on, but the diving board reminds me of Brian's front-flip dives, the yellow tablecloth on the picnic table next to the porch swing reminds me of my yellow prom dress, mom's pink begonias in pots perfectly lined up on the steps up to the pool remind me of the bouquet I held this afternoon, the grill reminds me of Brian and my dad grilling steaks. Enough looking around.

I close my eyes and remember taking the cake to the Jesus House with my little brother this afternoon. We took Michael's horrible little truck, because my car was parked in my parents' garage. I hadn't driven it to the church, because Brian and I were planning to go directly to the airport to leave for our honeymoon. Walt Disney World.

I think about all of the money spent on airfare and tickets, and I hurl again. Time to clean out mom's flowerpot. I ease off of the inflatable raft into the water and walk to the steps. I wrap up in my towel, then dump my puke in mom's flowerbed and head over to dad's outdoor sink next to the grill to wash the pot out.

Michael was driving and I was on the passenger side of his little truck. The four-tier cake was sitting between us in the big, white box. We drove downtown to the Jesus House

in total silence. Michael's not much of a talker anyway, and I
certainly didn't feel like talking.

Michael pulled into the parking lot, killed the truck,
and turned to me.

"It's all right." He nodded and pressed his thin lips
together. Then he placed his hand on my forearm
awkwardly. He looked at me with his deep chocolate brown
eyes that match both my eyes and our mom's eyes. "I think
you did good, sis. It's . . . it's . . . well, good job."

I smiled and patted my cute little seventeen-year-old
brother's hand. "Thanks, Michael."

We struggled to get the big box out of the truck. We
finally got it out and then started across the parking lot with
Michael holding one side and me holding the other. We
entered through the glass doors of the downtown Oklahoma
City mission and stopped at the reception desk. Seated
behind the desk is a woman with brown hair piled on to her
head with a dozen bobby pins.

"Oh my, what have you got there?" she asked.

"It's a cake. Would anyone here be able to eat it?" I
asked, not wanting to say that it is my unused wedding cake
that was supposed to feed the two hundred and fifty guests
at my wedding. That it's an Italian Crème cake with raspberry
filling that Brian and I picked out from Johnnie's Sweet
Creations. That we made an appointment, met with a baker
and a groom's cake designer, picked out this cake and
designed his OSU groom's cake, complete with Pistol Pete
on the top.

She lifted the lid and peeked inside. "Oh wow, that's
beautiful. Let me go check if we have any space in our cold
storage. If so, I'm sure they'll want to serve that for dessert
tomorrow. I'll be right back."

She walked out of the room through an open
doorway, weaving her way through tables filled with raggedly
dressed people until I couldn't see her anymore. Did she
look at me funny?

Michael and I looked at each other across the top of the lid. He gave me one of his sideways grins, the same kind of grin he gives the catcher just before he throws one of his famous pitches. I shifted my weight. The cake was getting heavy.

The woman came back, two men trailing behind. They looked like they must be homeless or residents of the shelter or whatever you're supposed to call them. They were slightly frightening with their dirty faces, long, stringy hair and ripped t-shirts.

"We have room in the cold storage. I'm so glad. Everyone's going to love the cake. Chuck and David here will help carry it."

The two men rumbled over to me and Michael and the cake. Michael and I carefully transferred the sleek white cake box to their rough leathery hands.

"Thank you girlie," Chuck or David said to me in a gruff voice.

"Didn't you even eat one piece?" the other one asked me.

With a nervous giggle, the woman with high hair scolded him. "Oh, Chuck, let's not ask her that."

I tried to think of an answer, but only came up with, "I guess I'm not in the mood for cake."

"But you ought to try it," Chuck said. "Hey Davey, let's set it down so the girlie can try a piece."

I shook my head and held up a hand. "No, it's okay."

But they ignored me. They sat the cake box on the desk and opened it.

"You got a fork?" Chuck asked us.

Michael and I looked at each other. Michael said, "Not on me."

"Wait, I have one." She opened her desk drawer. "Here, I keep plastic ones in my desk for lunch." She handed Chuck the fork.

Chuck grabbed it, leaned down into the big box and

cut a slice from the top tier. He pulled his hand out of the box. A small, perfect slice of the Italian Crème wedding cake with raspberry filling was resting on his rough, brown hand. He held the cake up to my mouth.

"Here you go, girlie. Take a bite."

That morning I thought I'd be eating this cake out of Brian's hand. Brian in his classic black tuxedo, freshly shaven face, every hair on his head in place; the freckles on his nose, freckles from the sun, even though he's twenty-two years old, his long golden eyelashes over his hazel eyes, wise eyes, the eyes of someone who considers things, a thinker, a smart, accomplished man who truly loves me.

"Thank you." I took the cake from Chuck the Homeless Man's hand and sunk my teeth in for a bite. It was delicious.

Now, hours later, I sit on the porch swing next to the pool in my parents' backyard. I have my trusty flowerpot in my lap. Behind me, the patio door opens. I hear my mom's voice.

"Missy, Brian's here."

I nod. Time to face it.

I turn around and there he is. I don't know why, but for some reason I expected him to still be in his tuxedo, but of course he's not. He's wearing jeans and an OSU T-shirt.

"Hey." I set the flowerpot on the ground and press my hands together, not sure what to do with them, since I usually hug him when I see him.

He takes two steps outside the door and stops.

Should I apologize? But what good would saying I'm sorry do now? Should I tell him that I love him? Do I love him?

He finally begins, "I thought you were okay, Missy. I mean, I knew you were a little scared, but I thought you were okay. Last night we had such a great talk . . . I . . . just," He puts his hand over his eyes. "Just tell me. Are we over?"

In the five years I've been with Brian, I've only seen

him cry a couple of times, once was at his grandpa's funeral and once was in church when he was praying. I don't know if I can bear to see him cry right now.

I'm an awful, awful person.

"I'm sorry." I scoot over on the porch swing. "Come sit here."

He walks across the concrete patio to the swing and sits next to me and faces straight ahead, staring at my parents' pool, refusing to look at me.

"I'm sorry. I don't know what's going on with me."

He picks up a Frisbee that Michael must've left on the ground next to the swing. He pats the plastic disk against his thigh. "Not even a year."

Not even a year? What does he mean?

"In less than a year we can afford a house, Missy. Probably about ten months." He keeps patting the Frisbee — pat, pat, pat.

"But the apartment's nice." Pat, pat.

"You start your job soon. I love my new job in the city. It's all set." Pat, pat, pat. Finally he turns to look at me and sets the Frisbee back on the ground. "Now what?"

What can I say? I'm honestly not sure if I love him. I respect him. I admire him. I think he's handsome and will make someone a wonderful husband one day . . . but do I love him?

I don't say all of that.

"I'm so sorry. I know that all of your relatives and our friends were there, and it's awful. I'm sure your parents and your brother and sister all hate me. I just couldn't do it, and I really, really don't know exactly why."

"Couldn't do it just today or can't do it ever or what? What should I do? Should I wait for you to get over this or should I leave you alone? My feelings haven't changed, Missy. I still love you. In my heart we were already married. I could see our future." He finally turns and looks at me. He smiles a faint smile and picks up my hands. "I've been looking at a house – I haven't even told you about it yet – it's right around the corner from my parents' house. I could see us buying that house, living in it forever."

Brian's parents live in a clean and friendly housing addition called Summer Valley, two housing additions over from my parents' addition, Lost Lake. Both additions are filled with beautiful, well-built brick homes stretched across a flat plain, and neither are anywhere near a valley or a lake. I'm sure the house Brian has picked out for us has at least three bedrooms, two bathrooms, a kitchen with a breakfast bar, maybe two living areas, a home office, and a good sized fenced backyard. Who wouldn't want that? There are people in this world who would consider that a mansion. It's just that lately I hear The Whisper every time I drive in the old part of town, the five blocks right behind Main Street. Every time I drive through that area I have to take a few minutes to drive slowly, up and down each of those five streets to see the houses that are as old as the town. The intricate brickwork, the second-story porches, the wraparound porches, the stained glass windows, the gated courtyards and brick pathways, detached garages with little apartments above them. Houses in the additions don't have any character like those old charmers.

Brian is still talking, "I could see you working for a couple of years and then taking a break so we could have kids. I could actually see the faces of the two or three children we talked about having. Remember when we used to talk about kids? We had names picked out at one time. What were they?"

He tilts his head, waiting for me to respond. Of course I remember. I can't bear to say the names, though.

"Hayden for a boy and Hadley for a girl. Remember babe?" He looks at me like he's trying to bring me back to life, like I'm lost somewhere inside my own head, and he's trying to make contact with the real me.

I drop my head and pull my hands out of his. What

can I say? That those names are meaningless now? That those names were connected to the images of a blonde haired, brown-eyed boy and a red haired, brown-eyed girl, but now those images are gone? I loved the "H" names we picked out, but lately I've been thinking about names that actually mean something for my future children, and I knew that Brian would think that was weird.

"Maybe it was all too much for you. Maybe the crowd looking at you and the extravagance freaked you out. Maybe we need to get married somewhere private, like here, in your parents' backyard - right here at the pool. This would be the perfect place for a small ceremony, just our families and us. What do you think?"

I know for a fact that The Whisper doesn't have anything to do with those things. But, I can't explain The Whisper at all, and his explanation sounds so much better.

"Maybe you're right." I hate myself for lying. Why can't I just be honest and tell him about The Whisper? "Maybe the crowd and the dress and the decorations and everything were just all too much." I'm such a wimp.

He takes my hands again. "Okay, that's okay." He's smiling now, happy to have an explanation for my ditching him at the altar. Nerves. Just scared, just overwhelmed at the spectacle of a big wedding, easily explained to all of our friends and family. "Why don't we call Pastor Kevin and see if he can marry us right now? We can do it right out here. It's a gorgeous night. What do you say?"

I open my mouth to respond, but nothing comes out.

He waits for me to respond, to say, "Yes! That sounds wonderful!" To say what any sane girl would say right now in this situation – a good looking, smart guy with a great job proposing marriage and a life filled with comfort and children in your hometown – What is my problem? This is the dream! Why can't I say yes?

Finally he gets it. He stands. "I still love you, Missy."

He turns and walks away.

*****

The house is quiet. My family debated going to church or not, didn't know if they should leave me alone. But was that the real reason they thought about not going? Was the real reason embarrassment? They didn't want to face everyone? In the end, their commitment and sense of responsibility won. Mom teaches the primary grades Sunday School class, dad is an usher, and Michael plays guitar on the worship team. So the Kolar Family went to church to fulfill their responsibilities, even though they would have to face the hundred or so people who had expected to see their daughter get married the day before.

They're the brave ones. I'm the chicken.

I'm lying in my bed, propped up on pillows, feeling sorry for myself and hungry, but not wanting to get out of bed and go downstairs to the kitchen to make a bowl of cereal. I'm a mess. What am I going to do now? Keep living with my parents? I guess I could. I could teach fifth grade all day and come home at night to my parents' house. Not exactly the life I'd envisioned, but what life do I want?

I desperately need to do something productive. I grab my red leather-bound journal on my nightstand and the pen setting next to it. I open my journal and start to write a prayer. The pen won't write. Of course.

I lean over to put the journal and pen back. This is the story of my life right now. The stupid pen doesn't even have ink. When I set the journal and pen on the nightstand, I see another pen there and grab it. Words flood into my brain and I know what I need to write.

You say you've planned my future
But from all the evidence I see
I'm not so sure
You know what to do with me.

What can be done with a pen with no ink?
With a flashlight with no battery?
I'm hearing a voice, but it's not distinct.
I feel like I haven't had my morning coffee.

From your lofty place in Heaven
How can you proclaim Jeremiah 29:11 over me?

I look at the clock on my nightstand. Eleven thirty-three. They'll be home by twelve-fifteen. The singing is probably over by now, and Pastor Kevin is probably preaching.

I re-read my little poem. No one else will ever see it. It's just for me and the Lord, in my journal along with lots of other poems, drawings, and prayers. I can't imagine what Brian or my parents or my friends would say if they saw my journals. They would probably think I had the swinging emotions of a dramatic thirteen-year-old girl.

I love to hear Pastor Kevin preach. His sermons are so down-to-earth and helpful. Maybe he'll say something today that could help me? I slide out of bed and cross my bedroom to my desk to get my laptop. I get back in bed, slide under the covers, prop my head up on the mountain of pillows, and open my computer. I go to our church website and click on the live streaming button. I'm expecting to see the face of Pastor Kevin and hear his voice.

But, when the live streaming window opens, Pastor Kevin is not on the screen. Instead there's a young guy in a denim shirt and black jeans standing behind the pulpit preaching. Ugh, of course. Everything is going wrong. I just wanted to hear my pastor preach, not some visiting minister or traveling evangelist, or whatever this guy is.

I almost close my computer, but stop when I hear the strange man quote a scripture.

"'For I know the plans I have for you, declares the Lord, plans to prosper you and not to harm you, plans to give you hope and a future.'" The man closes the Bible and looks at the congregation, at me through the Internet. "That is the scripture I have held on to for the last four years. I didn't know how God was going to build a mission and reach these people in the middle of nowhere. I didn't know how God was going to help me to build relationships with them. I didn't know how I could make any difference at all in their lives, but I knew that I had to do something, and I knew that God had a plan."

Oh my word. Is this a coincidence that he's preaching about the very verse I just questioned in my poem? Who is this guy? He must be some sort of missionary. I almost close my laptop again. No offense to missionaries, but this isn't going to help me in my situation. I've gone to church my whole life, and I know what it's like when a missionary comes to visit. For one thing, they talk too long. I guess they're used to the attention spans of non-Americans, which are probably longer than ours. They talk about their ministry to disadvantaged people somewhere, talk about how we can help them, and take up an offering. I know I sound self-centered, but I just had a huge heart-breaking event in my life, and I'm searching for answers. Hearing about this guy's ministry to . . . where did he say he was a missionary to?

Now he's pointing at something to his right while he's talking. "Just ninety miles northwest. This is all just ninety miles from here. Can you believe it? Can you believe that such poverty exists so close to home? I couldn't believe it when I first saw it. People live in houses with dirt floors. There was no church at all four years ago. Over eighty percent of the adults are alcoholics or drug abusers. Many houses have no running water. The school can't find enough qualified teachers who are willing to move there and teach in such a rural place, so many grade levels are combined and teachers must teach multiple grade levels at once. These people need *people*. They need ministers, teachers, teams of people to come and stay."

Wow, where is this place? He said it was ninety miles northwest? It sounds like another country. Is this really in Oklahoma? And this speaker – a missionary, I guess. He certainly doesn't look like any missionary I've ever seen. He has the tanned and lean looks of a guy who works outside doing physical labor. His denim shirt and jeans make him look more like a laid-back associate professor or something. He has short dark brown hair and jet-black eyes, and he looks so young. He doesn't even look thirty.

"You may be asking, how can I help? I can't just leave my job and move. Well, you can help in many ways."

Here we go, the plea for money. Like I said, I don't need this right now.

"At our mission we provide free hot meals, have a clothes closet, and we provide free after school childcare and tutoring. Can you please pray that we can find qualified teachers and childcare workers to help us? We have the facilities, and we have the income from generous churches like yours. What we really need are people to commit to move to Diniyoli Mission and minister with us."

And then I feel it. The familiar little tingle in the center of my chest and the almost audible hum. The Whisper.

"This is what I want to leave with you today, that God has a plan for you." His face on the computer screen looks right at me, and for half a second I wonder if he can see me. "Your plans will get messed up. Your plans will leave you feeling empty, but God's plan for your life is perfect. All you have to do is find it. God has promised that He will answer you when you call out to Him."

I can't believe I'm thinking this. Could this be God's plan for me?

He asks the congregation if any of them would like special prayer to find God's plan, and they pray. Then he closes the service by saying, "Thanks so much for letting me come here today. You all have a very nice church. I'll be leaving here today to go directly to the mission. Please keep us in your prayers."

And then he turns and walks down the steps, the same steps where 2 of my bridesmaids were lined up yesterday, and there is Pastor Kevin, telling everyone that they are going to take up an offering for the Diniyoli Mission and Reverend Chaney. "Church, you've always stepped up to help missionaries overseas, and now it's time for us to help a domestic missionary. I've visited Reverend Chaney's mission, and I can tell you that he and his team are making a real impact on the community there."

Pastor Kevin prays over the offering and then I close my computer. I stare at the ceiling of my bedroom, "Lord, what is<$n> your plan for me?" I lie there for a minute and wait for some sort of response.

I open my computer again, go online and look at a map of Oklahoma to see where Diniyoli is.

*****

Chapter Two

After a huge cup of overpriced coffee and an hour and a half on the road, I'm in desperate need of a bathroom. I should be seeing signs for Diniyoli by now, but I just see big, flat open fields with old, run-down houses here and there.

My phone tells me I have arrived in Diniyoli, but I still don't see any signs. Yesterday afternoon I called Pastor Kevin and asked him if he could give me the phone number of the missionary who preached that morning. Pastor Kevin gave me the number for Reverend Kirk Chaney, and then proceeded to ask me how I was doing.

"I'm fine, thank you."

"Do you need to talk to someone?"

"No thank you, Pastor."

"You're always welcome to come by the church and talk sometime, if you need to."

I knew he meant well, but talking about the wedding-that-did-not-happen is the last thing I want to do. I don't want to start throwing up again. I called Reverend Chaney, but he didn't answer. Instead a very grouchy female answered.

"Mission."

"Oh, ah, hello. This is Mis . . . Melissa Kolar from Cool Springs Family Chapel. Reverend Chaney was at our church this morning."

"Who?"

"Melissa Kolar from –

"No, Reverend? Oh, you mean Kirk. Yeah."

I'm a little taken aback. I would have thought that someone who answered the phone at a mission would be a little nicer.

"Well, Reverend Chaney, ah Kirk, said that you needed people to work there, and I wanted to drive out and check it out. I'm already contracted to teach here at Cool Springs this year, but I thought it might be something I could do next year, or even volunteer over the summer."

Silence.

"Are you there?"

"Yeah."

"Okay, so, will Reverend Chaney be there tomorrow so I can talk to him? Or maybe there would be someone else there that I could talk to about working with you? I can drive over there in the morning."

"He gets here at eight."

"I'll drive out there tomorrow then. Thank you."

Click.

One thing Reverend Chaney needs at his mission is a friendlier receptionist.

*****

A large blue metal sign on the side of the road reads, "Welcome to Diniyoli." There are brightly colored feathers underneath the words, like the feathers in a Native American headdress. Maybe now I'll see some stores or something, hopefully somewhere with a clean bathroom, but I'm not getting my hopes too high for that.

A few minutes later I see two buildings. I'm ready to turn in to their parking lot, but I see that both businesses are closed. A few more minutes pass and I see what looks like an old fashioned downtown main street, complete with sidewalks and big glass storefronts. I expected to see abject poverty, but this place doesn't look too bad. Cars parked in front of businesses, people milling around, a single flashing light hanging in the middle of an intersection. I park in front of a diner and go inside to use the restroom.

Back in my car, I find the mission on my phone GPS. Just five miles West. I turn left at the intersection, and

quickly realize that the single flashing light is probably the
only traffic light in town, and that the downtown businesses
on Main Street are probably the only businesses in town.
Right behind Main Street I see the school, Diniyoli Public
Schools, kindergarten through high school all on one
campus. The school doesn't look too bad. It's extremely
small, but it looks well maintained with nice, safe playground
equipment and a sign out front that reads, "School starts
August 18th!"

After the school, the houses appear. It seems like the
town was Scotch taped together haphazardly, not like the
evenly spaced apart neighborhoods of Cool Springs, where
homes are grouped together in additions by price range. On
my left I see a tiny house with weathered siding and a rusted
metal awning hanging over the front door. On my right there
is a newer trailer home on cinder blocks. About a block
down a house catches my eye. It's beautiful – or at least it
once was. I slow my car so I can look at it. Now in complete
disrepair, it must have been a beauty in the early1900s. It
looks like it's three stories tall with windows at every level, all
white exterior that looks like it hasn't been painted in
decades, and a huge porch with columns wraps all the way
around the house. It's exactly that kind of house I would
love to buy and bring it back to its former glory. Now, the
shutters are rotted and hanging, the windows are wide open
and bedsheets are flying in and out, and an old couch is in
the middle of the overgrown yard.

Brian said we could own our own house in ten
months. I swallow it down. I didn't bring mom's flowerpot,
so I'd better quit thinking about that.

I keep driving through the residential part of town –
I'm guessing the only residential part of town – past more
houses with weathered siding and rotting roofs and new and
old trailers, and every now and then a small well-cared for
home or trailer, but not many of those. After two blocks the
houses stop, and the road that was nicely paved and clearly

painted becomes a bumpy chip and seal road with a crumbling shoulder. After another mile it becomes a gravel road, and then I'm driving on a dirt road.

On my left I start to see a few more houses. All of these houses look alike and are evenly spaced apart, but these are not like the cookie-cutter houses in my suburban neighborhood. These tiny houses look like their siding is made of some sort of paper. Most of the houses look like they don't have a front door or their front door is open. Many of them have barrels for burning trash in the front yard. A few houses have motorhomes parked next to them.

My GPS tells me to turn left onto a street named Old Reservation Road. Now these paper houses with no front doors surround me. On either side of my car, on both sides of the dirt road little scraggly patches of weedy grass like welcome mats lay in front of each house. On the weedy patches are piled scraps of plywood, milk crates, and old furniture. Kids are everywhere. Through my closed windows I can hear them shouting and laughing. Riding bikes next to my car, playing in the little yards with each other, every one of them has different shades of dark hair and tan skin. They are beautiful.

At the end of the unnamed road I see a metal building with its double front doors open. A wooden sign sticking in the yard in front of the building says, "Church."

Next to the church is an open grassy lot. There are soccer nets, a basketball court, a backstop with spray painted baselines and squares painted in the grass to represent bases and a pitcher's mound with an intense game underway. I watch for a minute. A tall, thin boy in a red Cardinals hat who looks to be about eleven pitches a beautiful pitch and strikes out a boy who looks to about fourteen. The team in the field yells a cheer and runs in to bat. Next to the ball field is an acre of freshly mowed grass, filled with more kids. They are running wildly with their hands above their heads, arms stretched out wide with huge smiles on their faces and laughing like crazy.

    I pull my dark blue Honda Accord into the open lot and park next to the church. I can't help but smile. These kids are seriously happy about something right now. One of them runs into me and wraps her arms around me. Her head comes up to my waist. She looks up at me with blue eyes that are strikingly bright against her dark skin and smiles a huge smile that reveals the cutest gap between her front two teeth. She yells, "I got you wet!"

    She lets go and runs away. I look down, and sure enough, my clothes are soaked. Now I see what they are all going crazy over. Someone is standing in the middle of the open field with a water hose spraying every kid he can reach.

    I start to walk toward him, but I don't want to get wet. Then I recognize who it is. Standing there like a big kid with a huge smile on his face, laughing as much as any kid there and soaked to the skin in his T-shirt, shorts, and sandals, is the missionary, Reverend Chaney.

*****

    I think about walking out to the middle of the lot to talk to him, but I think better of it. I'd rather not get sprayed with a water hose right now. Instead, I go inside the church, where the air conditioning blows right into my face and is a welcome relief. One step inside the door, and I'm in the sanctuary, no foyer in this church. The sanctuary looks like it probably seats about a hundred and fifty people. An aisle goes down the middle, right up to the stage. There's a hallway to my left, so I turn, looking for someone. The first door in the hallway has a small sign on it that reads, "Church Office." The door is closed, but there's a window next to the door. The blinds are open, and I can see a sixty-ish year old Native American woman sitting at a desk, typing on an ancient desktop computer. I knock on the office door. Through the window, I can see her huff, roll her eyes, and continue typing.

Is she going to ignore me? This must be the lively conversationalist I spoke to on the phone yesterday. I knock again.

Eyes roll. She looks at me through the window. "The door's unlocked."

I turn the knob and step inside the tiny office, which only holds one cheap desk and two old wooden visitors' chairs in front of the desk.

"Hi, I'm Melissa Kolar. I called yesterday about—"

"I remember. You're the teacher, and you want to see what kind of help we need around here, but you can't help until next summer."

"Well, yes—"

She puts one arm on the desk and leans her large bosoms on it. "Look, we need help right now, honey. See all those kids out there? They need tutors, counselors, teachers, and people to play with them. The drug dealers in town know how to invest time in these kids, and we need church people to get off their—"

"Tess!"

She stops midsentence and slides her eyes up. "I'm sorry Kirk, but you know it's true."

I turn my head to look up at Reverend Chaney standing behind me. When I saw him on the computer I knew he was handsome, of course, but now that he's standing so close to me I'm surprised at how handsome he is in person, and I hope he can't tell that I've momentarily stopped breathing.

He smiles at her. "Can I help with something here?"

I stick out my hand. "Hi, I'm Melissa Kolar. I'm from Cool Springs, and I heard you yesterday. I just wanted to come out here and see what I can do to help. I'm a teacher, and I'm already under contract with Cool Springs Schools for this year, but I was thinking maybe I could come and do some work here next summer?"

He takes my hand and shakes it. "Nice to meet you, Melissa. I'm Kirk. I'd be happy to show you around and talk about the place. The kids are all occupied with their popsicle break. Janice, one of our mentors, is getting them all sugared up."

His hands are rough, like sandpaper. He has a towel draped over his shoulders, and he has a new, dry blue T-shirt on, and his super-short brown hair is already dry.

"Tess, could you please call Mr. Clemmons and tell him that I can meet with him later today about the afterschool program?"

Tess just says "Hmm."

"Come on. I'll show you around."

Reverend Chaney steps out of the office and waits for me to join him. Then he walks down the short hallway toward the sanctuary.

"This is our sanctuary, obviously. We have church services here on Sunday evenings at six o'clock. We also have a lot of meetings that take place here through the week. We have classes on overcoming addictions, parenting, personal budgeting, and several Bible studies that are taught here every week. We have volunteers from nearby churches and some people who live here who teach these classes."

He leads me down the center aisle of the sanctuary, and continues explaining, "We bought two acres for this church about five years ago." On either side the pews are the old fashioned kind, all wood with no padding at all. We walk through the altar area in front of the small stage. There are two wooden altars for people to kneel and pray. In the center of the platform there is a small wooden lectern. Assorted instruments everywhere—several guitars and tambourines, an electric keyboard, a drum set in the corner. There are also at least a dozen microphones in their stands, lined up on the side of the stage. I follow him to a door on the left of the stage, next to the drums. He opens it and holds it for me. I walk through and he follows.

"Back here we have our fellowship hall and kitchen."

This Janice must be some sort of kid-whisperer, because all of the same kids who were screaming and running around outside a few moments ago are now sitting cross-legged on a plastic tarp spread over the carpeted floor of the fellowship hall quietly sucking on brightly colored popsicles.

Reverend Chaney walks across the big room to Janice, a short, fifty-ish year old woman with shoulder length brown hair and warm brown eyes. He gives her a sideways hug and motions to me to join them.

"This is Janice, an angel on Earth."

She blushes and giggles and waves him away.

"Oh you," she says.

"Janice, this is Melissa. She's from Cool Springs. She came by to tour the facility. She's thinking about helping out next summer."

"That would be great! Would you want to meet some of the kids now? We were just getting ready to break up into reading groups. I have the older kids in charge of four to five younger ones. The older kids read a story to the little ones. I just walk around and monitor the groups. Want to help?"

"Sure." This is exactly the kind of activity I'll probably be doing a lot of in a couple of weeks when I start teaching. My job is fifth grade language arts, and I've been taught that reading aloud helps students' fluency and comprehension.

Then, Janice shows how a smart and calm teacher can control a roomful, even when she's outnumbered forty to one. She says, "Take out the . . ."

And the kids all get up and respond, "Papers and the trash," as they throw their popsicle sticks in the wastebasket.

Then Janice says, "Or you don't get no . . ."

"Spending cash," the kids all say as they find their assigned reading circles.

Then she says, "Yakkity yak . . ."

"Don't talk back!" they all finish. And the forty or so kids in the room have every single popsicle stick thrown away and are sitting in their assigned reading circle with their hands folded in their laps. Wow.

Reverend Chaney leans over to me and whispers, "She's amazing."

I just nod. I could probably learn a lot from this lady about classroom management.

She grabs a box of books from the kitchen countertop and starts handing books to the older kids who are the group readers.

"Okay, readers, remember to read with expression. You don't want to bore your listeners. Also, we have a visitor, Miss Melissa, so show her how good you are, and remember, I'll be walking around and monitoring, so do your best!"

All the kids look at me when she says my name, and I smile at them. I see the girl with the bright blue eyes in one of the groups across the room. She smiles at me and shows the gap between her teeth and waves at me to come over to her.

The older kids open their books and start reading aloud. The younger kids sit cross-legged or lean forward on their elbows or lie on their bellies and rest their chins on their hands and listen to the tales.

I walk through the groups toward my little friend. When I get to her group, she scoots over and pats the ground next to her. I sit where she has indicated. The boy in the red Cardinals cap, the pitcher, is reading to this group. He's turned his cap around with the bill on the back of his head, and there's a signature written on the cap stretched across his forehead – *Adam Wainwright* – I recognize the name. He's a player Michael talks a lot about. The good-looking, dark-skinned boy is reading *Holes* by Louis Sachar. I listen to the description of Camp Green Lake and smile at the descriptions of Armpit, X-Ray, Mr. Sir, and Stanley

Yelnats. I lean back on my hands, and my new little friend rests her head on my knee.

After twenty minutes, Janice says, "All right everyone. Reading time is over."

The kids all groan, and I suddenly realize that I stayed in the same group the whole time, and I was supposed to walk around and monitor the groups. The tall, thin boy who was the reader in our group did such a great job that I forgot.

Little blue eyes lifts her head up from my knee, rubs her eyes and looks at me.

"Did you like that book?" I ask her.

She nods. "Yeah, it was good. Have you read it before?"

"A few times."

"Really? You've read it more than once? You must like it. What happens? Is Stanley really bad? Did he do something bad? Does he make it out of the camp?"

I smile. "I can't tell you. Part of the fun of reading is finding out the ending on your own."

She rolls her eyes.

Janice uses another amazing singing call and response to tell the kids that it's time to clean up. The kids rush to obey. This lady definitely has a gift.

As my new little friend and I are helping Janice put books away and roll up mats, I ask her, "What's your name?"

"Whisper."

My chin almost hits the floor. "Well . . . that's a beautiful name."

It's just a coincidence that her name is Whisper. It doesn't mean anything. It's not like I told God that if a little girl was named Whisper I would move here or anything like that. It's not a big deal.

She's smiling at me.

"How old are you?"

"I'm seven. Hey, want to see my dog? He's cute."

"Uh, I'm not sure . . ." I look around. Where is Reverend Chaney? I wonder if he's going to finish the tour?

"Oh come on, I live right down the street. You can walk me home."

"Let me ask Janice if Reverend Chaney has anything else to show me."

Janice is stacking the books in a crate. "Kirk had to leave to meet with Mr. Clemmons, the school superintendent and principal. He was going to tell you where he was going, but he said that you looked like you were enjoying yourself and he didn't want to interrupt. He said to tell you that you are more than welcome to come and help anytime you want, even if it's before the summer. I think he could tell that the kids liked you." Janice says, winking.

I'm not sure why she winked. I thank her and turn to Whisper, "Okay, let's go see your dog."

Whisper claps and grabs my hand and we walk out the side door of the fellowship hall to the big grassy lot where the kids were playing earlier. She leads me to the dirt road in front of the mission, and we walk to her house. She's telling me about her dog.

"At first my grandma said I couldn't keep him, but after she saw how cute he was, she couldn't let him go. Now, my grandma loves him too. He's all black, except for a little white spot right here." She lifts her chin and points to a spot at the base of her neck. "I wish we could keep him in the house, but grandma says, 'No way.'"

"Do you live with your grandma?"

She nods.

"Which house is yours?"

"Just two more, mine's the one with the blue mailbox."

It looks exactly like all of the others, except the mailbox is a bright, Tiffany blue color, the same color of the box my engagement ring came in.

Whisper stops and looks at me. "Miss Melissa, are

you my friend?"

"Of course." I smile at the seven year old.

"Can I tell you a secret?"

"Sure."

She cups her hand next to her mouth, and I lean over expecting to hear a cute, little-girl secret. Instead, she tells me something that will haunt me for months to come.

*****

I'm out of staples in my staple gun.

I get down from the stepladder and get the box of staples out of the grocery sack and refill the gun, climb back up on the stepladder and resume stapling the light green butcher paper to the bulletin board. In one of my educational psychology classes I read a study about which colors you should and shouldn't use in classrooms. Some colors make kids hyper or angry and other colors are calm and soothing. I don't know if there's really anything to that, but I'm decorating my classroom in the calm colors of light green and pale yellow, just in case. I need all the help I can get my first year of teaching.

I finish the border and the letters on the board and stand back and look at my work. All three classroom bulletin boards are done; my desk is organized, and the student desks are arranged just how I want them. I wish the room had a reading corner, but I'll have to save money and take time to collect everything I want for that. But, other than the lack of a reading corner, everything else in the classroom is perfect. Now all I have to do is write my lesson plans, and school doesn't even start for two more weeks.

"Whoa, Missy! This is amazing!" My friend and maid of honor Staci steps into my classroom and admires my handiwork. My bubbly friend who I've known since elementary school still looks like a teenager in her T-shirt, shorts, and sandals, even though she's actually two years older than I am. I'm excited that Staci will be teaching right next door to me . . . Brian was right, everything is perfect.

"Want to grab some lunch?" Staci asks. She and I haven't talked since Saturday before the wedding that didn't happen. She was with me and my other two bridesmaids in the church nursery who were all three wearing knee length, chiffon dresses each with a darling little bow right in the back on their empire waists. Staci was in pale pink, Krystal was in silver, and Lisa was in fuchsia. My three best friends were in their matching dresses and strappy heels, in the rocking chairs the moms rock their babies in, and I was a few feet from them, standing in the nursery bathroom, staring in the mirror, as The Whisper in my mind grew louder than any of the real voices around me.

We each get a salad from City Bites a couple of blocks from the school. I'm putting raspberry vinaigrette on my spinach salad as Staci tells me about our school.

"Our principal is good. You'll love her. She's very well respected across the state. And of course you know about our test scores—some of the highest in the state. We're both lucky to start our careers in such a great school." She pauses to take a sip of her sweet tea. "I mean, I've thought about going on to become a school counselor or an administrator, and if I ever have to go to another school system, it is going to look so good on my resume that I taught at Cool Springs."

I am just nodding. I'm a total newbie, so I don't have anything to add. The school is perfect. The kids are perfect. My perfect best friend teaches next door. The town is perfect. The perfect man is waiting for me to marry him and move into the perfect house located in the perfect neighborhood so that we can have two perfect children and live a perfect life.

An image flashes in my mind. Whisper, with her dark skin and bright blue eyes and imperfect teeth. Whisper, with the secret that I've been trying to forget.

I'm just pushing my spinach leaves and strawberries around with my fork now. I've only been able to choke two berries down. I'm begging my stomach not to revolt again. I've lost seven pounds in four days, and while I'm actually thrilled to lose a few pounds, this is definitely not the way to do it.

"Okay." Staci tucks a long strand of her light brown hair behind her ear. "We need to talk about it, Missy."

I press my lips together and shrug. I taste stomach acid in my mouth.

"I don't expect you to tell me why. That's between you and Brian. It's not my business at all." She reaches across the Formica topped table and grabs my hand. "I've been praying for you."

I have to ask. "What have you been praying?"

Staci tilts her head and wrinkles her eyebrows.

"I mean, have you been praying for me to marry Brian, or to not marry Brian, to stop throwing up, to shake off the jitters, to break it off and focus on being a teacher— what? What have you been praying?" Suddenly it's very important for me to know what my best friend has been praying, almost like it's the key to everything. I might be losing my mind.

She squeezes my hand. "I've been praying that God will speak to you in His still, small voice and tell you exactly what you need to do."

*****

One of the perks of having a dad who is head usher is that I have access to keys to the church. My big six foot two dad who has no idea how to help his daughter right now was more than happy to give me his church key so that I could go and pray in the sanctuary alone.

"Is there anything else you need, Missy? Do you want me to go with you? Do you want to talk?"

I shook my head. "Not right now. Thanks though. Just the keys to the church." I smiled at my big bear of a dad and then gave him a hug. "I'm going to be fine, dad. Don't worry."

I could tell he wasn't convinced.

I don't turn the lights on. The sun is still up so light streams in from the tall windows that line the sanctuary walls. Family Chapel has been my family's church for my whole life. My dad's family has attended this same church for three generations, four counting Michael and me.

I wander around in the quiet sanctuary for a minute. I feel a little strange. I've never been at church all alone. It's a little creepy. I choose a spot in the second row and sit in the pew – a comfortable pew with patterned brown padding and think about the hard wooden pews in Diniyoli. I don't know what to say. I give up and just put folded arms on the back of the pew in front of me. After a few minutes an old song comes to mind and I start to sing. I'm not the best singer in the world, my singing voice is kind of raspy and monotone, but I know that God doesn't care about that.

"I surrender all. I surrender all.
All to Jesus I surrender; I surrender all."

My mom would know the verses, but I can't think of them right now. I sing those two lines a few times. We don't even sing that song in church anymore. I remember singing it when I was a little girl. We had a children's church leader who sang it with us every Sunday at the close of the kids' service.

"Lord, I will do whatever you want me to do," I whisper in the silent church. It's a short and simple prayer, but I truly mean it. I close my eyes and remember when I gave my life to Jesus. I was nine years old at a sleepover with the girls' ministry. I repeated the prayer Staci's mom led us in, such a childlike thing to do, but now that I look back at it, the most important decision I've ever made.

I feel someone touch my shoulder. My eyelids fly open, and I gasp sharply and sit up straight.

"Brian! You scared me to death!"

He chuckles. "Sorry babe, can we talk for a minute?"

"Sure," I scoot over on the pew, and he sits next to me.

We sit for a few seconds without talking. Just five days ago it was the night before our wedding, and we were sitting in this very sanctuary practicing the ceremony with our friends and family. Brian was teasing our pastor for being late to the practice, and I was aggravated at Michael for coming straight from playing baseball with his friends and not taking a shower and putting on clean clothes. That seems a lifetime ago.

He talks first. "I saw your car."

Funny. I wasn't even wondering how he knew I was here.

"Missy, I'm not going to pressure you to make a decision. I've been talking with Pastor Kevin and my parents, and they've helped me to see that I don't need to pressure you right now. I'm going to leave you alone and let you make your decision by yourself."

"Thank you." I say it so quietly that I don't even know if he hears it.

"I'm going to get an apartment in the city, near my work. I found one today. It's by a golf course." He turns his head sideways and grins at me. Brian loves to golf. I have always joked that Brian would never leave me for another woman, but he might leave me for a new set of golf clubs.

"I still love you, Missy. I still want to get married." He turns in his seat and looks right at me. "Do you realize how . . ." He stops himself. He clears his throat. "I'm trying to understand. I can't flip a switch and stop loving you so, of course, I'm going to wait, but . . ." He grabs my hands. "But Missy, I'm not going to wait forever."

I nod. Of course he won't wait forever. Was I thinking he would? How self-centered and egotistical of me to think that he wouldn't move on and find someone else.

He lets go of my hands, leans forward and kisses me lightly on the lips, and then he stands, turns and walks out of the sanctuary.

*****

I pull in to the Cool Springs City Park and get out of my car. As I stretch I feel a cool breeze on my face and admire the gorgeous moon. It's not right that I feel good right now. I shouldn't feel good. I shouldn't be enjoying the weather. I notice that my stomach isn't hurting. For the first time in four days I don't feel like I'm going to vomit.

I just started running a couple of months ago. I've never been a runner. I was that girl in P.E. class who couldn't run a mile or climb the rope, the same girl who hid behind everyone during dodge ball and was picked last for all the teams. But a couple of months ago, I decided to start running. I'm not sure what made me start. I've been increasing my distance every week. I can now run four miles without stopping, which is a huge accomplishment for me. It's been over a week since I ran, so I expect I'll be winded tonight and won't be able run as far.

This time of year the only good times to run outside are this late at night or really early in the morning, and I'm not going to get up before seven if I don't have to. It hasn't been that long ago that I was a lazy college student, after all.

I love being back in my hometown. I walk the path to the pair of benches in front of the fountain and stretch out my legs. The winding paths and flowerbeds are well lit throughout the perfectly planned park. I had my sixth birthday party here. I took my senior pictures here. Every fall we celebrate our family heritage at Czech Fest here and every Fourth of July my family claims a piece of ground here with our blanket and enjoys the fireworks overhead.

I finish stretching and strap my phone holster to my arm. I use an app on my phone that plays music and tracks my progress and route and tells me how far I've gone after each half mile. I get my phone and headphones out of my purse. I look at my phone before sliding it into the arm holster and see that I've missed three calls. One is from a number I don't recognize and my mom has called me twice. I have two voicemails. I'd rather start running, but I guess I'd better call my mom back. I don't listen to her voicemail and just touch the call back button.

It doesn't even finish the first ring.

"Missy? Where are you? What are you doing? Why didn't you answer my calls?"

I open my mouth to answer but she doesn't give me a chance.

"The missionary? The one from the Indian place? Reverend Chaney? He said he needed to talk to you. He said Pastor Kevin gave him your phone number."

"Mom, breathe." My mom can be a little high strung. "Reverend Chaney called? Did he leave his number?"

"Yes, oh my goodness, honey, that's not all. He said that someone named Janice is in the hospital and that the school superintendent told him he still needs a second grade teacher." She takes a breath. "Missy, he wants to talk to you about coming there this week!"

This week? I swallow. "That's crazy. Where would I live? I'd have to quit my job here."

Mom laughs. "It is crazy. I guess he's desperate. I get the impression that this Janice person was a pretty important part of the mission."

Take out the papers and the trash . . . forty kids throwing away their popsicle sticks and getting into their assigned reading circles . . . Yakkity yak . . . don't talk back.

". . . that a minister would be that presumptuous?" Mom is still talking, "I mean, I understand that he's in a tough spot, but to call and offer a teaching job, a role at the mission, a place to live and a roommate, like he's assuming you don't already have a life here. He rattled me. I was a little nervous that you'd—"

"A place to live and a roommate?"

"Can you believe it? The way he was talking it almost sounded like you had made plans with him, or, or . . . did you tell him about the wedding and Brian?"

"Why would I?" Of course I didn't tell him, but then why shouldn't I? Is it something to be embarrassed about? Is my mom embarrassed by it?

"Oh, thank goodness." She sounds so relieved. That answers that.

"What did he say about a place to live and a roommate?"

"Something about another first year teacher at the school who needs a roommate—renting a house in town and looking for someone to room with, something or other. I'm so glad you're not thinking of going there. It sounds so dangerous."

"Dangerous?" I think about Whisper's secret. What had my mom heard about Diniyoli?

"Didn't I say that part? That Janice woman? She was attacked."

*****

Chapter Three

She was hungry. Usually when people are sick that's a good sign, but Sierra knew that it was just the medicine causing her to want to eat. She looked at the clock radio across the room. Two-fifteen. For a moment she wondered if Jacob would bring something to eat upstairs to her, but she discarded that thought right after it crossed her mind. She would have to inch her way down the stairs herself.

In the first few weeks he had brought her food. He would bring her a bowl of cereal or toast or even a hamburger from The Green Parrot, but that stopped after a while. Not that she could blame him. He was taking care of the baby all by himself, while she didn't even have the strength to feed her.

Thoughts whirled in her head as she inched her way out of the bed, out of her bedroom and to the hallway along the old fashioned curved walls. "What kind of mother am I? I have a newborn and a four year old, and I'm not able to take care of either of them. I love my babies, but I barely have the strength to get out of bed, much less care for them. I'm dying and leaving them with a lousy father. What's going to happen to them? After everything I've done, who could blame God for killing me and ignoring my prayers for my babies?"

She gripped the banister at the top of the stairs, squeezed her eyes shut, and shook her head, as if to shake all of those destructive thoughts out. She hadn't known about the power of thoughts before she started listening to the lady on the radio. Now she knew that she could take control of thoughts like this. The lady preacher on the radio talked about taking control of your thoughts all the time, "putting on the mind of Christ" she called it. Sierra thought about that, and forced those thoughts out of her mind.

"I'm hungry," she thought. "I haven't had anything

to eat all day. I just need to make it to the kitchen and fix myself a piece of toast with grape jelly on it. I'll feel better if I can do that."

Hold on to the stair rail. Put left foot one step down. Put right foot one step down. She was climbing down the stairs like a toddler, planting both feet on the same step before stepping down to the next, all the time shakily holding the iron railing.

Last week the doctor said that she needed to come back in a week. That would have been today. Jacob knew that her appointment was for today, but where was he? All she heard was the television in the living room playing a cartoon. There weren't any voices. Jacob probably forgot to turn the TV off before he left.

She couldn't help thinking about it again. Dying. It was going to happen. She was going to die soon, and her kids were going to be raised by good-for-nothing Jacob. If only she had someone who could come and help Jacob, or even take the baby. But there was no one. Sure, she had a mom, but she wouldn't help, and who could blame her?

Sierra made it to the kitchen. There were dirty dishes piled all over the counters, and something sticky was all over the floor. She found the bread and toaster in the pantry. She stuck the bread in the toaster, wiped sweat off her forehead and remembered the phone conversation with her mom while she waited for the toast to pop up.

"Hello?" Ida's familiar voice had answered the phone.

"Mom? It's me, Sierra."

No answer.

"Mom, I'm sorry I haven't called you." She squeezed her eyebrows together and tried to remember the last time she talked to her mom. It had been at least three years ago. For the first year Ida had called her every week, but Sierra never answered.

"Are you still in Tulsa?" Ida asked.

"No, we moved back to Diniyoli. We live in Jacob's grandpa's old house." Of course Ida knew that house. Everyone in Diniyoli knew the big white house. "Are you still living with Aunt Anna?" Ida had moved from Diniyoli to take care of her elderly aunt five years ago.

"Aunt Anna died a year ago, Sierra. I'm living in her apartment still though."

"Oh," she felt terrible. Anna was her mom's only living relative, and she had loved the old woman. "I had another baby, mom."

"You did?" Ida's voice cracked. She was crying.

"A girl. She's beautiful. I named her Whisper."

"Whisper."

"Mom, I'm so sorry for everything. I was awful. I can't believe that I didn't answer your calls, and that I never called you. I'm so sorry."

Ida didn't say anything.

"I've been praying mom. I've been listening to this lady preacher on the radio. Anyway," she paused, not knowing what to say, "anyway, I'm kind of sick, and just, you know, thinking about things, and I wanted to call and tell you that I'm sorry."

The line was quiet for a few seconds. Then Ida responded, "Okay," and hung up the phone.

That had been three days ago. Ida had not called back, and Sierra couldn't blame her. Sierra had been a nightmare for Ida. She started up with Jacob Davis when she was only sixteen. He was eight years older, twenty-four, and he was still a baseball legend in Diniyoli – a boy wonder player who could've played in the major leagues if it hadn't been for the drugs. She was a sophomore at Diniyoli high school. She and Ida lived in a house with dirt floors on Old Reservation Road. Jacob lived in the big white house – the biggest house in town. He was a grown man who hung around high school kids – Sierra should have thought about that. He was good-looking and always the life of the party.

Ida begged her to stop seeing him. Ida tried to convince Sierra that she needed to finish school, but Sierra couldn't see any reason for that. She thought she loved Jacob. He had no problems with money and was always happy. Life with him was a party. So, of course, she ran away with him. They went to Texas, then to California. They lived in hotels and in cars. It was a blast – for a while.

But, of course, as these things usually go, after a couple of years it wasn't so glamorous. Jacob finally got arrested the first time for selling drugs and served a little over a year. By that time Sierra was pregnant. They lived in Tulsa for a while after he got out. He got arrested a few more times, and for a while Sierra thought he would be put away for good, but he made an important connection in Tulsa with a man who said that Jacob would "never get caught again, as long as he did what he was told." This new boss told Jacob to move back to Diniyoli. He had a plan. So, Jacob obeyed and now they live back in the big white house, and Jacob hadn't got caught again, like the new boss promised.

For Sierra, twenty-three felt more like eighty-three. She was tired. That was the sickness, but it was more than that. She now had two children and a husband who was still interested in high school girls. She took a bite of the toast and reached to the refrigerator to get the milk.

When she got sick, she couldn't do anything. There wasn't a television in her bedroom, so she started listening to the radio. You can only listen to music for so long, so she started listening to talk radio. She never cared about sports or politics, so the only thing left to listen to was preaching. At first it was just time killing, but after a couple of days she really started listening. How could it not have changed her? It seemed that the radio preachers were talking right at her. She started praying. She lay in her bed and prayed for days. The prayer was a lifeline. She hadn't had anyone to talk to for so long. It was literally life changing to have someone to talk to.

Her biggest prayer hadn't been for healing. Sure, she prayed for that, but the thing she prayed for the most was her little four-year-old boy and her newborn baby girl. She prayed that somehow, some way God would provide a Christian family for them, that somehow, some way God would transform this chaotic, depressing house to a house of peace and love.

She sipped her milk. She was starting to doubt. How could that ever happen? As she was taking another sip of milk, she heard it. Is that? She forced herself to move as quick as she could through the kitchen, left down the hallway, and into the living room. Then she heard it again. Was that her baby crying? Whisper?

In the living room, a cartoon was playing on the television. Sierra glanced across the dirty room. Her precious little boy was sleeping on the couch, a space had been cleared between heaps of cast-off clothing, overflowing ashtrays, and dirty cups. Her newborn baby was on a blanket in the middle of the floor. *Where was Jacob?* Surely he hadn't left them here alone. But, as soon as she thought it, she knew it was true. Of course he had left them here alone for who knows how long.

Sierra started to cry as she crossed the room to her baby girl. Whisper was crying, and Sierra knew she didn't have the strength to even pick her up. She went to the baby and lay down on the floor next to her. She put her hand on the baby's tummy and started to talk to her.

"There's my baby girl. Don't cry. Mama's here," she said as she rubbed her baby's tummy. She looked around for a bottle or a pacifier, but didn't see either in the messy room. Little Whisper looked at Sierra and stopped crying. Sierra still couldn't believe that a child of hers could have blue eyes. "Hello, princess. Mama loves you."

Behind her she heard her son from the couch. "Mama?"

She lifted her eyes to her sweet boy. Oh how she wanted to jump up and run to him and pick him up.

"Hey big boy! Did you have a good nap?"

He nodded. Then he pointed toward the big window. "Who's that?"

Sierra turned her head and looked where he was pointing. A strange small gray car was in front of the house, stopped at the curb. She didn't recognize the woman who was driving, but she did recognize the woman who got out of the car, retrieved a suitcase from the backseat, waved goodbye to the driver, and then started walking up the path to the front door.

Sierra smiled, "That's your Grandma Ida."

*****

I wish I didn't feel like the Clampett family moving with all of their stuff packed into the truck, including Granny in her rocking chair. Thankfully, I don't have that much stuff of my own. My only possessions are my clothes, my computer, my bed, dresser, desk, two beanbags and two bar stools. In college, I lived in a tiny one-room apartment. The whole place was literally one room, except for the bathroom, of course. The kitchen and living area were all one room, and there was a ladder you had to climb to reach a loft bedroom that was little more than a shelf with only room for my bed and dresser. There was just a bar in the kitchen, no room for a table. In the living area I had my desk and the beanbags. I didn't even own a television. If I wanted to watch something, I would just watch it on my computer. Of course, I also have six boxes of teaching and classroom stuff, which I delivered to my new second grade classroom at Diniyoli Elementary yesterday.

I'm sitting next to my dad in his big truck with all of my furniture loaded in the back. Michael and Mom are following in his little truck with all of the boxes. There have been fewer than two dozen words spoken during this peaceful drive, and I'm thankful for that. I feel a little sorry for Michael. I'm sure he's been getting an earful from Mom about how she can't believe I'm turning my back on Brian, our family, and Cool Springs to go live in a desolate wasteland.

As we pass the two empty stores at the edge of town, I pull down the visor to look in the mirror. I'm not wearing any makeup, but I want to check to make sure my hair isn't crazy. Since I'm not wearing any makeup, my freckles are shining all over my face. I have my dark red, almost brown hair pulled back into a ponytail. A few hairs have escaped on the sides, so I take out the elastic band and quickly redo it. I had been growing my hair out for the wedding for two years, so it's longer than it has ever been, almost to my waist. I do love it, but it's so hot and heavy in the summer. I ought to cut it. It'd be much more practical . . . especially since there's not going to be a wedding any time soon.

I snap the visor back up and notice my not-so-perfect French manicure, now two weeks old and grown out. I need to scrub the polish off my nails too.

Dad turns left at the town's single stoplight. We pass the school, and I see my classroom window on the far west corner of the building. We drive through the haphazard neighborhood, and again I look at the huge and stunning turn of the century white house, that I look at every time I drive by, and I remember Whisper's secret about the home again. We drive another block and pull into the driveway of my new home – a 900 square foot, two-bedroom rent house with red brick wainscot and peeling yellow siding. If I were planning on staying longer than a year I would re-paint that siding and put in a flowerbed. Maybe if I just put a few flowers in pots on the porch, and hang a flower basket that will make it a bit more cheerful. My new roommate, Chelsea, already painted the entire interior buff beige and scrubbed the inside of the house from top to bottom.

Dad kills the engine and takes his keys out of the ignition. He turns to me, "We're only an hour and a half away."

Is he telling me or is he reminding himself?

We open the doors to the truck, and my new roommate Chelsea swings the front door open and hops out onto the front porch, with a glass of iced tea in each hand. I've never thought of myself as tall; I'm only five foot seven, but Chelsea makes me feel like a giant. She's exactly five foot tall. I'm sure some of her fifth grade students will be taller than she is. She runs out to the truck to greet us.

"Hey! I'm so glad you're here! You must be Melissa's dad. I'm Chelsea. Want some iced tea?" She hands him one of the glasses.

"Thanks," He takes the glass and takes a long drink. "Nice to meet you. I'm Gary. Are you ready to live with our Missy? Your tea is wonderful; can you cook?"

Chelsea laughs, "Well, I can make a few things, spaghetti, hamburgers, tacos. I can make breakfast food, too. Oh, and I can bake cookies!"

I walk around the front of the truck and take the other glass of tea. "Dad, I lived on my own at college."

"That's true," he nods his head and takes another drink.

"But, I did eat a lot of McDonalds and Pop Tarts."

Dad laughs. "I didn't say it!"

I don't say it, but I think, "I also ate a lot of Brian's cooking." The plan was that when we married Brian would be the cook.

Is dad having doubts about me making it without Brian?

We start working together to get the furniture out of dad's truck. We each carry a bar stool into the house, and the three of us are working on getting the mattress out of the truck when Michael and Mom pull up. The sunlight reflects off of the side mirror on Michael's truck door as he opens it.

He and Mom get out with brown paper sacks in their hands.

"Lunch!" Mom calls out. "BLT's and French fries for everyone! We've got some for you too, Chelsea." Mom has decided that she likes Chelsea. She's not happy about me moving here of course, but when Mom met Chelsea, she instantly loved her and it made it better.

"I'm not sure how good the food will be. We got it from the diner on Main Street." Mom says as she takes the food in and heads to the kitchen.

"So, what did you think of the Green Parrot?"

"The what?" she asks. The Green Parrot is the diner that I stopped at and used its restroom on my first trip to Diniyoli. It doesn't have sign. All the locals just know its name, and there are green parrots painted in murals all over the inside of the restaurant. The last time I was here, I learned that Tess, the mission's grumpy volunteer receptionist, and her husband own the diner. They donate Green Parrot burgers and Indian tacos to all of the mission's events and dinners.

"It's the name of the diner. The owner volunteers at the mission, too."

Mom just says, "Mmm," and spreads the food out on Chelsea's table. The square table only has four chairs, so dad sits on one of my bar stools.

My new roommate is providing much more furniture to our new home than I am. She has a kitchen table and chairs, a sofa, and a television. The kitchen does have a bar, so I can use my college bar stools, and, since she only has a sofa and no other living room furniture, my beanbags can be used in the living room. I'll probably invest in some more chairs after my first paycheck, so that people can come and visit us and not sit in a beanbag, as if they were in a teenager's bedroom.

My desk, dresser, and queen sized bed fit snugly into my bedroom. I push the bed up against the wall and leave a path on just one side. Both bedrooms in this two-bedroom

house are about the same size, with the bathroom
equidistance apart, so there's no awkward discussion.

The one thing neither of us have much of is kitchen
supplies. I just have a few dishes and cups, and she doesn't
have much. We'll have to invest in a microwave and more
kitchenware after our first paycheck too. I don't have a chef
fiancé anymore.

Over BLT's, French fries, and Chelsea's sweet tea we
talk. Michael hasn't met Chelsea before, so we're telling her
all about his accomplishments in baseball. He keeps clearing
his throat, and his cheeks are turning red. I love
embarrassing my shy little brother.

"So, Chelsea, where are you originally from?" Mom
asks. "I know you went to college at Southwestern."

"I'm actually from right here. I was born and raised
in Diniyoli."

I'm surprised. I didn't know she was from here.

"Really? Where do your parents live?" I ask.

"Well, dad got a job in Tulsa, so they moved there.
They wanted me to get a job in the Tulsa area and live closer
to them, but I had to come back here."

"Why?" Michael speaks up.

"Michael, don't say that," I say. Michael's just
seventeen, but he should know better than to say that.

"It's okay," She smiles, "I know it's strange for me to
want to come back here. The truth is, I believe God called
me here."

Wow, I don't think I could ever say that, just boldly,
straight out say that God called me.

"I remember when I started kindergarten. There
were five Old Reservation Road kids in my class. Three of
them were girls, and I was so jealous of their long black hair.
Over the years those five classmates slowly disappeared. By
the ninth grade they were all gone. I believe God has a future
and a hope for these kids that is more than the life they have
now. I want to help these kids not only graduate, but also go

to college."

There's that verse again. A future and a hope, Jeremiah 29:11. That verse is following me everywhere.

"Of course there's the negative element, but there are a lot of good people here, and Kirk and the mission are making such a difference."

"Negative element? What are we talking about here? Drugs? Gangs?" Dad wants to know. I think about Whisper's secret.

"Yes, drugs, and yes, gangs by definition, but not any gangs you'd recognize. I'm sure you've heard about the number three that was painted on the inside of the kitchen door the night Janice was attacked, as if someone was claiming responsibility. But in the last four years the mission has made a huge impact."

"And that means that Reverend Chaney and the mission have enemies, right?" Dad asks and Mom closes her eyes.

"Yes, he does. I'm sure that's why Janice was attacked. We had just finished a big Back-to-School outreach, giving out new backpacks, school supplies, clothes and canned food. The mission had more people at the outreach than it's ever had at any event. We even had a lot of parents come with their kids. Kirk spoke at the end and invited people to pray with him to become Christians. He had several parents come and pray with him after the event. It was awesome." Chelsea sets down her tea glass, "Then, after everyone had gone home, Janice was by herself cleaning the kitchen. Someone broke in and hit her on the head and legs several times. She was unconscious when Kirk found her."

"How is she now?" I ask.

"Still in the hospital. She has a concussion and one of her legs is broken."

"Do you think she'll go back to the mission?" Although I don't know if I could return if something like that happened to me.

Chelsea shakes her head, "I'm sure Janice will come back when she can. She's so committed to the people here. I just don't know when she'll be able to come back. Her leg is pretty seriously broken. I think she's going to have surgery."

Mom turns to me. "Missy, are you sure you want to do this?" I know mom is freaking out about this place, and I can't blame her. "Mom, I'm only going to be here for a year, remember? Just a year. I won't be at the mission all the time like Janice. I'll be teaching school and just do some after school tutoring at the mission. I'll come home some weekends, okay?"

Mom nods her head. "Come home a lot of weekends."

"Anybody home?" Reverend Chaney knocks on the screen door.

"Kirk, hi, come on in," Chelsea jumps up and opens the door for him.

"Hello Mr. Kolar, Mrs. Kolar," He shakes my parents' hands. "And you must be Michael," He shakes Michael's hand. "Thank you so much for allowing Melissa to come here. I know this is probably hard on you."

Mom and Dad nod. Chelsea offers Reverend Chaney a bar stool and an iced tea. He sits and joins us. He is wearing an Oklahoma City Thunder baseball cap, a Nike shirt, and jeans that are paint-stained. I'm starting to wonder if this guy ever looks like a typical minister. I notice that he also has paint all over his hands. The paint on his jeans is white and the paint on his hands is blue. I wonder if he had been painting over the number three on the kitchen door?

Reverend Chaney sets his glass of tea on the bar and leans forward, his elbows on his knees, "I came by to tell you all that we have a new alarm system at the mission. The church I spoke to on Sunday gave us a special offering for an alarm. The security company installed it today." He drops his chin on his hands. "I just wish we would've had it before Janice was hurt."

The room is quiet. I think about Janice. I only saw her one time, but I remember her warm brown eyes and her singing with the kids.

"Reverend Chaney," my dad speaks up.

"Yes, Mr. Kolar?"

"You can call me Gary. Thank you for installing the alarm." He looks at my mom. "It's hard for us to leave Missy here, but we trust you, and we trust Missy, and we know God is going to take care of her." Dad covers mom's hand with his.

Reverend Chaney nods. "Thank you, sir."

Chelsea asks Reverend Chaney if he's eaten any lunch yet, and when she finds out he hasn't, she kicks it into warp speed to make sure the man gets something to eat. She finds some bread and cheese and a can of soup and produces a grilled cheese sandwich and bowl of chicken noodle in eight minutes flat. He polishes off the sandwich first and then moves to the soup – a compartmental eater.

"So Michael, did you go to any baseball camps this summer?" His dark brown eyes look intently at my brother, totally focused on what the teenager has to say about his two week long camp at OSU.

His leg is constantly bouncing as he's listening to my brother, and he keeps shaking the ice in his tea glass. I wonder if he was labeled ADHD as a kid.

He turns his dark eyes to me and asks me if I need any help finishing up my classroom, and I have to remind myself to breathe. Breathe in normally. Exhale normally.

"No, I think I'm all finished," I lie.

"Missy, you are not. You have at least a day's worth of work to do." Mom corrects me.

Ugh, busted. "Well, I mean I can handle it. I don't need any help."

"You're sure?"

Will he just quit looking at me please? I nod.

"Chelsea, Melissa, there's actually something I needed to come and talk to you both about today. I know that you both are going to be helping with the after school tutoring, and I appreciate it, but I was wondering if the two of you could possibly divide Janice's other duties?

"Of course, whatever you need," Chelsea blurts out before I even have a chance to say anything.

Kirk chuckles, "Thanks for your willingness, Chelsea, but let me tell you what it is first."

He stands up from his bar stool and starts pacing. "Janice did a lot, but the two areas I could really use some help with are the Wednesday night dinner and the primary Sunday School class. Both jobs are pretty – "

"I can do both of them. No big deal," Chelsea says with a big smile. I'm starting to feel embarrassed for her. Hasn't she ever heard of playing it cool? I can't blame her. He is gorgeous, dark eyes and dark hair, broad shoulders, well, pretty much everything girls find attractive. It's just odd. I mean, he's a minister. Not just a minister, a missionary. She's blatantly flirting with a missionary. Isn't that bad? I'd be afraid of getting struck by lightening or something if I tried to flirt with him.

"Tell you what, why don't I have you do the Sunday School class, Chelsea. Could you perhaps do the Wednesday night dinner, Melissa? The Green Parrot provides most of the groceries, but you would have to take a trip to the grocery store every now and then, and then, of course, you would prepare the dinner. The good thing is, you wouldn't have to clean up. Tess has organized clean up crews for each week."

"Uh . . ." He doesn't know he's talking to the girl who lived on McDonalds and Pop Tarts at college, and now I have to cook for . . . for . . . "Um, how many people are we talking about? How many would I have to prepare for?"

"We have about sixty. It's a wonderful outreach.

Some of these folks are malnourished, and it provides them a great meal, plus it gets them to church for our midweek service and small groups."

I look at my parents and Michael and can tell that my dad is trying not to laugh. They think I can't do this. I look at my family, dad, mom, Michael, and for the first time I realize that they don't think I can handle this at all, and not just the cooking, all of it – moving to Diniyoli, living with a stranger, teaching poor children, working at the mission, but who can blame them? I went to college, but I went with Brian. Brian's not here. My parents won't be here. I'm doing this all alone.

"I'll do it." I say and my dad's eyebrows go up. "When's my first dinner?"

"Can you do it tomorrow?"

*****

I'm reminding myself that in many places around the world entire families share one bathroom as I'm waiting in the hallway to use the restroom. Chelsea is bubbly, kind, giving, and all other sorts of wonderful qualities, but I'm afraid she's a bit of a bathroom hog. I've been waiting here in the hallway for thirty minutes, and my bladder has exercised about all of the control it can. I'm seriously thinking about driving to Main Street and using the bathroom at the corner convenience store.

Just when I turn to head toward my bedroom to get my keys, the bathroom door opens and out comes my roommate holding a bowl and looking like someone vomited on her face.

"It's an avocado mask," She smiles, "I made it myself. It nourishes and moisturizes your skin better than anything store-bought."

I look in the bowl and, sure enough, inside is an avocado peel, lemon rind, a half empty bottle of honey, and a fork. Was she in there mashing up avocado while I was out here in the hallway about to pee my pants?

I want to ask her to please make her facial masks in the kitchen from now on, but I can't wait any longer. I run past her and close the door as fast as I can.

It takes me less than fifteen minutes to use the restroom, brush my teeth, wash my face, brush my hair, slip into my comfy t-shirt and shorts and slide under the covers. As I lean over to switch off the lamp on my nightstand, Chelsea walks into my room and sits on the end of my bed.

"Hey, I have a question for you."

"Um, okay."

"I was thinking about asking Kirk out. What do you think about that? Do you think it's inappropriate? I was thinking that I would stick around after the staff meeting on Thursday and see if he wanted to grab some dinner with me, so that wouldn't seem like a real date. It would just be more like a convenient dinner that would maybe turn into a life changing conversation that would make him realize he's in love with me."

We both laugh. Is this what it's like to have a sister?

*****

A sad bird flits around the ancient birdbath in my new backyard looking for a drink. There's no water in it, of course, since it hasn't rained in weeks. The birdbath would be so cute painted a bright teal or yellow. Maybe I'll spray paint it today. Some former tenants also left behind octagon shaped pavers that curve from the back door to the concrete bench I'm sitting on. Some of the pavers have handprints and names and ages painted kid-style.

"Jonah, age 8" finger painted in blue below a painting of a smiling sun with sunglasses.

"Maddie, age 4" finger painted in pink below multi-colored scribbles.

I close my eyes and rest my head in my hands and continue praying. I can't remember what distracted me in the first place. No verbal prayer will come, so I pick up my pen and my red leather-bound journal setting next to me on the bench and start writing.

The little guy keeps walking and fluttering around,
But the concrete plate's bone dry.
It will be over one hundred today, and no water will be found,
But he keeps singing – why?
I've heard you know about tomorrow.
Is that why this little bird acts so free?
Your eye is on the sparrow,
But are you really watching me?

I close my journal and set down my pen. It's not the best poem I've ever written, but now I can pray.

"Lord, please help me. I'm not sure if I can do this. I'm supposed to make a meal for sixty people tonight, starting next week I'll be teaching kids who come from a culture that I know nothing about, and I'm supposed to be in charge of an after school program that I have no idea how to operate. I feel overwhelmed and underprepared."

As I'm praying about all I have to do here and then move on to the topic of asking God to help me know what to do about Brian, an image of the young girl named Whisper comes into my mind.

"Lord, be with Whisper. I can't imagine going through all she's been through. I pray that you would tell her how much you love her."

After I finish my prayer and Bible reading time, I go inside and get ready for the day. Grocery shopping and cooking are the main things I'll be doing today, so I throw on a pair of athletic shorts and a t-shirt and sandals and put my hair in a ponytail. I grab my keys and purse and go outside to my car. As I unlock it with the remote on my key ring, I notice my reflection in the window. I look like a teenager who just rolled out of bed.

Why do I care what he thinks of me? I don't. I get in and start the engine. I catch a glimpse of my dark red ponytail in the rearview mirror.

I turn off the engine, get out of the car and go back inside. Thankfully Chelsea isn't here to witness my bizarre behavior. Although, I know for a fact that every time she sees Kirk she makes sure to have on fresh makeup, perfect hair, and the cutest outfit possible. It makes sense for her to do that, since she's mildly obsessed with him, but it doesn't make sense for me. Why am I going back into the house, putting on eye shadow and mascara, pulling on a longer pair of khaki shorts, pulling out the elastic ponytail holder, brushing my hair and using hair spray? I don't care what he thinks I look like.

I tell myself that I'm wanting to look a little nicer to represent the mission better at the grocery store, and even I know it's lame, but it helps to give myself an excuse.

I drive to the mission and pick up a check from Tess, who is her usual grumpy self. Then I drive twenty miles to the next town, Clinton, because there's not a grocery store in Diniyoli. As I'm driving I think about my conversation with Tess. Have I done something to offend her? I know she's a good lady. She must be a Christian – she volunteers so much at the mission. She gives food to the mission. Tess and her husband just donated twelve pounds of hamburger meat, canned beans, and several onions for tonight's dinner. Tess suggested that I cook chili and cornbread. She said that all I would have to get from the store would be tomato sauce, cans of tomatoes, and cornbread mix. She said there were already eggs and butter and spices in the kitchen. She even made a shopping list for me that included all of the ingredients for the chili. So, I know she wants me to succeed in making the dinner. I just can't understand why she's always so rude every time I talk to her.

I thank the Lord for the GPS on my phone for the thousandth time as it directs me right to Buy For Less in Clinton, and load up my cart with the items on Tess's list. I purchase them with a mission check and show a tax-exempt card. Then I buy two cans of bright yellow spray paint – for the birdbath.

For the ride back I get my daily dose of caffeine, a huge Dr. Pepper from Sonic Drive-In. I think about the first time I drove to Diniyoli with my big cup of coffee. So much has happened since then. I was just checking the place out, thinking that I might come and help in the summer, and now here I am, living here, working here.

As I drive through Diniyoli to the mission road, I drive past the big old white house and look at it, like I do every time I drive by. This time someone is out on the porch. A man in his thirties or forties is sitting on a chair talking on a phone and smoking. He's wearing a sleeveless white shirt and jeans and has a backward ball cap on his head. I'm sure he's the one Whisper told me about. I quickly turn my head to face forward and drive a little faster.

I unload all of the groceries out of my small sedan and pile them up on the island in the mission kitchen. I look at the clock on the kitchen microwave, 12:15. Dinner is supposed to be at six. I don't think I actually need to start cooking until probably three. Although, I'm going to have to chop quite a few onions, so maybe I'd better start at two. What should I do now? At home I would go out to lunch with a friend or go run on my parents' treadmill (it's too dreadfully hot to go running outside) or go shopping for a few hours, but here in Diniyoli I don't have any friends, treadmills, or stores.

As I'm feeling a little sorry for myself, I hear it. The Whisper. It's been a few weeks, but there it is. I lock my purse in my car and walk down the dirt road to my friend's house.

*****

I spot the Tiffany blue mailbox halfway down the dirt road. As I walk I lift my hair off my neck and regret taking out my ponytail. You can sense the kids are squeezing in all the fun they can – riding bikes, yelling at each other, pushing toys around in their yards, chasing each other – desperately grasping onto their fleeting summer freedom.

As I get near Whisper's house, I see an elderly Native American woman in a lawn chair in the open doorway of the little house. Whisper's black puppy with the tuft of white hair on his chest is lying curled up under the shade of the old woman's chair.

"Hi," I call out to her with a big smile.

She nods once in response.

"It's pretty hot today, isn't it?"

"Sure is."

"I just wanted to come by and say hi to Whisper."

"Oh, she's in Clinton. Tess came by and picked her up. Took her to Clinton to get school clothes."

There it is, more evidence that Tess is a wonderful person, but why does she not like me?

"I'm Whisper's grandma, Ida. Want some tea?" She stands from her chair and heads for the kitchen, not even waiting for my response.

"Sure, that would be nice."

"Sit there, next to me," She says with her gray curls facing me. "It's sweet, that okay?"

"Oh yes, that's how I like it." I sit in the blue and white lawn chair just outside the door, next to her green chair. She has a fan plugged in to the wall next to the door, blowing right on her. She seems to have found the coolest spot in the house, sitting in the doorway she can feel any breeze that might blow by and the air from the fan right next to her.

She comes back and hands me a plastic cup with iced tea, and sits in her chair.

"Thank you," I take a drink. It is very sweet, just how I like it.

She takes a drink of her tea and then holds her cup in her lap. Her cup has a paper towel wrapped around the bottom. I notice her chubby fingers don't have any rings. I sneak a look around her house while she's watching two boys ride their bikes over a homemade ramp in the middle of the road. Her living room has an old, boxy television set on a little table and a brown corduroy couch, and the connecting kitchen is bright and cheery with yellow walls and white curtains around a small window fluttering in and out with the breeze. A hallway extends to the right, and presumably leads to the bathroom and bedrooms.

"Your house is nicely decorated."

Her smile reveals a couple of empty spaces where teeth should be. "Thank you. You're the new mission lady, right?"

"That's right."

Her smile grows and more empty spaces are revealed. "Tess giving you trouble?"

Had Tess complained about me to this woman? Has Tess been talking about me behind my back? I can't believe this! We work together for a missionary, after all. Aren't we supposed to act better than a bunch of middle school girls?

"Trouble?" Is all I say. I know better than to gossip about anyone in a new town. Who knows where real loyalties lie?

Ida chuckles and leans back in her chair. "Ole Tess is a good lady with a great big heart. She's seen a lot of cute city girls drop in for a few months and leave."

"What?"

"Oh don't get me wrong," She leans forward quickly and pats my hand. "I 'preciate all you gals do for our kids and the church folks, I really do. Any help we can get, I say!"

I take another sip of the tea that tasted so good a minute ago. Now, it has a sharp, metallic taste.

"I mean, who can blame 'em? Handsome missionary comes to their church, tells them about the poor Injuns, they suddenly envision themselves by his side helping out the poor brown kids, but then they get here, and see how it really is."

"Well, thank you for the tea, Ida." I stand and set the plastic cup on the seat of the chair. "It certainly hit the spot. I love sweet iced tea on a hot day." I'm already across the yard and almost to the Tiffany blue mailbox when I say, "Please tell Whisper I stopped by."

Ida takes another sip of tea.

*****

One o'clock. Actually three minutes after, to be exact.

After my "talking to" from Whisper's grandma, I feel lonelier than ever, and I'm refusing to go get a Band-Aid from Tess. I'm sure she has a box of Band-Aids in the office, but I can imagine her condescending look if I went into the office and asked for one.

Her lips would purse, and she might say, "Well, it looks like you're having some trouble cutting those onions. Does your mama usually do that at home?"

Or maybe she wouldn't say anything. Maybe she would just make a face that said it all. So, I'm wrapping my finger in another paper towel, because the bleeding hasn't stopped yet.

The truth is, I haven't cut many onions in my life. Of course my mom taught me how, and I did it a few times at home, but not enough to get good at it. I've only chopped two, and I'm supposed to chop six. Now the smell is getting to me, and my eyes are burning.

All alone in the very same kitchen where Janice was

attacked, groceries piled on the countertops all around me, I'm trying not to think about what it must have been like for Janice when the back door swung open and . . . what happened? A masked man with a baseball bat came in swinging? Were there two or three of them?

I look at the freshly painted spot right in the middle of the back door and imagine the big, black number three that is there hiding underneath the blue paint.

I shake myself, "Stop thinking about it." I tell myself aloud. I squeeze the paper towel around my finger to apply pressure to the cut. My phone rings. I fish it out of my purse with my good hand and see on the screen that it's my dad.

"Hey dad."

"Hey hon, what're you doing?"

"Oh, chopping onions." I don't know if it's the onions, or if it's the unexpected call from my dad. I honestly can't tell what causes the tears to start. "I'm making chili and cornbread for sixty people."

"In August?"

For some reason that makes me laugh. "Yes, it's over one hundred degrees outside, and I'm making chili and cornbread." I wipe my tears with the non-bloody end of my paper towel wad.

Dad laughs. "Well, don't use too much seasoning. You may have people pass out from heat stroke!"

"Oh Dad, I know you're joking, but I seriously hope I don't make anyone sick. I've nicked my finger while I was chopping onions, and now I'm waiting for it to stop bleeding. I don't want my blood to get in the food!" I'm pacing in front of the island in the mission kitchen. "I'm worried about the meat and the eggs, too. They were both donated, and I don't know how old they are. I just bought cornbread mix, so I'm not worried about how it will taste, but I am worried about cutting it up into perfect squares. I wish I had bought paper muffin liners so I could make cornbread muffins instead. Why didn't I do that? Although, I don't even know if they have a muffin pan here." I bend down and open a cabinet of cookie sheets and baking pans, looking for a muffin pan.

"Missy, you're going to do great. Stop worrying."

I stop looking for the pan and stand. "You really believe that?" I remember him laughing about my cooking. I remember mom's horrified face every time she heard another scary detail about Diniyoli. Brian saying he'd wait for me, like I needed to go on a little adventure before I would grow up, settle down, and marry him.

I notice that he hasn't answered. "Do you really believe that?" I ask again. I have to know if he believes in me. "You don't even think I'll last the whole year. Do you, dad?"

He clears his throat. "Honey,"

"Mom, Michael, Brian, even Staci, and probably all Cool Springs thinks I won't be able to do this, don't they? They all think I'll get overwhelmed, homesick, flake out, quit my job, forget the mission, go home, and marry Brian, right?"

"Missy, do you remember when you ran a fireworks stand?"

"Of course." I was sixteen and trying to save money for a car. My dad's cousin called him and asked if he wanted to open a fireworks stand in Cool Springs. He had stands in Chickasha, Tuttle, Mustang, and Piedmont, and he wanted to open one in Cool Springs, but he needed someone to run it. "Running it" included hiring and managing a crew of workers, guarding the stand at night, depositing the money nightly, paying workers, tracking inventory, ordering new inventory as needed, and taking care of any problems that might come up. According to city ordinances, it could only be open for the two weeks before July fourth.

"I didn't want to mess with it, but you were desperate to have your own car and not drive your grannie's old Taurus."

Despite myself, I have to smile at the memory. Grannie's Taurus would have been a good car. She only drove it twice a week – to the grocery store and to church. She had the oil changed and tires balanced right on schedule. The car was clean and safe and ran perfectly, but I thought I needed something more exciting than Grannie's Taurus. I had my heart set on a four year old Mitsubishi Eclipse. I would need about ten thousand dollars. I had saved my babysitting money for the last three summers. I was working at a snow cone stand, and I hadn't spent one penny of any paycheck. After all of that saving, I had just under four thousand dollars. I was looking under every rock for six thousand more dollars.

"I relented and let you do it, because you wore me down with your begging, even though I thought I'd have to bail you out after the first week, but do remember what happened?"

I nod, even though I know he can't see me.

"You only hired one employee, because you wanted to keep as much profit as you could – little miser. You and Staci worked day and night – slept in sleeping bags in the fireworks stand, even. I couldn't believe it. My girl who always wanted to be clean and whose hair was always brushed and clothes matched was sleeping in a sleeping bag in a fireworks stand!

I smile at the memory. Staci and I had so much fun those two weeks. Selling fireworks, eating peanut butter and jelly sandwiches, talking about everything in our teenage hearts. She told me about her all of her fears. She'd never told anyone how she panicked at the idea of eating food that might make her sick or germs she might catch in Wal-Mart. I confessed my secret dream of wanting to be a writer. We swore each other to secrecy, as we lay head-to-head in our sleeping bags on the floor of the fireworks stand.

"So then, Missy. Did you buy the Mitsubishi?"

I smile again, "Nope."

"No, you didn't. You bought that beautiful midnight blue Honda Accord that you still drive. And why did you buy that car?"

This story has become a legend in our family. The Story of How Missy Got the Honda is a tale that my parents both love to repeat. I bought the Honda, because I earned eight thousand dollars at the fireworks stand, even after I paid a percentage to dad's cousin and split half of the leftover profit with Staci. I added the eight thousand to the four thousand I already had, and took my money to a dealership in Edmond and bought the year old Honda."

I remember that my hands were shaking as I signed the paperwork. I remember thinking that if I ever wrecked it I could never make that much money again.

"So, yes, I know you can do it. I've seen you do incredible things. I know that you can do anything you want to do. What I'm wondering is, do you really *want* to do this?"

My phone buzzes in my hand signaling that I have a new text message. I use the opportunity to dodge dad's loaded question. "Someone is trying to get in touch with me dad. I'll call you tomorrow. Thanks for believing in me."

Dad told me that he meant every word, and I know he did. After I hang up, I look at my phone and see that the text is a group message from Reverend Chaney to Chelsea, Tess, another number, and me, reminding us of the weekly staff meeting tomorrow evening. I put my phone in my purse and check out my finger. No more blood. I turn to face the remaining four onions. I can do this.

I get a clean knife and set the next onion on the cutting board and commence the chopping. I get through that one with no tears, but in the middle of the second, I make a fatal error and wipe my eyes. Ugh, here come the burning eyes and tears again.

As I'm chopping and crying I think about the weekly schedule of the mission. There are Sunday School classes and church services on Sunday evenings, because Reverend

Chaney goes to preach at other churches on Sunday mornings to raise money for the mission. Several classes that meet throughout the week – from classes about overcoming addictions to parenting and personal budgeting, not to mention Bible studies. Of course, there is a free dinner on Wednesdays at five pm, and a church service at six pm. There are staff meetings on Thursdays at six. Starting next week we will have the after school tutoring program. There's also the clothes closet that's open on Tuesdays and Fridays and a day camp for kids that lasts the whole summer. It's so much work. I think about my dad's question. Do I want to be here? Is it worth all the work?

I'm almost finished with the final onion, ready to throw my arms in the air in victory, when there's a beep beep, signaling that someone is opening the door. I whirl around with my onion-cutting knife in the air.

The back door opens, and a blinding ray of sunshine bursts into the kitchen along with a whoosh of hot Oklahoma summer air, and I remember that it's over one hundred degrees outside. Reverend Chaney steps into the kitchen. He's carrying a big brown cardboard box with water guns poking out of the top, and he has a phone squeezed between his shoulder and his cheek.

"How many do you need?" He listens to someone answer his question as he walks through the kitchen on the other side of the island, to the pantry without even noticing me and my knife in the air. "Yes, we can do that."

As I pull the knife back down to the onion on the counter, I feel a little silly that I was ready to stab an intruder with my tiny knife. Reverend Chaney is standing in the pantry talking on the phone, unaware that anyone else is in the kitchen. I finish chopping and wash my hands. I guess I should start the cornbread, so I start hunting through the cabinets for a mixing bowl.

He comes out of the pantry, without the box. He walks right past me without seeing me again. I giggle to myself. This guy reminds me of The Absentminded Professor. His clothes are ripped and stained all the time; he's always doing five things at once, and he's often oblivious to things right in front of him.

He stops on the other end of the island with his back to me, puts his palms on the island, and hoists himself up on the countertop. "That would be great. Thanks Pastor Kelley. I am looking forward to it. Okay, see you in December, then." He takes the phone from his shoulder and touches the screen to hang up. Then he rolls his head around, like he's stretching his neck. He puts his face in his hands for a moment. Is he praying? Should I make more noise so he knows I'm right behind him? I open the cornbread mix box, but he still doesn't turn around.

He lifts his head and starts doing something on his phone. Then he starts singing an old worship song. His voice is definitely off-key, and he's getting about every fourth word of the song wrong. I can't help it. I laugh as I crack an egg on the side of the bowl.

He turns around sharply. "Melissa!" He jumps off the island and turns to face me. "I didn't know you were in here."

"Sorry, you were on the phone, and I didn't want to interrupt."

He walks toward me. "What are you making?"

"Well, I'm trying to make cornbread at the moment. We'll see how it turns out. I've never made cornbread." I stop stirring for a moment and look in his face. "To be honest, I've haven't done much cooking ever. You may regret asking me to do this."

He tilts his head to the side. "Melissa, have you been crying?"

Crying? I was upset before dad called. How could he know that?

"It's your . . . ah . . . right here," he reaches toward me and touches the side of my face with his finger, "You have black marks."

I take a quick step back and put my hand on my face where his finger had been. "Oh, my mascara must have run down my face when my eyes were watering from the onions." I explain. I rip a paper towel off the roll, turn on the water to wet it and wipe the mess off my face. I feel ridiculous as I remember that I went back into the house this morning to put on make-up so I would look good for Reverend Chaney and now he's seeing me like this.

"Oh, good. I'm glad you weren't crying." He reaches an arm around my shoulders and gives me a sideways hug. "You've made a lot of changes in the last few weeks. That's got to be tough."

This guy sure is a toucher – touched my face, gave me a hug. I move away from him toward the refrigerator to put the egg carton back.

"So," he claps his hands together. "How can I help? I'm not much of a cook either, but I'm sure there's something I can do."

He's going to help me? "Ah, well," I think for a minute. I'm almost finished with the cornbread. "I guess we need to start cooking the meat. Do you know anything about cooking hamburger meat?" I hold the refrigerator door open and show him the ten pounds of hamburger meat that Tess and her husband donated.

"I think I can handle that." He pumps some soap on his hands and rinses it off in the island sink, then crosses to a bottom cabinet and gets out two large skillets. "I've seen people drain the grease off and rinse the meat. Should I do that?"

I shrug, "I guess. My mom does that."

He sets the skillets on the cooktop of the mission stove and gets the meat out of the refrigerator and puts it in the skillets to cook. He continues singing as he works, making up his own phrases that make no sense on the verses of the old song.

I put two big pans of cornbread in the oven and set the timer. What should I do now?

I must have a confused look on my face, because Reverend Chaney laughs and says, "Are you lost?"

I smile and feel my cheeks get hot. "I guess I dump all of the chili ingredients together in some big pots? Tess just told me the ingredients. She didn't exactly tell me how to do it."

"You could go ask her. She's right down the hall in the office." He says as he stirs the meat with a wooden spoon.

I shake my head, "Nah, that's okay. I'll figure it out."

He nods. "So, your mom did all the cooking at home? And when you went to college you didn't cook much there either?"

I shrug, "I wasn't ever interested in learning." I find two big, deep silver pots with handles on the sides and set them on the burners on the stovetop, behind his two skillets on the front burners. "What about you? Didn't you ever learn? Who does all of your cooking?" I pick up an industrial size can of tomato sauce and a can opener.

His turn to shrug. "I can cook a mean frozen pizza." He looks down at the sizzling meat and moves it around with the spoon. "And, I didn't exactly have a normal upbringing."

I pour the cans of tomato sauce and wonder what he means. Should I ask? Is that being nosy? I guess if he wants to tell me he will keep talking. I open cans of kidney beans and dump them in to the pots. Next come the spices. I head to the counter to pick up the seasoning package. When I pick up the package, a thought strikes me.

"Uh oh."

He looks up from the sink where he is busy putting the cooked meat into a strainer, draining the grease, "What is it?"

"I think this seasoning was supposed to go on the

meat. Think it's too late to put it on there?"

"I have no idea." He rinses the meat. "But I don't guess it could hurt anything."

"Okay."

The two of us meet at the stove. He places the skillets with drained and rinsed meat on the burners, and I open the packages of seasoning and pour them on the meat. I can't help but notice that he has black stubble on his jaw line and he smells like freshly cut grass.

I finish with the seasoning and step back as quick as I can. I needlessly clear my throat. "Ah, did you mow today?"

He cuts his dark brown eyes to me and gives me an ornery sideways grin, "Why? Do I stink?"

"Oh! No, no, I just thought you smelled like grass."

He laughs.

"I don't mean that in a bad way, I promise. It smells good. You know, like freshly cut grass. They make candles with that scent." What a dumb thing to say.

"So, you think I smell good?"

I roll my eyes. "Looks like you've got the chili under control there, chef. Why don't I start the drinks? Tea and Kool-aide coming right up." I find the cabinet where the pitchers are and line up five next to the sink. Tess told me that Janice always made two pitchers of Kool-aide, two pitchers of sweet tea, and one pitcher of unsweetened tea.

As I stand at the counter measuring the right amount of red powder and pour it into the pitchers, I'm trying to keep my hand steady. In all my past experience, if a guy asks you if he smells good and smiles a sideways, crooked smile at you, he is flirting. Reverend Chaney cannot be flirting with me. This cannot be happening. I'm in some sort of weird limbo with Brian. Chelsea has a debilitating crush on Reverend Chaney. Then there's the fact that he's a missionary for goodness sake, a missionary! But, he is extremely cute. His short black hair, dark eyes, adorable smile . . .

With shaky hands I pick up the pitchers and cross the kitchen to the sink at the end of the island. I walk behind Reverend Chaney, just as he turns with the wooden spoon pointed out, like he's gesturing with it.

"You didn't answer my – "

I don't see the spoon and walk right into it and his arm. When I crash into him I tip the pitchers and spew the red Kool-Aid mix all over him. His eyebrows go up and he sputters. The red dust explodes all over his t-shirt and face. I freeze with my mouth open. He sets the wooden spoon down on the counter and lifts the front of his shirt to wipe his face, leaving dark red streaks all over his white t-shirt.

"Oh my goodness! I'm so sorry!" I set the pitchers down on the counter and run to the drawer with the washcloths, grab one, and go to the sink to wet it.

I hand him the damp washcloth, and he laughs, "Well, at least it wasn't grape. I hate grape."

"I can't believe I did that." He has red marks on his neck and next to his hairline that he's not getting at all. I grab another washcloth out of the drawer and run a little cold water on it. "Here let me help you." I start wiping the places he isn't getting.

"Is that all of it?" He looks at me with unguarded, trusting eyes.

I press my lips together, "Um," a giggle escapes. "You've got it right in your nostrils."

He wrinkles his eyebrows at me. "You sure got me good, Melissa."

"You kind of look like a dragon, you know with fire coming out of your nose." I'm laughing harder than I have in months. It feels like a valve has been loosened in my chest, like a faucet that was tightened with a wrench has been loosened and now giggles like water are flooding out of me.

He tears a paper towel off the roll and uses it to clean out his nose.

I put a tea bag in a silver pot and fill it with water and

shake my head again at this crazy missionary.

"Reverend Chaney, you don't have to stay in here and help me. You have to preach tonight. You might want to go clean up before you stand in front of people."

He tilts his head at me, "You've poured red Kool-aide all over me, and you've seen me clean out my nose. I think it's okay if you start calling me Kirk."

*****

I don't recognize the song until the chorus, but it's one that we sing all the time at Family Chapel. Of course, it sounds a little different here in such a small sanctuary with no padding on the seats or carpet on the floor to absorb any sound, and with five (*seriously five*) guitars, drums, an electric keyboard, and at least three tambourines rattling. This music could wake the dead, but I'm enjoying listening to them practice. The Native American man who leads the music is someone I haven't met yet. His voice is clear, beautiful, and easy to follow, and he sings with passion. I don't know where the stereotype "stoic Indians" came from, but whoever coined that phrase had never heard the praise and worship music at Diniyoli Mission Church.

After everyone had eaten, the clean-up crew shooed me out of the kitchen, saying that I had cooked and wasn't supposed to clean, too. I took no small measure of pride in the fact that every spoonful of chili and every crumb of cornbread had been gobbled up, that they kept coming back for seconds, and that so many people thanked me and told me the meal was delicious. My little blue-eyed friend Whisper had two bowls and said, "It's easy to pretend it's winter when we are eating chili in the air conditioning." Even Tess ate a bowl and said that I had done a good job. It may not be a big deal to anyone else, but to me, successfully cooking a meal for sixty people is a huge victory.

When the clean-up crew took over, I followed the

music down the hallway and through the door to the left of the small stage and into the sanctuary and took a seat on one of the hard wooden pews and enjoyed the music – somewhat rowdier than the church music I'm accustomed to, but certainly more fun.

As I'm trying my hardest to clap on beat, Chelsea enters my pew and takes a seat next to me. She is really dolled up. Her curly blonde hair is twisted into an intricate up-do, and she has added eyeliner to her regular make-up palette. I smile at my roomie. She smiles back and glances over her shoulder toward the back door and asks me something. I can't hear her over the deafening music.

"What?"

She asks again. Something about Kirk. I still can't hear her over the five guitars, drums, tambourines, and singing.

"I can't understand what you're saying."

"Have you seen Kirk?" She shouts over the music.

All of the team on the stage look at us with matching black eyes. I smile at them and turn to Chelsea and shake my head. "Not since before dinner. I think he had to go clean up for service and study."

She nods and looks at the back door again. We both clap along to the music till the end of the song. Then, when they start another one, Chelsea turns to me with a determined look on her face.

"I'm just going to do it."

"What?"

"Sing."

"What? Why? I think he's doing great." Is she thinking of grabbing the microphone out of his hand?

"He's singing the melody. If he had someone to sing the harmony part with him, it would make it so much better. I've been listening to him for a couple of weeks now, and he needs help." An errant blonde curl on the side of her face bounces with emphasis.

At that she stands, walks right up to the stage, grabs a microphone from one of the holders and starts to sing. I'm sure my eyes are as big as a first grader's on the first day of school. I could never do something like that.

The team finishes their practice. They smile at Chelsea, and she and the leader shake hands and talk for a few minutes. I'm thinking about how it would make sense for Kirk to marry someone like Chelsea, and a heavy hand lands with a thud on my shoulder blade.

"Good job on the dinner."

I open my mouth to say thank you, but before I can say it, Tess lumbers away, down the center aisle to the pews on the other side of the church. She sits in the second pew and doesn't look back at me.

More people are coming in now. I stay in my seat on the sixth row and smile at people as they pass in front of me. Chelsea walks down from the stage and stands in the center aisle, shaking hands with people as they come in. She knows everyone's name and she smiles a genuine smile at them all. She inquires about their health and remembers details about every one of their lives. Surely Kirk will notice Chelsea eventually. She is very cute, and clearly she would make a perfect missionary wife. It's so obvious where Chelsea fits, and I'm a little jealous of that. I thought I fit with Brian in Cool Springs, but I don't fit there, and I don't really fit here either. I would make a miserable missionary wife, can't cook, can't sing, a little awkward around strangers, not a great public speaker (unless it's elementary school-aged kids).

Chelsea is talking to a group of reservation ladies at the front of the sanctuary. It looks like she is telling a story. Her face is so expressive, and the ladies are hanging on every word. She raises her hands over her head and gives a big finish to her story, and all the ladies laugh. She laughs with her perfectly lipsticked mouth open wide and her blonde curls bouncing. Then in mid-laugh, she turns her head back toward the door near the stage. I follow her eyes and see what has caught her attention. Reverend Chaney, ah Kirk, steps inside the sanctuary. He has changed his clothes. Now he's wearing black jeans and a denim shirt, the same outfit I first saw him in, when I saw him on my computer screen that Sunday morning in my bedroom the day after I jilted Brian. His tan face is freshly shaven, and his short, black hair is combed and gelled into place – much different than the way he looked in the kitchen this afternoon with red Kool-Aid dust all over him. I chuckle to myself at the memory. Just then he looks at me, and grins, like he's thinking about the same thing.

*****

Their music stopped and now the missionary man is talking. He usually talks for about twenty minutes, and then the people talk for a while, and then the kids come out. Dreamer has discovered that if he'll stand in the grassy field next to the mission after their meetings that some kids will eventually come out and play ball with him.

He tosses his ball into his mitt while he waits. Then he tosses the ball up and hits it with the bat. Then he throws the ball up high and practices catching pop flies.

"Ugh, I'm bored. I wish they'd get out here already." He pushes his red Cardinals ball cap back and rubs the sweat off his forehead and then pulls the cap back down, subconsciously making sure the signature is centered on the back of his head. "I wonder what's going on in there now?" He thinks as he takes a few steps closer to the mission door.

The missionary man is still talking. The people laugh. Dreamer wonders what's so funny, so he moves a little closer. The missionary is talking about a man who wanted to talk to God. The man saw wind that shattered rocks, an earthquake, and a fire, but he said God didn't talk to him in those things.

"Finally, the Lord spoke to him in a gentle whisper.

Do you know what God said to Elijah?" the missionary man asks the people on the benches. None of the people on the benches raise their hands to answer or speak up. They all stare quietly at the missionary. "God said, 'What are you doing here, Dreamer?'"

Dreamer? Did he just say Dreamer? Of course he didn't. The missionary man said "Elijah," but when the man's lips formed the word Elijah, Dreamer heard his own name.

"This place is creepy," Dreamer says aloud to himself. Not even a chance to play baseball is worth this. I mean, I'll read a book aloud to some little kids, and I'll wait a while for them to come out of their meetings, but I won't stick around and hear voices. Dreamer folds his mitt in half and sticks it between his back and the waistband of his pants, hops on his bike, kicks up the kickstand and peddles away as fast as he can.

*****

My bottom is sore from sitting on this hard wooden pew for almost an hour. I've always sat on padded pews at church and never thought much about the difference they make until tonight. The uncomfortable wooden pews are pretty though. Someone must clean them and the walls with some sort of wood cleaner that makes them both shine. The pews and dark wood paneled walls gleam as they reflect the fluorescent lights in the sanctuary. The ceiling fans circulate their lazy orbs as Kirk asks everyone in the sanctuary to bow their heads. I'm supposed to have my eyes closed, but I peek. Kirk walks down the two steps to the altar area in front of the first pew.

"God is alive," Kirk says into the microphone. "He speaks to people today. He isn't a statue or a painting or a stained glass window. God is real, and He wants to talk to you. He has something to say to you. You just need to get still and quiet and listen to Him."

He looks right at me. Not the first time I've been busted for peeking during altar call. I quickly close my eyes and bow my head.

"So, if you would like to hear God's voice, I invite you to take time to pray at the altars or at your seats while the musicians play a soft song."

I guess I'm in some sort of leadership position here, but I don't know what's expected of me in this setting. As a leader am I supposed to pray loudly? Pray for other people? Pray at the altar or at my seat? Reverend Chaney, er Kirk, hasn't instructed me about this, so I decide to kneel at my seat and pray. I pray for my new students that I'll be meeting on Tuesday and for the afterschool program I'll be starting next week. Then, I pray for Brian, that he will be able to forgive me.

"God, help Brian to know—" Then I feel it. The Whisper. Through closed eyelids I see Michael's face.

"God, I don't know why, but I think I'm supposed to pray for Michael right now. God, please protect him. Help him make the right choices and the right friends. Please bless Michael in school and baseball, and Lord keep him out of trouble." I pray for my brother a few more minutes. Why would The Whisper tell me to pray for Michael? I need to get out of here and call him. I grab my purse and head out of my pew to the center aisle. Then two bony arms wrap around my waist. I look down to see blue eyes and the gap-toothed smile of my little Whisper.

"Miss Melissa! Aren't you so excited?" She claps her hands together and asks.

"Excited about what?" I'm happy to see her, but I keep thinking about getting out of here and calling Michael.

"Next week! Second grade! Duh!" She looks at me like I forgot my own name.

"Second grade? Are you in second grade?"

She nods, and her imperfect corkscrew curls bounce.

"And you're my teacher!"

"That's great! We are going to have so much fun!" My heart swells when I think about spending all day with this little one. What is it about her that has stolen my heart?

"Well, we didn't all die after we ate your food, girl." Ida walks up behind Whisper. "That's a good thing."

Is that supposed to be a compliment? What am I supposed to say? Thank you?

"I'm glad no one died." Is all I can think to say.

"Grandma, can Miss Melissa please walk me home? I promise I won't leave her side."

Ida tilts her head of gray wispy curls to the side and looks at me with narrowed eyes, "Can you keep a good watch on her?"

What's the big deal? Their house is less than a block from the mission, and most all of the kids walk home alone.

"Sure, I'll keep her right next to me."

Ida puts her hand on the back of Whisper's head and pulls her granddaughter's forehead close and kisses it, "God has His hand on you, child."

Whisper tells me that she has to talk to "Pastor" before she leaves. So, I go with her to find Kirk. She gives him a hug and tells him, "Thanks for reminding me to listen to God, Pastor." Then she has to say goodbye to every man, woman, and child, doling out hugs, "See you laters," and inside jokes with friends and we can finally leave.

Of course it's still over ninety degrees, because it is August in Oklahoma, but the sun has gone down, and there is a slight breeze. I breathe in the fresh air and look up at the stars that shine bright here in Diniyoli with no city lights to drown them out.

"How old are you Miss Melissa?"

"I'm twenty-two."

"My mama was twenty-three when she died. When's your birthday?"

I can't imagine how she must feel without a mother.

"November eighth."

"Just a few months and you'll be twenty-three."

"Yep."

We walk past a couple more houses, and Whisper's dog runs to greet us.

"Rocky!" She goes to her knees and pats his back, and his tail wags with delight.

I can't help myself. The little guy is so excited to get some love that I have to go to my knees and pet him too. He looks back and forth, from me to Whisper and pants, as if to say, "I love the attention, ladies, keep it up!"

We tell him he's a good boy and he rolls over and sticks his feet up in the air, wanting someone to rub his belly, so we give in and rub his belly and his ears, and he acts like he's in doggy-heaven.

We finish spoiling Rocky, and resume walking. I remind Whisper that her grandma will be expecting her home soon.

"Miss Melissa, do you remember that secret I told you?"

How could I forget? "Yes, I remember."

Still walking, but slower, "I didn't tell you everything."

Of course there's more to the story – grandma has stolen you away from your dad, a bad man who lives in the big house – I'm sure that's just the tip of the iceberg of this family drama.

"I have a brother." She stops walking and looks at me, smiling her trademark gap-toothed grin. "I know who he is, but he doesn't know who I am."

*****

Chapter Four

Last night mom assured me that Michael was fine. School started there this week. So far, he liked all of his teachers, and had lots of friends in his classes. He had plans to drive to Edmond Friday night for the first football scrimmage of the year.

"You're sure he's okay, mom?"

"Yes Missy, he's fine. Why are you worried about him? He's not the one who's living in a dangerous place all alone."

I can't explain the Whisper to her, even though Kirk's message last night made me realize that the Whisper is the Holy Spirit. I haven't ever been able to talk to my mom about spiritual stuff.

I try not to worry about Michael and focus on Tess's directions scrawled on the back of an envelope. East on Mission Road, past Main Street four miles – I've never driven on this side of Main. Apparently there's a whole neighborhood out here.

After four miles I see it, the grouping of half a dozen blocks of medium sized brick homes, Diniyoli's version of a housing addition. Tess's directions instruct me to turn onto the second street and down to the fourth house on the left. I park my car next to the curb in front of the neat and tidy house with its freshly clipped and edged yard and cheerful red geraniums in flowerpots on the front porch. I remember mom's flowerpot that I used to throw up in a couple of weeks ago and whisper a prayer of thanks to God for getting me out of that time of hopelessness.

As instructed, I don't ring the doorbell by the front door, but I go to the curved cobblestone pathway to the left of the garage and follow it around to the side of the house.

Next to the side door of the house hangs a sign hand painted on a piece of plywood that reads, *"Julie's Chop Shop."*

When I open the door I hear country music and laughter and smell the familiar mix of fruity and chemical smells that emanate from every beauty parlor. Tess had assured me that her cousin's wife's in-home beauty shop was the best in town. Then she added with a smirk, "It's also the only beauty shop in town."

"Hey there, are you Melissa?" a tall, drop-dead gorgeous Native American woman with green streaks in her hair and a nose ring asks.

"Yes," I seriously hope this isn't the stylist assigned to me. Green hair and nose rings aren't exactly my style.

"I'm Devin. My chair's over here." She nods her head in the direction of her chair, turns and walks to it.

Great, just great. The green haired girl is my stylist.

I follow her through the converted garage. There is one other beautician who is snipping a lady's hair and talking about a big back-to-school sale where she saved 75% on new jeans for all of her kids. I assume she must be Julie. I look longingly at her beautiful natural-looking brunette bob as I follow green haired Devin.

I sit in Devin's chair, and she spins me around to the mirror. I look in the mirror and talk to her standing behind me.

"Your hair is really long," she says as she picks up a section of my hair and examines it, "are you sure you want to cut it?"

"Yes, I'm sure." I look at my reflection and see the dark red cascading locks that were supposed to hold a headband veil and drape a few inches below the bateau neckline that perfectly followed the curve of my collarbone to the tip of my shoulders. Yep, definitely time to cut it off.

"Okay, and over the phone you said you wanted to cut it to rest on your shoulders, so," she leans her head over and measures with her fingers, "that means I'll cut about five inches off. Is that okay?"

"Do it."

She nods, puts a cape on me, leans my chair back and places my head in the sink. She turns on the water, pumps some yummy smelling shampoo into her hand and begins massaging it into my hair.

Her hands freeze mid-motion, she gasps and whispers a stream of obscenities only I can hear.

I jerk up. "What is it?"

She puts her hand on my shoulder and says loud enough for everyone in the salon to hear, "You need a smoke break right now, too? We can take a few minutes before we get started."

I almost say, "What are you talking about?" but she grips my arm and gives me a "hush" look and leads me with my half wet and soapy hair out the door.

As we walk past Julie and her customer, Devin tells her, "We're going to have a smoke real quick. Be right back." Julie nods to her and continues her story about the deals she found on back to school clothes.

Outside, Devin pulls me down the cobblestone pathway to the driveway and lets go of my arm.

"What are you doing? I don't smoke!" I'm pretty sure I'll have bruises on my arm where she gripped me.

"Sorry about that. Here," she hands me a towel.

I take the towel and wrap my hair in it. "Listen, I'll just go somewhere else."

"I'm sorry, I knew I couldn't say it out loud. You have lice."

"What?"

"Lice, head lice, you know?" She takes out a cigarette and lights it.

Then I feel it – tiny bugs all over my scalp, in my hair, on my neck crawling up and down my arms. I want to scratch and scream, but I keep my cool.

"That's no big deal." I shrug. "I'm an elementary

school teacher. It's just part of the job. I remember learning about it in college. I'm especially prone to get it with my long, thick hair. I've been working with kids some this week. It's to be expected."

Devin blows out a thin line of smoke. "You working with the mission kids?"

"Yeah, after school program, making their midweek dinner, stuff like that." It's hard to carry on a normal conversation when I know thousands of bugs are making a home on my head.

"Do you know how to treat it?"

"Sure, just get the medicated shampoo from a pharmacy, wash my hair, wash my bedding and get a new hairbrush, right?"

Devin laughs and stubs out her cigarette on the underside of her shoe. "There's a little more to it than that."

More to it? Like what? Am I going to have to throw out clothes? Burn blankets?

She sighs. "I'll help you out. I don't usually help people get rid of lice, but I'll help you, because you're working at the mission."

"Thank you."

"You know a big guy named Nelson? Sings?"

"I've seen the man who sings. I didn't know his name."

Devin takes another drag on her cigarette and blows out the smoke, causing a pause in the conversation. "He's my uncle. Used to go around beating people up for the local dealer, you know, the big white house guy."

I remember Whisper's secret. Her dad in the big white house is a bad man.

"Anyway, when that Chaney dude came a few years ago, somehow he got to know my uncle Nelson, and got him all straightened out with Jesus and stuff, and Nelson's like this perfect husband and dad now. He and my aunt have the two cutest little boys. Anyway," she pauses to suck in the chemicals and then blows smoke out, "you work at the mission, so I'll help you out."

"I appreciate that so much."

"We can't do it here, though. Julie would freak out if I let anyone with lice step into her salon. And, you can't get the shampoo in town."

She can't be serious. "Why? Lice is creepy, but it's not that big of a deal."

"You don't know what it's like to live in a town this small."

"I'm from Cool Springs, not New York City."

"Do you know how many people live here?"

I shake my head.

"Look it up on the internet." She says harshly. "If you go to the pharmacy on Main Street and get lice shampoo, everyone in town will talk about how the new schoolteacher has lice, and the town people will talk about the mission kids having lice." She shakes her head. "School starts on Tuesday. That's what all of the kids in your class will be talking about on the first day of school."

I know head lice isn't a serious disease, but now I feel like a leper. In Diniyoli does it really have the stigma she's describing?

"Tell you what," She looks back at the door to Julie's Chop Shop. "I have some medicated shampoo. I'll go back in there, get it and get your purse. I'll tell them that you got sick or something. I'll bring you your purse, and then I'll follow you to your house. I'll wash your hair and pick all the nits out. I'll show you how to wash your bedding and boil your hairbrush. Then we can do that haircut at your house, okay?"

"Okay."

She turns toward the cobblestone pathway. I reach out and touch her arm.

"Devin, I appreciate it."

She turns her head to face me. The sun glints off the

small gold hoop in her nose, and she smiles. "It's all good."

After forty-five minutes of nit-picking, two medicated shampooings, boiling all combs and hairbrushes, washing all bedding in hot water, calming down a panicked Chelsea (Thankfully, she didn't have any lice. Devin checked her – numerous times at Chelsea's insisting.), I'm finally getting that haircut. Sitting in one of Chelsea's chairs in the middle of the kitchen, and Devin is snipping away. I watch long pieces of my dark red hair fall to the floor. I told Devin to change my original plans. I want to make an even more drastic change.

"All finished." She takes off the cape and wipes my neck with her towel. "It's stinkin' sassy. Go look in the mirror right now."

You can just tell when some people are going to be a good friend. When I first saw Devin, I thought she was a bit strange with the green streaks in her hair and nose ring, and her somewhat bossy and abrasive way of talking, but when she called my new hair "stinkin' sassy," I knew we'd be friends.

In the mirror of our tiny bathroom I see a new me. The sides of my hair hang a little longer than the back in a Victoria Beckham-style bob. I've never had hair this short. I love how it makes my cheekbones pop out and really shows my dark, brown eyes. I feel so much lighter and cooler. In the bathroom by myself, I toss my head and swing my hair around like a model. I feel like a middle school girl and laugh at myself.

Devin dumps a dustpan full of red hair into the kitchen trash and puts her hand on her hip when she sees me. "So, what do you think?"

"I love it." I hug her with both arms, and she stands stiff through it. When I pull my hands back I feel something odd and metallic on her back, through the fabric of her shirt. "Thank you for everything."

She shrugs me off, clips the dustpan on the broom

handle and slides the broom back into its spot next to the refrigerator. "You're so tiny, you can pull the pixie thing off. I could never wear my hair like that with my wide face."

I laugh uncomfortably. What does she have strapped on her back underneath her shirt? A gun?

"Chelsea left while you were in the bathroom. She said to remind you not to be late to your meeting."

Of course Chelsea wouldn't wait five minutes for me. Our staff meeting with Kirk starts at six, and it's only five-thirty, but Chelsea has to show up at least fifteen minutes early to anywhere Kirk will be. Chelsea and Devin remembered each other from school. They remarked that they were both rare cases – Diniyolians who had left and actually returned. Chelsea left to attend college and then returned, and Devin had lived in Tulsa for a few years and had just recently returned home. Devin said earlier while Chelsea was out of earshot that Chelsea always seemed like a girl who knew exactly what she wanted and was going after it no matter what. Sounds like she hasn't changed.

"Yeah, I need to get going. How much to I owe you?" I find my wallet in my purse that's on the bar stool.

"Fifteen."

I drop my hands. "What?"

"That's what I charge for haircuts. Fifteen."

"But, what about the medicated shampoo and coming to my house, combing the nits out, helping me wash everything. You've been here over six hours."

Devin stuffs her hands in the pockets of her jean shorts and looks down at her flip-flops. "I'm a Diniyoli girl, one of the seven hundred and ninety-one residents." She looks up at me and grins, now I won't have to look it up. "I know how embarrassing it can be for the teacher to tell the whole class to stay away from you, because you have lice. I'm not a church person, but I see what Chaney is doing out there at the mission, how much he's done in just a few years, how it's helped my uncle, and it's . . ." She presses her lips together, then says, "it's awesome."

*****

  As I drive to the mission for staff meeting I pray for Michael. I can't shake the feeling that something is wrong with my little brother. I drive past Whisper's house, but don't see her. I remember what she told me about a brother and how her mother died when she was only twenty-three. How strange to live in a town of less than eight hundred, with your real dad and brother only a couple of miles away, but to live in two different worlds.

  Before I left the house, I paid Devin the fifteen dollars and gave her a thirty-five dollar tip. I'm still living off the dwindling dinky savings account I had built up from working on campus in the dean's office, praying that it will last until my first paycheck that I won't get until the end of September so I won't have to ask mom and dad for money, but I had to give her that much. She had spent so much time helping me that I had to pay her for her time.

  I park my car in front of the mission church and look at the car clock before killing the engine – 5:57, right on time. I walk around back to the fellowship hall, run my hand through my new short hair, and open the door to my first staff meeting. They have a round table set up and Kirk, Tess, Chelsea, and the song leader from last night are sitting on metal folding chairs around the table and have their Bibles open. Kirk is reading the Bible aloud. Note to self: they start early and bring a Bible next time.

  I sit next to Chelsea and my chair squeaks as I sit. She smiles at me and tilts her Bible to show me the page and points her finger to Matthew chapter twenty-one, verses two and three, so I can read along.

  " – you will find a donkey tied there, with her colt by her. Untie them and bring them to me. If anyone says anything to you, say that the Lord needs them."

He closes his Bible. "First of all, I just want to thank the four of you for all the work you do here. You aren't receiving any money for what you're doing, but your reward in heaven will be great." He motions to me. "This is Melissa's first staff meeting."

The four of them clap for me and Kirk continues, "Melissa, I know that you know Tess and Chelsea, of course. Have you met Nelson?"

I shake my head. Nelson, the Native American song leader and Devin's uncle, reaches a big hand over to me for a handshake.

"Welcome, Melissa. Good to meet you."

"Nice to meet you, Nelson. I enjoyed your singing last night."

He smiles. "Thank you. We have a good time in our worship."

"You sure do," I agree.

"I know this is a passage that we usually read the week before Easter when we celebrate the Triumphal Entry of Jesus, but I want to point something out to you." Kirk leans forward and rests his lean, tanned arms on the table and folds his hands together over the Bible. "What did Jesus instruct his disciples to do here?"

Chelsea, always ready to talk to Kirk, "He told them to get two donkeys."

"Right. Go get donkeys and bring them back. Do any of you have any experience with donkeys?"

I shake my head and shrug. When would a suburban girl like me ever have contact with donkeys?

Nelson raises one finger. "I have, Kirk, when I was a kid."

"And what is it like to work with donkeys, Nelson?"

Nelson laughs and rubs his chin. "Well, everything you've heard about donkeys being stubborn is true. They aren't dumb, and if they don't want to do something, it's pretty hard to make them do it."

WHISPERS & DREAMS / Martha Fouts/ 89

"I'm glad Nelson brings some actual donkey training experience to the table. I've never been around them, myself, but, of course we've all heard the phrase "mule-headed," and I'm sure it has some basis in truth."

Where is he going with this? I thought this was supposed to be like a devotional and planning meeting, and he's going on about donkeys?

"I wonder if Jesus' disciples felt like He was asking them to do something beneath them or something not "ministry-related?" I've had people come and volunteer at the mission, and think that they would do all church-type things, you know, like wear nice clothes and preach and sing and pray with people." Kirk smiles at the three of us. "Not that there's anything wrong with those things, but here Jesus is asking us to cook meals, mow grass, clean, hand out clothes, play with kids and teach them to read. I know that the three of you get that, and I want to let you all know that I appreciate you for it."

"Let's take a few minutes to pray. When we pray tonight, let's remember to pray for Janice. She's still in the hospital. The surgery on her leg went well, and she will be released soon. She'll have to do physical therapy for at least a month."

I look through the big window that opens from the fellowship hall to the kitchen. I look at the freshly painted blue spot where the ugly black three had been painted by whoever attacked Janice.

"Tess is going to visit her tomorrow. Melissa, would you like to go with her?"

How can I say I'd rather not ride in a car with Tess for an hour in a nice way? "Sure, that'd be great." I look at Tess.

She shoots me a look that lets me know she'd rather be in a car with a hyper toddler for an hour.

He invites us to pray, and we all bow our heads together and pray. I pray for Michael again, and think about what Kirk said. I tell the Lord that I'm willing to do whatever He needs me to do. Nothing God asks me to do is beneath me. I know that He can use even little things to make a big difference in people's lives.

After we pray, Kirk hands us the mission calendar for the next four months, September through December.

"Okay guys, I put our regular weekly events on here, with Chelsea and Melissa's afterschool program starting the second week of school, and then we just have three other events on here. He turns a page of his calendar. "We will do our carnival on Halloween, just like last year."

I write that down on October thirty-first and images of costumes and bobbing for apples and cakewalks appear in my mind.

"Pastor, I'm sorry to interrupt, but I have an idea."

It's hard for me to believe that this mild mannered man used to hurt people for a drug dealer.

"Sure, Nelson. What is it?"

"I wish we could put on a pow wow. It's been over a decade since there's been one in our community. I like the idea of a carnival, but I think a lot of the people here – white and native – would appreciate something that would honor our culture."

Kirk shoots both arms up in the air. "What a great idea. I don't know anything about a pow wow, but I'm sure we can figure it out, can't we?"

Nelson chuckles. "That's what I like about you, Pastor. You're not afraid to do anything.

Kirk laughs. "Well, I don't always get everything right, but I'm willing to try." He writes something on his calendar and turns the page. "We are also going to partner with the school and Clinton Community Church and Rural Outreach Ministries to do a turkey dinner giveaway the Sunday before Thanksgiving."

I write that on my calendar on November twenty-second. Chelsea had told me that before Kirk started the mission church four years ago, Clinton Community Church was the closest church to Diniyoli. It was twenty miles away. With most of the residents of Diniyoli not having a car, that may as well have been twenty million miles.

"In December," we all flip our calendars to the December page, "a church from Frisco, Texas is coming the week before Christmas. I talked to Pastor Kelley from there, and they have a huge event planned for us. They're bringing gifts for all the kids, and they're going to perform a Christmas musical for us."

"Wow, that's great. I love it!" Chelsea says what I'm thinking.

"Yes, he sounded very excited. And, I know Pastor Kelley, and he's trustworthy. If he says he'll do these things, then he'll follow through."

"So, do we need to put anything else on the calendar? Oh wait," he turns to November, "before I forget, the mission will be closed Wednesday through Saturday the week of Thanksgiving. I want you all to go visit your families. I will be here, and I can hold it together for a few days. Also," he turns the page, "same for the week of Christmas. I'll stay and keep the ship afloat. Chelsea and Melissa, you two are welcome to take two weeks off at Christmas, since that's how long you'll be out of school. You both need to make sure to spend time with your families for the holidays." He writes those things down on his calendar, and then flips back to September.

"Now, let's – "

"Ah – " I interrupt.

"Yes? Melissa?" He looks at me with his mahogany eyes.

"Oh, I'm sorry to interrupt, but I just was wondering when you were going to see family for the holidays. I mean, you said you're keeping everything running during Thanksgiving and Christmas. Aren't you going to visit family?"

One corner of his mouth lifts slightly. "My situation is a little different."

I look at the other three people around the table. They are all looking down, suddenly interested in their calendars. What did I say?

"Your hair is – ah, really nice, by the way." He looks at me only with that mischievous eye twinkle I saw in the kitchen.

I touch my hair. "Thanks."

His jaw twitches a little, like he's fighting a smile. He turns to everyone else, "I've saved the biggest news for last. I received a call from Rural Outreach Ministries. They are sending a team down next week to put up a one thousand square foot metal building for us."

Tess and Nelson gasp. Chelsea and I look at each other, confused. Why does the church need another building?

"We've been wanting a building to use as a nurse's station." Kirk explains to us.

"And a place to store the lawn mower." Tess interrupts.

Kirk nods at her, "Right, that too."

"And the weed eater." She adds. "Kirk spends half his life on the lawn mower and working the weed eater."

How much land did he say they have here, two acres? I wonder if Kirk could use some help with the mowing.

"Right, and we don't have a nurse or anyone to work the nurse's station yet, but we are all praying that God would send one our way. The nearest clinic is twenty-five minutes away. We need someone to treat and bandage wounds and dispense medical and nutritional advice and mostly just do basic things like –"

"Check for lice," I add, and reach up to scratch the back of my head.

"Yes, so please pray with us that we can get a volunteer nurse."

He reminds us to always set the alarm and lock the door when we leave, and he goes over the procedure for purchase orders and turning in receipts.

Then, he asks Chelsea and me if we have made any plans for the afterschool program, and Chelsea sits up a little straighter in her chair.

"I have lots of plans, Kirk. I made signs to hang at school. Mr. Clemmons already approved them, and he said that he would also announce it in his daily announcements. I have also made lesson plans for each day of the week — we will do the same activities every Monday, the same every Tuesday, and so on, and I have made timelines for units we will study for the whole year." She opens a binder as she speaks and takes out colorful posters, typed pages of lesson plans, and the timeline of the year.

Kirk looks over her plans. "Wow Chelsea, you've put a lot of thought into this."

"Thank you, Kirk." She beams. "I just want to help the kids."

I look at Nelson who's eyebrows are raised and lips are pressed together and at Tess who isn't even hiding her smirk. Oh Chelsea, everyone at the table is embarrassed for you. I want to tell her that she is a smart and beautiful girl, and that she doesn't have to try so hard. Kirk will notice her eventually, if he hasn't already, and he will realize that she's perfect for him.

"Pastor Kirk," Nelson mercifully shifts the focus of the table to himself.

"Yes?"

"Where will you be this Sunday? My family and I want to pray for your service."

"Thanks for that, Nelson. I'll be at a church in Fort Smith, Arkansas. It's a church I've never been to before. Please pray they'll start supporting us monthly."

We all say that we will, and then we fold our chairs and put them in the closet, and Nelson folds up the table and rolls it into the closet. Kirk explains that he has some studying to do, so he says goodnight and goes to his office. Nelson and Chelsea both parked out front, so they go through the sanctuary to the front parking lot. Tess and I exit through the side door of the fellowship hall together to our cars.

We walk out the door silently, and I lock the door after us. I walk to my Honda and put a hand on my door handle.

Standing next to her ancient minivan with her back to me Tess says, "You'd better tell me how to run this afterschool thing you're doing. I doubt Janice will be back before you and Little Miss Thing run home, and I'm sure I'll have to run it after you leave."

Then she opens the door, gets in, starts the engine and drives away without looking at me.

*****

"Rocky, shh!" Whisper scolds herself for bringing him. He's a good dog, but he whines a lot.

She reaches over and puts a hand on his head so he'll be quiet. He looks at her apologetically, and she scratches the white tuft of hair on his chest, letting him know it's okay.

After kneeling on the yard of dirt, rock, and weeds for nearly an hour, her knees ache and her legs are numb. She has found the perfect place to spy on the big white house – the backyard of an abandoned house across the street. The former tenants had left behind a pile of plywood that was perfect for Whisper to crouch behind. She knelt here three other times, and two of those times, like today, the dad and the son were playing baseball in the front yard across the street.

"I don't know a lot about baseball, but I think he's pretty good," Whisper thinks about the boy she supposes is her brother. He catches everything his dad throws at him, no matter how high, how low, how close, or how far. He jumps up and catches balls one-handed in the air. He bends over, scoops balls up into his glove, and fires them back to his dad all in one motion, it seems. It all seems so easy to him.

And the dad, a white man. He is kind of tall, not as tall as Pastor Kirk, but he seems tall. He has brown hair that touches his shoulders and tattoos on his arms. Whisper remembers when her grandma first told her that her dad was a white man. She'd been shocked, but of course she should have known. Her blue eyes had to come from somewhere. *"I was so dumb when I was little,"* Whisper thinks.

What are they doing now? They rested their gloves on the long front porch, and they went around to the back of the house, out of Whisper's sight. She cranes her neck to try to see them, but it's no use. If she wants to see anything, she'll have to move.

In the front yard of the abandoned house there is an old couch. She wonders if she should risk it. She stays in the backyard for a few more minutes, hoping they will come back around to the front, but they never do. She sighs. What would they really do to her anyway if they saw her over here? The dad actually seems nice. Does a bad man really play baseball outside with his son?

She bends over and shuffles to the side of the house, leans up against the peeling siding and peers around the corner, like an FBI agent in a movie. No sign of them. Between her and the couch, a pink sock, a few empty beer bottles, a blue flip-flop, and a white plastic grocery sack litter the yard. She gets down on her hands and knees and crawls through the trash and the dirt, rocks, and weeds to get behind the couch. Once there, she peeks around the corner of the couch to get a glimpse of them. She can see them now. They're in their backyard. The boy is hitting a ball that hangs on a string attached to the top of a pole. He hits the baseball, and it swings around the pole. The dad, her dad, is standing a few feet away, leaning against an old black car and talking to two men – both of them wear saggy jeans and sleeveless shirts. The two men look just alike, except that one of them has a backwards baseball cap perched high on his head. The boy hits the ball and the dad nods at him while he talks to the two men. Whisper imagines that the dad's nod means, *"Good job, son. I'm proud of you."*

What would they do if she stood up straight and tall and marched over there? She envisions herself saying, "Hi, I'm Whisper, and you're my dad and brother. My grandma told me that you were bad, but I can see that you aren't. I don't know why she told me that. Can I come live in this big house and play baseball with you?"

Her dad would give her a big hug and pick her up and hold her high in the air, like she's seen dads on TV do with their daughters. Her brother would teach her how to play baseball, and if anyone ever picked on her, he'd beat them up. She looks up at the windows over the porch of the big, white house and wonders how many bedrooms are in there.

A dog barks and brings her back to reality. Rocky. She had forgotten about him. She stays in her bent position, shuffles to the end of the couch, and prepares to dash across the yard to the backyard of the abandoned house where she'd tied Rocky's leash to a tree, but something comes over her. She stands up straight and tall and walks to the backyard. She unties Rocky and walks to the road behind the house that leads to her house on Old Reservation Road. She doesn't try to be sneaky or run. If her dad and brother see her, then, they see her.

*****

It is possible for two people to ride in a car together for over an hour in complete silence. For the first fifteen minutes of the trip to the hospital, I tried to think of something to say to Tess. I'd think of something, clear my throat, almost say it, and then realize it was something she'd criticize, so I wouldn't say it and try to think of something else to say. For the next ten minutes I just gave up trying to make conversation and stared out the window at the fields filled with cows, the occasional pond or stand of trees, and every now and then a farmhouse and barn or trailer house. I tried to focus on the scenery and not think about Tess or worry about why she doesn't like me. For the last thirty-five minutes of the ride I did the ultimate avoidance tactic employed by people my age and younger – I played on my phone.

The door to Janice's hospital room is standing ajar, so Tess lightly taps on it with her knuckles and says, "Hey Janice, it's Tess . . . and, ah, Melissa."

"Come in, come in," says the sweet voice from inside the room.

Tess and I enter the room. Janice is propped up in the bed, surrounded by a jungle of flowers. An arrangement of pale pink carnations adorns her food tray, a huge silk arrangement of purple and orange artificial flowers is on the windowsill, there are several baskets of flowers on the sink, and even more flowers are huddled together in the corner of the room.

"You ready to get out of here?" Tess asks as she trudges over to the only chair in the room and plops down.

Janice nods, "Past ready. I'm ready to be in my own bed, eating my own cooking." She looks at me, "Melissa, you can come right here and have a seat." She points to the end of her bed.

"No, that's fine. I'll just lean right here against the wall. I've been sitting in the car, so it's nice to stand and stretch my legs."

"How are my kids?" She asks me with a smile. I remember seeing her in action with her kids, the loving way she kept order and encouraged them. I hope I can be like that with my students.

"They're fine. They miss you and the summer day

camp. They're excited for school to start and for the after school program to start the week after that."

"Are you ready to get started?"

I think about Chelsea's binder full of plans. "Chelsea has a lot of plans. I think we'll be ready."

From her seat, Tess grunts.

Janice ignores her. "Reverend Chaney told me that you've been cooking the Wednesday night dinners. How's that going?"

"Well, I've only done it once. It went okay."

"Tess, have you given her any of the recipes they like?"

Tess just shakes her head and shrugs, as if to say, "Why would I do that? She's not going to stick around long."

"Give her the ham and cheese casserole recipe and the easy fruit cobbler recipe. Those are their two favorites." She gives me a wink. "Have you ever made either of those?"

"I'm not sure if I've had ham and cheese casserole. I love my mom's peach cobbler, but I've never made it myself."

"These are both very easy recipes with not very many ingredients, and all of the people love them. Tess will give you the recipe. Won't you Tess?"

Tess just grunts from her chair again.

Then Tess and Janice begin talking about Tess's husband Phil's blood pressure and about Janice's physical therapy schedule. A nurse who pops in to ask Janice if she needs a pain reliever, which Janice refuses, interrupts them.

Tess pushes against the armrest to lift herself out of the chair. "We'd better get going, Janice. I've got to get this one home to her roommate."

Janice clicks her tongue. "Home to her roommate. She needs to be getting home to her husband."

I'm surprised. This is the first time I've ever heard Janice say anything that wasn't genuinely filled with kindness.

I look to her face and expect to see a snide expression, but instead her face is filled with love, as always.

"I don't have any husband candidates lined up, Janice." I pick up my purse from the ground and pull it onto my shoulder.

"Do you need me to find you a man, Missy?" Janice's ornery eyes twinkle.

"I just might, Janice."

"Cause I've got the perfect one for you. Just say the word. I think he likes you already." Janice looks downright bubbly in her hospital bed, like she could jump out and dance a jig any moment.

I laugh. "Okay, I'll let you know when I'm ready."

"Don't wait too long. Someone's going to snatch that cute preacher up pretty soon." Janice clamps her hand over her mouth, pretending that she didn't intend to say it, and I feel my cheeks redden at the mention of Kirk.

Tess lets out a "Humph," and walks out the door.

*****

I've been smiling and standing perfectly straight for so long that I feel like a mannequin. My feet are already hurting. The heel on my pumps can't be more than an inch, but I'm so used to wearing athletic shoes or flip-flops all summer, that my feet are screaming for summer break. The yardstick in my hand has a laminated poster taped to it. The poster reads, "2nd Grade," in bright red with a yellow happy face underneath. I'm standing in the line behind Principal Clemmons with all of the other Diniyoli teachers. The entire student body of Diniyoli Public Schools – kindergarten through twelfth grade, one hundred and twenty-two kids – are sitting in the bleachers facing us. I was surprised that there were that many students in the school, and Chelsea explained that the population of Diniyoli didn't include the few hundred or so people who lived in the countryside surrounding the town, and those kids go to school here.

In this daily exercise known as the "Morning Rally," the whole school recites the pledge to the American flag, the pledge to the Oklahoma flag, has a moment of silence, and then Mr. Clemmons shares the daily announcements. To conclude the rally, he says that we will say our theme every day.

"So let's all stand and say our theme for the year together," Mr. Clemmons leads the student body in the theme that he introduced to us teachers at our Back to School workshops last Friday and yesterday, the theme that he told us would keep the whole school motivated toward a common goal, "Diniyoli Dragons Work To Discover Our Dreams." He and some teachers even came to the school over the summer and painted the theme over doors and painted starry skies and shooting stars and quotes about discovering dreams all over the campus.

After they recite the theme, he dismisses the high school and then the middle school students to their first hour classes. Then, he tells each elementary grade to come and meet their teacher, starting with kindergarten.

"Second graders, I have some wonderful news for you," the principal says in a tone that's just the right mixture of kindness, fun, and respect, "this is your teacher, Ms. Kolar."

He gestures to me and the row of second graders all slide their eyes over and up to me. I smile, give a little wave, and my heart jumps up to my throat – my first students. He directs them to line up in front of me, and I turn and walk to our classroom, and my future friends follow.

Every professor I had in college said that the first few weeks of school are critical, and that the first day sets the tone for the whole year . . . no pressure.

As we walk into the classroom, I tell my students to hang their bags on the hook that has their name above it, and to stow their lunchboxes in the cubby with their name.

Then, I tell them to find the desk that has their name on it. It took me a whole day last week to write out those name labels, laminate them, and affix them all, but it was definitely worth it. All of my fifteen kids easily find their names – poetic names I fell in love with when I first read them, names like "Spirit," and "Shanee," and "Cheyenne," and "Dakota."

As they come into the room and get their things organized, I notice worn-out sneakers with frayed laces, holey shirts, ripped shorts, and stained backpacks – all things that I didn't see much of as an intern teacher last semester in Cool Springs.

I'd planned to spend the morning putting our supplies in the right place, getting the lunch count, going over our class rules on a PowerPoint presentation, and then playing a game to reinforce the class rules. We finish it all in twenty minutes.

After our game Whisper asks, "What are we going to do now, Miss Melissa?"

Good question. I guess we will just continue with the lesson plans. Good thing I made a month's worth of lesson plans. Maybe they'll last a week.

At ten o'clock the kids go outside for their morning recess, and I'm thankful that there is a recess monitor, so I can have thirty minutes to straighten the classroom and figure out what we're going to do the rest of the day.

"How's it going?" Chelsea leans on my classroom door. She is barefoot.

"You've already kicked off your shoes?"

She nods. "You'd better believe it. It seems like things are going good over here. I haven't heard any screaming – from you or the kids."

"I think it's going good. I didn't plan enough to do, but we'll just do tomorrow's lessons if we need to."

"And the kids?"

"Great, so far." I'm relieved at that.

She gives me a wink. "It's the first day of school. They're on their best behavior."

Oh yeah.

After I tidy up the classroom, I pull three file folders with tomorrow's lesson materials inside. Always keep them busy – that's what I learned in student teaching. I look at the clock above the whiteboard. Twenty minutes until they come back. I sit at my desk and take off my shoes. I look around my classroom at my soft green and yellow décor and all of the kids' hanging backpacks and the supply boxes filled with spiral notebooks and crayons, and I'm filled with a calm peace. This is exactly the way I envisioned it . . . except the reading corner.

I've always wanted a classroom reading corner. I want a corner of the classroom to be a magical retreat from the world, a place where kids want to go, so they work hard and have good behavior so they can escape to the comfy spot to read a book. But, after I'd spent my own money on decorations and name labels and necessary supplies like pencils and paper, I just didn't have enough money to make the reading corner I've dreamed about.

Enough worrying about that, there's nothing I can do about it. I open my desk drawer and pull out the Bible I keep in there. I open it to the bookmarked page, where I left off the last time I read this particular Bible, John 14. I intend to read the whole chapter, but verse fourteen captures my attention. I read it again a few more times. Did God plan for me to read this particular verse right after I was wishing I had a reading corner? Maybe He did. I close my eyes and whisper a prayer. Then, I can't help myself. I have to write. I rip a piece of paper out of a spiral notebook on my desk and write.

Anything?
Salvation, I know.
Healing, I can believe.
But a magical reading corner where kids can read?
Yet I've learned to believe all your claims
So this must be the same
If I just ask in your name
Anything
Is possible for me.

I feel the hot air rush inside and hear the shouts and laughter and know that the outside door next to my classroom door has opened. I put my new poem in the desk drawer and stand. Time for their math lesson.

It took only a few minutes to get them on track for their group lesson on math tools. I walk around the room monitoring the groups as they take each math tool – a calculator, a ruler, measuring tape, a stopwatch, a protractor, and a compass out of the gallon size plastic bag and start hypothesizing about what each tool does and record their theories on the worksheet.

I stifle a smile as I overhear two boys trying to figure out how to use a compass.

"Hey, it's got a pencil in it."

"Yeah, put that pencil on the paper. Now what do we do with it?"

In the next group a boy is bragging that he knows exactly what a protractor measures – sunsets. He tells the two girls in the group with him that he saw his mom hold this tool up and look at the sky through it to measure the sunset.

The two girls take in every word with huge eyes. They believe every bit of his tale, and who can blame them? He speaks with such confidence that he must be telling the truth. He's also the tallest boy in class with long, black eyelashes and a deep dimple on the side of his face. The girls are mesmerized by him.

"I hope I don't look like those mooning second grade girls when I'm listening to Kirk speak," I think as I move on to the next group. I can't deny my attraction to Kirk. I think about his thin lips spreading into a slow smile every time he sees me, and force myself to put the image out of my mind. He and I are on two totally different planets – He's working his heart out to help a town, and needs someone who can roll up her sleeves and work alongside him. I'm a survivor of a wrecked relationship, and I just need time to heal. He needs someone like Chelsea. Someone who knows she's supposed to be here, and is ready to work here for the rest of her life. Sunday night it was as clear as the Diniyoli night sky. Chelsea sang with Nelson, and Kirk preached, and afterwards she stood as close as she could to him talking to everyone after church. No sense in me thinking about his cute smile.

We finish our math lesson and make an "All About Me" handprint with our birthday, our pet, favorite food, favorite color, and favorite hobby written on each finger. I make one too.

"My birthday is November eighth. I don't have a pet. My favorite food is coffee. My favorite color is blue, and my favorite hobby is writing poems. Now, who else wants to share?"

"Miss Melissa, coffee isn't a food!" Someone says from the back of the room. I guess I'm going to be Miss Melissa and not Ms. Kolar.

"Uh-oh, someone forgot to raise their hand. Remember, second graders don't blurt out."

The handsome lady-killer, Dakota, raises his hand.

"Yes, Dakota?"

"Miss Melissa, you said coffee was your favorite food. That's not a food."

"You're right Dakota, and I drink it too much, but I love it more than any other food or drink. Okay everyone, now it's time for me to teach you how we will line up for lunch."

After Chelsea and I swap first day stories over yogurt and pretzels, I take my kids to music class, and then we read a story about a boy named Max who is nervous about the first day of school. I call on students to read a page aloud, and I make notes about their oral fluency as they read.

"Whisper, it's your turn. Read the next page, please."

Whisper doesn't hesitate. She reads Max's conversation with his mom about his fears. She does a scratchy boy-voice for Max, and a high-pitched old lady voice for his mom. She correctly pronounces every word and doesn't have to pause or repeat any words. Whisper is obviously the best reader in the room.

We finish our story and have a discussion about it. I ask them about any fears they had about their first day, and we all laugh together about them. With only fifteen minutes left in the day, we play the Alphabet Back Game, where they trace a letter on someone's back and they guess what the letter is. Then we play Honey I Love You, but I Just Can't Smile, the game that makes them say that embarrassing phrase to one another without smiling. I feel a little sorry for the girls playing against Dakota. None of them can resist smiling when talking to him.

*****

I've never been much of a porch-sitter. Maybe that's because I always had something to do before I moved here — homework, wedding plans, dates with Brian, the coffee shop or the mall with Staci, run on my parent's treadmill or at Cool Springs Park, get a manicure or pedicure, church activities. Also, my parent's porch didn't have much of a view, in the middle of a neighborhood. My apartment at college certainly didn't have a view like I have now. There aren't any houses across the street from our rent house, just an open field. It's strange to me that there's an open field in the middle of town, but obviously Diniyoli wasn't laid out by a city planner.

Chelsea and I don't have chairs on our porch yet, but I'm totally comfortable sitting here on the front step drinking my evening mug of decaf and enjoying the sunset with its pink streaks across the huge sky. I think there's actually something planted in the big field across the street, but I can't ever recognize crops. Maybe the dark green leafy things are soybeans or maybe spinach? On the sides of the field a few wild crape myrtle trees add splashes of purple to the scene, and in the ditch in front of the field a row of bright yellow wild sunflowers are beholding the sunset, like I am. Behind me, the house is quiet. Chelsea is treating herself to a pedicure from Tess's cousin's wife, Julie, at her beauty shop. Beside me on the concrete, my phone rings. I look at the screen. It's dad, probably calling to ask about my first day.

"Hey Ms. Kolar, how was your first day?"

"They actually call me Miss Melissa. I think it's carried over from the mission."

"Ah, how'd it go?"

"Well, we did a day and a half's worth of lesson plans."

I tell dad about Whisper and Dakota and my other students, about my principal and how the school is organized.

"Is it . . . different?"

I think about that for a moment before I answer. I don't have much technology in my small classroom. Most of my students were not wearing new first-day-of-school clothes. Only three of my students don't have jet-black hair and matching eyes. Most of my students walked home at the end of the day, instead of being picked up by parents or riding a school bus. But, I still have smart kids, kids who struggle, sweet kids, hyperactive kids, fellow teachers who obviously care and work hard and those who don't, and a principal who's trying his hardest to motivate everyone.

"You know dad, it's really not that much different from my student-teaching at Cool Springs."

We talk a bit longer about my day, and then he says what I can tell he's been waiting the whole conversation to say.

"Honey, I need you to pray for your brother."

I swallow. I knew it.

"What's going on with Michael, Dad?"

"He and some other senior boys on the baseball team thought they needed to do some sort of hazing to incoming freshmen." Dad pauses. He continues and his voice breaks as he starts to cry. "They all went to an empty acreage outside of town and got drunk."

I pinch the bridge of my nose and stand on my porch. Michael got drunk? He hasn't ever done anything like that as far as I know.

Dad continues, "One of the boys had clippers and they shaved the freshmen baseball players' heads. Of course someone had a phone, videoed the entire incident, and broadcast it on social media. One of the freshmen boys' parents told the school administration, and now Michael and all of the other senior boys are suspended."

"Just suspended, not expelled?" I'm surprised. I can't believe my kindhearted younger brother would ever hurt anyone, but I would think an act of bullying like that would warrant expulsion.

"No, they aren't expelled, but they are suspended for ten days, and the landowner is pressing charges for trespassing, so they'll have to be punished for that. I don't think any of the freshmen boys are pressing charges, but they could, and I wouldn't blame them." I imagine my dad standing on the patio in the backyard, holding his cell phone to his ear. I can picture the disappointment that must be etched on his face as he talks to me. I wish I was there with him to take his hand and hug him . . . and wring my brother's neck.

"What kind of punishment will they have for trespassing?"

"We aren't sure yet. I don't know if they'll have to pay a fine or community service, or what they'll have to do."

"How's Michael?" I ask, concerned, even though part of me wants to smack him.

"He's . . . not himself. I never would have thought he would do anything like this in the first place, and now he's not even repentant. He's angry. He acts as if he didn't do anything wrong. He acts like he's a bigshot senior in high school and he's earned the right to sow his oats or something." Dad stops, then admits, "I don't know what's going on in his head, Missy."

"I should be there."

"No, I actually think it's better that you're not here. Now, your mom and I can focus on Michael, and, maybe you could offer him some sort of outside perspective."

"What if he came here this weekend? That would get him out of town for a few days, maybe help him get the perspective he needs? He can sleep on our couch." Hopefully Chelsea won't mind.

Dad voice brightens slightly. "That would be good, I think. He can drive there after school on Friday and come back Sunday night."

"What if I put him to work while he's here? A group is coming on Saturday to put up a metal building. Kirk always has mowing and weed eating that needs to be done. I could keep him busy."

"Perfect. I think some manual labor might be exactly what he needs." Dad says.

I tell dad that I love him and ask him to tell mom I love her too, and we hang up. Michael. My soft-spoken baby brother is acting like an entitled high school jerk. I knew something was wrong. I scoff, a lot of good my prayers these last few days did. Obviously my prayers didn't stop him from doing this idiotic thing. I slump back down on the porch.

I take a sip of my now cold decaf. As I set my mug back down, I get it. Of course. If I hadn't been praying something worse would have happened – a car wreck, someone seriously hurt, or perhaps worst of all, not being caught. Getting caught doing this stupid thing is actually the best outcome for Michael. I close my eyes and thank the Lord for protecting him, even in his stupidity.

I open my eyes and see Kirk's ten-year-old brown truck pulling up in front of me and parking. He crosses the yard and walks toward me with his trademark laid-back smile. He is holding a white plastic bag in one hand. He looks nice in dark jeans and a clean, crisp light blue short-sleeved, collared shirt, his lean tanned arms and face against the light blue shirt remind me of a day at a beach, a sandy shore and clean blue water. It's so seldom that I see him cleaned up without paint or grass stains that I have to ask if he's going out of town to speak somewhere.

"No, I just came from Oklahoma City. I had a few meetings with pastors set up there today." He sits next to me on the porch. His arm brushes against mine as he sits, and my skin tingles at the accidental touch. I'm surprised at my automatic reaction and tell myself it's nothing, but then I can't help but notice how nice he smells.

He asks me, "Did you have a good first day?" and it takes me a second to realize he's talking about school.

I tell him about my lesson plans not taking as long as I thought they would and about Whisper being such a good reader. He says that he's not surprised that Whisper is so smart and laughs when I tell him about my second grade Romeo, Dakota, and I impersonate the little girls batting their eyelashes at him.

"You've worked toward having your own classroom

for so long. Is it everything you hoped it would be?"

What a question. I tilt my head and think about it. "It's not perfect. The technology is twenty years old, which is not good for the kids, but I suppose we can make do with it until I can write a grant or something. I wish I had a cool reading corner, but I guess we can live without that." I realize the truth, but I don't want to say it. It's embarrassing.

Somehow he knows what I'm thinking. "What?" He asks. "What is it?" He lightly elbows me. "Don't be embarrassed. Is it what you hoped?"

I feel tears well up in my eyes and I look up at the sky to make it stop. "It sounds corny."

"Who cares? Tell me."

I think about the way they called me Miss Melissa even though Mr. Clemmons introduced me as Ms. Kolar, how the kids smelled sweaty when they came in from recess and how we all laughed together at story time and the games at the end of the day. "It was. It was exactly what I hoped it would be." I see an image of Whisper perched in her desk with her legs folded underneath her chair and wisps of her curly black hair tucked behind her ears as her finger trailed underneath the words as she read them aloud. "No, it was better than I hoped it would be."

Kirk smiles at me. "Not corny at all." He hands me the plastic bag sitting next to him. "A first day of school present."

My jaw drops. "You got me a present?"

He shrugs. "It's your first day of teaching ever. I think that warrants a present. Sorry about the bag. I don't know how to wrap presents."

I pull his gift out of the bag. It's a journal. It is leather bound and has wide black and white horizontal stripes and pink lettering across the front cover that says, "Follow Your Dreams." I look at him and see his sheepish grin. How did he know I use a journal and need a new one?

"The red one looked like it was getting full. I thought

you might need a new one soon." He explains.

I had taken my journal to church to take sermon notes in. He must've noticed it then. It's true that I only have a few blank pages left and the corners of the cover are wearing away. I can't believe he noticed that.

"Thank you, I love it." I open it and run my hand across a fresh white page.

"You're welcome." He says and then there's that slow grin of his followed by the melting butter feeling in my chest that I feel every time I see his thin lips subtly stretch into his trademark grin.

"So, how was your trip to Arkansas over the weekend?"

He tells me that it was a productive trip – that two churches from Fort Smith had pledged monthly support. He talks about his plans for the new building, and about a nurse who might come and volunteer two days a week.

"My brother is coming to stay the weekend with me. Can he help on the building construction or on yard work or something?"

"Michael? Sure, we'll have plenty for him to do, but don't you want to hang out with him? He probably doesn't want to come here and work."

"Well, he probably doesn't want to come here and work, but he's making some dumb choices right now and getting into trouble." I think about the incident with the other baseball players and make a fist, digging my fingernails into my palm. "I think some hard work will be good for him right now."

"Got it. Yeah, he can be my assistant for the weekend. We are getting started at five Saturday morning." He stands from the porch step. "What are you cooking tomorrow? After your chili and cornbread, I've been looking forward to your next meal all week."

"No pressure at all, right?" I stand next to him. "Every week it'll be a new recipe for me for a while, since I don't know how to make anything. Janice suggested I make her ham, cheese, and potato casserole and a fruit cobbler. Tess gave me the recipe. I'm sure I can't make it as good as Janice did, but I'll try my best."

Kirk puts his hand on his stomach, tilts his head and closes his eyes. "Mmmm-hmmm, that's one of my favorites. What kind of cobbler are you making? Please tell me peach."

I can't help but laugh. "Yes, peach."

"Oh, you're speaking my language now."

How can such a thin guy love food so much?

"Do you want my help in the kitchen again?" he asks with his ornery grin.

"No sir, you're too messy."

He laughs. "Guilty. I'm not the neatest person in the world."

I think about his perpetually stained clothes – "not the neatest person in the world" is an understatement.

"Well, glad you had a good first day. I'll see you tomorrow night." He starts toward his truck.

"Okay, and thank you for the journal. It's the perfect gift for me." I hold it up.

"Sure, you're welcome." He opens the door to his truck, gives a little wave and leaves.

I go inside and find a pen on the dresser in my bedroom. I want to write something about the view from the porch, maybe even sketch a picture of the field and the sunset. I go back to the porch and open my new journal to the first page. Then I see it - writing on the inside cover.

Melissa,
I really admire how you're chasing the dreams that God has given you, even though you aren't sure where they'll lead. Keep chasing those dreams. You'll discover that His plans are the best!
Kirk

His handwriting reminds me of Brian's — small and slanted, but nothing else about him is like Brian. Not only does Brian have all of his ducks in a row before he acts, he makes sure the ducks have had all of their shots and have been cleaned and brushed and are standing at attention in a precisely measured line before he acts. If Brian were in charge of the mission, he would have all of the volunteers and funding and buildings in place before he ever started the project. One might say that Kirk flies by the seat of his grass-stained pants.

But, Kirk has a passion that I never saw in Brian. Sure, Brian says that he loves me, and he loves the Lord, and his family, and he seems to enjoy his job as a physical therapist, but . . . passionate? Kirk is absolutely driven for the people of this community. The only thing I've ever known Brian to wake up early on a Saturday for was a game of golf.

I write and draw in my new journal. Chelsea comes home with pretty feet and hot pink toenails and a big, brown paper bag filled with take-out from The Green Parrot for both of us. We eat chicken fried steak, corn, and mashed potatoes and gravy with plastic forks out of Styrofoam containers. Far from fancy, but it tastes heavenly. I haven't had any meat for over a week, just eating what I can afford until my first paycheck.

"Chelsea, thank you for dinner. You didn't have to do that." I wipe my mouth with a napkin from the brown bag. "You didn't have to do that, but I'm so glad you did. Peanut butter and jelly sandwiches are getting old."

"We deserved a victory meal after our first day, sister." She winks at me.

We do the dishes together and then settle on the beanbags in front of the television and watch a chick flick that Chelsea owns on DVD. I can quote most of the lines of this movie, but I still tear up every time the two main characters realize they love each other at the end. The man's dog runs up to the woman and then she sees him coming up the path toward her. Her eyebrows wrinkle as if to say, "It was you?" He shrugs as if to say, "Yep, it's me." She shakes her head in wonder, and they kiss.

I wipe a tear from the corner of my eye. I do cry every time I watch this movie, but this time it's for a different reason. My happily ever after didn't happen.

Chelsea and I go through our nightly routines – I get the bathroom first to brush my teeth and wash my face for less than five minutes, and then she occupies the bathroom for about forty-five minutes for whatever beauty treatment she has lined up for that particular evening.

I'm sitting criss-cross on my bed with only the dim light of the lamp on my nightstand glowing, writing comments on my students' All About Me handprints, and Chelsea emerges from the bathroom with sparkling skin and a whitening strip affixed to her teeth.

"Your complexion looks gorgeous. What did you use tonight?"

"Cucumber mask. I got it at the pharmacy in town. My skin feels so soft." She says with a lisp through the plastic on her teeth.

"What, you didn't mash up cucumbers in there?" I laugh. "When you smashed those avocados, I thought, 'What kind of crazy nut am I living with?'"

She laughs. "It's okay, I know I'm crazy." She picks up one of the handprints. "Birthday, pet, favorite food, color, and hobby – these are great for introducing each other to the class. Mind if I borrow this and do it in my class, too?"

"Of course not, you brought me chicken fried steak tonight, after all."

She hands the handprint back to me, and I arrange all of them in a neat stack. "Are you going to hang them in the room?"

I shake my head, "Not yet. Tomorrow we're going to use them to write a paragraph about ourselves. Then we'll hang them."

"Ooo, I love that, too. Mind if I steal that, too?"

"You can use anything I have. You know that." I smile at her and put all of the handprints back in the plastic binder and zip it up.

Chelsea takes the plastic off her teeth and drops it in the wastebasket next to my bedroom door. "So," she takes the two steps to my bed and sits on the corner of it. "Remember how I said that I was going to ask Kirk to dinner?"

"Yeah, did you?"

She nods. "I did. After staff meeting last week I went back into the church to Kirk's office and asked him if he wanted to go out to dinner. He said that he couldn't go because he had to study." She runs her tongue along her newly whitened teeth. "I called him Friday and told him that I was going to drive to Clinton to get some new clothes for school, and," she mimics the aloof tone she must have used when she asked him, "'Did he want to tag along with me and maybe catch a movie?' He replied that he needed to get to bed early so that he could get up early on Saturday to get some things done. Then, I called him Saturday afternoon and asked him if he wanted to go to the lake with me. I even suggested we bring some fishing poles, even though I've never fished in my life, because I know for a fact that he likes to fish. He turned me down . . . again. He said that he already had plans. I guess he couldn't come up with a specific excuse." She puts a hand on my bed and leans over to me. "Are you counting, Melissa? That's three times. Three rejections."

Ouch. Poor Chelsea.

"I wasn't going to ask him out again. I really wasn't. I thought, 'That's it. He's obviously not interested. I'm not going to ask him again.' But then, I got to thinking that maybe he's just been busy and distracted and doesn't realize that he's been rude to me. Maybe after he's had a couple of days, he'll realize that he should have gone out with me. So, I thought I'd try one more time. This afternoon I called him and asked if he wanted to get a quick dinner with me at Green Parrot, and he said he had to go and visit someone."

"Oh, I'm sorry, Chelsea."

She shakes her blonde curls. "I don't understand. I really thought he wanted to go out with me. And not only that," she pulls her petite legs onto the bed and hugs them close, "I know this sounds crazy, but I thought it was God's will for me to marry him. I mean, I really do want to help the people here, and so does he. It makes sense that we would get married, right?"

"But, Chelsea, do you even like him?"

"Well," She props her chin on her knees and thinks about it for a minute. "He is hot."

I laugh. "Yeah, he's cute."

She smiles dreamily. "He's kind of a cross between a cowboy and a surfer and a professor."

We both break into giggles. Then Chelsea says something that changes everything. "But, now that I think about it . . . Don't you think he relies on good looks and charm sometimes? And, he's not a very good planner at all. I mean, a one-hour meeting to plan for six months? And, come on, a grown man who goes around with stained clothes?" She sits up straight. "You know what? I don't like him."

"You don't?"

"I don't." She stands up and puts her hands on her hips. "I'm not going to be a missionary's wife." She crosses to the mirror on top of my dresser and looks into it. "God's going to use me to help people here in another way." She walks to my bed and gives me a hug. "Good night Melissa. Thanks for the talk. You're so sweet to listen to me." She walks to my bedroom door and looks back at me. "And thanks for the handprint idea. I'm going to use that." Then she goes to her bedroom and shuts the door.

I lean back on my pillow and think about Chelsea's realization I just witnessed. I also marvel at the confidence Chelsea has concerning her future. I don't know that I've ever been that sure of myself and the direction I was going. I feel downright wishy-washy compared to her.

Everything she said about Kirk was true. But, all of those things could also be positive character traits. You could say he tries to get by on good looks and charm, or you could say that he's personable. You could say that he isn't a good planner, but you could also say that he gets a lot done because he doesn't take forever worrying about the details. And as for his clothes . . . well, I can't think of a positive spin you could put on those grubby clothes of his.

I lean over to switch off the lamp and see my new journal on the nightstand. I realize that I am the person Kirk told Chelsea he had to visit.

I pick up my new journal and write a prayer in it.

*****

Devin is also writing - not in a journal, but in the notes app on her phone. And not a prayer but notes about her interactions with the two men she's nicknamed "Dumb and Dumber."

"I accepted Dumb's invitation to hang out at Jacob Davis' house today." She types on her phone. "I sat on a couch in the living room for two and a half hours and watched Dumb and Dumber play video games. No criminal activity was witnessed, and Jacob Davis never appeared."

She turns off her phone and shoves it into her purse. "How long is it going to take to win the trust of these morons?" Devin asks herself. She leans forward and rests her forehead on the steering wheel. "What am I doing here?" She asks herself for the thousandth time.

Devin fishes cigarettes and a lighter out of her purse. She gets out of her car on the side of the country dirt road and lights up. She inhales and blows out the thin line of smoke like second nature, and is calmed by the familiar chemicals, but she knows the calm won't last long.

She silently curses herself. She curses herself for her big idea that she alone could clean up the town. She curses the miles of nothingness that surround her and her car in all directions. She curses the drug dealers who are smarter than businesses, politicians, churches, schools, and everyone else it seems, because they know just how to move in on a rural area and take it over.

*****

I'm sure that Janice can probably peel a potato in less than a minute, but I've learned that it takes me a lot longer than that, and when I saw that this casserole was going to require me to peel sixty – *yes sixty* – potatoes, I asked Chelsea to come and help me peel.

"How can you do this so fast?" I ask her as she finishes probably her twentieth potato while I work on my twelfth.

She shrugs. "Practice. My mom always worked, and I usually had dinner cooking by the time she got home. What about you? How come you never cooked?"

"My mom is a teacher, and she was always home by four and made dinner." I nearly cut myself and add, "I'm starting to wish she had taught me something, though."

We finish peeling the potatoes and then cut them into chunks and drop them in the huge steaming silver pot of boiling water on the stove. Chelsea asks if I've got everything under control, and I assure her that I do, so she leaves to go home to grade a few papers and re-do her hair and make-up before church.

I survey the kitchen. A pot of boiling potatoes on the stove, bags of grated cheese and diced ham on the island, margarine, flour, salt, pepper, milk all on the counter next to the stove – I double check the recipe to make sure all of the ingredients for the casserole are accounted for. Got everything. Okay, time to make the white sauce.

I measure everything and put it into the saucepan and pour milk on top. Janice's recipe says that I'm supposed to stir constantly while it cooks. Alone in the quiet kitchen, I watch the margarine begin to melt and the clumps of flour begin to disappear into the mixture. On Monday afternoon I found two index cards jammed into the metal mailbox that hangs next to our front door. One of them had the recipe for the casserole on it, and the other had the recipe for the cobbler on it. I could envision Tess's annoyance of me from the way the cards were shoved into the mailbox – crumpled by the bottom of the box and bent by the lid. The woman has decided that she doesn't like me, and I can't do anything about it.

I layer the partially boiled potatoes and diced ham and shredded cheese in the big aluminum pans, pour the white sauce over the top, and put the pans in the 350-degree oven. I wash my hands at the sink and look out the window. In the field outside I see the boy who was reading Holes the first time I visited here. He's wearing the same Cardinals baseball cap, and he's playing catch with a shirtless boy.

The shirtless boy holds up a hand to tell the red hat boy to wait a minute. Then, he picks up a water bottle on the ground beside him and pours the entire bottle over his head. I don't blame him. I'm in the air conditioning, and I feel like pouring a bottle of water over my head. With my hair so short, I can't pull it up into a ponytail, but it's still long enough to hang on my neck, so I have about a hundred bobby pins all over my head in a desperate attempt to lower the temperature on my neck. This morning, the daily news alert on my phone flashed a heat advisory warning for today.

*****

And just like it does every year, the weather stays hot until September and a few nights in October actually start to feel a bit cool and the school year inches along to progress report time. Janice progresses to a walking cast and then crutches and then walks with no aide at all, totally healed and helping in our after school program. Who am I kidding? It's Janice's program, and Chelsea and I are trying to keep up with the woman who is more than twice our age and learning more from her about everything than we ever learned about anything in college.

Something is different now. I'm waking up each morning fifteen minutes before my alarm, thinking about the kids who are reading better and whose bellies are being filled, and who are wearing new jeans from the clothes closet, the parenting classes being taught by our new twice a week nurse, and the constant reminders from Pastor Kirk to "Dream." I draw my dream classroom reading corner in my black and white striped journal. Devin even mentioned that she heard a rumor that the drug business from the big white house is declining.

It's not all perfect. The dirty looks and snide comments from Tess continue. But, every week a new index card is jammed into my mailbox – "Taco Salad for a Crowd," "Easy Lasagna Pie," "Beef Tips and Rice," "Chicken Spaghetti," and a delicious dessert recipe every week, "Sock-It-To-Me Cake," "Pecan Pie Bars," "Double-Decker Brownies." I've even started making some of these recipes at home for Chelsea and me. Around September I noticed that my waistband was tight, so I called Devin and asked her if she wanted to start running with me. I've learned that if I run at least three days a week, then I can eat Janice's decadent main dishes and desserts a few times a week and still button my pants.

My swingy bob turns into a misshapen pageboy, so Devin trims it. And Michael? He seems to enjoy his Fridays and Saturdays in Diniyoli hanging out with his sis and

Chelsea and working with Kirk. He's become a bit of a handyman genius – Kirk says Michael can fix anything. But Dad says as soon as he arrives in Cool Springs on Saturday night his attitude is surly, and it stays that way all week. What's it going to take to get through to him?

Chelsea has officially given up on Kirk. There's no one to date in Diniyoli, so she says that she's given up on dating, given up on men, given up on marrying, and will probably live a celibate life. We'll see. I'm happy that Brian doesn't creep into my dreams anymore.

Part Two – Dreams

Chapter Five

Should only have to mow a couple more weeks, Kirk thinks as he parks the mower in the new metal building and brushes the grass off his jeans. Thank the Lord. I'm seeing acres of grass in my nightmares, he chuckles to himself.

He pulls his phone out of his back pocket and checks the time. Five-fifteen. He is supposed to be at Chelsea and Melissa's house in fifteen minutes. Chelsea hadn't asked him out in a long time, and when she asked him to come over for pizza and board games on Friday night, he thought he was having déjà vu. He thought this was all over two months ago?

No, no, no, she'd quickly assured him when she noticed his deer-in-the-headlights look. It's a group thing – Melissa will be there, and Melissa's brother Michael, and some girl named Devin who cuts their hair. He hesitated – three women and a teenage boy? But, then again it wasn't like he had other offers to do something fun on a Friday night. Sometimes he went to Nelson's house and ate his wife's cooking and watched their sons play in the backyard. Sometimes he played basketball with a group of young men in the high school gym. But nothing tonight. And she did say that Melissa would be there.

"Sure, I'll be there at five-thirty, right after I mow."

He whistles as he locks up the building and jogs across the grass acreage to the parking lot next to the church where his car is parked. Going to have to hurry up and shower and change. Good thing he only lives a few blocks from Chelsea and Melissa.

He rounds the corner of the church and almost runs into him – a short guy in a black hooded sweatshirt with the hood pulled down low over face with a telltale can of spray paint in his hand. Kirk looks at the side of the church and sees another big, ugly number three painted there.

"Hey!" Was all Kirk could think to say.

The guy chunks the can at Kirk, turns, and runs. The can hits Kirk on the forehead and he instinctually ducks his head, but then quickly jerks his head up to see where the vandal went. He catches sight of the man sprinting to a black car. Kirk runs after him. The guy turns left to run through the open gate of the fence in front of the mission, but Kirk jumps over the fence, surprising himself that he could clear a fence that high, and is able to catch up to him right as he opens the passenger side door of the black car.

"You're going to fix that!" Kirk yells at the man as he points back to the graffiti on the side of the church.

The man pauses and looks at Kirk and snorts, "Sure thing, Preach." He slides into the passenger side and the driver, a man with a backwards baseball cap perched high on his head, points his finger like a gun at Kirk, backs out of the parking lot and drives away.

*****

The game is Scrabble, and Kirk is losing. He's blaming it on the fact that he's only had vowels all night. Melissa is killing everyone by at least fifty points. She's some sort of Scrabble savant – positioning letters just right on triple word score squares, adding prefixes or suffixes to words already on the board, clinking down tiles right next to each other to make multiple words so the tiles could be double, even triple counted.

"Melissa, you need to put these skills to use and enter a Scrabble tournament and win a million dollars for the mission!" He teases her with a pat on the back.

Next to him at the tiny kitchen table she grins.

"How did you learn how to play Scrabble like that?"

"We had game night every Thursday night, didn't we Michael?"

Across the table from her, Michael nods, "Yep, we played card games like Spades and Hearts and board games like Monopoly and Scrabble. Mom and Dad and I still do." Michael presses his lips together and shrugs one shoulder at Melissa. She replies with a shoulder shrug back. Must be a secret sibling language.

Kirk pictures the Kolar family on game night in a glowing home in Cool Springs. He can envision them playing games around a rich wooden table, eating cookies and laughing at the little trials of their day. A dream family. A girl from a life like that is as out of reach to a guy with Kirk's past as a princess or a movie star.

Devin and Chelsea step in to the dining area and interrupt Kirk's thoughts.

"Brownies are served," Chelsea announces.

"And milk," Devin adds.

Chelsea hands everyone a brownie square on a napkin, and Devin hands everyone a glass of milk. Kirk looks around the table – board game, brownies, milk, a beautiful redhead to his left – he never thought he'd be in a setting like this.

"Mmm," Melissa says as she takes a bite of the warm brownie.

"How are they?"

She closes her eyes and nods, "Mmm," she says again.

He can't deny his feelings for her. She's gentle and soft spoken and willing to try new things. Her heart seems so pure, always putting others before herself and never taking credit. Of course he can't ignore his physical attraction to her – warm brown eyes, dark red hair, full lips and slim build that he has noticed more often than he wants to admit.

"These are great, Chelsea."

"Thank you," Chelsea tells him without flirting. Thank the Lord.

"So, sis, I had nice conversation, and I played an entire game with you guys. Can I please turn the TV on now?" Michael begs across the table to Melissa.

She looks at her phone on the table to see the time and then sighs, "I guess."

Michael leaps out of his chair, runs two steps to the living room, and jumps over the back of Melissa's couch, lands right in the middle of it, scoops up the remote, turns on the TV and has the baseball world series on in less than three seconds.

"Hey! Don't jump on my new couch!" Melissa scolds him. "It's my first piece of adult furniture, and I want it to last."

Michael mumbles a distracted apology to his sister with his eyes transfixed on the screen.

Melissa rolls her eyes at him and turns to her friends at the table and starts talking about school, then the pow wow, then a movie that's coming to theaters next week while Kirk tries to listen and not watch the game over her shoulder.

"Kirk," she says to him, and he tears his attention away from a nail-biting eighth inning. She laughs, "It's okay, you can go watch the game with Michael."

"Great," he says as he repeats Michael's leaping, running, and jumping motion.

"Kirk!"

"Oops, sorry Melissa." He says without looking away from the TV, but he's not really sorry. He knew she'd holler his name like she had Michael's, and he'd do it again just to hear her say his name.

Michael and Kirk talk baseball during the game. Neither one of them like the teams that are playing, and they wind up talking about their favorite teams and players and the subject of conversation comes around to Michael's baseball career.

"So, you're a pitcher, right?"

Michael shrugs. "Yeah, maybe."

"Are you playing something different this year?"

Michael keeps his eyes on the screen, even though a boring law firm commercial is on. "I might have to play in the outfield this year. Don't know yet."

"Really? What happened?"

"Oh, there's this sophomore that everyone thinks is better than me. I've pitched all through high school, and now . . ."

What a heartbreaking blow. In the time Michael's been coming to help on the weekends Kirk has grown to like the kid. Maybe this disappointment has something to do with his rebellious behavior.

The women finish their conversation about movies and clothes and everything else under the sun and then meander into the living room.

"Do you play?" Michael asks, like he's expected to ask the question, still without looking away from the game that has resumed on TV.

"Yeah, not much anymore. I played third base in high school, didn't ever pitch."

"Oh yeah?" Micheal raises his eyebrows and looks at Kirk. "Cool. What school?"

"Memorial. Tulsa Memorial."

Devin speaks from her spot on a beanbag. "Really? When I lived in Tulsa I lived right behind LaFortune Park, right near there. How long ago did you live there? Maybe we were neighbors."

Kirk hesitates, not wanting to reveal too much. "I just went there one year, my senior year, and then moved right after high school, so it's been nine years since I lived there."

"Oh, I was in eighth grade here in Diniyoli nine years ago." She laughs.

"Are you saying I'm old, Devin?" He teases.

"Hey, I didn't say it – do you need me to turn up the volume on the TV so you can hear it, grandpa – I mean, Kirk?" She says with a wicked grin.

"Were you good in high school? Was your team good? Where else did you go to school?" Michael asks, suddenly interested in what kind of ball player the preacher was as a teenager.

"Uh, we were pretty good." Kirk rubs his hand on his knee.

"What other school? Did you go to Union? They have an awesome baseball program."

Kirk nods. "I went to Union in ninth grade."

"Just one year?"

Kirk figures he'd better come out with it. Michael wasn't giving up, and it was bound to come out sooner or later. "The truth is, I was a foster kid. I was in the system my whole life and bounced around from foster family to foster family. So, I went to seven different high schools." He stands. "I could use another brownie. Are there any more Chelsea?"

"Yeah, let me get - " She starts to get up from her beanbag, and he stops her.

"No, don't get up I got it. Anybody else need anything?"

No one needs anything from the kitchen. After he leaves the room, Chelsea gives Melissa a look. Who would have believed that Reverend Kirk Chaney had been a foster kid for the first eighteen years of his life?

He goes to the tiny kitchen and cuts himself a brownie from the pan sitting on the stovetop. After all these years, you'd think that he wouldn't be embarrassed about his past anymore. He'd done well in high school, graduated from Bible college in Texas, been employed as a youth pastor, and now was seeing lives changed as a church planter or domestic missionary – all of these accomplishments, and yet he still hated to talk about his chaotic upbringing.

He turns around and sees her step into the kitchen.

The sight of Melissa's beautiful face looking at him with pity sends an ache to his chest. "Are you going to eat that?"

He looks down at the uneaten brownie in his hand.

"Because, it's the last one, and if you're not going to eat it, you can give it to me." Melissa smiles at him, crosses her arms and leans against the refrigerator.

He takes a big bite.

"Oh that's just cruel. I thought you were a chivalrous gentleman."

He swallows the delicious brownie. "Not when it comes to the last brownie."

She looks down at her shoe, not sure how to start. "I – I just want to say that you – "

He interrupts her, "You don't need to say anything. It's no big deal, all in the past." The last thing he wants is Melissa's pity.

"No, I need to say this." She touches his arm. "I've always wondered why you were so driven, how you could go, go, go, never stopping, always working for the people of this community. I knew it wasn't that you are a workaholic, because I could tell that it wasn't work to you. It was a passion, a calling. Now that I know about your childhood," She pauses and nods. "You identify with these kids. God rescued you, and now you want to rescue all of them."

"Maybe there's something to that." He wipes his hand on a towel on the countertop. "But you know, Melissa, everyone needs rescuing, not just foster kids and kids from the middle of nowhere."

Her eyebrows shoot up. "I didn't mean to offend you. I'm so sorry if I did. I was just trying to say – "

Kirk interrupts her again. "It's okay, really. I know

you weren't." He steps in front of her and then steps out of the kitchen. "I think I'm going to go ahead and go home – got to get up early in the morning."

She opens her mouth to say something, but can't think of anything to say.

He says goodbye to the rest of them and jiggles his keys as he walks across the front yard to his truck parked on the street in front of their house.

He starts the engine and drives to his house while thoughts like hailstones pound against his mind. He would always be an outsider – bam. Melissa would never understand – bam. Something must be wrong with him for his own parents to give him up – bam. He would never have a family – bam.

He pulls into the driveway and parks his truck in the detached garage of his house and sits there for a few minutes.

"No more destructive thoughts," he tells himself aloud. "God is with me, and I'm here for the long haul. The people of Diniyoli are my family." He smacks the steering wheel with an open hand for emphasis and gets out of his truck. He pulls down the garage door, walks across his wood plank front porch, unlocks his front door and looks around his quiet house. How could he expect a girl like Melissa to stay for very long in a place like this? One thing was certain – he'd had a revolving door of authority figures in his life, and he's not going to do that to the people here, so he'd better quit thinking about the pretty redhead from the suburbs who will probably want to move back to mama in a few months.

*****

"Done." Whisper sets <u>Matilda</u> down on the table next to me.

"You finished the whole thing?" I pick it up to double check the grade level on the back, even though I already know that it is a fifth grade book.

Whisper beams with pride, showing the gap between her two front teeth. "It's so much better than the movie, but I think books are always better than the movie, don't you?"

"You read the whole thing? Did you answer the questions and define the vocabulary words in your book journal?" The second grader has only been working on this book for four days.

"Yep, I already turned it in to Ms. Janice." Whisper says with her chest puffed out, proud of herself. "And she said I got them all right."

"Girl, we are going to have to get more books. You are a reading machine!" I hold out my knuckles and she gives me a fist bump. "Go pick out another book. You'll need to get something out of the sixth grade level crate. You've read all of the fifth grade books."

Whisper floats over to the book crates on the other side of the fellowship hall, on a cloud after my praise.

I walk around the quiet room, weaving in and out of reading children, patting the backs of those whose eyelids are drooping, giving a thumbs-up sign to those who are working hard. Whisper's always the first one finished with her work at school, and she makes perfect scores on everything. Sometimes it's difficult to keep her occupied. I had to borrow a reading workbook from Chelsea's fifth grade classroom, because Whisper had already breezed through the second, third, and fourth grade reading workbooks. I also set up a table at the back of the room with Sudoku puzzles, crossword puzzle books, a brainteaser book, math puzzles, and art supplies. I call it the "Early Finisher Table," but it's really the Keep Whisper Busy Table.

I catch the eye of a boy sitting on the carpet. He's holding his book open, but he is looking around the room, obviously bored, probably wishing he was outside playing. I go over to him, kneel down on my knees next to him and whisper, "Just seven more minutes of silent reading, buddy. I know you can do it."

He rubs his eyes with the back of his hand. "Okay, Miss Melissa." He sits up a little straighter and focuses on his book.

I tousle his hair, stand, and resume monitoring. Across the fellowship hall Chelsea is having a similar conversation with another younger boy. Being still and reading silently for twenty minutes can be like twenty hours in a torture chamber to a little boy who just wants to run and jump around outside.

After the last seven minutes of silent reading, Janice sings a call and response song with the kids to signal that it's time to put the books away and go outside to play for twenty minutes. The kids put the books away as quickly as they can and rush to line up at the door. When Janice tells them that they did a good job putting the room back into order and they can go outside, they burst through the back door like prisoners released from the pokey.

Janice leads the line of children outside to the awaiting basketball goals, bats and baseballs, hula-hoops, jump ropes, and the empty acres of brown grass that's perfect for races and games of freeze-tag and Red Rover. Chelsea and I follow at the back of the line to catch any stragglers.

"Miss Melissa! Miss Chelsea!" an older girl runs from behind to us.

"What is it, Cheyenne?" Chelsea asks her.

"It's so gross. The toilet in the girls' bathroom is filled with . . . with, you know." Cheyenne's bottom lip curls in disgust. "I tried to flush it, but it just got more full, like it was going to overflow."

"Okay, thanks for telling us. We'll take care of it." Chelsea says, and Cheyenne goes outside to enjoy the beautiful autumn afternoon.

"I'll go fix it." I turn toward the bathroom.

"No, don't. It's fine. The kids will only be here

twenty more minutes after playtime. We'll just tell the girls to use the boys' restroom." Chelsea takes a step outside the door, into the sunshine.

I don't follow her. "It'll just take me a minute to plunge it and clean it up. It's no big deal."

"It's fine. Tess can do it tomorrow. Give her something to do besides gripe at everybody." Chelsea laughs.

I laugh. "It'll just take me a minute."

"Suit yourself." Chelsea shrugs and goes out to the kids.

I find a plunger under the sink in the bathroom and plunge the clogged toilet and then find paper towels and bleach spray cleaner in the supply closet, clean up the mess, and wash my hands. When I open the door, Tess is standing in the hallway with crossed arms, staring at the door, like she is waiting for me to come out.

"Oh, hi Tess."

Tess grunts.

"Well, see you later, I've got to go play." With the spray bottle and roll of paper towels in my hands, I have to turn sideways to make room to get past her in the narrow hallway.

We three teachers blow our whistles to indicate that playtime is over, and that it's time to line up, come inside and get a snack. All sixty sweaty kids find their assigned places on the carpet and start dipping their apple slices in yogurt and chomp their snack in happy silence.

"Everybody, don't forget that something very special is happening this week. Can anyone raise your hand and tell me what's happening on Saturday?" I ask them during the closing.

I call on a boy who has a line of white yogurt on his cheek. "Eddie?"

"It's the Pow Wow!" He stabs the air with a fist.

"Yes, that's right. The Pow Wow is this Saturday. Who's excited about it?"

Several kids raise their hands and some shout, "Me!"
"Remember it starts at – "
"My uncle said there's going to be drummers there!"
"That's right. It starts at ten in the morning and lasts
– "

"And dancers!"
I hold up a hand to stop the interrupter. "It will last
all day. There will be food and you can get – "
"Indian tacos and funnel cake!" another interrupter
blurts out.

"Guys, you need to stop interrupting me. I'm glad
you're excited, but you need to let me finish. The Pow Wow
will last from ten in the morning until six at night, and there
will be all kinds of yummy food and games and drummers
and dancers, so don't miss it."

Overwhelming joyful chatter breaks out around the
room.

"Never," Janice says to the talking kids as she walks
to the front to take my place.

"Give up!" they respond.

"Work hard."

"Do right!" they say back to her and all fold their
hands in their laps, sit up straight and face forward.

Once again, I marvel at Janice's Mary Poppins-like
ability.

Janice leads the rest of the closing program – sings a
song with a lot of crazy motions with them, plays a memory
verse game with them, and reads them a short story of
Abraham Lincoln's life. After she reads the story she asks
what we can learn from President Lincoln's life.

Whisper raises her hand, "Integrity."

"That's a wonderful word Whisper. Can you tell us
what that means?" Janice asks her.

"It's being good and doing the right thing all the
time, no matter what." She shakes her head for emphasis.
Her blue eyes are wide with conviction.

They talk about integrity and honesty and work ethic
for a few minutes before the subject of Halloween costumes
comes up. Then, of course, everyone has to tell the group
what they'll be wearing for Halloween tomorrow.

My big plans for Halloween include staying home
and handing out candy. Chelsea isn't going to be home.
She'll be in Clinton, meeting with the church team and the
Rural Outreach Ministries representative coming in
November for the turkey giveaway. Kirk asked her to
coordinate with their teams and plan the giveaway, and she
was more than happy to take the afternoon off from school
on Halloween – one of the most insane school days of the
year – and leave the candy-handing-out responsibilities at the
house to me. I'm kind of looking forward to it, though. I'm
planning on wearing sweat pants and watching romantic
comedies all night while handing out miniature chocolate
bars to every ghost, princess, pirate, witch, and monster that
comes to the door.

"What are you going to be for Halloween, Pastor
Kirk?" a little girl wearing an OU sweatshirt asks him as he
enters the fellowship hall.

"I think I'll go as a nerd." He tells the group. "I'll just
wear an OU shirt." He makes a face at her, and she sticks her
tongue out at him.

"OSU stinks!" a boy in the back shouts.

"Uh-oh, those are fighting words," Kirk tells him.

Didn't know Kirk was a Cowboy fan, I think. The
image of Brian's Pistol Pete grooms cake appears in her
mind, an image I hadn't thought about in over two months.

Kirk jokes around with the kids a little more and tells
them all to be safe when they go trick-or-treating tomorrow
night and then tells them to make sure to invite all of their
friends and family to the Pow Wow on Saturday. He ends
the day just like he does every day by asking the kids to bow
their heads and pray with him. He prays God's protection
and blessings for every kid there and for every kid in

Diniyoli.

"And everyone said – " Kirk prompts them with his standard line.

"Amen," all the kids respond.

Back in Cool Springs when kids were dismissed from school or church, they went through a pick-up line to be retrieved by awaiting parents mostly in SUV's. Here in Diniyoli, most of the kids walk home, and teachers just tell them goodbye, and don't have to worry with all of the rigid dismissal procedures of schools in a bigger town.

After the flurry of packing up and saying goodbye, Chelsea, Kirk, Janice, and I work together to clean the room and put it back in order.

"OSU fan, huh?" I ask Kirk as we work together to fold a table and carry it to the closet.

"Of course, orange power all the way." He smiles at me. "Don't tell me you're a Sooner fan."

"Ugh, never. I went to OSU, didn't you know that?"

He tilts his head as they stack chairs. "I don't know if I did know that. An OSU grad, I knew I liked you."

I pause stacking and look up over the back of a pile of six chairs into his face. Even though his comment – "I knew I liked you" – had a folksy, kidding-around tone, his face doesn't match that tone at all. His thin lips are in a straight line, and his dark eyes are leveled right at me – waiting for a response.

"I knew I liked you too." I finally say. "Right from the beginning."

*****

Knock, knock.

I look at the time on my phone next to me on the couch. Five-fifteen. A little early for trick-or-treaters isn't it?

I pick up the big orange plastic bowl filled with candy and head to the door. When I bought the bowl and the candy last Saturday on my weekly trip to Wal-Mart in Clinton, I made sure to buy only "good candy." As a trick-or-treater I always hated getting cheap candy or Halloween pencils, or, heaven forbid, fruit. As a child, I treasured the miniature chocolate candy bars that found their way into my treat bag.

"Tess?"

"Um," Tess is holding a large blue binder and shifts it to the opposite arm, "Here. You can have this."

I take the binder Tess holds out to me and open it – recipes, pages and pages of recipes.

"It'll be easier for you to just take the whole book of recipes. You don't have to get the recipe from me every week now, and you can pick out what you want to make."

I try to keep the shock from showing on my face. "Thanks Tess. This will make it so much easier." I flip through the pages and get excited when I see dozens of main dishes fit for a crowd.

"You earned it." Tess rubs her hands together. "You're doing a good job."

There was nothing I could do to stop my chin from dropping. I quickly snap my mouth shut.

A short laugh escapes from Tess. "I know I've been hard on you, but you aren't uppity, like I thought, and you seem to really care about the kids."

"I do care about them." Is it possible that Tess has decided to start treating me better? I wonder. Then I ask with a gesture to my living room, "Want to come in for a cup of coffee?"

Tess waves her hand. "Oh no, thanks. Phil and I are going to take the grandkids trick-or-treating." She steps down from the front porch.

"Thanks Tess."

Tess nods and walks to her ancient mini-van.

After nearly three hours of handing out candy, I haven't watched even fifteen minutes of the movie. The bright porch light, the pumpkins and yellow mums on the front porch, and the close proximity to both the "in-town" houses and the Old Reservation Road houses, all make my house a trick-or-treater magnet. And maybe word's getting out that I have good candy, I think with a smile of satisfaction.

Whisper and a few of my other students stop by. It's always funny to see their faces when they realize their teacher has a life outside of school.

Whisper is wearing a skirt and a white shirt and a red ribbon in her hair. "Can you guess who I am?"

It takes me a few seconds, but I finally get it. "Matilda!"

Whisper nods and her red ribbon bounces. "My favorite book character."

I load them all up with candy and tell them not to eat it all tonight and make sure to get to bed early so they'll be ready for school tomorrow. They say "Yes, Miss Melissa." A few give me hugs and say goodnight.

After the group makes it to the road, Whisper calls out, "Hang on," and rushes back to the porch to give me another hug. As we hug, she whispers in my ear, "I know you gave me more candy than everyone else." And she runs back to her friends.

That girl.

I try not to have favorites, but I just can't help myself. Whisper has so much potential and such a sweet attitude. Not only is she incredibly smart, but she's also a leader in the classroom, like a junior teacher, always helping other kids who need it. I haven't heard of a gifted education program at the school, but if there is one, Whisper needs to be in it.

At eight-fifteen the traffic on the front porch begins to slow. I sit on the couch and re-start Chelsea's DVD of the romantic comedy I'd seen at least a few dozen times. When it gets to the part where the girl has a cold and is in her apartment in her pajamas and the guy brings her a bouquet of her favorite flowers, all I can think about is yesterday – stacking the chairs with Kirk – telling Kirk I liked him from the beginning. Then, two boys got into a fight, rolling on the floor, punching each other, and the moment ended. It was over almost the instant it started, a millisecond of honesty.

Maybe too honest, I think. In my whole life I can't ever remember coming right out and telling a guy that I liked him before I was absolutely sure he liked me. Talk about setting yourself up to get hurt. And what did he mean when he said he liked me? I try to remember the context.

He had said, "An OSU grad, I knew I liked you." Then he had given me what I thought at the time was a serious look. But now that I think about it, I could have misread the look. That comment was an innocent, all-in-good-fun type of comment, and I blew it out of proportion. He was probably thankful the two boys started fighting – an excuse to get away from me before I proposed marriage. "I liked you right from the beginning?" What was I thinking? I bury my face in the soft animal print throw blanket next to me on the couch.

While I have my face in the blanket, there is a knock at the door. Ugh, late trick-or-treaters are probably older kids who aren't even in costumes and just want candy.

Just as I think that I might hide under the blanket and not answer the door, I feel the familiar tingle in my chest that I haven't felt in a while. The Whisper is back.

"Yes Lord," I say aloud and throw the blanket off and make my way to the door. I'll answer the door, but I definitely need to turn the porch light off after this one.

The pre-teen boy dressed as a Cardinals baseball player, the boy I've seen hanging around the mission usually throwing a baseball around is standing on my porch. When he speaks, I remember that he's also the boy who was reading Holes on that first day.

"Trick or treat," he says half-heartedly, as if to say,

It's late. I'm tired. We both know the drill. Just put the candy in the bag, lady.

"Hey, do you like chocolate?"

He shrugs. "Yeah, who doesn't?"

"Exactly what I say." I put a hand on my hip. "Tell you what, I'm ready to stop handing out candy for the night. Would you like the rest?"

His eyes light up, and he leans forward and looks into the orange bowl. There are seven or eight miniature chocolate bars left.

I put the orange bowl behind my back. "I've seen you outside the mission. Why don't you come to the after school program anymore?"

Another shrug.

"You're a good reader. We have some kids who struggle with reading. You could help them." An idea begins to take shape in my mind. "Would you want to help them? We're making a tutoring team, kids who help other kids – you'd be perfect for it." I'm making this up as I'm saying it, but I know it's a great idea. I know another student who would be perfect for it too.

"I don't know." He looks over his shoulder.

I look too and see what he's looking at - a black car parked in front of a house three doors down.

"Tell you what, if I give you the rest of my candy, you come to the after school program next week and give the tutoring team a try, deal?"

"Mmmm," he says as he looks at the car again. A man with a backwards baseball cap perched high on his head gets out of the car. When the car door opens, I can see three or four other adults in the car.

The boy looks back at the candy bowl and shrugs yet again. Then agrees, "Sure."

I give him the candy, and he hops down the porch steps.

"See you later . . . hey, I don't even know your

name."

He looks back and yells over his shoulder as he makes it to the street, "I'm Dreamer!"

I finished the movie, quoting several lines as I watched it, since Chelsea wasn't here to laugh at me for doing it, graded a few papers, and was curled up in bed with a paperback when my phone rang. I look at the screen. It's Kirk.

I fold the corner of the page, close my book, and let the phone ring again. Don't say anything stupid. Act like you never said you liked him, I tell myself.

"Hey Kirk."

"Hey . . . I bet I passed out more candy than you did tonight."

"Not possible. I think I saw every human being under the age of thirteen who lives in this town."

"Well, I think I had kids from other towns in addition to all the kids from this town."

"Maybe so, but I bet my candy was better."

"Candy was better? Candy is candy. Kids don't care about that. They just want sugar."

I laugh, "Oh you handed out bad candy, didn't you? You are marked from now on. You will have a reputation as the guy who hands out bad candy on Halloween."

"And I suppose you handed out good candy?"

"Of course. I will have a reputation as the lady who hands out good candy on Halloween."

"Sounds like a perfect match."

I don't know how to respond.

He doesn't say anything for a second either. Then, he finally talks. "I know we have the Pow Wow this weekend and have to survive that first, and then next week I'll be out of town for a few days raising money for Rural Outreach Ministries, but after that . . . . are you doing anything next weekend?"

I don't know how to respond. I actually am doing

something next weekend – a lot of somethings, in fact. My birthday is next Friday, November eighth, and I'm going home night for a birthday dinner and meeting some friends in the city to go shopping next Saturday.

"Uh, it's okay. Forget I asked." He finally speaks.

Oops, I took too long to respond. "No, it's not that. It's just that my birthday is next Friday, and I was trying to think about what I had planned."

"Your birthday is next Friday?"

"Yeah."

"Well, you've got too much going on. Don't worry about it. I just wanted to see if you wanted to grab some dinner or something. No big deal."

Great. Did I just ruin it? I can't leave it at this. "Well, since you're gone next week, why don't we go the week after my birthday? I'm free on Monday or Tuesday," I offer.

"Sure, we can do that." His voice brightens. "How about Tuesday?"

"I can go Tuesday." Are we planning a date?

"What kind of food do you like?"

"Every kind of food." I'm not kidding.

He laughs, "Good, me too."

"Hey, I had a nice visit from Tess this afternoon." I change the subject.

"I heard about that. It's amazing what a clogged toilet can do, huh?"

"What?"

"A clogged toilet – that's what changed her mind about you – when you fixed the toilet yesterday. I guess she thought you were a prima donna or snob when you first came, but how you interact with the kids, how you don't have to be in the spotlight, how you're cooking the meals – all that and then you fixed the toilet without a complaint – she's impressed with you . . . and to be honest – " he pauses, "to be honest, Melissa, I'm impressed with you too."

I swallow the knot in my throat and blink back a tear.

"Wow, thanks."

"I mean it."

We say goodnight, and I take extra time on my evening rituals, since Chelsea isn't here to hog the bathroom – brush my hair a little longer and spread moisturizer on my face (like my mom always tells me to, but I never do). It's kind of nice to be alone in the quiet house.

I turn off my overhead light, turn on the lamp on my bedside table, get into my bed and grab my black and white striped journal and a pen. A word has been churning around in my mind for hours, a name actually – *Dreamer.*

Not confined to visions in the night,
Not defined as a head in a cloud,
Not resigned to living by sight,
Not aligned with the voice of the crowd -
Dreams are designed by the Father of Light,
And dreamers know His dreams are where true living is
found.

The boy must have been dressed as Adam Wainwright, the starting pitcher for the St. Louis Cardinals. When Dreamer turned and walked to the road, I saw the name written on the back of his baseball cap. Wainwright is Michael's favorite player.

There's something else. Something about the car that was waiting in the street. The car door opened and I saw adults sitting in the car – one man was standing next to the car, and there were two men in the car and a woman was with them. She was in the back seat. When the door opened the woman turned her head – dark hair swung over her shoulder, she turned her head so fast, but I saw it. A flash of green. A green streak on the side of her hair. Devin.

*****

Devin sits on the closed lid of the toilet and types notes into her phone. So far, it's been a productive morning. She's learned that Saturday is their biggest day for business, and that business is done through a middle man, and never here at the big white house. She discovered that the drugs were dropped off at the convenience store in town, given to a certain clerk who would later pass them over to the middleman who then distributed to customers, all of the complicated passing around to confuse any cops who might get the crazy idea to clean up the town.

She's convinced Dumb to take her along to the drop off point later today, saying they needed to go by the convenience store for slushies – he's not the smartest guy in the world.

She saves the notes on her phone, and then forwards them to her lieutenant. Hopefully he would have enough information for an arrest, she's getting tired of hanging around Dumb, Dumber, and their boss, Jacob. Devin slides her phone in her pocket and checks her appearance in the bathroom mirror. She wants to be attractive, but not too provocative. She wants to get information from these losers, but isn't willing to give them anything in return.

Dumb and Dumber are on the couch playing video games, and Jacob is on the phone, as usual. Jacob's son Dreamer is usually outside throwing a baseball around, but Devin hasn't seen him today.

"It's almost noon, boy. You've been at that place for hours. Get yourself here – now." Jacob slams his beer bottle on the table next to the couch where Devin is sitting. Devin forces herself not to jump and looks up at Jacob with a blank expression.

"Where's the kid?" She says with the affected persona of a criminal's groupie.

"Why do you care, Pocahontas?" Jacob looks at her with disgust and stomps out of the house, slamming the front door behind him, pulling his keys out of his pocket as he crosses the long front porch, gets into his black car, squeals out of the driveway and accelerates toward the mission.

"What's with him?" She asks the moronic video gamers.

Dumb shrugs. "Dunno."

"The kid's been at the mission Pow Wow all day. Jacob hates that place." Dumber says without moving his eyes from the screen.

Devin thinks about Melissa, Kirk, and Chelsea all working at the Pow Wow today, unaware that a ticked off, half-drunk criminal is headed their way. She tries to think of a way she can warn them without compromising her relationship with the white house gang.

"What's he care if his kid's at that place? Keeps the kid out of the way. Free babysitting, right?"

Dumb snorts. "Not to Jacob. He's funny about the kid."

Eyes still glued to the screen, Dumber chimes in, "Yeah, he's gotta know where the kid is all the time. No deals around the kid. He thinks that kid's gonna play in the MLB one day." He shakes his head. "Yeah, right."

Dumb puts his arm around Devin's shoulders. "Why do you care anyway? We're talking too much." He leans toward her and kisses her mouth. His tongue tastes sour from beer, and there's sugar on the top of his lip, probably from a donut.

She kisses him back, trying to think of an escape.

"Here," she grabs his empty bottle from the couch next to him, "let me get you a new one." She stands up.

He grabs her arm and pulls her back down. "Don't take too long." He kisses her again.

Devin smiles at him, but wants to punch his face. "Just a minute. I'm going to grab a quick smoke."

She tosses the empty bottle in the kitchen trashcan and steps out the back door. On the square of concrete outside the back door, she fishes a pack of cigarettes out of the back pocket of her jeans and lights up.

She takes in a drag and casually pulls her phone out of her pocket. She taps on the icon to send a text. She types Melissa's name in the space next to "To:" but then pauses. *What can I type?* She wonders. *A crazed meth dealer is headed your way and is angry? How would I explain my relationship with him?* She presses "cancel" and puts the phone back in her pocket.

Devin looks out over the haphazard arrangement of houses and trailers behind the big white house and thinks about the irony of the situation. Jacob is a horrible person — cooks and sells drugs and rules the rural town with fear tactics, but he's a concerned parent with big dreams for his son. How can such a bad guy appear to love his son? Devin wonders as she stamps out the cigarette butt with the toe of her boot.

From her pocket, her phone vibrates. A text. She gets her phone back out and reads the text from her lieutenant.

Find the lab.

*****

"Last night when Jarrett and I were talking he said the funniest thing."

"Did I tell you that Jarrett said the mission can use the Rural Outreach Ministries' van anytime?"

"Jarrett said he wishes he could have come to help today, but he already had plans."

Jarrett said . . . Jarrett said . . . Jarrett said . . . I've never met Jarrett, and I'm already sick of him.

Not really. I'm happy for Chelsea. I really am, but my word, she's only known him for two days, and I feel like I already know him. His name is Jarrett, and he works for Rural Outreach Ministries and lives in Clinton. She met him Thursday night at the meeting about the turkey giveaway, and apparently there were heart-shaped fireworks that exploded in the sky the instant they met. Not only is she quoting him constantly, but also they talk on the phone and text incessantly. If I'm happy for her, then why do I feel so irritated?

Chelsea and I are in the kitchen assembling Indian tacos – piling ground beef, beans, lettuce, and chopped tomatoes on top of fry bread and stacking the plates on a wheeled cart.

Michael sticks his head in the kitchen. "Hey," he yells, "you guys know where a hammer is?"

Ever the big sister, I tell him, "Michael, you're yelling."

"Sorry, I've been talking over the drums all morning." He lowers his voice. "You know where a hammer is? One of the stakes of the game tent came up. I need to hammer it back in, but can't find one. The ones from the out building are missing."

"Kirk always keeps extra tools in the bottom left drawer of his desk." I say as I ladle a spoonful of diced tomatoes on top of an Indian taco.

"Thanks." He turns and jogs to Kirk's office.

Chelsea and I roll the cart outside to the bright yellow food tent. There are four huge brightly colored tents on the grassy acreage, a yellow one for food, a blue one for dancing and drummers, a green one for games, and a red one for arts and crafts. A banner tied between two trees declares, "Diniyoli Pow Wow – Everyone Welcome!" in bright red letters that Kirk and I painted last night. The noon sun, high in the baby blue sky shines bright on the colored tents and on the hundreds of people streaming in and out of the tents. It's sixty-eight degrees and there's a light breeze. It's a gorgeous early November Saturday.

In the food tent, Janice tells us they need about twenty-five more Indian tacos. As Chelsea and I head back to the kitchen to make more, my phone vibrates in my back pocket. The screen tells me that it's Michael. He's running a game in the green tent today.

"Hey, did you find the hammer?"

"Yeah, but sis, do you think you could come and help with crowd control over here?" He asks, and I hear kids yelling in the background. "Some kids are cutting in line, and there's been a few arguments."

I can imagine. Chelsea says that she can handle twenty-five more plates by herself, and I jog over to the green tent. As I pass through the middle of the grassy acreage, I see Kirk, but he doesn't see me. He's got a circle of fifteen or so people around him, and he's obviously telling some outrageous story. His ornery dark eyes light up as he talks and gestures with his hands. The people around him wait for one of his famous punch lines with wide eyes, and they aren't disappointed – slapping knees and throwing heads back in laughter. He catches me looking at him and gives me a secret smile over the shoulders of his audience.

In the game tent, Michael has completely lost control of his game – yelling at kids to get back in line and to stop fighting.

"Absolutely not." I turn on my teacher voice and put my hands on my hips. "This is absolutely not the way my kids behave." The dozen or so kids in line give me sheepish looks. "I want to see a straight line in three seconds." I count to three, and the kids form a perfect line.

"Whoa, that was impressive," my brother tells me in awe.

I've picked up a few things from the master ninja teacher, Janice.

Michael's game is, of course, a baseball game. He has empty glass bottles stacked on a table for contestants to pitch at and try to knock down. After the fifth pitcher hasn't gotten close to touching the bottles, I ask him if we should move the kids closer to the table to make it easier.

Micheal won't hear it. "No way, regulation distance

from mound to plate is sixty feet and six inches. This is less than half that. It's already too easy."

I roll my eyes. My brother and baseball.

Next up to pitch is Dreamer, wearing his Cardinals baseball cap, as always. From behind the table, I nod at him, and he pretends not to recognize me.

Like a professional baseball pitcher in the middle of a major league game, Dreamer raises his leg, rares back, and overhands a beauty of a pitch that crashes into the center of the pyramid of bottles on the table.

"Way to go, Dreamer!" I can't keep myself from cheering. His tan neck shows a hint of red as he turns to the prize table to collect his prize.

"Wait a minute, kid." Michael stops him. "That pitch was perfect. Want to make things a little more interesting?" Michael smiles his sideways grin with a double-dog-dare-look at Dreamer.

Dreamer shrugs. "What you got?"

"Step back." Michael tells him. "All you kids in line, make room. Let's see if – Your name is Dreamer?"

Dreamer nods.

"Let's see if Dreamer can do it again, but ten feet farther away this time. Do you guys think he can?"

The kids in the tent all cheer as Michael gets them fired up. This is completely uncharacteristic of my usually quiet brother. I guess the key is baseball. If baseball's involved, he's bound to be passionate.

Michael estimates ten feet by walking ten paces and shows Dreamer where to stand. He's in the middle of the tent now, and people at other game tables turn to see what's going on. Michael walks back to the table and re-stacks the bottles. Once again, Dreamer launches a perfect pitch that crashes right in the middle of the stack.

The whole tent erupts in applause and cheers.

Michael holds up his hands and addresses everyone in the tent, "Okay, okay, that's about thirty feet away.

Anybody want to go outside the tent and see if he can do it from sixty feet?"

All of the kids in the tent shout, "Yeah!" and Michael leads them out of the tent into the sunshine, telling some older boys to grab the table and the bottles. I follow the crowd that has now started to chant, "Dreamer, Dreamer, Dreamer!"

The older boys set the table in the open area in the middle of the tents. Michael makes a big show of measuring off sixty feet and telling Dreamer exactly where to stand. I stack the bottles on the table and stand next to them. Michael turns and walks back toward me at the table, and Dreamer eyes the target, waiting to be told when to throw.

"You see his form?" Michael whispers to me.

"Is it good?"

Michael shakes his head. "How did we grow up in the same house? Can't you tell?"

"Can you interpret or write poetry?"

He snorts. "Yeah right." He turns his head to look at Dreamer then looks back at me. "Just look at him pitch. This kid is probably on a really good travelling tournament team. He's probably got a private pitching coach, too."

"He's that good?"

"Either he is, or he just threw two lucky pitches. Let's see if he can do it again." Michael turns around to talk to Dreamer. "Whenever you're ready, kid. Show us what you've got."

Once again, Dreamer bends his knee, pulls his arm back, and throws a powerful pitch, and, once again, he sends the baseball straight to the center of the pyramid of bottles. Now, his crowd of spectators has grown to include people who have come out of the others tents to see what's going on, and they all cheer for him.

"Good job, Dreamer, good job." Michael tells him. "Hey, come here. Let's go get your prize." Michael directs the older boys to put the table and bottles back in the game tent. Dreamer jogs over to Michael and me, and the three of us walk back to the game tent.

"You take pitching lessons?" Michael asks him.

Dreamer shakes his head. "No. My dad taught me."

"You on a team?"

Dreamer shakes his head again. "No little league here in the middle of nowhere."

"Really?"

"Nah, my dad tried to find me one, but the closest one's in Clinton, and that's too far."

Michael gets him his prize and tells him that he did a great job. Michael and Dreamer talk about baseball for a few minutes. When Michael tells him that he's a pitcher for Cool Springs High School, Dreamer is impressed. Dreamer leaves to go play more carnival games, and then Michael and I tell the kids where to stand in line, and get the game going again. At least a dozen more kids want to play now, after Dreamer's success. They all want to do the same thing.

After four or five kids pitch and hit air and nothing else, Michael asks me, "Does that Dreamer kid come to your program?"

I tell Michael about Halloween and Dreamer telling me that he'd start coming to the after school program to be a peer tutor.

"Man, he's a gifted pitcher. Too bad the town doesn't have little league."

Across the tent, things are heating up at another game. "Pastor Kirk, let's see if you can do it."

I look across the tent and see that a group of eight to ten year old boys are challenging Kirk at the foam dart shooting range. They're holding their bright orange toy guns out to him, begging him to play.

"All right, you don't know what you're asking. I'm a master at this." He tells them.

The boys laugh, and Kirk shoots at the aluminum can targets randomly spaced in the shooting gallery. He hits most of the targets, but the boys make fun of the ones that he misses, and he teases back with them and watches a couple of them shoot. I can't help but watch him interact with them as I continue to help Michael at the pitching game table.

The young boys finish playing at the shooting range and ask Kirk if he wants to get some funnel cake with them.

"You guys go ahead." Kirk tells them as he walks over to our table. "I'll stay in here and make sure Miss Melissa knows what she's doing."

A few of the boys say, "Woo – woo," the universal sound made by all elementary school students to indicate that they think something romantic might be going on.

"Woo – woo," I accentuate the syllables with raised eyebrows.

Kirk laughs. "I guess they think there must be something fishy going on for me to turn down funnel cake to talk to a girl." He looks at Michael standing at the other end of the table. "Thanks for getting here so early this morning to help me set up."

"No problem," Michael tells him.

Kirk, Michael, Nelson, and Tess's husband Phil got here before anyone else this morning and set the tents up. We still have a few hours until the Pow Wow is over, and then they'll have to take the tents back down. Kirk is going to preach at a church in Texas tomorrow, so he'll have to wake up and leave pretty early in the morning. I wonder sometimes if he ever feels sleep-deprived. He never complains of being tired, though.

Sounds of jingling bells join the sounds of beating drums from the blue tent, and a woman sticks her head into our tent.

"The jingle dance team just got here, and they're starting their show in five minutes!" She tells everyone in our tent. All of the kids and adults waiting in line to play games rush out of the tent to see the show.

"Want to watch the jingle dancers?" Kirk asks me, but Michael, who happens to be looking the other way, thinks he's asking him.

"Not especially. I think I'll go find a quiet spot in the church and take a nap." He rubs the corner of his eye. "Can I crash on the couch in your office for a while?"

Kirk gets his key ring out of his pocket and tosses the keys to Michael. "Here you go. You earned it."

As Michael turns to go, a man with slicked-back hair and a white t-shirt grabs his shoulder.

"You the jerk that used my son like some sort of rodeo clown? My son's going to go places. He's not some stray kid you can push around." He shouts at him.

"What?" Michael squints his eyes at the strange man.

Kirk steps forward. "Can I help you, sir?"

The man lets go of Michael's shoulder and turns his attention to Kirk.

"You're the snake oil salesman himself, aren't you? You like to parade twelve-year-old boys in front of people, like they're some sort of freak? He's not a freak. He's got talent. You probably charged everybody to watch him throw that baseball. Just like a preacher – " the man steps in front of Kirk and thrusts his face inches from Kirk's face, "all about the money."

Kirk doesn't flinch. He speaks in a calm, even tone. "I'm sorry if you think your son was exploited. I saw the whole thing, though, and I can promise you that it was just for fun. And no, we didn't charge anybody. In fact, this whole event, food, games, everything, is one hundred percent free to everyone." He takes a step back and smiles, "What's your name?"

The man scoffs with a grunt. "Like you don't know who I am." He folds his tattooed arms, and I recognize him. He's the man who was standing next to the black car when Dreamer was trick-or-treating at my house, and he's also the man who sits on the front porch of the big white house, always talking on the phone and smoking – Whisper's dad.

He's yelling at Kirk about stealing people from him, and the second realization hits me – that means Dreamer must be Whisper's brother.

As he is yelling at Kirk and Michael, I hear something even louder than his insults. His voice has more volume, but the Whisper has greater impact on my heart.

"I have an idea." I interrupt his rant, and the man stops yelling and turns to me, and Kirk and Michael look at me too. I can't believe what I'm about to say, but I've learned to always obey when I hear it.

"We're going to start a baseball team."

All three men look at me like I've lost my mind.

I focus on Kirk. "Think about it. We've got the coaches." I point to Kirk and Michael. "We've got a place to practice." I open my hands to indicate the two acres we're standing in. "We've got transportation to games. Jarrett from Rural Outreach Ministries told Chelsea we could use their van anytime we need it." I put my hands on my hips. I think I've proven my point.

"A team . . . in Diniyoli?" The hard man has his arms folded across his chest and his head cocked back in contempt, but his voice cracks a little when he says the name of his hometown, revealing that perhaps this tough guy has a vulnerability to the hope of a little league baseball team in Diniyoli.

Kirk senses it to. "We could do that." He claps Michael on the back. "You thought you were done here since mowing season is over, but we need you to coach, bud."

Michael rolls his eyes and groans.

*****

Jacob woke up from a nap. He didn't sleep much last night in the rocking chair next to Sierra's bed, and it's only nine in the morning, so maybe it wasn't technically a nap.

As the hospice nurse added painkiller to the hanging plastic bag of liquid, she told them it would make Sierra go to sleep in about twenty minutes. "After that," the nurse added, "I'm not sure if she'll wake up. It would be a good idea to say goodbye to her now." The nurse said the last sentence in a sympathetic whisper and patted Jacob on the shoulder as she left the bedroom. She closed the door behind her and probably sat on the old wingback chair at the end of the hallway, where she had taken to sitting the last couple of days in the Davis Home. She would sit in that chair and type on her computer. The hospital had arranged for her to come in the mornings and evenings to make Sierra comfortable in her own home for the last week of her life. Jacob had no idea how he was going to pay for it. He didn't exactly have any extra money lying around.

It wasn't supposed to be like this. Trey had promised him complete autonomy in Diniyoli. He would help him get started, take a little cut in the beginning, and then Jacob would be on his own. *Yeah, right,* Jacob thought.

Trey was a visionary. "Oklahoma has all these towns in the middle of nowhere – ripe for the taking." He'd told Jacob years ago. "These towns are miles from civilization, might have two or three police officers, and absolutely nothing for anyone to do for fun." Trey had promised Jacob that in six months he'd be running the town of Diniyoli.

"Especially since you were a star baseball player there. People in those small towns remember that. You'll own the town in a few months," Trey had told Jacob.

But there were a lot of things Trey didn't tell Jacob. He didn't tell him that he'd be sending thugs to collect payment weekly. He didn't tell Jacob he'd be sending goons to take up residence in his house, to spy on him. And he didn't tell him he couldn't quit. Ever. He didn't tell him there was no way out.

Sierra's eyes fluttered open. She looked at Jacob

sitting in the rocking chair by the door. She turned her head and saw her mom, Ida, sleeping on the loveseat in front of the window.

"Hey, can you hear me?" Jacob scooted his chair closer to her bed.

She nodded.

He reached over to her hand at her side and covered it with both of his hands. "I love you, honey."

Sierra lifted her other hand and covered the top of his hands. "Jesus . . . please, Jacob. Jesus."

This again? This now? This Jesus nonsense? Her final words and she doesn't talk about their two kids or ask him one more time to quit breaking the law. No, she brought up the only thing she can talk about lately – Jesus.

Jacob shook his head. "Let's not talk about that right now, okay?"

She closed her eyes for a few seconds and then opened them. "Take care of Dreamer."

"You know I will. That boy's my life."

"And Whisper."

Guilt stabbed his heart like an icicle. He hadn't had much to do with the baby. He wasn't a baby kind of person. And, besides that, she was a girl. One day he could teach Dreamer to play baseball and hunt, but what could he do with a girl? Even though he couldn't stand Sierra's mother, he was glad she had moved in to take the baby girl off his hands.

"I'll look after her." He promised. He kissed her forehead. "I haven't been a perfect husband, but I love you, Sierra."

Across the room, Ida woke up from her nap.

Great, the old bat will be sobbing in a minute, Jacob thought. Got to get out of here before it starts.

"She's awake?"

"Yeah."

Ida talked to her daughter as she rose from the

loveseat and crossed the room to sit on the corner of the bed. "Sierra, it's mama. Don't you be worried none. Jesus is waiting on you. We're going to miss you, but we're going to see you soon."

Jacob rolled his eyes and stood. "I'm going to check on the kids."

"You don't need to do that. My friend Tess has them – came and got them when you were sleeping earlier."

Got to think of another way to get out of this room. He rubbed his chin, maybe he could say he needed to shave.

Just as he was about to use the lame excuse, the sound of unfamiliar voices came up the stairs from the living room below. Two, no three men. Jacob lifted the back of his shirt and placed his hand on the gun in his waistband. He looked at Ida and Sierra and put a finger to his lips – *Be quiet*.

He deftly left the room and pulled the door closed. Ida looked at Sierra. Tears streamed down her daughter's face. Oh, what her life must've been like for the last several years with this criminal.

She reached up and stroked Sierra's hair. "It's okay," she whispered, "the babies aren't here."

Sierra nodded.

"I just hate it that you've had to live like this, baby. I should've contacted you. I should've made you come live with me and Anna." So many regrets for such a brief twenty-three year life.

Sierra shook her head, "No, nothing could have – " she stopped talking and inhaled as deeply as she could.

"Don't try to talk."

"Mom, I have to . . . " breathed in, "tell you. Jacob is going to . . ." Sierra closed her eyes and inhaled sharply.

"Baby, you don't have to say anything. I've already been thinking about what I'm going to do with Whisper after – " Ida couldn't bear to finish the sentence.

Sierra lifted her head from the pillow and looked right into Ida's eyes. "Jacob will change . . . he will . . . I've prayed, and he will come to God . . . he will." She closed her eyes and laid her head back on her pillow, exhausted.

The voices from downstairs grew louder and then Ida jerked to cover her ears as the air was pierced by the ear-splitting sound of gunfire ripping through the house and by the screams of the hospice nurse in the hallway.

*****

Half a dozen pink helium-filled balloons are tied to my parents' mailbox – mom's annual tradition for my birthday.

One thing in my old neighborhood stands out to me – sidewalks. I don't think I ever even thought about the sidewalks. They were just always here. I'd strap on roller skates when I was a kid and skate down the sidewalks. I'd draw hopscotch squares on the sidewalks. I've gone on countless runs on these sidewalks. I've gone door-to-door selling fundraiser items to my neighbors using these sidewalks the whole time, and it never even dawned on me that there were neighborhoods in the world that didn't have sidewalks.

I park in my parents' driveway behind my brother's truck and look at the house for a few minutes. The front porch is bedecked with friendly-looking scarecrows, yellow pillows tied with burlap bows on mom's iron bench and on the white wicker chair next to the door, pumpkins, potted mums, and twin fall colored wreaths on the double front doors. Dad's yard lights are shining on every tree in the yard and spotlighting some of the bushes and trees in the flowerbeds. Not a single leaf litters the perfect lawn, even though leaves have been falling all week.

I get out of my car and walk up the driveway to the porch and realize it's been almost three months since I've been home – the longest I've ever been away from my family. I push the glass storm door open and don't ring the doorbell. My mom's beautifully decorated entry hall is the same – a silver framed mirror hangs above a dark wooden table, and two hurricane lamps flank the sides of the table with mom's collection of blue and white ginger jars in the center. One thing is different, though – several strange boxes of all sizes are stacked under the table. I hear mom and dad's voices coming from the kitchen.

"Mom . . . Dad . . . I'm here!" I call to them as I cross into the living room on my way to the kitchen.

"Melissa!" Mom says as she runs out of the kitchen to me with her arms open. "Give me a hug!"

"My girl's home," Dad says as he wraps his long arms around mom and me in a warm group hug.

I try to let go, but my dad won't let us separate for a few seconds. "This feels too good to let go yet," he says to mom and me, "I've got my two girls here, and I just want to keep hugging them a little longer."

He finally lets go and mom puts her hands on my hair, commenting on how "smooth" and "healthy" it looks. It feels like such a long time ago that I got my hair cut, but I guess they haven't seen me since I cut the long wedding-hair off.

"I love how the front is slightly longer than the back. Did you get it highlighted?" She says as she looks it over.

My hair does have streaks that are a slightly lighter shade of red. "No, I've been outside a lot the past couple of months – I've been running again, and then the Pow Wow, playing with the kids in the after school program, and I try to give the recess monitor a hand a couple of times a week. I guess it's sun streaked."

"Mmm," she intones thoughtfully, and then, "are you hungry?"

"I'm hungry for a meal cooked by someone else and not from the Green Parrot."

They laugh, but I'm not kidding.

We go to the kitchen. Dad and I sit at the round,

glass table and watch mom put the finishing touches on the dinner. She has a pan of spinach manicotti cooling on the stovetop, a Caesar salad in a huge bowl on the counter, a round cake on a cake stand, and she opens the oven and pulls out two loaves of buttery and cheesy garlic bread.

"Is that cake red velvet?"

"Mmm-hmm," mom affirms with a smile.

"With cream cheese frosting?"

"Yes, it is. I made all of your favorites. It's your birthday, after all."

"Wow, you out-did yourself, mom. Everything looks perfect. I think I just gained five pounds smelling it."

Mom laughs and asks dad and me to set the table. Dad and I get the placemats and dishes and silverware and place them on the oak table in the adjoining dining room while mom makes the tea.

"Where's Michael?"

"Running an errand. He'll be back in a couple of minutes." Mom says offhandedly as she stirs the tea.

"What are those boxes in the entry hall? Under the table?" I ask as I put ice in the glasses.

"Oh, well, honey, that's actually something I need to talk to you about while you're here. Those are wedding gifts that we couldn't figure out what to do with. I mean, most of the presents we just gave back to the people who gave them to you, but there were a few gifts from the wedding shower that got separated from their card, and we didn't know what to do with them. I thought if you could look at them you might remember who gave them to you. It was quite a job, returning all those gifts." Mom finishes stirring the tea. "Honey, make one more glass of ice and set one more place at the table while I cut the bread, please."

I automatically obey, reach into the cabinet and pull out a glass before it clicks in my brain. "One more?" I pause with the ice tea glass in my hand and look at mom's guilty back as she is cutting bread and intentionally not looking at me.

"What errand is Michael running mom?"

"Hmm?" She still won't turn around.

I remember that Michael's truck is in the driveway. "Is Michael coming here with someone?"

"Now, Melissa," she starts in her most reasonable, logical tone.

"Brian? He's coming here with Brian, isn't he?" I set the glass on the counter, because I feel like throwing it.

"Honey, don't get upset." She puts the knife in the sink and starts to arrange the garlic bread slices in a basket.

"Don't get upset? You invited my ex-fiancé to my birthday dinner?"

Mom and I freeze when we hear the front door open and voices in the entry hall.

Mom leans toward me and whispers, "Set another place on the table and make another glass of iced tea. I've been cleaning up your mess for almost three months. The least you can do is sit down to a civilized meal with your family and the young man you dated for seven years and should have married."

*****

"Would you like another cup of coffee?"

"Sure, thank you."

"Still one cream and two sugars?" Brian asks me as he picks up my coffee cup and heads to the kitchen.

I nod – that's still how I like my coffee.

After mom's fantastic meal we talked around the table for a while. Then Brian offered to make us coffee to go with the red velvet cake. Brian always made the best coffee.

Surprisingly, dinner wasn't too awkward. We all tried to stick to innocent topics – mainly Michael's plans for college next year and Brian's recent promotion at the clinic. They all told me about the Czech Fest – this was my first

year to ever miss it. Michael and I also told them about the
Pow Wow. Dad and Brian acted interested in the event and
in the people and culture of Diniyoli, but mom kept silent
while we talked about it.

"Michael, can you take out the trash, please?"

"Sure, mom." He gets up from the table and heads to
the kitchen to get the trash.

"Gary, could you come in here and help me with
these dishes? If we both work on it, it won't take as long."
Mom asks my dad sweetly from the kitchen. Dad smiles at
Brian and me. We all know what she's doing.

"Would you like to take our coffee to the front
porch?" He asks me.

"Sure." We pick up our coffee cups and walk
through the house to the front porch. I'm glad he didn't ask
if I wanted to go to the back patio. I remember our last
conversation out there.

I sit on mom's iron bench on one side of the front
door, and Brian sits on the wicker chair on the other side of
the door. It's late, but it isn't that dark out here, with my
parents' porch lights and yard lights, the street light on the
corner, and all of the neighbors' lights spotlighting their
perfectly manicured lawns and sculpted bushes. The lights
make the stars invisible. This may be the same sky that is in
Diniyoli, but it doesn't look like it.

"So . . . I'm sure your school is a lot different than
Cool Springs, huh?"

I'm glad he started the conversation at an easy place.

"Yes, it is . . . the school's different, the town's
different, the church is different . . . everything is . . .
different." I sound like a broken record. I smile weakly.
"Sorry, I'm a little tired and can't think of a better adjective."

He chuckles. "It's okay. I've had a long week, too.
Basically, my promotion means more paperwork for the
same money." He takes a drink of his coffee.

I can't think of anything to say, so I drink my coffee

too. We sit in silence. In the past we would talk about future plans most of the time. Now that I think about it, that's mainly what we talked about. Strange that two people supposedly in love didn't talk about what we loved about the other person or we didn't engage in playful banter. I guess that isn't real life – that kind of romantic conversation must just be in books and movies.

I finish my coffee and try to think of another safe conversation topic. "Are you golfing much?"

He nods. "I am. I've taken five strokes off my game since . . ."

The reference to the wedding that didn't happen hangs in the air.

"That's good," I finally say. "You'll be ready for the tour soon."

"Yeah, in my dreams." He laughs. "You want me to re-fill your cup?" He stands and holds out his hand to take my coffee mug.

"Sure," I hand it to him. "You don't have to wait on me, though."

He turns toward the kitchen and pauses.

Don't have to wait on me. Why did I say that?

Brian clears his throat and turns to me. He hands my cup back to me and sets his down next to his chair. "No, Missy, I don't have to wait on you. And, you know," he grabs the back of his neck and squeezes it. "That's what I've wanted to tell you all night. I've been patient. I've waited. I haven't gone out with anyone else, and at the same time, I've given you space – haven't contacted you at all since August. But, I'm letting you know right now that that won't last forever." He reaches in his pocket and retrieves his keys. "I've decided to give you until Christmas break to make up your mind. You can finish the semester. They can find a new teacher to take your place in January. Lots of people graduate in January and are looking for a teaching job. They won't have trouble finding anyone."

A deadline.

"Tell me what you've decided at Christmas. Then we can have a Valentine's Day wedding. We won't have to do much to prepare. Your poor mother kept all of the decorations and everything. I helped her carry the boxes to the attic. But, just so you know," he points his keys at me. "I'm not waiting any longer than that. I've got a life too, Missy, and it's selfish of you to make me wait."

I look down at my hands in my lap – my naked hands – no engagement ring, no paint on my nails. There are two noticeable marks on my hands, though – a small burn on my pinkie finger from when I took a pan out of the oven at the mission with an oven mitt that had a hole, and a smidge of red paint on the knuckle of my left ring finger from when Kirk and I painted the Pow Wow banner. I smile as I think about the Pow Wow, the mission, my students, and Kirk.

"What?" Brian asks with raised eyebrows and the beginnings of a smile. "What do you think, babe?"

Of course he thought I was smiling about getting back together. How could he know that I was smiling about a missionary with paint-stained jeans?

I stand and put my hand on top of his. "Brian, I'm sorry."

"Fine." He nods. "Fine. Tell me at Christmas then. I'll wait until then." He pulls his hands away from mine and turns toward his car parked in my parents' driveway.

"No, Brian." I step toward him and touch his shoulder. He turns to face me. "I know now. We won't be getting back together."

*****

"What do you think?" I come out of the dressing room at Natalie's Boutique on Main Street in Cool Springs and stand in front of my three friends. I'm wearing the fourth outfit I've tried on today. I want something to wear when I go to dinner with Kirk that he hasn't seen before. I want to impress him, but I don't want it to look like I'm trying too hard. I want to look good, but I want to be modest. I want an outfit that's dressier than what I usually wear, but not overly fancy. This is complicated.

This outfit is a simple emerald green dress. It's solid color with a V-neck and belted waist, and it goes to the top of my knees. I stand in the center of the three mirrors in the sitting area of the large dressing room, in front of my friends in the plush chairs across from the mirrors. I feel beautiful.

Staci gasps. "That is your color Missy. Your skin is positively radiant. You definitely need to get this and wear it Tuesday."

Lisa and Krystal look confused. "What's Tuesday?" Lisa asks.

I shoot Staci a look. *You weren't supposed to say anything.* She raises her eyebrows and shrugs sheepishly. *Oops.*

"Actually . . . I'm going on a date."

Both of my friends' mouths drop open. Then they start asking questions at the same time.

"Who is he?"

"Does Brian know?"

"So, are you and Brian completely over?"

"Is he from that little town?"

"Do you have a picture?"

I hold out my hand like a traffic cop. "Okay, okay. I'll answer all of your questions. But first, tell me what shoes I should wear with this."

After an hour more of shopping and talking, I tell them all of the details about Kirk and we find the perfect shoes – leopard print flats. I don't usually go for animal prints, but I love the brown and black spotted shoes paired with the deep green dress. I'd never have thought of the combination, Lisa suggested it.

"He sounds amazing." Krystal says for about the hundredth time while she stirs the sugar into her iced tea.

We're taking a break at a café a few doors down from
Natalie's.

"He sure does." Lisa says dreamily. "Show me that
picture one more time."

I laugh as I pass her my phone. I only have one
picture of Kirk on my phone. It's from the Pow Wow. He
doesn't know his picture is being taken. I was actually taking
a picture of Michael pitching at his game in the green tent.
Kirk was in the background talking to a group of boys. In
the picture, he's wearing his usual t-shirt and jeans and his
arm is resting on the shoulders of a middle school aged boy
and he is listening to another boy talk. He is looking at the
boy with total focus. The candid snapshot reveals one of my
favorite things about Kirk – the unguarded way he loves all
people, regardless of age, race, or social position.

"He's a hottie." Lisa says as she passes the phone
back to me.

Of course the fact that he's extremely handsome is
something else I like about him, I admit to myself.

"What are you all smiling at? He is. Can I not say a
missionary is a hottie? Is something wrong with that?" Lisa
asks us with her hands palms-up.

"Nothing wrong with that at all. I think he's a hottie
too." I tell my friends.

"Missy's lucky. Brian's a hottie too. I'm not gonna
lie," Staci looks down at her lap. "I'm a little jealous of you
Missy. Guys aren't falling out of the sky for me, like they are
for you."

Do I sense an edge in Staci's voice?

"If you can't be open and honest with your friends,
who can you be open and honest with? Am I right?" Lisa
holds her tea glass up, and we all clink our glasses against
hers, and we all say, "That's right!"

"Speaking of friends, have you made any friends in
Diniyoli? What about your roommate? Is she nice?" Staci
asks me.

"She is. We get along well together. She's very extroverted, can't sit still . . . kind of opposite from me, but we've gotten to know each other and get along great now. There's another girl named Devin who's hung out with us a few times too."

My friends nod and move on to the next topic of conversation – their dating lives. As they discuss a blind date Lisa recently went on, I think about Devin. I didn't tell them that I haven't spoken with Devin since before Halloween when I saw her in Dreamer's dad's car. I've texted her a couple of times, but she hasn't responded. I'm not sure why she's ignoring me.

We finish our drinks and walk down the block to another boutique, and I buy a pair of small gold stud earrings to go with my outfit. Krystal and Lisa both find cute shirts on the bargain rack. While they pay for them Staci and I tell them that we'll meet them outside.

We step out of the boutique on Main Street and sit on the bench in front of the store. I'm thankful for my boots and jacket – it's a chilly day.

"Listen, Staci, are you mad at me? For breaking up with Brian? Or for leaving town?"

She shakes her head. "Not at all. I do miss you. I wish we were working together." She looks across the street at an elderly couple exiting the hardware store.

I look with her. The little bald man holds the bag of their purchases and walks his gray-haired wife to the passenger side of the car, opens the door for her, and then walks over to the driver's side and gets in.

We watch them drive away and she continues. "I guess what I said earlier is true. I'm jealous of you. You were going to marry Brian, who would've been the perfect husband – a Christian, great career, nice guy, good-looking. Now you've moved off to an exciting new adventure, and, low and behold, you've met another perfect man. Meanwhile, I haven't had a date in over a year. I'm sorry for sounding hateful. You know I love you, Missy. I guess I'm just jealous."

*****

Michael bends over and gets another baseball out of the bucket on the ground next to him and pitches it to his practice net in the backyard. I'm sitting on a patio table chair that I drug out to the middle of the yard so I could watch him practice, and I'm writing a prayer in my journal as I watch. In the last twenty-four hours that I've been home I haven't seen a hint of his old bad attitude. I write a message of thanks to the Lord for that.

Michael's phone, which is lying on the ground next to my chair, buzzes with an incoming call.

"Hey, get that, sis. I'm expecting a call."

"Sure." I answer his phone. "Hello?"

"This is Bud Granger from Clinton Parks and Recreation. I'm returning a call from Michael."

Michael has jogged to me. I tell him who it is, and he takes the phone.

"Mr. Granger? Thanks for calling me back." He walks to the back fence of the yard to talk.

As I look around my parents' yard at the pool, the patio furniture, grill, outside sink, shed, and all of their gorgeous shrubs and flowers, it makes me think of my dinky backyard in Diniyoli with only a yellow birdbath and a concrete bench and a walkway with concrete pavers. Chelsea and I could plant a flowerbed around the birdbath, but I hate to put money into a rent house. I wonder if the landlord would ever think about selling the house? I've already saved some money, and by next year I'll have enough for a down payment.

The image of the big white house – Dreamer and Whisper's dad's house – appears in my mind. I wish I could buy a house like that. It's in horrible shape and would need a

lot of work, but it could be beautiful. I sketch a picture of
the house in my journal and pray while I draw. I draw the
home with flowerbeds full of flowers and no broken
windows or rotten wood or trash in the yard. It's the house
of my dreams.

"You want to know who that was?" Michael
interrupts my praying and drawing.

"It was Bud Granger, whoever that is."

"Smart aleck." He lightly kicks my toe.

I laugh and close my journal. "Who was it?"

"Mr. Granger is the head of Parks and Recreation in
Clinton and is the baseball commissioner for the Clinton
Little League. I called him yesterday, and he was returning
my call. He was telling me how to get a team started in
Diniyoli."

"Really? You're thinking about doing it?" Surely he
realizes what kind of commitment that would be.

He shrugs. "Yeah, those kids need a team. I want
that Dreamer kid to definitely be on the team."

Michael thinking of starting a Little League team in
Diniyoli, and me thinking of buying a house in Diniyoli – are
the two of us seriously considering putting down roots
somewhere besides Cool Springs? Our mom is going to flip
out.

*****

I drive past the blue Diniyoli sign with the Indian
feathers painted on it and admire the sunset framed by my
windshield. Then I see them. Two rainbows on either side of
the sun – sun dogs. I remember learning about them in
eighth grade Science class. I pull my car over to the shoulder,
turn on my hazard lights and get out to take a picture. I share
the unfiltered picture on Instagram with the caption, "Sun
Dogs over Diniyoli."

I lean on the hood of my car for a few minutes

admiring the twin colored bands. This morning my pastor from Cool Springs, Pastor Kevin, preached about Joseph from the Old Testament and how long he had to wait to see his dreams become reality. It was uncomfortable to be in church after not getting married. When I walked into the sanctuary, I felt everyone's eyes on me and thought I heard some whispers. I should've just worn a sandwich board that read, "Yes, I left him at the altar." on the front and "Yes, I moved to the middle of nowhere." on the back. I could have paraded back and forth in the foyer before and after service. Maybe that would've stopped the whispers.

But, then again, maybe I'm imagining things. Maybe no one was talking about me.

I drive down Main Street, turn, and drive past the little yellow house that now feels like home. I continue driving toward the mission. They would be in the middle of their church service now. Kirk went to Texas this morning, and would be back now, preaching to the people who now feel more like family to me than the people I grew up with. I pull into the grassy lot next to the church alongside the few cars parked there, a lot of the congregants walk to church, so there are never many cars. I turn off the engine and listen. I can hear the guitars. I can hear Nelson's powerful voice and Chelsea's perfect harmony. They are singing a rowdy song and clapping as they sing. They finish the song and I hear Kirk's voice next. I can't understand what he's saying, but I can tell that it is Kirk speaking. I imagine that he is wearing a denim shirt and black jeans – the first outfit I saw him in.

After a few minutes, I start my car and drive home to grade spelling tests and make my lesson plans for the week.

*****

It's a Monday – hit the snooze button three times and finally get out of bed thirty minutes late, not enough time to wash my hair, so I just take a quick bath and pull my hair into a ponytail, not enough time for a complete make-up job, so I just put on mascara and lipstick and call it good, pull on a pair of black slacks and boots and a solid gray shirt and tie a pink floral scarf around my neck, grab a mug of Chelsea's coffee and run out the front door, start the car and get to the street – forgot my bag of graded papers and lesson plans, so have to go back into the house to get them, back in the car, drinking coffee on the way to school, a car pulls in front of me out of a neighbor's driveway and I slam on the brakes and spill coffee all over myself, pull into the school parking lot six minutes late, the principal just happens to be standing at the door when I walk in and says "Good morning" in a tone that really says, *"Nice of you to make it to work this morning, Ms. Kolar. Rough weekend?"* At my classroom door I struggle to dig my keys out of my purse and drop my bag on the floor, spilling all of the students' papers. I gather up all of the papers and put them back in my bag, find the key, unlock the door and exhale as I finally make it to my classroom. I leave the lights off and put my purse and bag in their places in the closet and the table behind my desk and plop into my teacher chair and look at the clock on the wall. The students will be in here in twelve minutes. I groan and lean back in my chair in the dim classroom.

Then I see it.

In the corner of my classroom by the wall of windows . . . it's . . . how can that be? I get up and walk to the door, turn on the lights and look at it in the bright lights. In the exact place I'd imagined is the reading corner of my dreams. Hanging from the ceiling is a hoop with light green and pale yellow sheer fabric tied to it. The sheer fabric hangs from the hoop all the way to the floor, encompassing the semi-circular reading area. There's a fluffy tan rug that students will want to take their shoes off on while they're sitting in one of the half dozen green and yellow beanbags. The two walls at the back of the reading corner have three shelf bookcases that are painted white and big green and yellow wooden letters that spell "READ" hang on one of the walls.

I walk to it and sit in a yellow beanbag. They are miniature beanbags – the perfect size for my second graders to cuddle up in and read a book. It's absolutely perfect.

Chelsea pokes her head into my classroom.

"Just checking on you, roomie."

"Get in here right now. Did you do this?" I gesture to the reading corner.

She shakes her head and holds up her hands in innocence. "Not me. Don't you like it?"

"It's perfect." I stand up and look at it. "But, it's creepy. It's like someone has been spying on me. How would someone know exactly how I wanted this?"

She shrugs with feigned ignorance. "Who knows?" Then she points to one of the bookcases. "What's that?" She asks innocently.

I give her a look that says, *You're not fooling me, sister.* And go to the bookcase. There's an envelope on top of it with *"Melissa"* written in the center in small, slanted handwriting – Brian's handwriting. I open the envelope and read the birthday card. *"Hope you like it. Happy birthday – keep dreaming."* The card is unsigned.

"Anonymous." I raise an eyebrow at Chelsea. "It's not signed."

"Really? Well, I guess the teacher fairy made it magically appear in your classroom for your birthday." She twirls out of the room.

Before the door closes, Whisper sticks her head in. "Miss Melissa? Can I come in?"

"Of course Whisper."

She walks into the classroom and stops in her tracks when she sees the reading corner. "Whoa. What's that?"

"It's a reading corner. We can take turns using it for silent reading. Do you like it?"

She nods.

"You've still got seven minutes before everyone gets in here. You can try it out, if you want."

She drops her backpack and practically jumps into the reading corner in a single bound. For a book lover like Whisper, I'm sure this is like a slice of Heaven.

She picks out a book and sits in a beanbag. I grab a dry erase marker and write some daily instructions on the board.

"Miss Melissa," she says after a few seconds.

"Yes?"

"I'm kind of tired."

"You are?" I talk as I write, trying to get all of this written on the board before the rest of the students arrive. "Did you not get enough sleep last night?"

"Not really. Grandma made a lot of noise."

"She did? What was she doing?" It's hard for me to imagine that Ida would be loud at night and interrupt Whisper's sleep. She was probably just snoring. I smile at the thought of Ida's snores shaking the house.

"Coughing and making lots of noise when she breathes."

"Is she sick?" I turn around and face my little friend who has her eyes closed.

"Mm-hmm. She's been sick for a while." She opens her eyes. "Miss Melissa, can you pray for my grandma?"

"Of course." I go to the reading corner and sit criss-cross on the rug in front of Whisper's beanbag. I hold my hand out to her and she grabs it. We bow our heads and pray together for her grandma to be healed.

She sits up out of her beanbag and gives me a hug. "Thanks, Miss Melissa. Your reading corner's nice, but you gotta make sure kids don't fall asleep in it."

I laugh. Whisper is right, as always.

"Miss Melissa, can I tell you a secret?"

"Sure."

"I know who my brother is. He's the boy who always

wears the red baseball hat – the one who won that baseball pitching game at the Pow Wow. His name is Dreamer."

*****

Chelsea comes over to my classroom and shares her leftover pizza with me for lunch.

I open a bottle of water and eye her suspiciously. "You know who did the reading corner, don't you?"

"Please don't ask me." She has her blonde curls piled on her head today, and they shake as she talks. "I promised I wouldn't tell."

"Okay, okay. Just tell me this." I gesture with my water bottle toward the reading corner. "The hanging fabric? The beanbags? The rug? The bookcases? The word "Read" on the wall? It's exactly what I wanted. How did this person know that? I never told anyone."

"No, you didn't, but you did make a drawing of it . . ." Chelsea slides her eyes to my desk.

"I had a drawing on my desk."

"Yep."

"And you gave it to Brian."

She closes her eyes and shakes her head. "I'm not telling you who it was. You can't trick me." She takes a bite of her pepperoni pizza.

"I can't believe he did this after we talked on Friday night. I guess he's trying to get me to change my mind." He didn't beg me to reconsider in the card, though. He told me to *"Keep dreaming,"* which sounds opposite of Brian, now that I think about it. It sounds more like something Kirk would say. In fact, it's something Kirk has already said.

"Wait a minute." I go to my small classroom closet and retrieve my purse from the hook. I get my black and white striped journal out of my purse – the journal that was Kirk's first day of school gift for me. I open it to the inside cover and read his note again. *"Keep chasing those dreams."*

Written in small, slanted handwriting that looks just like Brian's handwriting, just like the handwriting on the card. I turn the envelope over and look at my name written on the front. Melissa.

"Brian calls me Missy."

*****

Rocky always waits for her by the fence in front of the school. Whisper walks as fast as she can out of the building and down the sidewalk to her dog. She doesn't run, because Mr. Clemmons is watching and he would tell her to slow down if she did. She makes it to Rocky and bends down and pets him.

"Good boy, did you have a good day?"

He wags his tail in response and the two of them start walking toward Whisper's house on Old Reservation Road. There are kids walking in front of her, behind her, and on the other side of the street. She waves good-bye to friends as they get to their houses and go inside. There is a group of four older boys on the other side of the street, and her brother is with them, her brother who doesn't know he is her brother. As Whisper walks she sneaks peaks at him under her eyelashes. He has a baseball, as usual, and he is throwing it up into the air and catching it as he walks. He and his friends stop in front of a house, so she stops too, pretending to tie her shoe.

"Look out, stupid!" A boy runs into her.

"Oh, sorry, I didn't know you were behind me." She stands and moves out of the way so the older boy and his friends can pass.

"Try paying attention next time, little brat." The boy grabs Whisper's backpack and throws it. It lands in the middle of the street and all of her books fall out. The library book she checked out today lands with the cover on the ground and the pages flutter in the wind.

Her mouth falls open. Why did this big boy do that? He and his two friends laugh. She looks both ways and then steps into the street to gather up her books and get her backpack. She walks a few feet into the road when a car turns onto the street, clearly exceeding the speed limit.

"Hey!" From across the street her brother yells at her. "A car!"

Whisper turns and sees the car speeding toward her precious books, and she freezes.

Dreamer runs into the street, grabs the books and the backpack before the car reaches them, tucks them under his arm, grabs Whisper's arm with his free hand, and pulls her to the grass on the side of the street. The car whizzes by, and the driver never looks back.

"Are you okay?" Dreamer asks as he stands over her.

"Yeah," she rubs her arm where he grabbed her. "Thanks."

Dreamer shrugs. "Whatever." He looks at the bully who threw her bag into the street. "You," he says sharply as he walks to him. Dreamer is several inches taller than the boy. "You like to pick on little kids?"

The boy and his friends look at the ground.

"Well guess what?" Dreamer grabs the boy's jacket and pulls him to his face. "You're a little kid to me." Dreamer shoves the boy to the ground. "I'd better not ever see you picking on her again."

The boy looks at his two friends who have matching expressions of terror. He gets up and the three of them run down the street as fast as their nine-year-old legs will carry them.

Dreamer turns to cross the street to go back to his friends.

Whisper sits up. She can't let this opportunity to talk to him pass. "I guess I owe you my life."

He looks back at her and snorts. "That's okay."

She stands up. "Well, at least let my billionaire dad

pay you a reward for saving my life." She smiles her trademark gap-toothed grin.

He smiles at her and looks at her books. "Is all your stuff okay?"

She looks at her books. Everything seems to be fine. "Yeah, I'm Whisper. What's your name?" She asks even though she already knows it.

"Dreamer."

"Our names are kind of alike."

"I guess." He steps into the street to go to his friends who are waiting on him on the other side. Then he stops. "Don't let those bullies pick on you."

"What am I supposed to do when they're bigger than me?"

"Just tell them that Dreamer will beat them up if they mess with you, okay?"

She nods and watches him cross the street. His friend tosses him the baseball and he starts tossing it and catching it as he walks with them toward his house – the big white house with the porch and the windows and the dad, and Whisper goes to her tiny, creaking house with the baby blue mailbox and the sick grandma on Old Reservation Road.

*****

Devin pulls open the last kitchen drawer and rummages through it looking for a piece of paper, a receipt, a picture, a business card, anything that would provide evidence about Jacob's boss, Trey. Nothing. She looks around the kitchen and tries to think of somewhere else to look. She's already looked in every cabinet and drawer and the pantry. She's already searched the bedrooms and bathroom and living room. She walks out of the kitchen to the hallway between the living room and kitchen that leads to the front door on her right and the winding staircase on her left. The house has peeling paint, crooked cabinets, carpet with holes and stains, and several inches of dust on every surface, but you can see that it was once a showcase of a house. The staircase with wooden steps and an iron railing with intricately designed iron spindles winds its way up to the wide landing where an old wingback chair sits, covered in cobwebs. Devin studies the staircase. She walks behind it — no closet under the stairs like a lot of homes have. She walks back around to the front of the steps, gets on all fours, and knocks on a step with her knuckles.

Hollow.

But how can I get under there without making a noticeable mess? There's got to be a secret door somewhere. Behind her she hears noise coming from the front yard. She stands and whirls around. She was so focused on her search that she didn't hear people outside until they were close. Hopefully whoever it is didn't see her searching the house through the front windows. She looks through the glass in the front door.

It's Dreamer and some friends. She tries to think of Dreamer as just "Jacob's kid" and not by his name. She wants to be ruthless in her takedown of Jacob, but the kind-hearted twelve-year-old has made her look at Jacob as a father with a soft spot. She doesn't like that. Compassion might make her slip.

Just remember all of the people Jacob has hurt over the years, she tells herself. That should help when she starts to get softhearted.

The boys are playing baseball, as usual. Too risky to continue searching with them right outside. She'll have to try to get into the area underneath the stairs another time.

"Hey Devin," The boy says to her. Not Dreamer — just a kid with no name who always wears a Cardinals baseball cap.

"Hey punk." Devin wants to ask him how school was, if he made good grades and stayed out of trouble. The kid needs someone to ask him those questions. Instead she sits in one of the folding chairs in the yard and lights a cigarette.

She gets out her phone and types more notes. She knows so much now that she could arrest Jacob, Dumb, and Dumber, but she wants to keep her line dangling in the water – there's a bigger fish out there.

As she's typing, her phone tells her that she has a new text message. It's from Melissa.

Hey,
Want to hang out this weekend?
Miss you!

She hasn't seen Melissa since Halloween night when she saw her from the backseat of Jacob's car. Hanging out with Melissa, Chelsea, Kirk, and Michael was fun, but there's no way she can do that anymore, not with how Jacob feels about Kirk and the mission. It's like he thinks Kirk is out to get him personally. Some of Jacob's former customers turned their back on the drug scene because of whatever Kirk's got going on at that mission – God or whatever. And now those people are trying to get more of Jacob's customers to join them, so Jacob hates Kirk.

She deletes Melissa's message without responding to it.

"When's your dad coming home?" She asks the boy playing catch with his friends.

"Dunno." He catches the ball and immediately throws it back without missing a beat.

Devin takes a long drag off her cigarette, drawing the smoke into her lungs and looks at the street with no cars or noise. This job requires patience.

She finishes her smoke, and waits a while, but Jacob and his dummies never come home. The boy's friends go home, and he stays outside. Now he's pitching the ball, aiming at a black X spray-painted on the side of the house.

"I guess I'll go."

He doesn't respond. Devin doesn't blame him. She does treat him like he's a kid with no name after all.

"Do you know where they went?" Maybe the kid has information that'll be useful.

Dreamer shrugs again. "Tulsa, I guess."

Could the boy know something about the bigger fish?

"Why do you think they went to Tulsa?"

Whack, the ball hits the house. He gets another ball out of the bucket next to him. Whack. "Today's the twelfth? They go there second week of the month, every month."

Like a pay period? "What do they do there?"

Gets another ball out of the bucket. Whack. "I dunno. It's been a long time since I went with him. I was little."

The kid went with him to Tulsa? Could he possibly be a witness? Devin's head is spinning, thinking about children testifying against their parents, thinking about dragging testimony out of children, thinking about everything it would take to turn the boy into a witness against his father when a truck pulls into the driveway. A horrible little truck of a teenager. Melissa's brother, Michael gets out of the vehicle.

"Hey!" Dreamer drops the ball into the bucket and runs to the driveway.

"Hi Dreamer," Michael wrinkles his eyebrows at her. "And Devin?"

"She's just my dad's friend. What's going on? Why are you here? Don't you live really far away? Did you have baseball practice today?"

Michael laughs. "Hold on, hold on. No, I didn't have practice today. It's November, dude, not everyone practices all year like you do. I do live kind of far away, but I had to come here to take care of some stuff, and I had to see you to tell you something."

"What?"

"Is your dad here? I was hoping to tell him too."

"Nah, he's not home yet."

"Okay, well, you can tell him. Guess what we're starting right here in Diniyoli?"

Dreamer shakes his head.

"Come on, you have to guess."

"I don't know . . . a taco place?"

"A taco place? Really? No, what do you wish you had here in Diniyoli? Something you've always wanted?"

Dreamer is silent for a moment. Then his eyes light up. "A baseball team?"

"Yep!" Michael holds his hand up and Dreamer smacks it. "You've got to convince your dad to let you play."

"Oh, he'll let me, and even if he doesn't, I don't care – I'm playing!"

"No, you've got to have his permission."

"He will, he will." Dreamer assures him. "When do we start?"

"Well, we've got to recruit a team first. Know any ten, eleven, and twelve year olds who might want to play?"

"Oh yeah, I'll get em." Dreamer says with a serious nod.

"Let's try to get about twelve players, and then we can start working on fundamentals on Saturdays. I just talked to the principal, Mr. Clemmons, and he said that we can use the school gym when it's cold."

"Can we start this Saturday?" Dreamer asks, bouncing on the balls of his feet, like he can't wait to run to his friends' houses and tell them the news.

"Sure," Micheal says, loving the kid's enthusiasm, "you and your buddies meet me in the mission lot at nine o'clock Saturday morning."

"Nine o'clock." Dreamer starts heading across the yard. "Saturday morning."

"Where are you going?"

"I'm getting us a team!"

"Okay, see you later, Dreamer."

"See you Saturday!" Dreamer runs a few houses down and starts beating on the door of an eleven year old neighbor.

"Baseball team, huh?" Devin asks with her hands on her hips.

"Yeah, he loves baseball, and they don't have a team here." Micheal explains.

"Kind of early to start baseball isn't it?"

"Yeah, but I figure these kids will need time to learn the basics."

"Season starts when? April?"

"Yeah, late April."

"Hmm," Devin presses her lips together.

"Well, I'd better get going. I'm heading back to Cool Springs. Good to see you again, Devin." He opens the door of his truck and slides into the driver's seat.

"Yeah, you too, Michael."

He drives off and Devin feels sorry for Dreamer. He'll never get to play on that baseball team.

*****

I poke and prod the pasta on my plate with my fork. I can't force myself to eat.

Kirk isn't eating either.

"Is it not good?" He asks me.

"No, it's good. I just can't eat for some reason."

He took me to a popular Italian restaurant in Clinton. I've been here a few times, and I love it. I have no idea why my throat is closed and my stomach is flip-flopping.

Kirk reaches across the table and puts his hand over mine.

"You look pretty tonight."

"You look nice too." He's wearing a brown sweater

with dark blue, un-stained jeans. His sweater has a shawl collar with two wooden buttons at the neck. It's the kind of sweater that makes me think of hot chocolate, a blanket, and a fireplace.

I take a sip of my water and push a tomato around on my plate.

"Do you want to go? I have somewhere else I was going to take you tonight." He looks at his plate that's just as full as mine. "And it doesn't look like either one of us are very interested in eating."

"Sounds good to me, but don't you want to finish your dinner?"

He shakes his head and takes the cloth napkin out of his lap and puts it on his plate. "I'm not in the mood to eat right now."

"I never thought I'd hear you say that." I tease.

He asks the waitress for the check and pays. He takes my hand and guides me out of the restaurant to the parking lot. We walk a few feet into the parking lot and he stops and faces me.

"In case I don't say it later, I just want you to know that I'm glad you agreed to come with me tonight, and I think you're a really special person." He says and then leans over and squeezes my shoulder in a sideways hug.

He grabs my hand again, and we walk to his truck. I can't think of anything to say in return. I feel the same way about him, but I can't bring myself to open up that much.

"You said you had somewhere else you wanted to go tonight. Where is that?"

He opens my door and jogs around to the driver's side as I get into his truck. He starts the engine and answers my question.

"When I saw you admiring the sunset from your porch, I thought you might like to see something. Have you ever been to Lake Foss?"

"No, is it near here?"

"About twelve miles. Want to go?"

"Sure," I say as I buckle my seatbelt.

"Great." He buckles his seatbelt and pulls out of the parking lot.

Kirk drives through Clinton to the east side of town. The town ends and we drive along the highway for a couple of miles by pastures and wooded areas. We drive in contented silence – neither one of us feel compelled to talk. I look out the windows at the sun setting in the wide Oklahoma sky. I turn to him and catch him looking at me. He smiles, unembarrassed. I don't think this guy ever gets embarrassed. He covers my hand that's resting on the seat next to me with his hand and drives with one hand.

"My family used to go to the lake all the time. My dad had a boat when I was younger. We'd waterski and fish a little. We'd go to Lake Murray."

"One of the families I lived with lived near Lake Tenkiller. We'd go there every day after school and fish and swim." He chuckles. "One day it was so hot we couldn't wait to go swimming. We were talking about jumping in the lake the whole school bus ride. I think I was in . . . that would've been fourth grade. We started daring each other to strip our clothes off and jump into the lake. Of course we started saying that whoever didn't do it was a sissy, and those are fighting when you're a ten year old boy."

"You didn't." I put my hand over my mouth.

"As soon as the bus let us off – the family I was staying with had two boys about my age – we ran to the lake. The house had its own dock in the backyard. We ran to the end of the dock, pulling off clothes the whole way and we jumped off the end of it. We were laughing and yelling and didn't hear or notice anything until we were already in the water. Then we heard it. People were laughing at us. We looked around and saw that it was coming from the public dock about fifty yards from us. There was a wedding ceremony in progress and we had just interrupted it."

I gasp. "No!"

Kirk is laughing. "Yep, they were all dressed in their tuxedos and fancy dresses. The bride's mouth was wide open and the wedding guests were either in shock or laughing."

I can't help cracking up. I don't know what's funnier – the story or watching him tell it. "What did you do?"

"What could we do? We didn't want to climb up the ladder to the dock, of course. We swam down to our friend's house and yelled at him to come outside and bring us clothes."

"Did you get in trouble?"

"Oh yes, we had to do yard work for the people who got married."

"I was just thinking that I don't think you ever get embarrassed. Were you embarrassed?"

"A little, but I was even more embarrassed when I found out later that people were videotaping the wedding, and they filmed the whole thing."

I burst out laughing. I can imagine someone's perfect wedding video interrupted by three naked boys running and jumping off a dock into the lake.

"You know, there's something even crazier about that." He says as he turns the truck into the entrance marked by a big wooden sign reads, "Foss Reservoir."

"How could it get any crazier?" I take off my seatbelt as he parks.

He pulls the keys out of the ignition and turns to me. "When we mowed their yard and worked in their flowerbeds as our punishment, that newlywed couple talked to us. They were the nicest people. They invited us to church with them. We went, and that was when I first heard the gospel and accepted Jesus."

I turn in my seat and put both of my hands in his. "What a story, and I want to tell you that I'm glad you agreed to come with me tonight, and I think you're a very special person."

Kirk pulls my hands to his lips and kisses my fingers. "Let's go look at something."

We get out of the car and walk across the parking lot to a floating sidewalk with handrails. Kirk leads the way on the narrow walkway, and I follow. We walk past a marina store that advertises bait and cold drinks, and then we reach a long wooden dock with a couple of empty benches. All of the boats are empty and swaying in the water, except for one. An elderly man is in a small fishing boat near us, cleaning up his boat and packing his gear. He must be a die-hard fisherman if he's been out fishing on a chilly November night like tonight. I shiver thinking about it.

"Are you cold?" Kirk asks me. "I have an extra jacket in the truck."

"I'm fine." It's a little cold, but I don't want him to have to go get a jacket. I almost wore black leggings with this green dress, but I thought it looked better without them. Ah, the price of looking good.

"We'll just stay a minute. I know you're freezing. I just want to show you something. Sit here." He indicates the empty iron bench, and I sit. He sits next to me.   "Is it okay if I put my arm around you – just to warm you up?"

"Sure."

He puts his arm around me, and we look at the sun setting over the water. The sky almost looks like it's on fire with streaks of yellow, burnt orange, red, and pink stretched across the expanse. The water reflects the colors, and the mirror image makes it look like the sky is twice as big.

"It's beautiful," I say, already feeling warmer with Kirk's arm hugging my shoulders.

"Do you see it?"

I'm not sure what he means. The sunset? Of course I see it. "Um . . . see what?"

Kirk points straight out toward the water. I follow his finger and try to see. "On the other side of the lake."

"Are those?" I look at Kirk.

He smiles and nods.

I stand up. I don't care if I get cold. On the other side of the lake, below the gorgeous sunset is a line of buffalo.

*****

Over the next couple of weeks I try to draw a picture to capture the beauty of the sunset and the buffalo at Lake Foss, but I can't even get close. I drew a few pencil drawings in my journal and purchased an eleven by fourteen sketchbook with high quality paper that won't show eraser marks and draw a beautiful picture, but it doesn't come close to the beauty of the real sight.

Not only does the image stay with me, but the feelings of that night do as well. The feeling of electricity when Kirk kissed my fingers in the truck, the feeling of my heart skipping a beat when I looked at him after seeing the line of buffalo, the feeling of losing breath when he lightly kissed my lips on my front porch at the end of the evening, and the feeling of pure joy when he waved good-bye to me out the window of his truck when he drove away from my house – my drawings can't compare to the real image, and no feelings I've ever experienced can compare with the feelings I have for Kirk.

The last two Wednesdays he has helped me cook – or, rather, he's made me laugh while I cook, actually slowing down the whole process. He tried to convince me to serve chocolate chip pancakes with chocolate chip cookies this last Wednesday. He said, "It'll be a theme night. The kids will love it." I just rolled my eyes at him and made chicken alfredo with chef salad. We went to a movie in Clinton last night, a chick flick that Kirk made fun of afterward, and I feel just as dewy eyed and ooey gooey for Kirk as the girl in the movie felt for her leading man.

"Melissa, we need a few more cans of vegetables in

this bag. Can you grab those, please?" Chelsea's boyfriend, Jarrett, asks me.

Jarrett and his team from Rural Outreach Ministries are in the mission kitchen helping us package turkey dinners for tomorrow's giveaway. Jarrett is shorter than me and quite muscular with a flat top haircut and perfect teeth. He kind of looks like a college wrestler or a marine or something, and Chelsea is absolutely swooning over him . . . but, I guess she could say the same thing about me. I hope I don't look flush faced and big-eyed around Kirk, but I probably do.

After we get all of the packages containing canned vegetables, instant potatoes, boxed stuffing, and brownie mix lined up on the counters and all of the turkeys stuffed in the refrigerators, Kirk addresses the volunteers. "Thank you all so much for giving your Saturday morning to help us with this." Everyone in the kitchen – Tess, Janice, Nelson and his wife, Chelsea and Jarrett and his team of five people stand still to listen to Kirk, this missionary who has dedicated his life to making life better for the people of Diniyoli.

"Jarrett, you and your team have been a great blessing to us, bringing us all of this food. I know that tomorrow is going to be an amazing day. The people of Diniyoli are going to see God's love in a tangible way." Kirk starts clapping his hands in appreciation and we all join in clapping for Jarrett and his team.

"Got plans for today?" I ask as I put my chin on Kirk's shoulder after he says good-bye to Jarrett and his team, and their van pulls out of the grassy lot and drives away, headed back to Clinton.

He turns to me and puts his hand under my chin, lifting my face up to his. "I need to go to the school gym and help your brother with the baseball team."

"Oh yeah, I forgot about that."

He gives me a light kiss. "Want to come?"

Over Kirk's shoulder I see Tess and Janice walking out of the mission to their cars. Janice gives me a conspiratorial smile and a thumbs-up. Tess gives me a look that says, *Exactly as I thought – the city girl just wanted to snag a boyfriend.* Of course she's wrong, but I can't help feeling a little guilty. Tess and Janice get into their vehicles and I try to shake off Tess's disapproving look.

I look back at Kirk and shrug. "Sure, I don't know much about baseball, but maybe I can help."

"We can use your kid-wrangling skills, I'm sure."

I find my gloves in my pocket and walk to my car as I put them on, and Kirk follows me. "I'm no Janice, but I'm learning."

"You're amazing with the kids. They all love you. After baseball, I have to prepare for tomorrow. I'll be finished by six tonight. Want to eat dinner together and hang out?" He leans on my car and asks me.

"I'd love to." I open my car door and get my keys out of my purse.

"Tell you what – you cook for me all the time. Why don't you let me cook for you?"

"I didn't think you knew how to cook."

"I don't, but you've inspired me. If you can learn, then I can too." He scratches the back of his head and gives me one of his trademark grins. "I've been looking at recipes online, and I think I've found one that I can do."

I laugh at the mental picture of Kirk surfing the web for recipes. "You've been looking at recipes?"

"You think you've already got me figured out, don't you?"

I laugh and shake my head, but don't answer. "See you at the school in a few minutes. I'm going to swing by my house and change into my baseball clothes."

He waves good-bye to me, and I drive home and change out of my jeans and boots into athletic pants and shoes. I check the time on my phone – ten o'clock. Michael's been practicing with the kids for an hour, and I'm sure he could use some help.

The school is always strange on the weekends. The empty hallways and classrooms seem lonely without the little people and their backpacks and ponytails and their shouting and giggles. In the gym, Michael and Kirk are trying to control what looks like a mutiny by ten, eleven, and twelve year olds.

"Listen! Hey, get off him now!" Michael yells at two boys who are dog-piling on top of another boy.

"Everyone please stop talking and listen to Michael." Kirk tries the nice approach.

"One, two, three, eyes on me," I say in my best Janice-voice.

"One, two, eyes on you," the boys and girls all say. They stop talking and all turn around to look at me.

"Coach Michael and Pastor Kirk want to teach you to be better at baseball. You need to give them your full attention. Coach Michael, were you wanting to tell them something?"

The dozen or so kids turn to look at Coach Michael. I see Whisper in the crowd, and she gives me her cutest gap-toothed smile. She's the youngest one here by two years, at least, but I'm not surprised she's here. That girl is always in the middle of the action in this town.

"Um, ok, thanks Melissa." My brother seems shocked that I was able to get the kids to quiet down in a matter of seconds without raising my voice. "For the second hour of practice, we're going to divide you up into groups. I'm going to work on throwing and catching. Kirk is going to work on scooping up grounders and throwing them –"

"What about batting?" A bigger boy interrupts.

"We're going to work on batting today too. We'll be hitting whiffle balls, since we're inside. Melissa, do you think you could work on batting with them?" Michael looks at me with a pained expression. He knows that there's no way I could ever teach anyone to hit a baseball. He must be desperate.

"Ah, sure . . . I guess." I pick up a bat on the ground and look at it like it's an artifact from an alien life form.

"I'll do it."

Michael, Kirk, and I turn around to the bleachers behind us. Dreamer's dad – actually I guess he's Dreamer and Whisper's dad – in his white t-shirt, slicked-back hair, and tattooed arms, walks down the steps toward us.

"Great, thanks," Michael says. "Dreamer's dad is going to help out with the batting. What's your name, sir?"

"Jacob."

Michael divides the kids into three groups. The groups go to opposite corners of the gym and start practicing. My job is to retrieve as many errant balls as I can and throw them back to the proper group. After twenty minutes, Michael tells everyone that it's time to switch, and then after another twenty minutes they switch again, and then they repeat the process twenty minutes later.

In the last rotation, Dreamer is in his dad's group, and he's the first kid to bat. Of course he smacks the whiffle ball to the top row of bleachers on his dad's first pitch. I started to run up the steps before he even hit it, though, because I figured that's what he'd do. By the time I get back to the court, Whisper's up to bat. Jacob tosses a ball at her underhanded to make it easier for her to hit. She misses it by a mile.

"Keep your eye on the ball, kid." Jacob tells her.

"You can do it, Whisper!" Dreamer yells from his place at the back of the line.

Jacob jerks his head around to Dreamer and demands, "What did you say?" in a low, even voice.

"I was just telling Whisper that she can do it," Dreamer explains to his dad.

I watch as realization spreads across Jacob's face. He looks at little determined Whisper, with her blue eyes – eyes just like his – wide open, ready to watch that ball.

Jacob tosses a soft, underhanded pitch to his

daughter.

She misses again, laughs it off, and Jacob stares at her as she finds her place at the back of the line. The kids have to yell at Jacob to get his attention. He shakes himself and pitches to the next one.

At the close of practice, Michael calls all of the kids to center court.

"You guys did awesome today. Some of you this was your first time to ever play baseball, and you already showed a lot of improvement. Some of you," he looks at Dreamer, "could teach me how to play baseball, and you did a great job working on your skills and helping other kids."

As I stand behind the circle of kids with Kirk on one side of me, and Dreamer and Whisper's dad Jacob on the other side of me, I can't help getting teary-eyed at seeing my brother working with these kids. Gone is the entitled, egotistical high school jock who had replaced my sweet brother for a few months. I thank God for working on Michael's heart.

"We're going to end every practice with a scripture and prayer, guys." Michael presses the screen of his phone to open the Bible app. "Today's scripture is Second Corinthians five and seventeen, "Therefore, if anyone is in Christ, he is a new creation; old things have passed away; behold all things have become new.""

He puts his phone down and talks to the kids. "To me, that means that when I gave my life to Jesus, He made me a new person, and He did away with the bad stuff I did in my past."

Every one of the ball players, and all of the adults – Kirk, Jacob, and me – we all listen intently to Michael. Michael tells the kids that if they want to give their lives to Jesus that they can come and talk to him about it any time. He closes in a prayer.

As we leave the school, a familiar hand slips into mine. I look down and see my star student.

"I noticed you got a really good hit out there today."

She rolls her eyes. "After I missed it about twenty times."

"You're just starting. I'm sure you'll get better."

"Today was the first day I ever played baseball, and I did hit it. I think I'm already getting better." As she talks she hops to accentuate her words.

I laugh. "That's right. I'm proud of you." She continues hopping and holding my hand as we walk out of the school into the bright sunshine. A bone-chilling November wind blows her wild curls in every direction, and whips my short ponytail around. I let go of her hand and put my gloves back on and zip my coat. She hops next to me with no coat or gloves as I walk across the parking lot to my car.

"Is Grandma Ida coming to pick you up?"

She shakes her head. "Nah, I'm just gonna walk."

I survey the parking lot. All of the other players either have a car picking them up in the parking lot, or they jump on their bicycles and pedal home as fast as they can. I don't see any other kids walking home.

"Let me drive you home."

She doesn't even answer. She runs to the passenger side of my car and yanks the door open as soon as I unlock it.

"You got a heater in here?" She asks as she rubs her hands together.

I turn on the heater. "Yep."

We drive for a few minutes and let the hot air of the heater warm us up.

"Is your grandma feeling better?"

Whisper shakes her head. "No, she went to the doctor, and he said she's got pneumonia. She has medicine, but it's not working yet."

"Oh, I'm so sorry for her. Tell her I'll be praying for

her."

"Okay," Whisper says as she looks out the window.

"Hey, do you have a coat and gloves?"

"I've got my coat from last year, but it's too little, and it looks really babyish, because I was in first grade when I wore it. Grandma or Tess usually take me to get clothes in Clinton, but Grandma's sick and Tess's husband Phil is real sick too."

I didn't know that Phil was sick. I knew he battled with poor health at times, but I didn't know anything was going on right now.

The Whisper tells me what to do.

I call Ida and get permission to go to Clinton to go winter clothes shopping. Four stores and three hours later, we've got two new pairs of jeans, a few sweaters, a couple of adorable hoodies, a new coat that doesn't look babyish, a few sassy knit hats and three different pairs of gloves, because a girl has to match. We stop at a charming bakery and recharge with cupcakes and hot chocolate. If the Lord blesses me with a daughter one day, I definitely want to have days like this with her.

Whisper licks the frosting off of her cupcake, falls back into her chair, and says, "Mmmm, this is the best thing I've ever tasted."

"What kind did you get?"

"Peanut butter with chocolate icing. What'd you get?"

"Red velvet with cream cheese icing. It's so yummy." Red velvet with cream cheese icing makes me think of my birthday dinner, only two weeks ago, but it feels like two years ago.

We eat our cupcakes and drink our hot chocolate, and Whisper talks. She tells me about Dreamer rescuing her from the bullies after school, and about him walking behind her every day, and how he says "Hi" to her in the hallway at school every day.

"Miss Melissa, I've been thinking about telling him. Do you think I should?"

*****

I tell Kirk that his grilled cheese sandwich is the best I've ever tasted. Apparently he tried to make the recipe he found online, and it was a disaster, and the only thing he had ingredients for was grilled cheese sandwiches, but that's completely fine with me. These sandwiches absolutely melt in your mouth.

"I've made these since I was a kid." He shrugs in mock modesty. "I guess some of us are just natural chefs."

"You know, you may have something there. I think since you've got such a natural talent for cooking that you need to start making the Wednesday meals." I get up from the table and take our plates to his kitchen and put them in the sink before he can respond.

"Oh, I'm a natural, but you're a prodigy." He says as he follows me to the kitchen with the rest of the dishes from the table.

I laugh. "Yeah, right."

"A cooking prodigy." He kisses my cheek. "Scoot over. I don't want you doing dishes. I asked you to dinner, and I'm going to do the dishes, too."

"Well, okay. I'll let you do it."

Kirk does the dishes and I lean against the cabinets and tell him about Whisper and Dreamer being brother and sister and about Whisper wanting to tell him.

"Do you think I should talk to Jacob?" He asks me as he dries a plate and puts it in the cabinet.

"If he were a regular person I'd say yes, but I've heard some pretty scary stuff about him. I'm sure Ida had good reasons for keeping her from her father all these years." I pause, debating with myself. "But, then again, she knows who he is anyway, and she'll see him at baseball practices and around town. I can't imagine how that's going to affect her — growing up knowing that her dad didn't want her."

Kirk scoffs. "It affects you all right." He puts the spatula in a drawer. "Let's just leave the rest of the dishes and watch the OSU game."

"Sure," I agree. Do I detect offense in his tone? Did I offend him by talking about Whisper's dad not wanting her?

We watch our Cowboys play for the last half. Every good play, every bad play, every bad call, every funny commercial, everything goes by without one comment from Kirk. A few times I make observations about the game, but all he does is grunt.

With only two minutes left in the game, we are winning by more than two touchdowns, and I decide to leave. I guess this isn't going to work out between us if he's going to get offended every time I mention a child who doesn't live with his or her parents. I wipe a tear from my eye and stand and collect my purse and start for the door.

"Melissa." He touches my wrist. "Wait a minute." He switches off the television.

I stop walking but don't sit down.

"I'm sorry. Would you sit down and talk to me for a minute?"

I sit down. I try to stop the tears, but I can't. They are slipping out of my eyes and sliding down my cheeks, even though I don't want them to. I wipe my face with the corner of my sleeve and try to pretend that I'm not crying.

"Please don't cry." He reaches over and covers my hands with his. "I'm sorry. I'm oversensitive about being a foster kid. I know I am. It's an insecurity I have, and something I need to get over. I logically know that you weren't talking about me, and that you didn't intend to offend me, but this is an issue that I don't think about logically. I'm sorry."

He's sitting across from me on the couch, his deep

brown eyes pleading with me to forgive him. It was such a small thing, just a misunderstanding, an over-reaction on his part. If it's such a small thing, then why do I feel so upset?

I lean toward him and kiss him on the cheek. "Don't worry about it. We'll figure it out."

He smiles and touches his forehead to mine. "Thanks for understanding, Melissa."

I say goodnight and leave his house. As I drive home, I think about Kirk – always so strong, always wise, always knows the answers, always funny – that was the Kirk I thought I knew, but that was just the surface. I pull into my driveway next to Chelsea's car and sit in the car for a while and think about Kirk, not Kirk the Missionary or Kirk the Preacher, but Kirk the regular human.

*****

Some men carry in all of the chairs from the fellowship hall and line them in the back of the sanctuary behind the pews, and there are still people who don't have seats. There's an undeniable energy in the air as the people in the over-stuffed church worship the Lord this morning. Bright rays of warm sunshine flood the sanctuary, as if God is smiling on us today, happy that we're giving away big, fat turkeys and non-perishable food to anyone who needs it on this perfect Sunday.

Kirk preaches an uplifting message about hope, and many people respond to a call for salvation. After service, people line up against the sanctuary wall in a line that extends through the back door of the sanctuary down the hallway to the fellowship hall and snakes around the main room of the fellowship hall.

My arms are getting a much-needed workout from lifting turkeys out of the refrigerator and passing them to Chelsea who places them on the countertop. Nelson, Tess, Phil, Janice, and Kirk distribute to people in line. Jarrett from

Clinton is also here helping, and Chelsea can't stop smiling.

Kirk is in his element. I watch him as he gives out the food. He talks to everyone who passes by him, and he doesn't say the same phrases to any two of them, nor does he use clichés when talking to them. He remembers details about their lives and comments on them. He asks questions about their family or their health. He notices people he's never met, and he introduces himself and asks their name. He plays with kids and jokes around with teenagers. This is Kirk at his best.

After the food is distributed, we go outside to help people load their cars. I see Whisper struggling with a turkey and a sack of food.

"Whisper!"

She turns and faces me. She's wearing her new coat with her new purple knit hat and gloves. The purple makes her dark skin glow and her bright blue eyes shine.

"Wait, let me drive you home." I get my keys out of my pocket and push the button to unlock my car doors. "Go ahead and put your stuff in the car. I'll be ready to leave in a little bit."

"Okay," She says and then she turns to my car and loads her bounty.

I turn to go back inside to retrieve my purse and see if there's anything else Kirk needs me to do. In the grassy lot next to the church I see that we have a guest. If he wanted to be invisible, he should've worn a different color hat. Dreamer is on the far edge of the property, viewing everything that's happening while tossing a baseball up and catching it repeatedly.

"Dreamer!" I call out to him across the grass.

"Yeah?" He yells back.

"Come here." I motion for him to come. I look through the door of the fellowship hall and see Tess and Phil are still in the kitchen. "Tess, Phil, is there any food left?"

"Yeah, there are six meals left."

The plan for the leftover food is to take it to The Jesus House in Oklahoma City tomorrow. There isn't an outreach that takes perishable food anywhere near here. They will be fine with five turkeys.

"Let's get a turkey for your family." I tell Dreamer when he gets closer.

"Ah . . . I don't know." A mixture of doubt and fear crosses his face.

"Just tell your dad I forced you to take it."

"He won't like it, Miss Melissa."

"Oh, come on. How can he get mad about a turkey?" I smile a conspiratorial grin at him until he smiles back.

"Okay, okay, but do I have to carry that heavy thing home?" He asks as he sees the monstrous bird Phil carries to us.

"I can give you a ride." I offer.

Phil helps load the turkey, and Dreamer carries the sack of non-perishable side dishes. Tess follows us out to the car, nagging at Phil the whole way, telling him he's not supposed to be lifting heavy things. We get Dreamer's food loaded in the car, and Dreamer sits in the backseat. Whisper has already claimed the front passenger seat. The two kids recognize each other and start talking immediately.

"Melissa, wait." Tess tells me when she sees the two kids in the car together.

A deep line is set between her dark eyebrows and her jet-black eyes are filled with worry.

"What are you up to? Why are these two kids together in your car?"

"I'm not up to anything. I was just going to help them get home with their turkeys."

"Be careful." She says sincerely.

"I will."

I get into the car and fasten my seatbelt. Dreamer is giving Whisper pointers on hitting better in baseball, and I don't interrupt. I start the engine and begin to back out. I look in my rearview mirror and see Kirk standing behind my car with his hands up.

I roll down the window. "What are you doing, crazy man?"

"Trying to stop you." He walks to the driver's side door and leans in through the window. "What's going on? You guys having a party without me?"

Whisper laughs. "Pastor Kirk, we're not having a party. Miss Melissa's just taking us home."

"Well, it looks like a party to me. Can I come with you?"

I look at Whisper and Dreamer. "What do you think, guys? Should we let him come with us?"

Dreamer shrugs, and Whisper says, "Yeah" with both her arms raised over her head.

"I'll go sit in the back with Dreamer. I won't make Whisper give up the shotgun seat." He walks around the front of the car to the back door.

Before he gets in the car, Whisper says, "Pastor Kirk is so funny."

I nod in agreement. Pastor Kirk is funny.

Kirk gets in and buckles up. I pull out of the parking space and head to Old Reservation Road. Kirk gets the kids talking about which Thanksgiving foods they like the best. Whisper and Dreamer seem to share Kirk's love of sweets, and we all come to the conclusion that pecan pie is the best Thanksgiving food.

I find the Tiffany-blue mailbox and park in front of Whisper's house. Kirk and Dreamer follow Whisper and me across the lawn to the front door. Kirk carries the huge turkey, and Dreamer carries the sack of groceries.

Whisper opens the door, and we wait to go in. "Grandma?" She walks in and peers into the bedroom to the right of the living room. "She's sleeping. Come on in."

We quietly walk into the house. The television in the corner is on with the volume down low, a pile of laundry is on the couch and dirty dishes are in the sink. The house is clean, but clearly Grandma Ida is having trouble keeping up with everything. We put the turkey in the almost empty refrigerator and stack the boxes of instant potatoes, stuffing, and brownie mix and canned goods in a kitchen cabinet. Kirk gives Whisper a hug, and Dreamer gives her a fist bump and heads for the door. I kiss her on the forehead and follow them to the door. As I walk past Ida's bedroom, I feel the familiar tug on my heart that I've come to recognize and learned to obey.

"Whisper, would it be okay if I checked on your Grandma?" I stop in the doorway and turn back to her and ask.

"I guess that would be okay."

She peeks into Ida's room. "Grandma, can Miss Melissa come in to check on you?" She waits a few seconds. "Hang on," she tells me and goes into the room.

I look at Kirk on the front porch. He gives me a questioning look.

"We need to check on Ida." I tell him with a certainty that he immediately understands, and he and Dreamer come back into the house.

Whisper comes out of Ida's bedroom. With wide eyes she says, "Miss Melissa, she's not waking up."

I touch Whisper's shoulder and guide her to Dreamer. "Dreamer, could you keep Whisper company here in the living room while Kirk and I check on her grandma?"

Dreamer nods, looking almost as scared as I feel. I've never been in a situation like this. I think a desperate prayer asking the Lord for wisdom and guidance.

Kirk follows me into Ida's bedroom. The elderly woman's ragged breaths are shallow and rapid. Her eyelids flutter open as I enter the room, but she doesn't say anything.

I sit on the edge of her bed. "Ida, I'm so sorry you're sick."

She simply closes her eyes and opens them in response, as if to say she's too tired to reply.

"Your throat hurts?" I feel Kirk standing behind me.

Eyes close and open again.

"I'm going to feel your forehead, okay?" She responds with her eyes again, and I feel her forehead. She's burning up. "Do you have a thermometer, Ida?"

Outside the door Whisper answers, "It's in the kitchen. I'll get it."

She's in the room in seconds with the thermometer. I show it to Ida, and she obediently opens her mouth. I slide it underneath her tongue. She keeps her eyes closed while waiting. Her gray curls are matted to her head with dried sweat. Her normally beautiful dark complexion is the pallid color of someone who's been sick and in the house for a long time.

The thermometer beeps and I take it out of her mouth. Her temperature is one hundred and three. I show it to Kirk.

"Ida, when did you go to the doctor last?" He asks her.

"Two weeks ago," she rasps.

"Ida I think you need to go to the doctor."

She shakes her head at him.

"Ida your temperature is dangerously high, and you have been on medicine for a while, so it should be down, right?"

"Whisper . . . what about Whisper?" She asks.

I speak up. "Ida, Whisper needs you to get better so you can take care of her like you always have. I will be happy to babysit Whisper at my house, if I need to."

She looks up at me with a cocked eyebrow.

"I promise I'll take good care of her." I pat Ida's hand. "I love her, Ida. I won't let anything happen to her."

A tear escapes Ida's eye and slides down her cheek. She nods.

Kirk goes into the living room with the kids, and I help Ida get dressed. I call Kirk back into the bedroom when she's ready, and we both help her out of bed and help her walk out of the bedroom into the living room, and Kirk tells the kids to get in the car.

"Do we need to grab her coat? It's kind of cold out there," Dreamer asks.

"Yep, good thinking, Dreamer." I look around the tiny living room. "There it is on the couch. Would you grab it please?"

Dreamer gets Ida's coat and gently lays it across her shoulders.

"Here you go, ma'am," he says respectfully. Then he goes out the front door and races Whisper to the car.

Ida looks at me and then at Kirk. "Dreamer?" She asks us.

"Um," I look at Kirk. How can I explain? "It just happened, Ida. He and Whisper are friends."

She points an accusing finger at us. "No!" She says with all of her strength.

Kirk speaks up. "We won't let Jacob hurt Whisper. You have my word, Ida."

She sighs and then nods.

We load her into the front passenger seat, and Kirk and the kids sit in the back. I drive to the big, old white house in the center of town, Dreamer's house, the house Ida snuck baby Whisper out of all those years ago, to take Dreamer home. On the way, Kirk sings a song about boogers and gets the kids to laugh. He asks them about friends at school, and they start talking. Both of Ida's grandkids, with their matching black hair and high cheekbones chatter about kids at school, sometimes talking at the same time in the backseat of the car.

I look over at Ida. She's smiling.

I park on the street in front of the house. Kirk helps Dreamer with his turkey and groceries, and we all tell

Dreamer that we'll see him later.

After they get out, Ida asks, "Does he know?"

I shake my head.

"No, Grandma, I haven't told him." I look at Whisper in the rearview mirror, and see that she's smiling. "I haven't even told him yet, and he's already a good big brother."

****

Chapter Six

"Everyone who has read at least ten books and has finished the quizzes over the books, may now be dismissed for the Reading Dragons reward party." The school secretary announces over the intercom throughout the elementary school.

"According to my list, these are the students who qualified to be Reading Dragons," I read from my computer, "Spirit, Addison, Cade, Jayden, Jaxon, Shanee, Cheyenne, and Whisper."

The star readers smile at each other and bounce with excitement as they put their supplies away and line up at the door to go to the extra recess they earned. I tell them that they may go, and the rest of my students look at them enviously. Maybe next quarter they will remember this feeling and finish their reading, I hope.

"All right everyone," I get the attention of the remaining fifteen students. "We are going to get into three groups and rotate through three centers – math at this table, science at this table, and silent reading in the reading corner." I put the students into groups, and then I float between the groups, monitoring and answering questions. The students' favorite center is the reading corner. They love relaxing in the cozy spot with its beanbags and floating rainbow.

I use a timer on the smartboard to signal when it's time to switch. Each rotation is ten minutes long, so we should be finished by the time the reward recess is over. My students have had focusing problems today, and I have, too. It's difficult to focus on the last day of school before a break. Everyone is ready for the Thanksgiving break. I'm excited to be out of school for a few days, but I'm not really looking forward to going back to Cool Springs. I'm nervous that my mom might try another Brian intervention. And I don't know what I'm going to do about Whisper. Hopefully Ida will be out of the hospital before then, but if she isn't, I guess I'll have to tell my mom to set another place at the table.

Right after we get settled into the third and final rotation, Chelsea steps into my classroom. I tiptoe to her, making sure not to interrupt my students who are hard at work.

She whispers, "They need you in the office. I'll stay with your class."

I nod and make my way to the office at the end of the hallway. I open the wooden door of the office and see Whisper sitting in the waiting area. She's sitting in one of the plastic waiting area chairs and has her leg propped on another chair. The school secretary, with gloved hands, is doctoring a nasty scrape on Whisper's shin. Whisper is silently sobbing.

"Miss Melissa!" She reaches out her hands to me when she sees me.

"Oh no, what happened?" I go to her and put my arm around her shoulders.

"I was playing baseball," She tells me with a shaky voice and quivering lip, "and I got a real good hit," she stops and smiles through her tears, "so I ran as fast as I could, because I wanted to get a home run, and I tried to slide into home base, like Dreamer does, but I hurt my leg."

"Oh goodness, that does look bad." The secretary has cleaned the scrape and is spraying something medicated and antibacterial on it. "Was it worth it? Did you get a home run?"

"I sure did," She smiles her perfectly beautiful gap-toothed grin.

"I'm so proud of you, girl." I embrace her and then sit in the chair next to her as the secretary puts a bandage over the wound.

The office door swings open, and Dreamer steps in.

"Where is she?" He asks, and then he sees us on the other side of the door. "I heard about what happened. Are you okay?"

Whisper nods and wipes the tears off of her cheek. "Yeah, I'm fine. Guess what? I got a home run!"

"Are you serious? That's awesome!" He holds out his fist and she bumps it with her fist. "You had to slide in to home to get it, huh? Was it worth it?"

Her curls bounce as she nods, "Definitely."

The brother and sister talk for a few more minutes, and Whisper doesn't cry anymore. As I watch the two of them talk, I'm amazed at how they've bonded over the last few weeks, and I wish Dreamer knew that the precious little girl he's befriended is actually his sister. Somehow I don't think he'll be all that surprised, though.

"Looks like you're all better. Are you ready to get back to class? As much as I'd like to stay and talk with you two, I have a class full of second graders who need to learn some stuff this afternoon."

The last couple of hours of the day go according to my lesson plans. After three months of teaching, I've finally figured out how long it takes my students to do things. We do a math reinforcement mini-lesson and end the day with reading aloud. As we read, I notice tiny bits of paper are being thrown from somewhere. I don't ask where they are coming from. Instead, I pretend not to notice and peek over the page while Whisper reads aloud. I see Dakota, our resident Romeo, slyly reach into his desk and toss paper bits onto a girl's desk in front of him.

"Dakota," when I say his name, he sits up straight in his chair, "I need to talk to you when we're finished."

He doesn't respond and grabs his book and stares at the page, well aware that he's been caught.

We finish reading and I talk to Dakota while the kids gather their backpacks and jackets. I assign him ten minutes of detention during Monday's recess, and he hangs his head as if he's been given a life sentence. When the bell rings, I dismiss my students and receive the daily good-bye hugs from most of them. Whisper stays in the classroom, since she's going home with me, and she cleans the desks with disinfectant wipes while I answer emails and prepare to leave.

I'm writing tomorrow's plans on the whiteboard when Mr. Clemmons, the principal, sticks his head into the room.

"Miss Melissa? May I speak with you for a minute?"

"Yes, Whisper, would you take these books back to the library?" I hand her a stack of books and then open my desk drawer and pull out a dollar. "You can buy a snack from the fundraiser sale, too."

"Awesome!" She takes the books and the dollar and rushes out of the room, excited to get a cookie and a drink from the library.

Mr. Clemmons pats Whisper on the head and tells her that he hears good things about her, and she beams from his praise. After she leaves, he sits in one of the student desks, and I sit in one across from him.

"So, she's staying with you?"

"Yes, we're going to visit her grandma today. They say she's getting better."

"That's good. It's also good that Whisper didn't get hurt badly enough to have to go to the emergency room today. It was just a scrape, but we would've had some trouble if it had been worse. The school can have her transported to a hospital, but who would've been her legal guardian at the hospital, since her grandmother can't be there? How long is she staying with you? What if she does get into a situation where she needs a legal guardian? What if she makes abuse accusations against you? You need legal protection, Melissa. I've seen other teachers in the same place you're in. The situation dragged on much longer than they expected, and they didn't become emergency legal guardians or get their home approved by the department of human services, and there were problems because of it."

Emergency legal guardian?

I thank him for his advice and promise that I'll consider it. Whisper gets back from the library with chocolate smeared on her face, and Mr. Clemmons tells us to be safe as we travel to Clinton to see her grandma. We finish cleaning the room, gather our things and head out the door.

"How about Green Parrot for dinner?" I ask as I lock the door.

"Yes, I love their chicken fried steak," she answers.

Some parent I'd make, I think, chocolate chip cookies and chicken fried steak.

We toss Whisper's backpack and my canvas bag full of papers to grade into the backseat, and drive to the mission for the afterschool program. The kids are not in the mood to work since they are out of school for the rest of the week. So, after I read a story aloud to them and Chelsea times them on math facts, we fold up all the chairs and play games. Red Light, Green Light, Simon Says, Mother May I, and Freeze Tag – they love all of those old games.

After the kids leave and we clean up, Whisper and I drive to the café on Main Street. Whisper wants to sit at the counter, so we sit on two round stools, rest our elbows on the Formica countertop and watch the cook flip sizzling patties, scramble mounds of eggs, and fry bacon right in front of us. We order without a menu and talk about our day. Then Tess emerges from the back room.

"Well, if it isn't my Whisper!" She exclaims and comes around the counter to give Whisper a hug. "How are you Melissa?" She asks sincerely.

"Doing good. We're having an early dinner and then heading to Clinton to check on Grandma Ida."

Tess puts a hand on the countertop and leans on it. "I was there today. Doctor said she'll probably get to go home tomorrow, just in time for Thanksgiving."

"Yea!" Whisper cheers. "I love staying with Miss Melissa and Miss Chelsea, but I miss my grandma."

"I know you do," I tell her. "I'm going to miss you, but I'm glad she's better."

"Whisper, hon, can you do me a favor?" Tess asks her. "Can you go back there and tell Phil that we need more napkins out here?"

Whisper says, "Sure," but she looks at me and rolls her eyes. She's not fooled. She knows this is the second time today that she's been sent out of the room so the grownups can talk.

"I just wanted to tell you that I'm sorry for the way I've treated you. You've proven to be a hard worker, and now you're taking care of Whisper . . I – " She stops and claps her big hand on mine and pats it. "Thank you, that little girl is special to Phil and me. I wish I could take care of her, but with Phil's health, and I'm not in the best shape . . . I just don't think we could do it."

"Thank you, Tess. That means so much." I mean it. It really does mean a lot to finally have her approval.

We enjoy a delicious "greasy spoon" style dinner and chat with Tess and Phil. Tess's eyebrows go up when Whisper talks about Dreamer, but she doesn't say anything. When we're finished eating, Tess and Phil won't let us pay, joking with Whisper that she can come back and wash dishes sometime. Later, when we're driving to Clinton, Whisper asks if she'll really have to go back and wash dishes.

"No, honey. They were just kidding."

"I'll do it if I need to."

I assure her that it was just a joke, and she turns on the radio. She knows the song playing, something very repetitive being sung by pre-pubescent boys, and she wiggles and waves her arm as she sings, telling me that it's a popular dance that teenagers do. I laugh to myself, remembering the days when I knew all of the words (of course it isn't very hard to know all of the words to these songs) to the latest songs and knew all of the moves to the latest dance fad. Whisper spins the dial on the radio, and every time it lands on another station, she sings along for a little bit and then spins it again.

"I can't believe that you know all of the words to every song." I tell her after she's displayed her knowledge of hip-hop, country, rap, and Christian music.

She shrugs. "I love music."

I marvel at her ability to memorize all of the lyrics to these songs and know that it's not normal. I tell myself again, I have got to demand that this child be tested for a gifted program.

I slowly open the door to Ida's hospital room, not wanting to wake her if she's asleep. A game show is playing on the television.

"Ida? Are you awake?"

"Yes, come in."

Whisper rushes ahead of me. "Grandma, are you okay?"

"I'm much better than I was, that's for sure." Ida is sitting up in the bed. Her complexion is back to its beautiful caramel color, and her gray curls look freshly washed. She has an IV in her arm and oxygen tubes taped under her nose, but she looks a million times better than she looked two days ago. When she sees Whisper she smiles brightly, showing empty spaces in her grin where teeth should be.

"What's that under your nose?" Whisper asks.

"Just air to help me breathe. Sit here," Ida pats the bed, "right next to me and tell me everything that's going on with you."

Whisper sits on the bed next to Ida and tells her about scraping her leg and making a home run. She tells her about Dreamer coming to the office to check on her, and then she talks about Dreamer for several minutes – he's so funny, so good at baseball, so nice to me.

"Grandma, do you think it's time?"

"Time for what, child?"

"Time to tell him."

Ida kisses Whisper's forehead and looks at me over Whisper's head. "Maybe it is time." She says.

"Really? When can we – "

Whisper is interrupted when Ida's doctor comes into the room. He tells them that Ida's condition has improved, and that she will get to go home tomorrow, if she has a good night's rest. A respiratory therapist will come and check on Ida at home every other day for the next week. Everyone is thrilled with the news, and Ida tells us that Tess had already promised to drive her home when she is released.

"Tomorrow is the day before Thanksgiving, Ida. What will you and Whisper do on Thanksgiving?" I ask after the doctor leaves.

She sighs. "I don't feel up to cooking a big meal. We can have that turkey the mission gave us next week."

I can't stand the thought of Whisper not having a Thanksgiving meal. "What if you came to my house? We could have Thanksgiving together." I'm supposed to go to Cool Springs for Thanksgiving at my parents' house, but maybe they'll understand, but even as I'm thinking it, I know the idea of me skipping a family Thanksgiving will be blasphemous to my mother.

"That'll be nice." Ida smiles. "I bet you can make a delicious Thanksgiving dinner. Your Wednesday meals at the mission are always wonderful."

Oh yeah. I'd have to cook it, won't I?

We say goodnight to Ida and leave the hospital. As we're getting into the car, I feel my phone vibrate in my purse. It's a text from Devin.

Sorry I haven't responded – been busy. Wanna hang out sometime?

Before I pull out of the hospital parking lot, I type a response to her, telling her that I'd love to hang out and ask her if she's going to her parents' house in Tulsa for

Thanksgiving. It's been a month since I've seen Devin, and I wonder what she's been up to. We've only hung out a couple of times, but I still feel like she's a good friend, and I worry about her spending time with Jacob.

Whisper doesn't feel like singing songs on the way home. As soon as we get on the road, she drapes my jacket over herself and falls asleep in the backseat. The ride home is quiet. I admire the huge moon and the bright stars as I drive the winding roads to Diniyoli. As I'm thinking prayers of thanksgiving to the Lord, a poem comes to me. Hopefully I can remember it when I get home, so I can write it in my journal.

A healthy body and well fed,
Family, friends, and a warm bed –
So many reasons to give thanks
To the Father I give my praise.
You're the One who takes care of me.
Because of You, I live abundantly!

Whisper awakens when I pull into the driveway and asks what time it is.

"It's nine-thirty. You had a nice, long nap."

"Yes, but I'm still tired. I just want to go to bed as soon as we go inside."

She's slept the last couple of nights on the couch. I'm going to be sad for her to go home tomorrow. I think Chelsea will, too. We've enjoyed our little roommate. "You can go to bed right after you brush your teeth."

She rolls her eyes. "Ugh, can't I just skip that tonight?   "Oh, come on, it just takes a couple of minutes to brush your teeth. Don't complain." This is no surprise that she doesn't want to brush her teeth. She's tried to get out of brushing every night she's stayed with us.

I open the front door and almost run into Chelsea.

She's standing less than a foot in front of the door. Whisper steps in the house behind me, but neither of us can get past Chelsea.

"You're home!" She hugs me. "You're home!" She hugs Whisper. "You're home, you're home, you're home!"

Whisper and I share a look and read each other's minds. We are in total agreement that Chelsea is a spaz.

"Sit, sit, sit." Chelsea grabs my shoulders and steers me to the couch, and then she grabs Whisper's shoulders and seats her next to me.

She stands in front of us. "Notice anything different, girls?" She parades back and forth in front of us like a runway model.

"Did you do a facial mask?" I ask, remembering the avocado smashing experience.

"Did you get a haircut?" Whisper guesses.

"No . . . no. Come on, look a little more carefully." She acts like she's modeling and gestures with her hand around her face.

Then I see the ring.

I stand up and scream. Chelsea runs to me and grabs my hands and screams with me. We stop screaming and hug, and then we start screaming again.

Whisper has her hands on her ears. "You guys are too loud. What's all the screaming about?"

Chelsea holds her left hand out to Whisper to show her the diamond. "Jarrett asked me to marry him! I'm getting married!"

*****

"Kirk's the winner!" His foster mom shouted when he crossed the finish line first.

"What? No fair." The nine year old shoved his hands into his pockets in disgust. "He always wins just because you guys feel sorry for him."

"Nick, be quiet. I don't ever want to hear you say that again. Kirk won fair and square. Now, I told you boys that I'd be the judge, and I was, now I have to go in and finish setting the table. Everyone will be here in less than an hour." Kirk's foster mom looked at him and at her two sons. "Do not get dirty. I want to take good pictures this Thanksgiving."

The three boys decided to walk down to the dock and throw rocks at turtles until the guests arrived – surely they wouldn't get dirty doing that. They skipped rocks and found an albino catfish and tried to catch it with their hands, but missed him every time. They all got wet and their hands got dirty, so they decided to sneak into the house and wash their hands and dry their clothes with their mom's hair dryer before any relatives arrived. The three boys entered the laundry room through the garage, and stealthily opened their parents' closet door, which connected to the laundry room. Nick's brother, Stephen, put his ear to the door to hear if anyone was in his parents' bathroom.

"I don't hear anything." He whispered.

The boys tiptoed into the master bathroom and opened the cabinet under their mother's side of the sink. Nick found the hairdryer, pulled it out, and plugged it in. Just when he was going to turn it on to dry their clothes, Kirk pulled the plug out of the wall.

"Wait a minute." Ten-year-old Kirk whispered like a secret agent in a spy movie. "That thing is loud. If we turn it on they'll hear it."

Nick slapped his forehead. "What was I thinking?" He put the dryer back under the sink.

"Hang on." Kirk had a plan. "What if we sneak it to my room? No one will hear it from up there." Kirk's bedroom had been the attic before his foster parents remodeled it for him. It was twice as big as Nick and Stephen's rooms, a fact that irritated the brothers. They often told their parents it wasn't fair that the kid who wasn't really theirs got the best room.

"Great idea!" Nick pulled the hairdryer out again.

"I'll be out in a minute. I'm going to take this call in the bedroom," Kirk's foster dad's voice came from the adjoining master bedroom, and the boys froze in fear.

Stephen was closest to the closet door, so Kirk pointed at him and silently mouthed, "Go!"

Stephen obeyed and crawled to safety.

Kirk nodded at Nick, jerked his head in the direction of the closet, telling him to save himself. Nick obeyed too.

As Kirk started to follow them, he overheard his foster dad say something that made him stop.

"We aren't interested in adopting at this time."

That phrase carried clearly through the bathroom door. Not interested in adopting at this time. Kirk knew that he could be adopted. His mother had given up all rights. He had hoped that this family was the one – two brothers, parents that acted like they cared, a house on the lake – but now he knew. They aren't interested in adopting.

"It's a tough situation, and we feel terrible. We've only had him for four months, and he's a good boy, but our family will have to make so many other changes with the move to Louisiana, that I think if we adopted him it'd be too much for us. I'm sure Kirk will be fine. He's a survivor."

Kirk turned and crept out of the bathroom undetected. He snuck through the laundry room to the stairway and found the other two upstairs in his attic room waiting for him. They dried their clothes with the blow dryer, and a few minutes later were seated at the Thanksgiving table alongside cousins, aunts, uncles, and grandparents, and no one suspected that they had disobeyed and gotten wet and dirty, and no one suspected that Kirk had overheard his foster father tell someone that his family was moving, and they weren't taking Kirk.

*****

There was no arguing with her. When I called my mom and told her that I was going to stay in Diniyoli and have a Thanksgiving meal at my house with Ida and Whisper, it was like I hadn't even said it.

"It won't be a problem at all to set a couple of extra places at the table. Your Aunt Diane and Uncle Steve and cousins are coming, plus Grandma and Grandpa and Grannie, so I'm already setting up an extra table. The more, the merrier!"

"You don't have to do that Mom. I can make a Thanksgiving meal for us. I'm sure I can figure it out."

"We are eating at noon, so the three of you be here a little before then."

It was like talking with a crazy person.

So, when I found out that Kirk was planning on spending Thanksgiving alone, I knew she wouldn't care if I invited him as well.

Last night I'd washed my face and brushed my teeth and slipped into my sweats and t-shirt, turned off my bedroom light, switched on the lamp on my nightstand and propped myself up on my pillows on my bed and wrote in my journal as I waited for his nightly call. My phone rang at 9:55 pm.

"How was your day off?"

"Relaxing. Chelsea left early with Jarrett to travel to his parents' house and make some wedding plans. I slept in until nine and then cleaned house and did laundry for a couple of hours. Then I went for a run at the high school track and the rest of the day I was blissfully lazy – watched three romantic comedy movies in a row.

"I'm jealous."

He had driven to Oklahoma City for meetings.

"What's wrong? Were your meetings not good?"

"They were fine, great actually. I'm not exactly a meetings kind of guy."

I chuckle. The image of Kirk in a suit and tie sitting around a conference table is hilarious. I'm sure he bounced his leg the whole time, and probably drove the other men in suits crazy by shaking the ice in his cup or tilting his chair back.

"Did you get some good news?"

He met with the mission oversight board – a group of pastors and businessmen and church lay leaders that he'd recruited a few years ago to review all of the finances and activities of the mission.

"Do you remember telling me that you wished we had a completely stocked and furnished nurse's station?"

In the new metal building that Rural Outreach Ministries put up for us, we have a room designated for the volunteer nurse who's been coming twice a week. The furniture in this makeshift nurse's station consists of camping chairs and a card table.

"Yes, we need it so badly . . . are you telling me what I think you're telling me?"

"The board approved my proposal to furnish and stock it."

"Oh Kirk, that's wonderful." I imagine the room outfitted with a padded patient bed, locking cabinets, a rolling chair for the nurse, and comfortable waiting chairs.

"Not only that, but I told them about Ida getting sick last week, that if we had a nurse who was here all the time, Ida probably could've received care before she got so sick, and guess what they said?"

I think I know what he's going to say. "Oh my . . . "

"Three of the board members said they wanted to pay the salary for a full time nurse for us."

"That's incredible! We can have health fairs for the kids, give immunizations, flu shots, classes for new parents, screening for – "

"Hold on a minute," Kirk laughs at me, "Let's get the room set up and find a nurse first."

"I'm just so excited. We'll be able to help so much more."

"I'm excited too . . . and there's another thing too."

"Something else? Wow, it was a good meeting."

"We're getting a backstop and real bases and a machine to mark the chalk lines for our new baseball field."

My chin drops, and I can't think of anything to say. I can only envision Michael and his Diniyoli Dragons little league team playing a game on their very own home field. I can picture Dreamer seeing the field for the first time, and my eyes well up with tears.

"Melissa?"

"Yeah," I wipe the tears from the corners of my eyes. "I'm here."

"Are you okay?"

"Yes, I'm just imagining how Dreamer will react when he sees our very own home field."

"He's the first one I thought of, too. I love that kid." Kirk's voice cracks with emotion. "Such a sweet spirit, even though he's been raised in a horrible home – he's a miracle."

We talk for a long time. Somehow we get started talking about Thanksgiving and then we start listing things we're thankful for. We start out being serious – thankful for a house, food, clothes, health, but maybe because it's almost eleven and we're getting tired and silly we start listing the random and obscure things we're thankful for as well.

"I'm thankful for caffeine." I'm not joking at all.

"I'm thankful for college football." He adds.

"I'm thankful for my new microwave." Seriously, it's changed my life.

"I'm thankful that I have a job that doesn't require me to go to meetings every day."

I laugh at him. "When you were talking about your meeting earlier, I could just picture you in a suit sitting around a conference table bored out of your mind."

He laughs at himself. "Yeah, I would go crazy if I

had to do that all the time."

I smile and don't say anything, but I imagine that my smile is communicated over the phone, and that he's probably smiling, too.

"I'm thankful for something else." He adds but then pauses.

"What's that?"

"I'm thankful that I have you to talk to every night."

Even though no one else can hear us, I blush. "I'm thankful for that, too."

"You're going to Cool Springs tomorrow?"

"Yes, I'm taking Whisper and Ida. Mom's setting two extra places." I almost ask him if he's going to his family Thanksgiving, but stop myself. Of course he isn't. He doesn't have a family to see on Thanksgiving.

"Do you want to come with us to my parents' house?" I can't believe I didn't think to ask him before now. I should have thought about him not having anywhere to go for the holiday.

"Are you sure it will be okay if I come? Do your parents know we're dating?"

"It will be fine." I avoid his question.

We make plans for when to meet and who will drive and talk about how we can't believe Chelsea's getting married. I warn him about some of my eccentric relatives and tell him to stay away from my Grandma's dressing, but to definitely eat my Grannie's homemade macaroni and cheese.

We say goodnight, and as he's hanging up he tells me, "Don't think I didn't notice that you didn't answer my question earlier."

I don't know how to respond. I haven't told my parents. I assume that Michael has probably told them, but for some reason I just haven't been able to tell them.

"Good night, Melissa. See you in the morning."

*****

"Need a re-fill?" Phil asks Nelson, who is in his usual spot at the counter, drinking his morning coffee before he heads to work in Clinton.

"Please."

Phil tops his cup with hot coffee, and Nelson spoons in some sugar and stirs it before heading out the door.

"See you later, Phil." He calls back and waves. He exits the restaurant and gets into his car, starts the engine, buckles his seatbelt, and prepares for his daily forty-five minute morning commute to work.

He puts the car in reverse, and then he feels steel against the back of his head and the telltale click, the sound of a gun being cocked.

"You know where to go."

The person holding the gun to his head doesn't introduce himself, but Nelson recognizes him. He could never forget Jacob's voice.

Nelson hesitates.

"Don't even think about going anywhere else. Your nine year old – Jesse? He's been asking for you."

Nelson turns around and faces Jacob. "You'd better not do anything to my boy."

"Turn around and drive then, Nelson, and I won't have to."

Nelson obeys. He doesn't protest, because after all those years working for Jacob, he's learned that he doesn't make empty threats.

The place he knows Jacob wants him to go to is a clearing in the middle of a soybean field owned by an old farmer who is paid to keep his mouth shut. Nelson drives the familiar dirt road to the field and wishes he'd never started working for Jacob all those years ago. He'd given his life to God about a year ago, and he'd never known such a peaceful and joyful life could be his. Images of his little Jesse appear in his mind, and his heart races with despair. Why should I have given my life to God, if it was going to end up like this? He asks himself.

Then he hears it. It's not really aloud, but the words are so strong and clear to his heart that they seem almost audible.

I am your help in time of trouble.

As Nelson pulls his car into the clearing and puts it into park, he still feels fear, but he knows that his God will help him. He turns to face Jacob, who still has a gun pointed at his head. Jacob looks different than how he used to look when Nelson worked for him. Back then, Jacob was scary. He was a crazy man who'd hurt anyone who got in his way, but now, Jacob doesn't look scary . . . he looks scared.

"You're going to start working for me again." Jacob says.

Nelson shakes his head. "No, I'm not."

"Thought you were a family man. Thought those boys and that wife of yours meant something to you. I told you – I've got Jesse right now." Jacob accentuates his words by stabbing the air with his gun.

"Where is he?"

Jacob shakes his head. "No, you don't get him back until you're working for me again. The first thing I want you to do is send that preacher friend of yours a message. You can keep singing at the church with him – it'll be a good cover. We're gonna shut that mission down."

Then the silent voice whispers to Nelson's heart again. *"Trey . . . tell him you know about him stealing from Trey."*

"I'm not going to work for you, Jacob. You see, I know all about you stealing from Trey, and I just have to make one phone call and you're a dead man."

Jacob's jaw twitches, but otherwise he remains expressionless for several seconds. He finally responds to Nelson's threat.

"You don't have any proof of that."

Nelson thinks a quick prayer. *Of course I don't have proof. I didn't even know it was true until you told me to say that, Lord. Tell me what to say, God.*

The words appear in Nelson's mind, and he doesn't hesitate to speak them aloud.

"Old Reservation Road."

Jacob can't keep his face from reacting this time. His eyes widen, he lowers the gun and asks, "How did you know that?"

Nelson considers telling him that God told him, but instead says, "It doesn't matter how I know it. I know it, and you're going to leave my family and me out of your business, and you're going to tell me where Jesse is right now."

*****

My grandma's dressing is even worse than I remembered, but my grannie's macaroni and cheese is creamier and more heavenly than I remembered, too. Mom has strategically placed extra tables and chairs and removed furniture, so that all fifteen guests have enough room and are all part of the group – no one has to be relegated to a table in the garage. She moved the couch and loveseat out of the living room and moved her dining room table and kitchen table both into the room to accommodate everyone. Both tables have gorgeous centerpieces mom made out of glass punchbowls filled with artificial fall leaves and three brown and white pillar candles tied together with raffia ribbon. The lighted caramel corn scented candles join the smells of her homemade rolls, turkey and grandma's pecan pie.

"Can you ask your grannie for her macaroni and cheese recipe? I think the kids at the mission would love it." Kirk tells me as he piles a third helping onto his plate.

"The kids will love it or you will love it?"

From behind us, sitting at the other table, Whisper replies, "The kids will love it, and Pastor Kirk will love it.

You need to make this stuff Miss Melissa. I think we need to call it Cheesy Gold."

Next to me, Kirk says, "Cheesy Gold Deliciousness."

"Cheesy Gold Deliciousness That Makes Your Mouth Smile," Michael adds from the end of our table with a spoonful of the much-lauded mac and cheese lifted in the air.

At the other end of the table Grannie waves a hand at them, "Ya'll are silly," but we can all tell that she relishes the praise for her famous dish.

I finish the turkey and macaroni and cheese and sweet potato pie and green bean casserole and pecan pie and put my napkin on my plate and lean back in my chair, feeling fat, but telling myself - *this day only comes once a year – enjoy it. I can count calories and exercise regularly until Christmas, and then I can feast again* – and it helps to soothe my guilty feelings.

To my right, Dad is still eating, and to my left, Kirk is still eating. Across from me, Mom has also finished and has also leaned back in her chair with her eyes closed.

"Are you tired, Mom?"

"Mmm . . . a little bit." She opens her eyes, leans forward, puts her elbow on the table, and rests her cheek on her hand.

"What time did you have to get up this morning to do all this?"

"Oh, I was up by five. Your dad and Michael moved the furniture for me yesterday, and I made the centerpieces yesterday, but I didn't start on any of the food until this morning." She closes her eyes again, and then opens them. "Except for the rolls. Of course, I had to make them yesterday, so they could rise overnight."   "Why don't you go take a nap? We can all do the dishes and clean up." She looks so tired, I want to help her.

"No, I don't want to sleep while you're here. I hardly ever get to see you. I don't want to waste the time sleeping."

I feel guilty. I haven't come home much at all since I

moved, and I promised that I would come home often.

Kirk puts his napkin on his plate. "You and your mom and dad sit and talk. I'm doing the dishes." He stands up, stacks dishes and turns to carry them to the kitchen.

"Kirk, you don't need to do that." I protest.

"I don't mind. You need to talk to your parents. Michael and Whisper can help me, right guys?" He asks them with a smile.

"Right!" Whisper says and jumps up and starts collecting dishes.

"What?" Michael asks, not looking too excited to do all of the dishes.

"Come on, we'll make it fun." Kirk says to him. He looks down at me. "You work so hard all the time. Let me do this for you." He leans down and kisses me on the forehead.

He freezes.

My cheeks get hot and my eyes widen. I cannot believe he just kissed me in front of my parents.

I look at my dad next to me. His jaw has dropped open. I look at my mom across the table. One side of her mouth is curled up in a knowing grin.

Kirk clears his throat. "Um, I'd better start those dishes." He rushes out of the room.

Chicken.

"Whatever will we talk about? I don't believe there's anything you haven't told us, Missy." Mom says sarcastically in her perfect Scarlett O'Hara impersonation.

I look around the room and notice that every pair of eyes – Grandma, Grandpa, Grannie, Aunt Diane, Uncle Steve, my three little cousins, Ida – are all staring at me. I know all of my family members must think I have a scandalous love life. I jilt my longtime boyfriend at the altar, and now here I am at the family Thanksgiving dinner three months later being kissed by some strange missionary.

"Mom, Dad, it's such a pretty day, and I ate so much,

why don't the three of us go on a short walk around the neighborhood together?" I say so everyone can hear.

Diane and Steve invite Whisper to play outside with them and their kids, and Ida, Grandma, Grandpa, and Grannie volunteer to help Kirk and Michael with the dishes. As everyone scrambles from the table, I go to my old bedroom to grab my coat that I'd laid on the bed when we first got here. Kirk follows me.

"I'm so sorry."

"Did you do it on purpose? I mean, I'm not mad. I was going to tell them, but . . . did you?" I have to know.

"I didn't do it on purpose, I promise. It hit me just as I kissed you what I was doing. I'm sorry. I'll be honest, this whole day I've wanted to hug you or grab your hand, but I kept reminding myself that I couldn't. I'm not very good at pretending."

I wrap my arms around him. "I'm so sorry that I asked you to. I should've told them before we came today. It's just with all of the drama from the wedding, I didn't know how to – "

"Missy? Are you coming?" My dad asks from the entry hall.

I lean my head forward and rest it on Kirk's chest for a moment before answering. "Coming, Dad."

The three of us walk down the driveway and to the street. We walk with Dad on the outside and Mom in the middle and me closest to the houses. This is just how it was when I was growing up. Whenever we'd go on a walk around the neighborhood Dad would always insist to be on the outside, closest to any cars. Of course, in the middle of Lost Lake housing addition there's not a lot of traffic to worry about. The big established trees in the neighborhood have bright orange, yellow, and red leaves. These beautiful trees stand in the yards of the tasteful and well-maintained houses of my parents' neighbors, most of whom I've known the majority of my life.

"Oh look, the Martinez's painted their shutters and front door black."

I look at the house that's a few doors down from ours on the cul-de-sac.

"It looks much better." Mom voices her opinion. "I should've grabbed a jacket. Gary, can I wear yours?"

Dad smiles at her. "Sure," He slides off his jacket and hands it to her without a thought.

I remember my first date with Kirk. As we watched the sunset on the dock, he put his arm around me "just to warm me up." Pretty smooth move. I smile at the memory.

"What are you smiling about, Missy?" Mom asks, next to me. Before I can answer she infers, "Kirk?"

I shrug. "I'm sorry I didn't tell you guys that we were dating, but it's only been for a couple of weeks. I wasn't trying to hide anything."

On the other side of the street two women in their thirties pushing baby strollers approach us.

"Happy Thanksgiving," Mom says to them as we walk by.

"Happy Thanksgiving," they respond. The toddler in one of the stroller waves at me, and I wave back at him.

After they get out of earshot, Dad responds to me. "I'm not mad at you, Missy. Kirk seems to be a great young man. I was surprised, but I approve."

"Thanks, Dad." I look over at my tall and strong dad and silently thank the Lord for him.

We walk to the stop sign two blocks from our house and automatically cross the street and head back to the house. We've walked this path so many times after dinner or on a Saturday or Sunday afternoon or when we needed a few minutes for a talk, like now, that no one has to say, "Let's turn around here," we just know the Kolar family walking route.

After we turn and started heading back, Mom says, "Well, I wasn't surprised."

"Really? How did you know?" I find it hard to believe that my mom suspected and never said anything about it.

"I don't know . . . lots of things. When we first met him, he was so handsome and driven and I thought, 'Now, there's a guy who'd be a perfect match for Missy.'"

I laugh. "Mom, I thought you didn't even want me going to Diniyoli."

"I didn't, but not because I didn't think it was perfect for you. In fact," she stops walking. We're four doors down from our house, and I can see that Kirk and the rest of our guests are in the backyard. "maybe it was too perfect for you."

"What do you mean?" How could it be too perfect? If any place is perfection it's Cool Springs, not Diniyoli.

"It was just a fit for you. Your love of kids, your strong work ethic, your open-mindedness about new people, and then when I met Reverend Chaney . . . I just knew."

"What was it about him?" Now I believe her. I wonder how she knew he was perfect for me.

"He's as strong as you are – a challenge. Brian's a great young man, but, let's face it, you were much stronger than he was. Reverend Kirk was obviously passionate about his work, and he had that twinkle in his eye that told me that he knew how to have fun. Honestly, Missy, he scared me."

"Scared you? How?"

"Not that he was bad or would hurt you or anything, but I was scared that I would lose you. With Brian, I knew I'd never really lose you."

"Mom, you'll never lose me."

She brushes a strand of hair back from my face and tucks it behind my ear. "But I'm supposed to. I've realized that I was wrong."

"We were wrong." Dad says as he puts his arm around my mom's shoulders. "We were wrong to try to hold onto you. You're supposed to grow up and fall in love and have a life of your own." Dad puts his other arm around my shoulders and pulls me in tight. "With Kirk you'll definitely have an adventurous life."

"That's for sure," I agree, "but you guys are getting ahead of yourselves. We're just dating. It's only been a couple of weeks. We aren't really serious."

Mom and Dad look at each other. Then Mom speaks.

"Honey, we're your parents, and we aren't blind."

*****

"Goal!" My dad yells and throws his arms in the air. "Way to go, Whisper!"

He gives her a high five, and she beams as Ida, Grandma, Grandpa and Grannie cheer from their seats on the patio.

Mom retrieves the soccer ball from the net and tosses it to me. "Sorry, everyone," she says, "I'm not a very good goalie."

"It's alright Mom, we'll get 'em. Okay, everyone, come over here. Let's huddle." I tell my team. Two of my cousins, Uncle Steve, my mom and I get into a huddle. A few feet away Kirk, Whisper, one of my cousins, Aunt Diane, and my dad also put their heads together in a huddle. So far, their team has scored three goals, and our team hasn't scored at all. Kirk has proven to be a brick wall as the goalie on the other end, and my mom, well, she's not exactly effective as goalie.

"Here's our plan," Uncle Steve tells our team, "we're going to form a ladder down the field. You just have to get the ball to the person on the next rung of the ladder. Missy, you stand to the left of the goal and I'll stand to the right of the goal. When you guys get the ball to me, Missy you distract Kirk with your feminine whiles."

"What? Feminine whiles? What are you talking

about?" I protest. "Are you saying the only thing I have to contribute to the team is being a distraction to Kirk?"

Uncle Steve gives me a sheepish look, like he doesn't want to hurt my feelings, and my eleven-year-old cousin, Carson, answers for him.

"Missy, you're our only hope of getting anything past him. All you have to do is shake your pretty red hair at him, and we'll score." Carson explains to me like a general explaining the battle plan to a soldier. "Can you do that?"

I roll my eyes at my fifth grade cousin. "Sure, I'll do it."

We all put our hands on top of each other and push our hands down and throw them up together in the air as we yell, "Go Kolars!"

Uncle Steve's game plan unfolds perfectly. I position myself to the left of the goal, and the rest of our team forms a ladder down the soccer field, also known as my parents' backyard. My youngest cousin, Carson's brother, kicks the ball to Carson. Carson will have to move the ball about ten feet down the field and then pass it to his dad, Uncle Steve. I guess I'd better use those feminine whiles that Carson and Uncle Steve seem to think will distract Kirk.

"Hey Kirk," I whisper, just a couple of feet from him.

"Hmm?" He asks, not taking his eyes off the ball, which is now being kicked by my uncle.

"It's only an hour back to Diniyoli. What do you say we get out of here and watch the sunset at Lake Foss?" I say in my best conspiratorial tone.

He smiles, still not taking his eyes off the ball, which Uncle Steve is moving closer to the goal. "That sounds good." It's supposed to be a ruse, but it actually sounds like a wonderful way to end this perfect Thanksgiving Day.

A million things go through my mind to say. I could say something flirtatious. I could say something silly, but instead I decide to say something real. I decide to say what I really want to say.

"Kirk,"

"Yeah," he's still focused on the ball.

"I love you."

He turns his head and looks at me.

Uncle Steve scores a goal, and my team cheers. They jump up and down whooping and high fiving, but all I can hear is Kirk.

"I love you, too."

He walks away from the net and wraps his arms around me and kisses me.

My three little cousins say, "Woo woo," in unison.

"Way to go, Missy!" Carson yells.

*****

In the backseat of Kirk's truck, Whisper and Ida are sound asleep.

"Anybody need to visit the restroom or get a drink?" Kirk asks us as he pulls in front of the gas pump at the gas station on the edge of town.

No response from the backseat.

"I think they're comfortable," I tell Kirk. Whisper's head is on Ida's lap, and Ida's head is back against the seat. "I'm going to get a bottle of water. Do you want anything?"

He shakes his head at me. "Nope. I don't need a thing." He leans over the center console and kisses me lightly on the lips. "I'm completely content."

I touch my forehead to his for a moment. I don't regret telling Kirk that I love him. I guess I could've waited for him to say it first, but I'm so glad that I didn't. I squeeze his hand and then get out of the truck to get a water bottle from the gas station, and Kirk gets out to fill the truck's tank with gas.

I enter the small store and find the water bottles in the refrigerator at the back. I get one out and start down the aisle toward the cash register to pay. I freeze when I hear a voice I know very well coming from the next aisle.

"You don't like gum? You're kidding. Who doesn't like gum?" his familiar voice asks.

"I don't. It's messy, and when people blow bubbles it's just gross. I mean, that's their spit hanging out of their mouth." Her voice explains her reasoning to him – part of the phobia I remember her telling me about all those years ago as we laid in sleeping bags in the floor of a fireworks stand.

"You're hilarious," he tells her.

"And that's why you love me."

"It's one of the reasons I love you, Staci."

I can't move. I don't want them to see me, but I need to get out of here and get back outside to Kirk. I try to think of the best escape route from the store to avoid them. I set the water bottle on the shelf in front of me. I'll just leave it and get outside as quick as I – "

"Missy?"

Shoot. I didn't move fast enough.

"Hi Brian. Staci."

My former fiancé and best friend quickly drop each other's hand when they see me.

"Um . . . " Staci tries to think of something to say.

I say the first thing that comes to mind. "Happy Thanksgiving."

"You too," they both say at once.

After a moment, Staci steps forward and gives me a hug. "It's good to see you, Missy."

I hug her back. It is good to see her. It's only been three months, but as I'm standing here looking at my former maid of honor and my almost-groom with guilty expressions, I realize that it's been a lifetime.

"How are you guys?"

They look at each other, and then look at the ground.

Brian finally speaks, "Fine, Missy. How's Diniyoli?"

I look out the glass storefront at Kirk standing by his

truck pumping gas and Whisper and Ida still asleep in the backseat.

"It's perfect."

Chapter Seven

Devin checks the time on the clock in her car. Three-fifteen in the morning. When she told Melissa that she'd like to hang out sometime, this was not what she had in mind at all. She considers honking her horn to tell Chelsea and Melissa that she's here, but decides that their neighbors probably don't want to hear her horn honking in the middle of the night.

A stream of yellow light slices through the darkness as their front door opens. Chelsea and Melissa come out to the porch, turn off the light, lock the door and head to Devin's car.

"What have I gotten myself in to?" Devin asks herself.

"Ever been Black Friday Shopping?" Chelsea asks as she and Melissa get into the car.

"Never," Devin answers. The closest thing I've been to it is arresting shoppers who assaulted people so they could get their hands on some popular toy. Thank goodness I don't have to patrol the mall anymore, Devin muses. "Why are we doing this again?" She asks aloud.

"We're going to the craft store in Clinton. I need to get ribbon, artificial flowers, and some material for my veil, and it's all marked down eighty percent at four am." Chelsea says as she waves her list. "And Melissa wants to get a Christmas tree."

Melissa nods. "I've never had my own tree, and the same store has six foot tall, pre-lit trees eighty percent off at four. I also want to get some tree decorations. They're eighty percent off, too."

"Okay, okay, just don't get violent like those people you see on the news," Devin tells them as she backs out of their driveway and heads toward Clinton.

During the twenty minute drive Chelsea talks wedding plans, and Devin surprisingly finds herself interested. She's never thought of herself as a girly-girl. She was always the girl who raced the boys at recess and played football with them. She never stood around and talked with the girls and never played with dolls. And, she always wanted to be a cop. Even when she was in high school and had temporary insanity and went to cosmetology school, she still wanted to be a police officer at heart. She just thought since she was a girl she should do something more girly. But, after a few years the police officer dream wouldn't stop, so she enrolled in the academy.

As Chelsea talks bouquets and guest book table decorations though, Devin finds herself thinking about what kind of wedding she'd like. Probably an outdoor wedding, she thinks, but I definitely want a traditional dress. She imagines herself in a floor-length, white satin halter dress. Great, I know what kind of dress I want, now I just need to find the guy. She thinks as she enters the city limits of Clinton. But how am I ever going to find him if I have to keep hanging around losers like Jacob and Dumb and Dumber?

She told her lieutenant everything she'd learned so far and her suspicions about a secret room under the staircase. He told her that if she could get into that secret room and find evidence that she should arrest Jacob then. Originally the plan was to use Jacob to get to his boss, but her lieutenant was getting impatient. She'd been in Diniyoli seven months and hadn't produced an arrest yet, and he was ready for her to get whomever she could and come back home to Tulsa.

He was also getting nervous. It's a miracle that no

one has told Jacob that she's a police officer. Only a couple of people know, and none of them talk to Jacob, but, still, it's a miracle that someone hasn't said something to him. Her lieutenant told her to get what she needed and to make the arrest this week. Devin still wanted to get Jacob's boss, though. He was the reason she came out here. He'll just replace Jacob with someone else after he's gone.

"What do you think about that? Devin?" Melissa and Chelsea both look at her, awaiting a response.

She hadn't heard the question. "I'm sorry. What?"

"Are you tired?" Melissa asks her. "Do you want me to drive?"

"No, I'm fine. I was just thinking."

"I just asked if you would do my bridesmaids' hair. Could you give them all up-dos?" Chelsea asks.

She nods. "Sure, I can do that." The year long cosmetology program back in high school has certainly come in handy for this undercover job.

As Devin pulls into the shopping center parking lot, she can't believe how many cars are here.

"Okay, let's divide and conquer," Chelsea tells them. "Devin, are you getting anything?"

Devin shakes her head. "Nope, I'm just here for the show."

"Okay, then you go get the material for my veil." She hands her a piece of paper. "Here, this says the type of material I need and how much."

"Melissa will get a shopping cart and get her tree and ornaments, and I'll get ribbon and artificial flowers. I've got copies of a map of the store for each of us." Chelsea hands Devin and Melissa the maps.

Melissa laughs. "Where did you get maps?"

"They were online." Chelsea says, completely serious. "There was a Black Friday survival guide online, and it included maps of all the stores with the biggest sales."

Devin looks at the paper Chelsea handed to her. *100*

inches of tulle. Shouldn't be too hard, but it seems like a pretty important job, getting the material for Chelsea's veil. A terrifying thought crosses Devin's mind – What if I get the wrong thing?

"Okay, are we ready? Looks like there's a line forming at the front door. Let's get in it!" Chelsea says as she opens the door and gets out.

Devin looks at the clock. "It's just three-forty. Are we really going to stand in line in the dark for twenty minutes? And what if I don't get the right material for her veil?" She's more nervous about buying tulle than taking down a group of drug dealers.

"Oh come on, Devin. It'll be fun." Melissa gets out of the car.

Fun, she thinks, maybe that's my problem. I haven't had much of that in a while.

She looks out the window. Melissa's standing at her door waving for her to hurry up. She opens the door and the two of them run to catch up with Chelsea.

"Look at all these people already in line." Chelsea tells them. "Next year we're bringing sleeping bags and setting up a tent."

"And hot chocolate!" Melissa adds.

Devin smiles in spite of herself and thinks, Oh yes, I definitely need to hang out with these two nuts more often.

*****

Michael wants to make sure the kids can round the bases quickly, and in the month he's been practicing with them, he's learned that competition is the best motivator for these kids, even better than candy. So, he's made two diamonds on the school basketball court, one on each half of the court. He laid the bases out and made baselines out of painter's tape, because he doesn't want to leave marks on the gym floor. When he blows the whistle, a player carrying a tennis ball takes off from home and runs to first, second, and third. When they get to third they throw the ball to the next kid who's standing on home base. When that kid catches it, they take off and run the bases. Michael says he's teaching them to run the bases quickly, but the kids don't really care what they're learning, they just want to beat the other team.

Michael, Kirk, Dreamer and Whisper's dad Jacob, and I stand outside the diamonds and cheer for the kids as they run. A boy named Dakota runs hard and, even though the runner from the other team is already past first when Dakota catches the ball, he pushes so hard that he pulls ahead between third and home and wins the relay for his team. His team yells and runs to him after he wins, and they all run and jump and chest bump each other, like they've seen older kids and professional athletes do.

"You know what I love about these kids?" Jacob says, standing next to me. "It's not even a game, just a drill at practice, and look how excited they are. Look how hard they try at practice. That's cool."

I nod in agreement. Michael's done an amazing job of motivating them. I marvel that Jacob and I are standing here talking and agreeing about something. It's hard to believe that a man guilty of all the things I've heard would help a kids' baseball team. He's good with the kids and a loving dad. Surely he isn't a drug dealer and a criminal like Whisper told me and I've heard other people say.

"Okay guys, let's huddle up," Michael announces, like he does at the end of every practice. "Prayer and devotion time." He tells them.

The kids immediately obey, and Kirk, Jacob and I follow. I sit criss-cross on the gym floor next to Whisper.

Michael takes out his phone and swipes the screen with his finger. "I want to read you guys a Bible verse." He finds it on his phone and reads, "It's from Deuteronomy thirty-one and six. Be strong and courageous. Do not be afraid or terrified because of them, for the Lord your God goes with you; He will never leave you nor forsake you."

Michael returns his phone to his back pocket, and then goes to the first row of bleachers and picks up a stack of papers. "I want you guys to think about that verse and try to even memorize it, so I brought papers that have the verse on them. Maybe you guys can hang them in your room or something, you know, to help you learn it." He hands the papers out to the kids. "This verse has really meant a lot to me at different times when I was going through stuff, and I hope you all will use it in your life, too."

I look at Whisper's paper. I can't believe Michael took the time to type and print the verse. I imagine him using the computer at our parents' house and looking up the verse, typing it, and printing it on our parents' printer. I'm so proud of him.

On the other side of Whisper, Jacob reads her paper. "Be strong and courageous. Are you strong and courageous?" He asks her.

"I try to be. Are you?" She asks him.

He shrugs. "I guess."

"Know what's my favorite part of this verse?" She asks him.

"What?"

"Where God says that He will never leave us. That's nice." Whisper looks up at her father, and he rubs his chin.

"Never leave us, huh?"

Michael prays with the kids and then instructs everyone to help clean the gym before they go. As I peel the painter's tape off the ground, I watch Whisper and Jacob out of the corner of my eye. He does seem like a nice man, but everything I've heard about him is terrible, and I'm sure Ida wouldn't want Whisper talking to him. I know that Whisper knows he's her father, and I'm sure he knows who she is if he knows her name.

There aren't any other seven year olds named Whisper in Diniyoli.

*****

From the loading dock of the hardware store, Kirk waves at me to keep coming. I barely press on the accelerator to nudge his truck a little further back. He keeps waving for me to come closer, and I back up a little more. Then he smacks the back of the truck and yells, pretending like I hit him with the truck. I smile at him through the rearview mirror, unfazed. Doesn't he realize that I have a little brother, and I've had all of the immature tricks played on me a thousand times?

Kirk and the hardware store worker load tile, bags of thinset, and grout into the back of the truck. Someone is coming next week to lay tile in the nurse's station, so Kirk is picking up the supplies tonight. After baseball practice this morning he asked me if I'd like to come with him.

"Do you want to go somewhere with me tonight?" He asked, leaning on my car door, talking to me as I sat in the driver's seat with my window down.

"Sure, where?"

"It's extremely exciting. You've probably never been on a date as extravagant as this." He said sarcastically.

I laughed. "Where?"

"The big home improvement and hardware store in Clinton."

"Wow, you really know how to show a girl a good time." I matched his sarcastic tone.

"Hey, a guy can spend a lot of money in a store like that." He bent over and put both of his arms on the window ledge of my car and rested his chin on his arms. "A girl sees all of those light fixtures and refrigerators and starts getting ideas."

I leaned forward and kissed his nose. "Tell you what. Take me to that Italian restaurant where we had our first date after the hardware store, and I won't get any ideas."

"What if I want you to get ideas?" he asked.

"Well then, let's look at granite countertops." I teased back, and he groaned.

"Do you think you can eat this time? Last time we went there you were so smitten with me that you couldn't even eat." He said with an ornery grin.

I rolled my eyes. "I think I can handle it."

The new tile will make the nurse's station so much cleaner. Right now the floor is just the concrete floor of the new building, which can get so dusty and is hard to clean. The white and gray tile and dark gray grout that Kirk and I picked out will be so much easier to clean, and will look much better.

After we load the supplies, Kirk walks to the front of the truck and opens the driver's door. I still have my hands on the wheel and the engine running.

"I'll drive. I'm already here." I tell him.

"Uh . . ." He doesn't move to the passenger side.

"Is that a problem?" I can tell by the look on his face that it's definitely a problem. "I'll just scoot over then, no big deal." I start to move over to the passenger side, and he stops me.

"No, it's fine. Go ahead. You can drive." He shuts the door and walks around the front of the truck. I laugh to myself at his clenched jaw. He opens the passenger side door, gets in, and buckles the seatbelt.

"Stefano's?" I ask him.

He nods in response.

Stefano's restaurant is only a few blocks from the hardware store, and I'm thankful, any further than that, and Kirk may have had a heart attack. When I changed lanes he thought I didn't see a car and loudly warned me, even though I had already seen it and was avoiding it. When I stopped at a light, he said something about the intersection actually starting behind us. When I parked the truck, he made a noise to let me know that he disapproved of my parking.

"What's wrong?"

"It's nothing. I just wouldn't have parked so close to this car on my side."

"Do you have a problem with my driving?" I hand him his keys.

"No . . . can I drive when we're together though?" He asks with a pained expression.

"I'm a good driver. I've never had a wreck." I protest.

We both get out of his truck and meet behind it. He gives me a hug.

"I'm sure you're a good driver, but I just need to be the one driving." He kisses me on the forehead and grabs my hand as we walk to the front door of the restaurant.

"Oh my, I think someone has control issues." I'm not a psychiatrist, but Kirk definitely likes to be in control.

He smiles at me as he holds the door open for me. "Melissa, I have a lot of issues, but you love me even though I have issues, right?"

I nod, and he gives his name to the hostess.

This time I don't have any trouble eating. I've ordered chicken marsala, and it's delicious. Kirk doesn't have any trouble eating his manicotti, either. We laugh about how we both acted on our first date about a month ago.

"It was like my stomach closed and said, 'Sorry, you can't eat anything.' It was so weird. I don't know why I was so nervous." I remember that I just pushed the food around on my plate with my fork, because I knew I couldn't take a bite.

"I'd thought about asking you out for so long, and I couldn't believe we were actually sitting in a restaurant at a table across from each other on a date. I remembered that first time I ever saw you – the day you came to tour the mission. You were sitting in Tess's office, and we talked for a minute and I showed you around for a little while. I knew instantly that you were gorgeous, of course, but I think the day I started falling in love with you was the day you spilled red Kool-Aide all over me. Remember that?"

Of course I do. I smile at him as I recall the image of him with the red dust smeared on his handsome face.

"You made me laugh. For three months I watched you work so hard to help other people – I love that about you. I watched you get lost in beautiful scenery and then write and draw in your journal. I watched you win the heart of the biggest cynic of all – Tess. She often spoke condescendingly to you, and you never said a hateful thing in return." He shakes his head. "I couldn't believe that I'd finally had the guts to ask you on a date, and I couldn't believe that you said yes. So, it's no wonder that I couldn't eat."

My stomach tightens up again, and I set my fork down. I don't think anyone's ever said anything like that to me before. My eyes fill with tears, and I wipe them with the cloth napkin from my lap.

"I don't think I can eat now."

"I'm sorry." He reaches across the table and grabs my hand.

I shake my head. "No, don't be sorry. That's the nicest thing anyone's ever said to me."

"I'll stop being nice so you can actually finish your dinner." He laughs and picks up his fork and starts eating again.

"I never told you who I saw in the gas station on the way home from Thanksgiving at my parents' house." I haven't told anyone about overhearing Brian and Staci in the convenience store and seeing them standing in the aisle with guilty expressions.

"Who?" He asks innocently.

"Brian."

Kirk puts his fork down.

"And Staci . . . my best friend . . . together."

His eyebrows go up. "How do you feel about that?"

242

"On one hand I feel relieved. I'm glad he's moved on, but – "

"What?"

I shake my head. "It sounds silly."

"Come on, you can tell me."

"I guess I kind of feel betrayed by Staci. I mean, we were best friends, and I move away for a few months and she starts dating my ex-fiancé? I know that makes me sound immature."

He reaches across the table and holds my hand again. "It's completely understandable. I know it sounds immature for me to say this, but I'm glad he's dating someone else. I've had this secret fear that you might go back to him."

"Never, I never felt this way with Brian. My relationship with him was . . . convenient. My relationship with you is . . ." I think of a few adjectives to finish my sentence, but can't bring myself to say them.

"Yes?" Kirk asks.

I'm embarrassed to say what I was thinking. I shake my head.

"Come on, what? Say it?" He's smiling at me. He knows he's embarrassing me.

"Nope, I'm not going to say it."

He grins at me and lets go of my hand so he can finish his dinner. My stomach finally lets me eat, and I'm glad because the food is so good, and I don't go out to eat that often. Kirk and I stay at the table for a while and talk after the waitress takes our plates. Then we decide to go ahead and leave, even though we'd rather stay and talk, and let someone else take our table so the waitress can get more tips.

We drive back to Diniyoli and Kirk talks and I listen. Kirk is a master storyteller. He tells me stories about some of the foster homes he lived in, stories of when he played baseball, and stories about starting the mission. I love watching him tell a story. He uses his hands to talk, which makes me nervous a few times, considering he's driving. He makes hilarious facial expressions and mimics people. I could just sit and be entertained by him for hours.

When we drive in front of Jacob's house, Kirk stops talking for a moment and looks at the big old beauty. All of the lights are on inside, and in the dark you don't see the trash in the yard or the peeling paint, and you can see the shadow of the grand house that it once was.

"I love that house," he says. "If someone put some work into that house, it could be awesome."

"I know. That's what I think every time I drive in front of it." I agree.

"It'd be fun to fix it – paint, new windows, flooring, I don't know what the inside would need. I've never been in it, but I imagine most everything would need to be updated."

"Granite countertops?" I ask.

He smiles at me. "See what I mean? Those home improvement stores give women ideas."

He pulls in front of my house. The porch light and the living room light are both on, so Chelsea must be home.

He puts his hand on the handle to open his door.

"Don't worry about walking me to the front door." I tell him.

"What? That's not very gentlemanly." He opens his door.

"No, it's just that you're the pastor at the mission, and I live on one of the main streets in town. If you walk me to the front door and kiss me, someone will see it, and it will be all over town."

He opens his door and steps out, closes it, and walks around the front of the truck to my side and opens my door. He holds out his hand to me.

"I don't care what anyone says. I'm single. You're single. We can go to dinner, and I can walk you to the front porch and kiss you goodnight. There's nothing wrong with that."

I take his hand and walk to the front porch with him. He kisses me and tells me goodnight, just like he said he would.

I open the front door of my house, and he turns around and says loudly to me as he's walking to his truck, "Next time we'll look at those granite countertops."

I go inside and talk to Chelsea for a bit before brushing my teeth and heading to bed. I think about the words I was going to use to describe my relationship with Kirk. My cheeks get red, even though I don't say it aloud to anyone. The words I was going to use to describe our relationship were *Passionate and Undeniable.*

*****

Someone is banging on the front door of Jacob's house. He rolls over in bed and picks up his phone from the nightstand. Three-thirty. The person on the front porch keeps beating on the door. Probably some junkie needing a fix in the middle of the night. Even though everyone in town knows they're not supposed to come to his house to buy drugs, sometimes people get desperate and come banging on his door in the middle of the night. He swings his legs out of bed, reaches into the drawer of the nightstand and gets out his gun. He grabs his pants that are lying on the floor, pulls them on and heads to the front door.

He quietly shuts Dreamer's door as he walks past his bedroom. Dreamer was the reason he didn't want these people coming to his house. Of course it also protected him if they didn't come to his house, but the main reason was Dreamer. He didn't want Dreamer around that stuff.

In the living room, he slightly moves the curtain in the big window with his finger and sees a skinny woman on the front porch. Her stringy blonde hair's a mess, wearing a ratty t-shirt and sweatpants and no shoes. The way she's rubbing her hands together and looking back and forth and clenching her teeth tells him exactly what he suspected. A desperate junkie in need of a fix.

She beats on the door again.

He drops his hand, lets the curtain go back, leans against the wall and sighs. She's probably harmless. He tucks the gun in the waistband of his pants.

Jacob wants to ignore her and go back to bed, but he knows that she won't quit. He opens the door.

"What do you want?"

"You Jacob?" She asks with the halting, quivering voice of a meth addict.

"Yeah, don't ever come to my house – especially not in the middle of the night."

She gives him an eerie grin and then steps to the side of the door.

Jacob's eyes follow her, so he doesn't see the man come at him until it's too late for him to react. A man the size of a linebacker rushes to Jacob, grabs him by the neck and pushes him to the floor. The huge man pins Jacob to the ground with his knee on Jacob's chest and his hand on his neck. He whispers to Jacob.

"We'll come to your house when we want. Got it?"

Jacob tries to speak, but the man is choking him. He tries to get his gun out of the back of his pants, but he can't move under the weight of the huge man.

"We're delivering a message from Trey. Your profits are down, man. Don't know what the problem is – don't care. Just fix it." The huge man leans down closer to Jacob's face. "And if you're stealing from Trey, then you'd better have your will written, because you're a dead man. Trey will find out." He looks back to the porch. "Lorraine?"

The skinny blonde woman appears in the doorway, still fidgeting. "Yeah? He got the stuff?"

"Yeah, he's got it. Where's your hiding place? I know you keep some stuff here at the house." He lets up off of Jacob's neck a little so he can respond.

"Fourth step. Under the fourth step."

He looks up to the stairway. He drags Jacob by the neck to the stairs. He pulls a gun out from under his shirt and hands it to Lorraine.

"Here, hold this on him. Shoot him if he moves."

Jacob stays on the ground and stares at the twitchy, blinking woman. The gun is obviously heavy to her, she acts like she can barely hold it, and it keeps slipping in her hand. Jacob closes his eyes. His life is in the hands of a woman whose brain is scrambled and can barely stand. His son, Dreamer, the most important person in the world to him is lying in bed in his bedroom just down the hallway, mere feet from this crazed woman with a gun and this hired thug.

Desperate thoughts sear his brain – How did my life come to this? What's going to happen to my boy? What kind of father am I?

The man finds the stash under the step. He takes his gun back from the woman, and gives Jacob one last warning.

"Trey said he's almost done with you. He said he'll send more than just a message if things don't change soon." He barks a short laugh and asks Jacob on his way out the door, "Didn't you used to be a big deal around here? Look at you now." He laughs again and holds the gun on Jacob as he and the woman back out the front door and leave.

Jacob gets up and turns around. The man didn't put the wood cover back on the step. Jacob snaps it back into place. He walks back to the window in the living room and moves the curtain back again. The man and woman drive away in an old white car. Jacob walks down the hallway to Dreamer's room. He opens the door to check on him and sees the boy is still asleep. Jacob goes back to his bedroom and sits on the edge of his bed. He takes the gun out of his pants and puts it back in the nightstand. He leans forward and puts his elbows on his knees.

He'd been stealing from Trey for years. How could he be so stupid? Could Nelson have told Trey? Why would

he do that? The house on Old Reservation Road had been a
gold mine for Jacob – dealing to the down-and-outers in that
shack had profited Jacob handsomely for several years, and
he hadn't given Trey any of the cut. Jacob had also lost some
business because of the mission, and, who knows, maybe his
men were stealing from him like he was stealing from Trey.
As he sits with his head in his hands the voice of Michael
comes into his mind.

God will never leave you or forsake you.

"Yeah, right," Jacob whispers, then slides his legs
back into the bed without taking his jeans off.

In the living room, across the room from the big
window with the curtain is Jacob's old couch – the same
couch that had sat in that same spot since Jacob's parents
bought it and put it there over thirty years ago. There was a
quilt spread on the couch, and Devin lay underneath it.

*****

Pastor Kirk is preaching like a crazy man today,
Whisper thinks as she follows along in her Bible.

Next to her, Ida keeps saying, "Amen," making
Pastor Kirk preach louder and longer, and all Whisper can
think about is the fact that she might starve to death if she
doesn't get out of this church in the next few minutes and
get something to eat. She looks around the big room called
the sanctuary. Mrs. Tess and Mr. Phil are sitting in front of
Whisper and her grandma, and Mr. Phil's head is tilted back
and his mouth is open and his eyes are closed. Mrs. Tess
nudges him in the side with her elbow, and Mr. Phil opens
his eyes and sits up straighter.

Pastor Kirk must be wrapping it up, because the guy
who sings, Nelson, and the lady who plays the keyboard
come up to the stage. Whisper's noticed that they always do
that at the end, and it seems like Pastor Kirk always asks
people if anyone wants to come to Jesus at the end of his

talking, too. A lot of times nobody comes, but Pastor Kirk keeps asking every week anyway.

Now he's doing it. He tells everyone to close their eyes and bow their heads, and he asks them if anyone wants to come to Jesus, they can walk right up there to him, and he'll pray with them.

Whisper obeys and closes her eyes and bows her head. She remembers when she walked up there to Pastor Kirk when she was a little kid. She wasn't scared at all. She didn't really hear a voice, but it was kind of like she did. She felt kind of a tingle in her chest and it was like she almost heard the faintest voice saying, *"Come."*

As she's standing here now a few years later, listening to Pastor Kirk give that same invitation, she hears it again. It's like a whisper. The voice must be God. He tells her one word, *"Pray."*

Whisper doesn't know who or what she's supposed to pray for, so she just silently prays for God to help someone in this room give their life to Him right now.

Then, after she prays, she hears something else. Another one word command silently, not really aloud, but definitely clear, *"Look."*

She opens her eyes. She doesn't see anything at first, no one walking down the aisle. She turns her head to see if anyone is coming from the back, and she sees him. With his eyes fixed on Pastor Kirk, her father is walking down the center aisle of the church.

When he gets to Pastor Kirk, he bows his head. Pastor Kirk puts a hand on his back and begins praying for Jacob. Nelson starts singing, and Whisper can't hear anything they're saying. She desperately wishes she could run to him. She wishes that she could squeeze out of this row and run down the aisle to her dad, wrap her arms around him and say that she's been praying for this day – the day he would give his life to God and stop all of the bad stuff that made her grandma keep her from him.

She taps her grandma's hand. "Grandma," she whispers, "Grandma, look."

Ida opens her eyes and sees Jacob standing at the front of the church praying with Kirk. "Oh Lord Jesus," she says as she puts a hand over her mouth.

Ida and Whisper watch in amazement as Jacob's eyes are closed and his lips move, obviously praying. Whisper grabs Ida's hand when she sees a tear run down the side of Jacob's face.

"He's praying, Grandma. He's crying and praying." She pumps Ida's hand up and down. "He'll be different now. I know he will."

"Hmph, we'll see," Ida says with a scowl.

Whisper watches Jacob pray and then go back to his seat. Pastor Kirk dismisses the congregation, and she tells Ida she'll be back in a minute. She says, "Excuse me," to the people sitting on her pew and maneuvers her way around people to get to Jacob. He was sitting by himself on the back row, and now he's almost to the back door. The throng of people in the aisle is at a standstill – too many people stopping and gabbing to each other, so Whisper steps on the seat of a pew and climbs over the last few pews.

"Whisper, you know you're not supposed to do that," Miss Melissa tells her.

"I'm sorry," Whisper tells her but keeps climbing to the back. She knows she's not supposed to climb over the pews, but this is an emergency.

She gets to the back of the church but can't see him. I can't let him get out of here without talking to him, she tells herself.

She goes out the door and scans the gravel parking lot. There he is.

"Jacob!"

He stops and turns. His expression is one Whisper's never seen before. He waits for her.

"I saw you pray with Pastor Kirk."

He nods. "Yeah, Whisper . . . I need to tell you something."

She puts her hands on her hips. "Wait, I need to tell you something." She takes a deep breath. There are so many things she wants to say. She's dreamed about this moment for years. She's prepared multiple speeches for the day she finally met her dad. Some of the speeches are mean and hateful, some are sad, and some are happy and forgiving. What she has on her heart to say now though, is not anything she's ever prepared to say.

"For years I've asked God for a dad. I didn't want a bad dad though, I wanted a good one. I wanted a dad who loved God and did good things."

Jacob looks at the ground.

"I thought maybe somehow someone would come to me and say there was a mix-up at the hospital, and my dad was really someone else, or I even thought that maybe some amazing dad would swoop in and adopt me. Those things didn't happen." Whisper's voice shakes as she recounts her eight-year-old lifetime of wishful thinking about a dad. "I think I know now how God is answering my prayer."

With tears in his eyes, Jacob asks her, "How?"

She stops and takes a deep breath, preparing to say the strange thing she thinks God told her. "He's making you the dad I always prayed for."

*****

Tuna fish casserole night.

I absolutely hate tuna fish casserole, but Tess told me that the people who eat the mission dinner on Wednesdays love it, so I found Janice's recipe in the folder and now I'm sitting at my kitchen table making my shopping list. We have milk that's still good in the mission kitchen, and we have cans of cream of chicken soup and noodles. I write down cans of tuna and then stifle a gag reflex as I write down a bag of frozen peas. I'm trying to remember if there's any bread left in the mission pantry that I can use to make breadcrumbs when Chelsea opens the front door and comes inside with a big box in her arms. She shuts the door behind her and dramatically falls back against it.

"Melissa!"

"Yes?" I put my pen down and smile. I love being entertained by Chelsea's nightly dramatic re-tellings of her life events, and it looks like she's got a doozey she's going to act out for me tonight.

"Guess who came to see me after school."

"Jarrett?"

She stops like I stole her punch line. "Yes, Jarrett. How did you know?"

I laugh at her. "I saw you guys after school, remember?"

It was ten minutes until the bell was going to ring. I had my classroom door open and I was reading aloud to my students. Out of the corner of my eye I saw something tall and red in the hallway, just as one of my students gasped and said, "Miss Melissa, look!"

I turned and saw what made her gasp. Jarrett, Chelsea's fiancé, was in the hallway headed to her classroom carrying the biggest arrangement of long stemmed roses I've ever seen in my life. My students started giggling and making kissing noises and comments about Miss Chelsea's boyfriend.

"Okay, everyone, that's enough." I told them as I went to my classroom door. As I pulled the door shut, I whispered to Jarrett, "Wow, those are beautiful. Good job, fiancé."

He lowered the huge arrangement a bit to talk to me. "You think she'll like them?"

"Definitely."

"Good, I'm going to ask her something."

He knocked on Chelsea's classroom door, and I

couldn't help myself. I had to wait there to see her reaction to the roses.

She opened the classroom door and gasped. "Jarrett! What are you doing?" She took the flowers and looked at me. "Melissa, can you believe this?"

"You've got a good one, Chels. You need to hold on to him." I teased and then closed my classroom door and went back to reading to my students. It wasn't until after we had finished reading, and the students had cleared their desks and retrieved their backpacks from their hooks that I thought about what Jarrett had said. What could he be asking her? He's already asked her to marry him.

"So what did he want?"

"How do you know he wanted something?" She asks me as she sets the box on the kitchen table and sits in a chair beside me.

"He told me this afternoon, before you opened the door that he was going to ask you something."

"Well, he definitely knows the way to my heart is with flowers – especially three dozen long-stemmed roses. I left them at school so I can keep them on my desk and look at them all day."

I think about that for a second and do the math in my head as Chelsea sighs and lays her head on her arms, fantasizing about her ever-so dreamy Jarrett, no doubt. "Chelsea, do you realize how much three dozen long-stemmed roses probably cost him?"

"I know," she smiles, "he's so amazing."

I'm happy that Chelsea is happy, but I think that if Kirk brought me three dozen roses I'd probably be aggravated that he spent that much money on something that was just going to die.

"Are you going to make me guess what he asked you?" I push my shopping list away and turn to her. "Come on, tell me."

"He asked me to marry him."

I groan. "Well, duh, Chelsea. He already asked you that." I pick up my paper to continue making my shopping list.

"In December."

"December? Next December, right? Like next year December, not December like next month December, because next month December literally starts in two days."

"Next month. The twenty-eighth."

"Thirty days from now." I'm quick with the math today.

"I said yes. I told him that I would love to marry him as soon as possible, and we're having a Christmas wedding – it'll be beautiful. Of course, I've already picked out my dress and the bridesmaid dresses and they're sleeveless, but that's okay, right? I mean, we'll be inside. It's not like we'll be outside in the cold."

"Chelsea," I grab both of her hands and look her in the eyes and say to her what I wish someone would've said to me in August. "In a few weeks you are getting married. Are you one hundred percent sure that you want to spend the rest of your life with him? If not, you need to be honest with him and end this before it's too late."

She lets go of my hands and hugs me. "I'm one-hundred percent sure, Melissa, I promise. I love Jarrett, and he loves me, and I know for sure that he's the one God has picked for me to spend the rest of my life with."

"Okay, as long as you're sure," a little blonde curl has fallen over her face, and I tuck it behind her ear, "then I'm happy for you."

"I'm sure, and Melissa, there's actually one more thing."

"What?"

"Would you be a bridesmaid?"

"Of course." I agree and think about the dresses she chose. They're cute, but sleeveless in December?"

"And, I need you to help me with something else, if

you don't mind."

"Anything, roomie, name it."

She opens the big box and pulls out ribbon, artificial flowers, and vases.

"Help me make the centerpieces for the reception?"

"Sure." I listen to her instructions on how to assemble the centerpieces, and we work for over an hour and finish all twenty of them. Then she calls Jarrett and they work out the wording for the invitations while I look online for alternatives to pew bows. She said that she wants something tied on the chairs next to the center aisle, but not satin bows, but she doesn't know what exactly.

Kirk calls as I'm researching.

"What are you up to tonight?" It's comforting to hear his laid-back voice.

"Affirming that I don't want an elaborate wedding ceremony." I say as I rub my eyes that have looked at a computer screen too long.

"Sounds good to me."

*****

Devin knows it has to be done quickly. She doesn't think Jacob or the two goons will put up a fight, but you never know, so she's thankful that her lieutenant called in two other Tulsa officers to assist her and the Diniyoli police with the arrests.

She made sure it would happen while Dreamer was at school, and when all three men were in the house alone. Dreamer would be picked up from school by a child services caseworker. She hated for him to have to go into the system, but what else could she do? He didn't have any other family.

She's leading the operation. She and the other officers parked their cars half a block away so they wouldn't be heard. One of the Diniyoli officers stayed with the vehicles and will drive to them when he's radioed after the arrest is made, so they can put the perps in the car immediately and take them to the Diniyoli jail for booking.

She'd hoped to get evidence on the Tulsa connection, but still had nothing, just the threats from a man named Trey, voiced by a man she couldn't identify because she was hiding under a blanket – not the most solid evidence. It's great that she's stopping a bad guy like Jacob in Diniyoli, but she's afraid she might have to go back to Tulsa empty-handed. The only thing that could change that is if she could get Jacob to talk about his boss, Trey. She'd need leverage to get him to talk, and Saturday night as she lay on the couch under the quilt in Jacob's living room and heard where the stash in the house was hidden, she realized that she had the leverage she needed - the thing in this life that means more to Jacob than anything – Dreamer.

She motions to the three officers with her and they go where they are supposed to go – one to the back door and one around the house to the other side of the front porch from Devin. When the officer gets to the other side of the porch, she sees him and nods. He goes first. He's a big guy with a lot of experience in breaching doors and arresting dangerous suspects, and Devin feels confident in her ability to hold her own in any situation, so she's not nervous at all.

She falls in behind him. He swings the ram and the old door opens without a problem. They go in. Jacob, Dumb, and Dumber are sitting in the living room, drinking beer, napping, and playing video games – living the high life.

Devin and her colleagues handcuff the men while she reads them the arrest warrant and their rights. One of the officers radios the driver to come and pick them up. The whole process takes less than thirty seconds.

Dumb spews curses at Devin, and Dumber, in a drunken haze, doesn't seem to comprehend what's happening.

When she's finished talking, they begin walking the three men to the car waiting outside. She's escorting Jacob.

The once big man in town is now reduced to a common felon with his skinny white wrists helplessly behind his back in the silver cuffs. He talks to her as they walk to the car.

"What'll happen to Dreamer?" He asks in a ragged, defeated whisper.

"You should've thought about that before you started dealing drugs, Mr. Davis. Your son will be in child services." Devin is all business.

"No." A tear escapes the hard man's eye and blazes a trail down his face. "I deserve this. I know it, but Dreamer deserves better. Is there anything I can do?"

Exactly the response Devin was counting on. "Yeah, you can tell me everything you know about Trey."

They get to the car and he turns to her. "I'll tell you whatever you want to know, but I want Dreamer to live with his grandma, and I want to give her this house. I don't want this house going up for sheriff sale. I want to call my lawyer and make sure he's got all of this is in writing, and then I'll tell you all about Trey."

"Sounds good." She reaches in her pocket and pulls out her phone. "What's your lawyer's number?"

*****

"Do you know what's going on?" Kirk asks me for the third time.

"No, I have no idea. I told you that."

We round the corner and head for the door of the school office.

Devin called me five minutes before the school bell rang. I don't normally answer my phone during class, but she called me twice in a row, and I thought since there was only five minutes left I'd go ahead and answer her second call. She asked me to call Kirk and tell him to get here to the school as soon as possible. She told me that as soon as he got here we were supposed to come to the school office. She said that she would explain everything when we got there.

The tone of her voice told me how serious it was. When I called Kirk, he said he was in the middle of building a cabinet for the nurse's station. I told him that I thought it was urgent. He showed up at the school five minutes later with sawdust in his hair and wearing jeans stained with wood varnish.

"Why would Devin be at the school? Does she know someone here?" Kirk asks as we get to the door.

I shrug. I have no idea why Devin would be in the school office.

Kirk opens the door, and the secretary says, "In the conference room," as soon as she sees us.

I open the door to the conference room, and Devin is there with the school counselor and with Dreamer. Dreamer has obviously been crying, and he's drinking a soda.

"Hey guys," I say, still not sure what's going on. The image of Devin in Jacob's car on Halloween flashes in my mind. Could she be here on behalf of Dreamer?

"Hey buddy," Kirk says as he sits next to Dreamer.

I sit next to Kirk, and Devin starts talking.

"First of all, Melissa, Kirk, I need to let you both know that I'm a police officer with the Tulsa Police Department."

Kirk and I look at each other with wide eyes.

"I came back to Diniyoli to stop a drug ring that's linked to a large crime operation in Tulsa. I made three arrests today and was able to get the information I need to arrest the head of the operation in Tulsa."

Next to Kirk, Dreamer drops his head on his arms.

"And one of the arrests we made today was Jacob . . . Dreamer's dad."

Kirk puts his arm around Dreamer who is crying again.

"What's going to happen to Dreamer?" I ask. My heart breaks for him. His dad may be a criminal, but

Dreamer loves him. I can't imagine how crushed Dreamer feels right now.

"He's going to be placed with a relative, and his dad is giving the relative his house." She looks at Dreamer with her warm brown eyes, and she places a hand on his shoulder. "You get to stay at this school, so that's a good thing."

He sniffles and looks up at her. "How long will my dad be in jail?"

"It's hard to say, Dreamer. It will be a long time, though, bud, a long time."

He puts his head in his hands. "What relative will I be with? I don't even know any relatives."

Devin looks at Kirk and me. "You're going to live with your grandma."

He looks up at her, confused. "What grandma? She's dead."

"Your mom's mother, and – " She puts her hands on his shoulders. "you'll live with your grandma and your little sister."

He shakes his head. "That's not possible. This is a trick. I don't have a grandma or a sister." He pulls away from Devin and stands up, his hands shaking at his sides. "I'll just live by myself in my house. I can take care of myself."

"Dreamer," I still the precious boy's shaking hands in mine, "she's right. You do have a grandma and a little sister. Your grandma wanted to keep her away from Jacob, so she'd be safe."

"What are you talking about, Miss Melissa? I have a grandma and a sister? Who are they?"

*****

I still have a hard time believing that Devin is a police officer. I look at her sitting next to me, driving a police car to Ida's house. She doesn't look like a police officer to me – nose ring, long, straight black hair with a green streak by the side of her face, with long legs and long arms that make her look like a Native American Barbie doll. In my mind, she's still the beautician who got rid of my head lice and gave me a cute haircut.

"Turn here. It's the one with the bright blue mailbox." I tell her as I point to Ida and Whisper's house.

She pulls in front of their house and parks. Dreamer, sitting in the backseat of the police cruiser next to Kirk, has been silent the whole ride. When Devin told him that Ida was his grandmother and Whisper was his sister back in the school conference room, he didn't speak either. His only reaction was to rub his eyes with his palms. When Devin asked if he was ready to go and talk to them, he didn't say anything. He just nodded.

"Are you ready, Dreamer?" Sitting in the car parked in front of Ida's house on Old Reservation Road, Devin asks him again

He nods.

"Dreamer, do you want me to say a prayer with you before you go in? I'm sure you're having a tough time with all of this, even though you're not saying it." Kirk asks him.

Again Dreamer only nods.

Devin and I bow our heads, and Kirk puts his arm around Dreamer's shoulder as he prays. He closes his prayer by asking the Lord to remind Dreamer that He is with him always.

When the prayer is over, Dreamer looks up at Kirk and finally speaks. "Just like Coach Michael's verse last week."

"Yeah, it is. God won't ever leave you. It's the truth, Dreamer."

"I know it. Thanks, Pastor Kirk." He leans in to Kirk and Kirk envelops the boy in a hug.

Dreamer leans back and wipes the tears from his eyes. He looks at Devin in the driver's seat and bravely tells her, "I'm ready."

We get out of the car. Devin and Dreamer walk side by side, and Kirk and I follow.

"I called Ida after everything with your dad this morning and told her that we're coming, so they're – "

Before Devin can finish her sentence, the front door of the house swings open, and Whisper runs out the front door. She runs to Dreamer, jumps on him, almost knocking him down, and wraps her arms around his neck.

"Dreamer! You're here! You're my brother and we get to live together! I'm your sister!"

He looks down at his little sister with her crazy brown curly hair, gap-toothed smile and beautiful blue eyes, and he laughs.

"Of course you're my sister. I recognized the family baseball talent in you a long time ago." He says with a grin.

Her eyes widen. "Really?"

He laughs and looks up as Ida walks to him.

"Hello, Dreamer."

"Hi."

"You've got your mama's eyes. Whisper's got her daddy's eyes, but you . . . you've got Sierra's."

"I've seen a couple of pictures of my mom, but I don't remember her. Do you have more pictures?"

Ida's eyes well with tears. "I do. I've got boxes and boxes of pictures of her when she was a little girl. They're right here in the living room. Come on in, we can look at them now, if you want."

Dreamer looks questioningly at Devin.

"It's okay, go on in."

He turns back to Kirk and me. "You're going to be fine." Kirk tells him.

He walks to Ida, and she puts an arm around him and an arm around Whisper, and the three of them walk into the house. Devin, Kirk, and I stay on the scraggly patch of brown grass in front of the house.

"I can go to his house and pack his clothes, if you

need me to." I tell Devin.

"You'll have to wait. They're still processing the house. Finding all of the evidence will take a while. They'll probably be working the house for a few days. I'll grab him a couple of changes of clothes, and you can come and pack for him in a couple of days." She looks at Ida's tiny house and runs a hand through her long black hair. "Although, they may want to move in a few days. They can take possession of the house as soon as we're done. The lawyers probably already have the house in her name. Jacob's house is falling apart, but it's better than this shack." She turns to Kirk. "That scripture you told Dreamer in the car?"

"'He will never leave you or forsake you.' Michael shared it with the kids at baseball practice on Saturday."

"Yeah, it's funny. Jacob actually said that to me today. I can't tell you the details, but let's just say that he lost some friends today. He told me that he felt strangely at peace about it, though. He said he knew that the Lord would never leave him or forsake him. I didn't think he was religious at all, so it was weird." She turns to me. "Thanks for being a friend to me while I was here. I was living a double life – one with you and Chelsea, and then one with Jacob and his idiots. Hanging out with you and Chelsea was the only good thing about living here these past few months."

"Do you have to move back to Tulsa?"

"Yeah, I'm leaving today. There's a lot to do to get this guy behind bars where he belongs, but the information we got today should make everything easier."

I reach up and hug Devin while she stands stiff through my hug, enduring it, and I remember the first time I hugged her, after she'd cut my hair in my kitchen.

"Come back and visit sometime?"

"Definitely." She tells me with such certainty that I know she will.

"Devin," Kirk says to her, "thanks for what you did today. I think Diniyoli's going to be a better place because of it."

"I hope so. I hope someone else doesn't take his place tomorrow."

"Well, that's why we've got officers like you looking out for us."

"Thanks, Kirk. That means a lot. Can I take you guys home? I'm going to get those clothes for Dreamer."

"Sure, let me say goodbye to Whisper." I tell her.

I walk to the front door and lightly tap on it. Whisper answers less than two seconds after my knock.

"Miss Melissa, it's so awesome about my brother living with me, isn't it?"

I chuckle at her. I have a feeling she's going to be calling Dreamer "my brother" for a while. "It is awesome. I just wanted to say bye. We're going to go home."

"Okay, Grandma, Miss Melissa and Pastor Kirk are leaving." She yells to her grandma in the living room behind her.

"Tell them to wait a minute." Ida says from inside.

Ida's face appears in the doorway above Whisper's. "Y'uns can come in for a minute. Have some tea."

"Oh, that's all right. We're going to let you guys catch up." I say, not wanting to interrupt this overdue reunion.

"He's a good boy," Ida says and looks back at Dreamer, who is sitting on the couch going through a box of old photos.

"He is," I agree.

"Just wish I didn't have to move to that dad-burned house. I don't know how I'm s'posed to live there. Everything needs fixed. I can't fix all that."

Devin walks up behind me. "Do you mean you don't want to live in the house, ma'am?"

"No, why would I want to? My house's not good, but that house's worse. Got windows out, porch is sagging, and who knows what it's like on the inside. Probably ain't even fit for children to live in."

"You know, she's right." Devin says to Kirk and me. "It might not be fit for children to live in. Before Ida officially becomes his guardian, someone from Department of Human Services will come and inspect the house. If it's not deemed suitable, it could mess everything up."

"Well, we're staying here then. That big old house can rot to the ground, for all I care. I can stay here in my little house with my two grandkids."

Devin steps forward. "Ms. Ida, can I come in and talk to you for a minute about this? I want you to be aware of your options."

The three of us stay at Ida's house for about fifteen more minutes as Devin explains to Ida that Jacob's house is hers to do with as she wishes. If she wants to live in it, she can, or she can sell it. Devin tells Ida that if she sells Jacob's house and her house, that she can afford a very nice house for her and the kids, and Ida gets excited about the idea. She says she'll visit a realtor tomorrow to put both houses on the market and to start looking for a new house.

We tell the reunited family goodbye and load up in the police car. Devin starts the car and puts it in gear when Dreamer comes running out of the house to us. Devin rolls down the window next to me.

"What is it buddy? Are you all right here?" I ask him.

"Yeah, I'll be fine here, but I forgot to ask you a question, Devin." He runs a hand through his hair, and I realize that it's one of the few times I've seen him without his Cardinals baseball cap. "Can I visit my dad? Will he be somewhere close that I can go see him sometime?"

"He'll be a couple hours away from here, but they do have times that you can come and visit him."

"Okay," Dreamer looks back at the house. "I don't know if Ida can take me."

Kirk tries to roll his window down, but, of course it won't, since he's in the back of a police car. He leans forward and talks to Dreamer through my window.

"I'll take you, Dreamer. Anytime you want to go, just tell me, and we'll go see your dad, okay?"

"Yeah, okay Pastor Kirk." He says, then he smiles. "Hey Pastor, you need to be careful in the back of that police car. Those lady cops might take you to jail."

Kirk laughs. "Tell me about it, bud. I need to hurry up and get out of here."

Dreamer laughs and waves to us as we leave. Devin takes us back to the school where our cars are, and she leaves to finish her paperwork of the arrest. Kirk has to get back to the mission to finish his work on the cabinet in the nurse's station, and gives me a kiss before I leave the school. I drive the short distance to my cozy rent house and park in my driveway. The lights are on, so Chelsea is home. I smile as I think about what project she'll have me doing tonight. Addressing wedding invitations? Making boutonnieres or bouquets?

*****

She can't believe her new house has a fireplace. She's always wanted a fireplace on cold nights to sit in front of and read a book, or to roast marshmallows in, or, like she's doing right now, to hang Christmas stockings over. She's never had a Christmas stocking before, because she didn't have a fireplace, and because Grandma said she just never thought of it before, and Dreamer said he's never had one before either.

Grandma's friend, Mrs. Tess, made stockings for Whisper, Dreamer and Grandma, and gave them to them when they moved into their new house. She said it was a housewarming gift. Grandma's is dark red with sparkly rhinestones all over it and has 'Ida' sewn into the top of it in silver thread. Dreamer's is a St. Louis Cardinals stocking, of course. It has a picture of Santa Claus with a fluffy beard playing baseball on the front of it and Dreamer's name sewn on the top in red. Whisper thinks Mrs. Tess spent more time on hers than any of them. It is covered in sparkles. There's not an inch of it that doesn't have a sparkle. On top of the sparkles, Mrs. Tess sewed hot pink flowers and bows, and the top of the stocking has shiny hot pink material with 'Whisper' sewn into it in sparkles. Whisper thinks it's the prettiest thing she's ever seen.

"Did you finish your homework?" Grandma asks.

"Yes," they tell her.

"Did you clean your rooms?"

"Yes," they tell her again. It's easy to keep such a pretty room clean, Whisper thinks. When grandma sold her dad's big, old house, she had enough money to buy this beautiful new house in a nice neighborhood and all new furniture. Whisper got a bed with a canopy and a dresser and a desk and a pink fluffy rug. When they first moved out here, she didn't think they were in Diniyoli anymore, because she'd never seen these houses, but Grandma said they were still in Diniyoli, just four miles east of town, still in the school district, which is good, because she wouldn't want to leave Miss Melissa's class.

"Did you do your chores?"

Again they tell her, "Yes." Dreamer and Whisper hurried and finished taking out the trash and feeding and walking Rocky and doing the dinner dishes, because the movie comes on at seven and they didn't want to miss it.

"Okay, then let's watch the show."

"Yes!" Dreamer and Whisper say. They run to their shiny new kitchen and cook popcorn in the microwave, and come back to the living room and get comfy on their new furniture. Whisper lays on the leather loveseat, Dreamer gets on the couch with flowers on it, and Grandma turns on the TV from her big recliner, and the funny Christmas movie they've been looking forward to all week starts. It's a movie Grandma and Whisper have never seen, and Dreamer said they haven't had Christmas until they've watched this movie, so it must be good.

"What do you want for Christmas, Dreamer?" She asks her brother as the movie starts.

He shrugs. "Can't think of anything."

"How about a new hat?" Whisper points to the red baseball cap that never leaves his head. "That one's getting grungy."

"Never." He takes off the hat and turns it around to show Whisper and Ida the back of it. "See this signature? He's my favorite player. My dad made a special trip to St. Louis to get me this hat." He puts the hat back on his head and twists it to position it just right on his head.

"He loves you a lot, Dreamer." Whisper says from her spot on the loveseat.

He looks at his little sister. "He must've been really messed up to make Grandma Ida take you away. I think God's going to help him, and he's going to become a dad to you, too."

"I know he is. I already prayed about it." She juts her chin out with assurance.

Christmas is still three days away, but this year is different than any Christmas Whisper has ever had. Usually she has a list of toys she wants, but this year she can't think of a single present to put on a wish list. She already has everything anyone could ever want.

*****

I get out my phone and type a note to myself. "Talk to Kirk about buying more chairs."

I'm standing in the back of the sanctuary, against the wood paneled wall, with three rows of metal folding chairs between the last pew and me. Everything that could be used as a chair, including the chairs from the offices and fellowship hall is being used. I feel unsure of what to do with myself, since I'm not supposed to do anything. It's a strange feeling to not be responsible for anything. The church from Frisco, Texas came in yesterday and taught kids and adults how to do different parts in their musical, and they have plenty of people to wrangle the kids and manage costumes and sound. I'm not even supposed to cook anything, which is weird. Ida and some of the other ladies from the mission came to me a few days ago and said they wanted to make meals for the team from Texas.

"You do so much, Melissa. Let us bless these people like you bless us," Ida had told me.

So, they shooed me out of the kitchen and made breakfast, lunch and dinner yesterday, and breakfast this morning for the visitors, and they're making lunch for them after service this morning, too. After that, the group will head back to Texas. It's been a whirlwind trip for them. They drove five hours to get here early yesterday morning. They stayed and worked extremely hard for about thirty-six hours, and then they're leaving this afternoon and driving five hours again to get home.

A few of our teenage girls are performing choreography now as the people from Texas and some of our teenagers sing "O Little Town of Bethlehem." They brought pastel dresses with strips of sheer fabric hanging from the sleeves for the girls to slip over their clothes and wear as they perform. I'm amazed that they were able to teach our kids and teenagers the choreography and the songs in just a few hours.

The song is over and "O Come Let Us Adore Him" softly plays as Whisper walks to the microphone. She reads lines from a notebook on a lectern in front of her. I'm not at all surprised that they chose Whisper to narrate. She's adorable and can read as good as an adult.

**"God gave us a present who came from above –
Jesus, our Savior, the newborn king**

**He is the one we celebrate and love.
May we always remember the joy He brings!"**

After she reads her lines, she smiles and looks at Ida, who is sitting on the second row beaming. Then, she goes back to her place with the choir. They sing "Carol of the Bells," and a group of my precious elementary school aged kids play the bells while they sing. A woman from the visiting group holds up colored cards, telling the kids which bells to play at the right time. Genius. I take out my phone and type a note to myself to ask where they got those bells and the colored cards. I'm not musical in the least, but I'm pretty sure I can do that with my students at school or with the kids in the afterschool program.

Peppy music for "Little Drummer Boy" starts to play, and a group of six older boys step in front of the choir. Dreamer is one of them.

The music has a strong beat, and the boys start bopping their heads and waving their arms, dancing the latest craze I've seen kids doing on the playground in perfect time to the Christmas classic. People across the congregation smile and bob their heads as the boys dance and the choir sings.

Then the other five boys move back and Dreamer moves to the center. The singing stops and only drums play as Dreamer drops to the ground and spins on one hand, then jumps up and goes upside down, standing on one hand with his legs frozen in a bent position. Then he drops to the ground and spins on his shoulder and then his head!

I never knew Dreamer could do anything like that. I'm thankful I'm standing so that I can see the whole thing. People in the pews and the chairs crane their necks and raise up to try to see Dreamer better. When he finishes, the sanctuary explodes with applause, and Dreamer blushes and tries not to smile.

They end the program with "Joy to the World," and

everyone sings along. The congregation gives the team a standing ovation at the end of the song.

"Wasn't that amazing?" Kirk says as he walks to the stage.

People in the congregation respond with "Yes," and "Yeah, it was," and nod.

"We want to thank Pastor Kelley and his team for everything they've done, helping our teenagers and kids put together this program, and for something else. Does anyone know what else they did?"

All of the kids in the church yell, "Presents!"

"That's right. They brought presents for all of our kids."

Members from their team bring several large black trash bags to the stage, and kids all over the room giggle and squeal with delight.

"Pastor Kelley, would you come up here and say a few words before the big moment?"

Pastor Kelley comes and stands next to Kirk and speaks to everyone for a few minutes. He explains how his church in Texas started out as a mission church in the middle of a poor neighborhood years ago, and how his church and the people there had been blessed over the years by churches from other cities coming and working on their property, giving them clothes and food for their people, bringing them gifts at Christmas, and now that their church has grown, they can help other churches. He says a prayer and then gives instructions for how the gifts will be handed out, telling the boys to stand on one side and the girls on the other. Then his team divides the boys and girls by age and then starts matching the presents to the appropriate age.

After each child has three presents, Kirk talks to the kids who are anxious to start ripping them open.

"Okay, guys, when I say 'Go,' you rip that paper off – none of this careful opening like an old person. You just tear into those presents. On your mark – "

The kids are deciding which one to open first.

"Get set – "

The grins on their faces are huge as they have their hands on the presents ready to rip the wrapping paper to shreds, and the Diniyoli grownups and the visitors from Texas hold up their phones videoing the countdown to chaos.

"Go!"

The sanctuary is filled with the sound of ripping as wrapping paper goes flying. I laugh at kids who yell, "Yes!" when they open their present or who want to open it and start playing with it right then and don't care about opening the second and third gift.

I feel a tug on my heart, like a string is tied around it and someone is pulling the string. I look in the direction I feel the tug, and see the one whose heart is tied to the other end of the invisible string. He looks over the happy madness at me leaning against the back wall. With tears in his eyes he smiles at me, and I give him a thumbs-up sign. Way to go, Kirk.

*****

It is not possible to make s'mores in the microwave.

I thought it was a good idea. Kirk and I had been planning to celebrate Christmas together tonight at my house on Christmas Eve. I'm driving home to Cool Springs after he leaves, because my mom wants me to wake up with the family on Christmas morning. I thought it would be fun for Kirk and me to make s'mores and open presents together.

"Melissa?" He hollers from the kitchen, with a tone that tells me something is wrong.

"Yeah?" I'm almost finished wrapping his present in my room.

"Um, I think the marshmallow is exploding."

"What?"

Turns out, marshmallows expand in the microwave. So, our s'mores turned into a gooey mess of chocolate and marshmallow and graham crackers all over the plates, which, isn't a bad thing actually, if you're willing to use your fingers and lick it all off the plate, and we decided we weren't above that. So, we stand in the kitchen and eat the delicious disaster, and get chocolate and marshmallow all over our fingers.

"Yum," Kirk says, licking a finger. "I think we should do this again. Who cares if it's messy. It is s'mores after all."

"I totally agree." I wash my hands in the kitchen sink and turn around to him. "Want to open presents now?"

He laughs.

"What?"

"You've got chocolate on your nose." He grabs a dishtowel and wipes the smudge off my nose.

At that moment my heart takes a snapshot of the sensory details that surround me – the smell of Kirk's aftershave, the feel of the towel rubbed on my nose, the sound of our laughter, the sweet taste of chocolate, marshmallows, and graham cracker, the sight of Kirk looking down at me. I add this memory to the others I've collected the past few months with Kirk – Kirk with red Kool-Aide all over him, the journal he gave me for my first day of school, the line of buffalo underneath the sunset over the lake, Kirk smiling at me over a sea of happy kids opening Christmas presents.

"Are you ready to open my present?" He asks me.

I tell him I am, and he washes his hands and I retrieve his gift from my bedroom and meet him on the couch in the living room. I hand him the two rectangular boxes that I've wrapped and tied together with ribbon.

"Two? I only got you one."

"Well, they go together." I explain.

He unties the ribbon and rips the wrapping paper and opens the top present. He pulls the jeans out and smiles.

"Jeans, thank you."

"I know it's not very exciting, but look, they're nice jeans. They don't have any rips or stains." I point out, feeling like I have to explain my present.

"Yes, I definitely need that." He leans to me and kisses me. "Thank you."

"Now, open the next one." I put the opened present on the ground and lift the other gift to him.

He opens the second gift and laughs. "Coveralls, I've never had any of these." He stands and holds the heavy, thick brown coveralls in front of him.

"See, you can wear these over your clothes while you're working, and you won't mess up your nice clothes." I feel bad for buying him clothes. I should have gotten him something fun instead.

"This is perfect. I'll use these a lot." He sits back down. "Thank you for taking care of me." He kisses me again. "I love you, Melissa."

I rest my forehead on his. "I love you, too."

"Okay, now it's time for you to open your present." He picks up a square medium sized package and hands it to me.

The gift is wrapped in silver wrapping paper with a gorgeous red velvet ribbon tied around it, forming a beautiful bow on the top.

"Did you wrap this?" I ask, impressed.

He laughs. "No, I had the lady at the store wrap it. I could never do that."

I open the present and see a wide, leather bound book. I pick it up and open it. It's a Bible with extra-wide margins. In the box, underneath the Bible is an envelope. I open the envelope and find colored pencils and markers.

"It's called a journaling Bible." He explains. "Have you heard of it?"

I shake my head. I haven't heard of it, but it's definitely something I know I'll love.

"You can draw in the wide margins as you read. I thought you might like it."

"I love it. I know I'll use it. It's such a thoughtful gift. Thank you." I kiss him, and we make some hot chocolate and talk for a while longer. I wish I didn't have to go. I tell him that I don't have any problem driving late at night, but he doesn't want me falling asleep on the road, so he leaves, and I head out of Diniyoli to Cool Springs.

During my hour drive, I don't turn on the radio. I reflect on the evening with Kirk. I do love the journaling Bible, and I can't wait to start using it. I honestly admit to myself, though, that I was disappointed when he handed me the medium-sized package. I didn't realize until that moment that I was hoping for a Christmas present in a much smaller box, delivered to me by Kirk kneeling on one knee.

******

My favorite part of Chelsea's wedding is the lighted garland. Chelsea told me that Clinton Community Church, the church she was raised in, decorates their sanctuary for Christmas every year with the clear lights entwined in greenery hanging high on the walls, near the ceiling, encircling the room.

My dress is emerald green, like the other bridesmaids' dresses, and her adorable little cousins who are her flower girls wear ruby red dresses. Jarrett and his groomsmen wear classic tuxedos. The whole ceremony is flawless, but of course it is, Chelsea had a minute-by-minute agenda, a wedding coordinator who was determined to carry out all of Chelsea's wishes, and we practiced four times yesterday.

As I stand on the stage smiling and holding flowers, I sneak a peek at the audience to look for Kirk. It doesn't take long to find him. He's sitting next to Nelson in the middle of the congregation. He looks handsome with his fresh haircut and shave, listening attentively to the minister. I wonder what he's thinking about.

From where I'm standing, I can't see Chelsea's face, but I can see Jarrett's. He's totally fixed on what the minister is saying. I've never seen a more intent groom, and I'm thankful that my friend is marrying someone who is taking this commitment so seriously.

All of us girls in the wedding party are perfectly comfortable in our short sleeves in the heated church, and when the time comes to go outside and head to the reception, we bundle up in our coats and scarves, and our friends and family drive up as close as they can to the door to rescue us from the cold.

The snow started falling three days ago, on Christmas day, and it has stopped and started a few times since then. The wind is blowing so hard, though, that the snow isn't accumulating much, just whipping around and seeming to blow away. There are about two inches of crunchy snow on the ground now, and we navigate through it with our high heels to get to the reception.

Fun music, great food, conversations with Chelsea and Jarrett's friends and family last for hours at the reception. Chelsea and Jarrett change their clothes, and all of the guests gather outside the reception hall to wave goodbye as they drive away in Jarrett's car that the groomsmen wrapped in toilet paper and wrote with shoe polish on the windows.

As we hurry inside to get out of the cold, Janice runs to me and wraps her arm around my shoulder.

"You must be cold, sweetie. Pastor Kirk needs to get over here and put his coat over your shoulders."

I laugh and look over at Kirk. He's talking to a group of men. Of course, he's the one doing the talking, and the rest of the men appear to be listening to him tell a story.

"I'm fine, Janice. It was a pretty wedding, wasn't it?"

"Sure was, honey. Now, when do we start planning yours?"

The cold weather only lasted a couple more days, and it warmed up for New Years. Michael and I went to Bricktown in downtown Oklahoma City on New Year's Day and rode the boat in the canal and ate dinner at a nice restaurant. My two-week break from school and working at the church was refreshing, and I was ready to see my precious students and get started when the second semester began.

January was one of the coldest on record, with temperatures below freezing for three weeks straight and two horrific ice storms. I don't know how people who live in places that are cold for months and months survive. I'm usually freezing December through February, piling the blankets on my bed, wearing layers of clothes, and eating lots of stew and chicken and dumplings and drinking lots of hot coffee. (I guess I actually drink lots of coffee year-round, though.)

It's odd to have the house all to myself. I'm not sure what to do with Chelsea's room. I don't need a sitting room or an office. Maybe I could get a treadmill and put it in there?

Chelsea moved into Jarrett's house, which is on this side of Clinton, but still forty-five minutes away. She's got a long commute to school every day, and they haven't decided what to do about her job next year. They'll either move closer to Diniyoli, or she'll get a job in Clinton. I know Chelsea's heart is to minister to the people of Diniyoli, so I hope she stays at the school and the mission. Of course, I hope she stays because I'll miss her terribly if she leaves, too.

At the beginning of February, we get the third ice storm of the season, school is closed for three days because the roads are so icy, and Kirk gives me the best gift anyone has ever given me.

"It's a space heater," he tells me after I open it.

He drove to my house in his four-wheel drive truck, which doesn't slip and slide on the ice. He knocked on the door, and I opened it to see him standing on the porch with a huge box wrapped in brown paper.

"Why are you giving me a present? It's not my birthday." I had told him.

He shrugged. "I don't know. It's just what I do."

It is what he does. I remember the journal he gave me, and the journaling Bible and art supplies, the reading corner that magically appeared in my classroom. He loves to observe me and give me gifts that he thinks I'll like.

After I open it, I plug it in immediately and stand in front of it.

"Just remember to unplug it when you're not here, and don't put anything on top of it or let anything touch it. I'd feel terrible if it caught your house on fire." He says.

At school, Whisper shows me a letter from her dad. He tells her that he is praying and talks a lot to chaplains who visit him. He tells her that he is becoming the dad she always wanted.

"That's what I told him – that God was making him the dad I always wanted," She told me one day after school, "and I know he is. Maybe he had to get arrested and put in jail. Maybe it was the only way he would ever come to Jesus."

I'm amazed at the maturity of my little second grader.

"How do you like your new house?" I ask her.

She tells me that she loves it, and tells me about her new bedroom with the fluffy pink rug and that she met a girl her age who lives down the street.

"I'm so happy for you and your grandma and Dreamer. You guys deserve a nice house like that. It's such a blessing, and it happened so fast. I can't believe how fast the houses sold." They sold both houses in less than a month, which is unreal to me. I've noticed that the new owner of Jacob's house has been working on it. Every time I drive by, I can tell that work is going on.

Whisper shrugs. "Yeah, they sold fast. I don't know how that happened."

Chapter Eight

"Can you help me with something?" Kirk asks me over the phone one cold February day right after school.

"Sure," I'm sitting at my desk making my shopping list for this week's Wednesday meal. "What do you need?"

"I'm installing a countertop for the sink in the nurse's station, and I need your opinion. Would you care to meet me somewhere and look at a countertop and tell me your opinion?"

"I can do that. Where do you want me to go?"

"It's Jacob's old house. The new owners have re-done the kitchen and have installed beautiful new countertops. Can you meet me there and tell me what you think?"

I tell him I can, and finish a few things at school and put on all my layers – coat, gloves, hat, scarf – before leaving.

I've been wanting to meet the new owners of the big, white house, and I wonder how Kirk met them. Knowing Kirk, he probably just rang their doorbell one day and introduced himself. A part of me is sad that someone bought the house. When Ida put it on the market, I looked over my finances to see if there was any way I could buy it. I could've handled the monthly mortgage payments, but I didn't have enough cash to cover the money down or the closing costs. I figure that I'll be able to buy a house next year. I'm already looking for real estate signs every time I go to the neighborhood a couple of miles out of town to get my hair cut at Julie's or to visit Dreamer and Whisper, but none of those newer homes compare to the old beauty.

I pull into the driveway behind Kirk's truck and can't avoid admiring the house. The new owners must be hard at work on the interior. On the side of the porch are bags of thinset, cans of paint, and a pile of lumber.

I place a foot on the first step leading up to the wide porch and marvel that I'm finally going to see inside the place I've ogled for seven months.

"There you are," Kirk says as he comes from the side of the porch and kisses me hello.

"Want to go on a tour?" He asks as he opens the front door.

"Where are the new owners? They probably don't want strangers traipsing through their new house."

"They don't mind. I promise." He says with such a bright grin that I have to believe him.

I follow him in the front door and take in the grand entry hall and wide, winding staircase in front of me.

I suck my breath in and put a hand on my heart as I view the room. "How tall do you think these ceilings are? Twenty feet?"

"Twenty-four," Kirk tells me as we both lift our chins and admire the high ceiling with its intricate network of decorated tiles.

"Wow," is all I can say. I move to look at the room to the left. "I'm assuming this is the living room?"

"Mmm . . . " Kirk nods. "How would you arrange the furniture in here?" He asks with a mischievous smile. "Come on, let's pretend."

I laugh at him. "Okay, I'll play." I show him where I'd put the couches and tables and rug and where I'd hang the television. Then we move to the room on the other side of the living room. I'm assuming it's the dining room, since it's connected to the kitchen and I tell him where I'd put the rug and dining table and china hutch. I start for the kitchen, but Kirk stops me.

"Let's go look upstairs first." He tells me, and we go upstairs and look at the four bedrooms and bathrooms.

I stop on the landing and put my hands on the railing and look down to the rooms below. "It's like a house from an old movie. I can see a family living here, getting this place all cleaned up and decorated and organized. I imagine family pictures hanging on the wall going up the stairs and the whole house smelling like cookies baking in the oven." I turn and see Kirk smiling at me.

"Oh, hush. I know I sound cheesy, but can't you imagine that?"

He walks to me, stands behind me and encircles my waist with his arms. "Yes, I can." He puts his chin on my shoulder. "Of course you have to see past the broken light fixtures, dingy walls, and crumbling porch."

I shrug. "It's not that bad, just a little work required."

"You should've seen it before the new owners cleaned it up."

I turn to him. "You saw it?"

He nods. "I won't tell you all the details. I'll just tell you this and you can imagine the rest." He makes a face that tells me to get ready for the worst. "Dead animals."

I shudder and cover my mouth with my hand.

He laughs at my reaction. "Let's go downstairs and look at the kitchen. I want you to see the countertops."

I follow him down the steps to the kitchen. I run my hand along the curved wall that leads to a pantry door and open it. I gasp when I see how deep the pantry is.

"Kirk, did you see this pantry?"

He doesn't answer me. He walks around the island sits on a window seat on the back wall of the kitchen.

"Oh my word," I take in the whole room. "This is big enough for a full-sized table in the kitchen. The window seat could be the seating for that side of the table. You could stand here and cook and talk to people sitting at the table, and there's room for bar stools at the island. This place is more amazing than I thought." I look at him studying me. "I can see a family with three or four kids living here, can't you? Kirk, tell me the people who bought this have a big family."

"Not yet, but they will."

"What about the countertops?" I look down at the tops of the cabinets, where the countertops should be, but only open space is there.

"Stay right there." He goes to the huge pantry and comes out with a large book. He balances it on the top of the island cabinets. He flips the book open to pictures of different types of granite countertops.

"Which ones do you think you want in here?"

I tilt my head at him. "What?"

"I have no idea about this kind of stuff. I need you to pick it out. I thought since the cabinets are light, you might want a darker countertop, but I wasn't sure. Of course, you have to think about what kind of backsplash you'll want and what kind of sink you'll want too. So, I need you to make some decisions, because after I got everything all cleaned up, I thought I'd start remodeling the kitchen first."

"Kirk, are you telling me – "

His grin tells me everything.

"You did!" My chin drops.

He comes around the island to me and wraps me in his arms again. "Do you want it?"

"Do I want it? The house? What?"

"I figure that I can fix it up and then, maybe one day, you'll agree to marry me, and we can fill it up with that family you were describing. Cookies baking in the oven sounded perfect to me."

*****

I'm so thankful that a couple of dads have volunteered to help with baseball practice. Now, I can sit in the bleachers and read my book while they practice, and I don't have to chase errant balls or act like I know how to swing a bat. I still love to come to practice, though. I help the coaches get the kids to listen, and I play team-building games with them. I also love that I get to see my brother every Saturday.

They're playing a real game now, with Kirk and Michael on one team, and the two dads on the other team. Michael pitches and a boy hits it and runs to first. Whisper is on third, so she runs as fast as she can to home to score a run. Kirk is the catcher, and he gets up and runs to Whisper and lifts her up. Her feet are still running in the air, like a cartoon character.

"Put me down, Pastor Kirk!" she yells at him through her giggles, "Put me down!"

"Why? Then you'll score, and we'll lose."

The outfielder throws the ball to Michael and he runs to Whisper and tags her out while Kirk holds her.

"She's out!" Michael yells.

The kids on the other team yell and scream and run at Kirk and Michael. They let the kids jump on them and soon there's a big dog pile in the middle of the school gymnasium.

They get the kids back in control and practice a little more. Then they have their Bible devotion, like always, while I help pack up all the equipment.

"Are you and Pastor Kirk working on the house today?" Dreamer says as he hands me third and fourth base, and I put them into a bag.

After Kirk surprised me with the house, he told me that Ida, Dreamer, and Whisper had been in on the secret from the beginning. He told me it was killing Whisper not to tell me.

"Yep, Kirk's installing backsplash, and I'm painting."

"Which room?"

"Do you want to come to the house with me and see what we're working on? You can hang out there with us for a while, maybe have lunch and see some of your old neighbors. I can take you home later."

His whole face brightens with his smile. "Sure."

Dreamer loved seeing his old house cleaned up. He

kept commenting that he'd never seen it so clean. He visited his old neighbors for a while and then came back for a grilled cheese sandwich and a bowl of tomato soup.

Kirk had to get more supplies from the hardware store, so Dreamer and I sit on the new bar stools at the kitchen island and enjoy our soup and sandwiches together.

"I think my mom would've liked to see this house fixed up," he says between bites.

"Do you remember her at all?"

"Sometimes I remember things. They just flash in my mind for a second and then they're gone. I remember her making me a bowl of cereal one time. I was sitting in here at the table, and she gave me a bowl of cereal and sat down next to me. She had long, black hair."

I slightly lift the bill of his red baseball cap and look in his eyes. "She would've been proud of you, Dreamer, the way you take care of your little sister, how you work so hard at school and lead other kids to do the right thing. She would've been proud."

He smiles at me. "I think she's in Heaven, Miss Melissa. Grandma Ida says she knew the Lord, so I think I'll see her again one day."

"You will, buddy."

We continue eating our lunch in silence until we hear a crash in the living room.

"What was that?" He puts his spoon down.

"I don't know. It sounded like something broke." I start in the direction of the sound, but freeze at the kitchen entry. Standing in the living room are four men. The front door is open, warm air streaming into the house hitting me with the realization that something is very wrong. The men, all four wearing jeans and ratty t-shirts, see me when I see them. Then one strides forward in front of the group. They all watch him as if waiting for direction. His upper lip curls in a sneer. Then I see it. His short sleeves are rolled up, revealing his toothpick arms with little balls of muscles on them. On his left arm a big, black, ugly number three tattoo tells me everything I need to know.

I want to scream, but I can't seem to form any words. Dreamer . . . he's here. He's in danger.

I snap out of my shock and scream, "Run!" I turn to Dreamer. He's staring, frozen, jaw slack. "Run!"

I hear a deep voice behind me, too close. "It's him – wearing a Cardinals baseball hat, just like Trey said."

*****

The next few minutes are a blur. I'm grabbed and pushed face-first against the wall by one of them who smells like body odor. All I can see is the wall and the edge of the kitchen cabinets, but I hear Dreamer try to run, and I hear them catch him. I yell at them to leave him alone, to let him go and take me instead.

They ignore me.

I hear a scuffle, probably Dreamer trying to fight them off. But they are four grown men, and he is one twelve-year-old boy. What can he do?

They manhandle us to a car parked on the front lawn, right in front of the porch. I look around for someone, anyone outside who might see us and help, but no one is in sight. The shove us into the floorboards of the old car, one of those heavy, long four door cars like my grandpa used to drive. They keep yelling at us to keep our heads down. A big, rough hand grips the back of my neck and holds my head to the floor of the car. My face is smashed against tan carpet, and I can hear Dreamer next to me crying. I try to lift my head to look at him and say something to him, but they yell at me to shut up and the hand on the back of my neck rams my face deeper into the floorboard.

I want to succumb to the churning in my stomach and the pulling in my mind that's trying to take me to a dark place of complete panic, but I push those thoughts and feelings away, because I tell myself that Dreamer needs me . . . Dreamer needs me . . . . it's the only thought that's keeping me sane.

I'm trying to make sense of all this. Our four kidnappers must be somehow connected to Jacob, because they were obviously after Dreamer and not me. The one in the driver's seat keeps yelling at the other three that "Trey" will be mad that they "grabbed the girl." That's not the only thing they're fighting about – taking a wrong turn, not speeding so they won't get pulled over, and like a couple of kids, the two in the backseat who are holding our heads down are actually fighting about staying on their side of the seat and not touching each other.

I try to tell where we are by sounds and judging distances. After two hours of being folded and jammed into the floorboard, my legs are cramping and I'm sure I'll have a bruise on my neck where he keeps pressing me down. I'm guessing we're in the Tulsa area. A lot of the drive felt like the smooth interstate. Then again, we could be in Texas, too. I'm not sure which direction we're driving in.

While my head is pushed down, someone ties a blindfold over my eyes. I try to open my eyes and find a place in the fabric to peek through, but it's tied so tight that I can't even open my eyelids. When we park, they hustle us out of the car just a few steps. I feel concrete under my feet and then carpet. Then, I'm shoved onto a bed, and I feel Dreamer pushed down next to me.

Our captors argue with each other about where to put us, and then they decide to tie our hands behind our backs. One of them ties a thick rope around my wrist. Then, Dreamer and I are shoved into chairs with our backs to each other and our shoulders touching. Someone ties my ankles to my chair, and then he moves to Dreamer, instructing him to be still while he ties his ankles, too.

Then it's quiet.

"Dreamer, don't be scared, we're – "

A big, rough hand slaps the side of my face. "Shut up," the man says.

My face stings, and I obey. We sit there in silence for a while, and then I hear the door open and more voices fill the room.

"What's this?" A new voice asks.

"We were just going to grab the boy, but when we saw this little piece of eye candy, we thought she'd sweeten the deal."

A loud smack makes me jump in my seat. The new man must've hit the man who called me eye candy.

The new man yells at them. "Idiots! You were just supposed to grab Jacob's kid. Now we're going to have more people after us, and I've got to figure out where to put two bodies."

I feel Dreamer's back straighten in the chair behind me. I twist my hand around in the rope and poke it through the back of my chair. I find Dreamer's hand and squeeze it. He squeezes back.

*****

Kirk finally found Devin's number, his trembling fingers no help as he'd searched through Melissa's purse to find her phone and then through her phone contacts to find Devin's name.

The Diniyoli police were at the house just minutes after Kirk called them. They examined the broken door and the big, black number three spray-painted on the door. The sheriff mentioned tracking down Jacob's old boss from Tulsa. That might work, but Kirk knew who could solve this faster than anyone.

"Hello?"

"They took Melissa and Dreamer, Devin." Kirk is embarrassed at the obvious fear in his voice, but he can't help it. "I came home to a broken door with a three painted on it, and Melissa and Dreamer were gone."

"I'm on it."

The confidence in Devin's voice calms his fears, if only slightly.

"I know exactly who has them," She continues, "Jacob gave me a lot of information on his old boss, and the guy was arrested today. It had to have been his second-in-command who got Melissa and Dreamer. It's a message to Jacob, and this guy is telling everyone that he's in charge now." Her voice softens. "Don't worry, Kirk, and don't try to do anything. Just trust me and pray, okay?"

"Yeah." Kirk runs his hands through his hair, looks around the half-finished kitchen, and tries to stop imagining what could be happening to them right now. He shakes his head, as if to shake those thoughts out, and whispers a prayer as he pulls his phone out of his pocket and dials Ida's number.

*****

Trey's second-in-command is just another moron, like Dumb and Dumber, and countless other bad guys Devin's put behind bars – mean, violent, intimidating, but not much on brains, and not very creative. The new guy trying to take Trey's place is his brother-in-law, runs in all the same circles as Trey, frequents the same bars, pays the same thugs, uses the same hideouts, and lives in the same neighborhood. Shouldn't be too hard to find Melissa and Dreamer if she digs up information about Trey's old crimes. If Trey ever kidnapped anyone, then his brother-in-law is probably following the same plan.

Devin is seated at her metal desk, ready to pick up her laptop and throw it against the wall. The Wi-Fi isn't working right today, and she keeps having to re-start her search. She bangs the top of her desk in frustration.

"Got it," Devin's lieutenant comes to her desk with a

folder. "Four years ago, Trey was charged with kidnapping." Devin pulls her long, jet-black hair into a ponytail while she heads outside to her car. Her lieutenant keeps talking and follows her through the maze of desks and officers, out the side door to avoid the usual craziness at the front of the stationhouse. "The charges were dropped. A fourteen-year-old girl whose father worked for Trey was kidnapped. She was missing for two days. The first day, her family insisted that Trey was behind it. Second day, they changed their story. Said the kid ran away with a boyfriend. They even told the detectives the motel she was probably at. They found her at the motel, and the dad is still a member of Trey's gang."

"Trey was sending a message to her dad." Devin says as they take the concrete steps down to the parking lot two at a time.

"Yeah, and dad got the message loud and clear. Now this new boss wants to send Jacob a message."

They reach her car and climb in – Devin behind the wheel and her lieutenant in the passenger seat.

"Plug the motel address in the GPS." She starts the car. "How far away is it?"

"Fifteen minutes. I'll call for backup."

*****

The room's been quiet for a long time, and Dreamer takes a chance that they're gone. "Miss Melissa?" He whispers and tenses for a possible blow.

"Yeah, honey?"

Dreamer thanks God they're alone. "You scared?"

"Yeah." She squeezes his hand. "Are you?"

"Yeah."

Dreamer thinks about Grandma Ida and Whisper and Pastor Kirk and Miss Melissa's brother Michael, and he blinks back tears. Do they even know he and Miss Melissa have been taken?

"Dreamer, I bet we've been gone for four hours. It's probably late afternoon. Kirk must've come home by now and seen the front door kicked in. I'm sure he called the police, and they're working on it."

He tilts his head back until he feels the back of her head. He closes his eyes and imagines her face. Miss Melissa's eyebrows are probably scrunched together like they get when she's worried. He feels her shoulders go up and down in a deep breath.

"Can we pray?" He asks her.

"Of course, sweetie."

Miss Melissa prays aloud, and Dreamer whispers his prayer.

Before they finish praying, the door opens with a loud crash and a blast of cold air rushes into the room.

The five men are yelling at each other. Their insults and instructions to each other are peppered with expletives.

"Get everything out. Everything," the voice of the man in charge tells them.

"What about them?" another voice asks.

Dreamer hears another loud smack.

"Idiot. There's no way we can take them. Benny said the cops are on their way here now. We leave them."

A wave of relief sweeps over Dreamer. They're going to let them live.

"But they've seen our faces. They could identify us. We need to get rid of them."

Twelve years old. Dreamer always knew he would die young, probably because he was Jacob's son, but he thought he would at least make it to twenty.

I'll never see my dad again, he realizes.

I'll never see my new little sister and grandma again. I'll never play baseball again, he thinks. Dreamer can't see with the blindfold over his eyes, but he imagines his captors are readying their weapons.

Will it hurt?

He swallows down the hard knot of vomit rising in his throat, and twists his wrists in the ropes until he feels it rip his skin.

How will they kill me?

I will never leave you or forsake you.

The quiet voice is almost audible and is clearer to him than any other voice in the room, certainly clearer than his own thoughts. Dreamer knows who is with him. It doesn't make any sense, but the knot in his throat disappears and his breathing slows down.

"We're going to be okay." He squeezes her hand, and he doesn't care if they hear him. What can they do? Hit him? Kill him? It doesn't matter. God is with him.

*****

I want to believe Dreamer. I want to believe that we're going to be okay. I desperately want to believe that I'll see Kirk again. I'd lived for years thinking I knew love, but with Kirk I've learned what true love is. As bleak as our situation looks right now, I actually feel . . . grateful. *Thank you, Lord for letting me know true love. Even if I don't live much longer I'm thankful —*

"Get down!" My prayer is interrupted by one of the men yelling. "There's something going on outside."

The voice of the leader tells him, "Let me see." I hear movement across the room and the rustle of drapes. "Didn't take them long to find us."

"We know you guys are in there. We know you guys have the woman and Jacob's boy. Make this a lot easier on yourself and let them go now."

It's Devin's voice. It sounds like she's talking into a megaphone from outside. I'm so glad to hear her voice that I actually smile.

Our idiot captors argue about different ways they can escape from the room. They discuss escaping through the air

vents and come to the conclusion that they're all too fat for
that. One of them suggests cutting a hole through the back
wall, and the smacking sound that follows tells me his reward
for the suggestion was a backhand.

"It's over," the leader sounds frustrated, and the rest
of the guys are silent enough that I hear the beeping of a cell
phone. After a few phrases, I can tell he's talking to his
lawyer. He ends the call, then tells the others his plan.

Warm air rushes in. Someone must have opened the
door. The leader's voice is confident as he yells, "We're
sending them out. We put our weapons down. They aren't in
any danger."

Someone's rough fingers untie the rope around my
wrists. A moment later, I feel the ropes binding me to the
chair loosen. He grabs my shoulders, yanks me to my feet,
and pushes me toward the warm air. I take a few steps on
carpet, then I take a step on concrete. I feel the wind as soon
as I step outside.

I step forward tentatively, then, before I can remove
the blindfold, someone grabs me and pushes me inside a car.
I feel a rush of movement behind me and feel Dreamer
being pushed into the car with me.

I reach up and pull the blindfold off my head,
anxious to see my surroundings. The first thing I see is Kirk.

"Are you hurt?" he asks.

The sight of Kirk – the one who makes me laugh, the
one who understands me better than anyone else, the one
who holds my heart – after I thought I'd never see him
again, is just too much. A sob escapes, and I can't speak.

He puts his hands on my cheeks and puts his
forehead against mine.
He pulls me to him and kisses me, and I don't ever want him
to let me go.

We're tightly packed in the backseat of a police car
with Devin and Dreamer. Next to me, Devin has taken off
Dreamer's blindfold and is checking to make sure he's not

injured.

"Are you okay, bud?"

Dreamer nods, head up and down slowly and deliberately.

I sniff and wipe away my tears. "He was so brave. He was the one telling me we were going to be okay."

"I heard . . . something."

Devin, ever the detective, asks, "What did you hear?"

"God told me that He would never leave me or forsake me. When I heard that, I knew we'd be okay." Dreamer's dark eyes, somber and wide, communicate his sincerity.

Devin turns to me on her left, and then to Dreamer on her right, "I think He was with you guys today. He kept you safe."

I hug Devin, and for the first time my non-hugging friend hugs me back.

*****

There was no convincing my dad. He would not go home.

I tried explaining to him that Trey and all of his gang had been arrested, and that even if some of them were out, I wasn't the real target, anyway, Dreamer was. I was just in their way. Kirk told him that he would stay on the couch in my living room all night to stand guard, but I think that actually made my dad even more protective – even though I'm a grown woman, he still doesn't want the man I'm dating to spend the night at my house.

So, after hours of mom crying and hugging me, and Michael, Kirk, and Dad fixing a broken lock on one of my windows, replacing a burnt bulb in my back porch light, and installing a deadbolt lock on my front door, Mom and Micheal drove home to Cool Springs, but not dad. He's planted on my couch, and I'm not sure when he'll leave.

"Do you want another blanket?" I ask him.

"This one will do. It's thick." Dad tells me, as he stretches out on my couch and spreads the quilt over his body.

"Okay, I'm going to bed." I pause in the hallway. "Dad, you really don't have to stay. Devin assured me that I wasn't in any danger."

"When you have kids one day, you'll understand," he says as he closes his eyes.

He's probably right.

I hear my phone, and find it on the nightstand in my bedroom.

"Hey Kirk."

"Are you okay?"

I sigh. Between Kirk and my parents and Micheal, I've been asked that question about a thousand times today. I pull the covers back and slide into my bed.

"Yes. I'm fine. I've told you and everybody that. It was scary, but it was only a few hours, those guys are all behind bars now, and Dreamer and I are safe. Will you quit asking me that?"

"No."

"What?"

"No, I won't quit asking you if you're okay," he says stubbornly. "Every day for the rest of our lives I intend to make sure you're okay."

"Fine," I respond, irritated.

"Fine," he fires back.

We're silent for a few moments. It's late, I'm tired, but I don't want to go to sleep. I keep saying I'm fine, and I think I am, but I'm afraid of the possible nightmares if I go to sleep.

Somehow Kirk seems to read my thoughts. "Want to keep talking?" He asks.

"Yes . . . tell me a story."

He laughs. "Like a bedtime story?"

"No, a Kirk-story, you know, one of the stories you're always entertaining people with."

I hear the smile in his voice. "Okay, let's see. What do you want to hear? The story of when I dove headfirst into a cellar? How about when I ran the wrong way in a football game?"

"Tell me about your first kiss."

He groans. "That's not a good story."

"Come on. Tell me." I insist.

"All right, but just because you were kidnapped today."

"Oooo . . . I've got something I can use as leverage now, don't I?" I lay my head on my pillow and pull the blanket up to my chin.

"Great," Kirk mutters. "She's going to get everything she wants from now on."

"Spill it."

"I was five years old," he begins.

"Five?" I interrupt. "Man, you started early."

"Hush, let me finish," he says. "I was playing in the backyard by myself, swinging on a swingset. The little girl who lived next door came outside. She walked to her side of the chain-link fence, and we started talking. I jumped off the swing and walked over to the fence. She asked me if I would kiss her, and I said, 'Sure,' so I met her at the fence and poked my lips through, and so did she."

"Aw, that's so cute. I can see little Kirk kissing the neighbor girl through the chain link fence." I say. "Tell me another story."

"How about the story of the time I almost lost a kid when I was a youth pastor?" He asks.

"I've heard that one." I pause. I know what I want him to talk about, maybe after what we've been through today he'll be more willing to share about his past. "Tell me about your parents, Kirk."

He's quiet for a little bit, and I'm afraid I've pushed

too far, but then he begins. "I don't have any memories of a father . . . only a mother. She gave up her parental rights when I was three years old. I have a few memories, but they're so faint, just images really . . . I remember long brown hair, like a curtain down her back. I remember sitting next to her outside on a concrete step. We were eating orange popsicles. I remember lying next to her in the bed, watching cartoons. That's about all I remember."

My heart aches for him. I can't comprehend the pain he's felt over the years from his mother's absence. "Did you ever hear from her?"

"She sent me a few birthday cards through the years, but that's it. I was told later that she went to prison for a while." He's quiet for a few moments, and I don't know what to say. "I kept her cards though."

"Have you ever thought about contacting her?" I ask him.

"I used to think about it. Maybe I will . . . one of these days. I'd like to make sure she's been told about the Lord." He says.

I shake my head. I don't know if I'll ever get used to his constant concern for people's souls. It's always the first thing he thinks about. I've never known anyone like Kirk Chaney.

*****

Valentine's Day fever is rampant at Diniyoli Elementary School. The student council is selling buttons, and the kids proudly pin the pink and red buttons they get from their friends or their sweetheart on their clothes all week. I buy Dreamer and Whisper buttons, and write "From your secret admirer" on the attached cards. Dreamer's has a baseball on it and says, "You're an All-Star," and Whisper's has a kitten on it and says, "You're a Cutie."

I devote our lessons to the holiday – I give them each a piece of Valentine candy, and they write a descriptive paragraph about the candy using all five senses, they do a math page that has a puzzle on it with the numbers representing letters that spell out the phrase, "Someone Loves You," and we make Valentine card bags so they can collect their cards at our afternoon party.

At lunchtime, I'm sitting at my desk, eating yogurt, and my dad gives me a call.

"Happy Valentine's Day to my sweetheart."

"Happy Valentine's Day to you to, Dad. What's going on?"

"Just wanted to hear your voice. Are you having a good day?"

In the ten days since the kidnapping Dad's called me every day, just to hear my voice.

I tell him a couple of stories of my second graders and ask him if he got mom anything for Valentine's Day. He tells me that he got her a basket of different kinds of tea with a teacup and a couple of new books in it. A reader like me, mom will love the gift. He tells me about Michael's new love interest, a girl at school that he's bringing over to the house tonight for Mom and him to meet. I tell him a little about how well the mission is doing and about the new nurse's station.

"Yeah, Kirk told me that it should be ready next week. That's great. It'll be a blessing to the people of Diniyoli," he says.

"Yes, it's almost finished." Then I realize what he said. "Wait a minute. When did you talk to Kirk?"

"Oh . . . ah, today."

"You talked to Kirk today? You two talk?" Kirk and my dad talk?

"Oh, yeah, he had to come to town to get some supplies for something he's working on." Dad says quickly.

"He had to go to Cool Springs to get supplies?" That sounds odd.

"Yeah, he just swung by the house and talked to us

for a few minutes while he was here. He, ah, had to ask us something." Dad clears his throat. "Well, love you babe, I'd better get going. I need to get out of work early to take your mom to dinner tonight, so I'd better get busy."

I tell my dad that I love him and put my phone down on my desk. I imagine Kirk stopping by my parents' house in Cool Springs and shake my head at the strange picture.

Love is certainly in the air all over Diniyoli Elementary. Jarrett concocted a Valentine's Day plan for Chelsea, and got me in on it.

"Did you write the note?" He asked me on the phone last night.

"Yes, I've got it, and I'll put it on her desk when she leaves the room to check her box in the teacher's lounge after school." I told him.

"How do you know she'll check her box?"

"Don't worry. I'll give her a reason to, if she doesn't." I reassured him.

"Okay, so right after school you're going to leave your classroom to put the note on her desk."

"Yes, it'll be fine, Jarrett."

At two-thirty we put away our books and clean up our desks. Then, a couple of my students' moms serve snacks and supervise the Valentine card delivery and play games with the kids. When the bell rings at three, I'm considering taking a sick day tomorrow – not because I'm sick, but because I'm exhausted.

I only missed two days of school after the kidnapping, and my parents and Kirk keep telling me that I need to take more time off. Even Mr. Clemmons has said that I need to take more time off. At first I thought I could make it another month till spring break, but I think everyone's right. I need a couple more days to feel normal again . . . honestly, though, I don't know if I'll ever feel normal again.

I get tomorrow's lesson plans out of my planbook,

and head to the office to make copies for a substitute tomorrow. I get halfway down the hallway when it hits me – I forgot to get Chelsea out of her classroom and put Jarrett's note on her desk.

I run back to my classroom, and get the note out of my purse. Across the hallway in Chelsea's classroom, she's straightening desks.

"Hey, did you have a good day?" I ask, out of breath.

"Yeah, our party was good. I had a mom bring a cookie cake – yum."

"Yum – we had cupcakes." I do some quick thinking to get her out of the room. "Did you see the memo Mr. Clemmons put in our boxes?"

"No. What was it about?"

Ugh, now I have to think of something. "Um, I think it may have been about new procedures for recording absences."

"Really? We're changing that this late in the year?"

Rats. I should've come up with something better. Before I can think of something else to say, she changes the subject.

"Come look at this." She points to the bulletin board next to her desk.

Next time Jarrett needs to recruit someone who's better at subterfuge. I'm not doing a very good job getting her out of the room to put the note on her desk. The note has an address written on it with driving directions and instructions for her to go to that address as soon as she leaves. It's a spa in Clinton. Jarrett has an appointment for her to get a massage at four-thirty, and then he'll meet her there to take her to dinner.

"You know Evan? He made this for me. Isn't it the sweetest thing?" She shows me a portrait of herself illustrated with crayons hanging on the bulletin board next to her desk. It has a caption above it that reads – "Happy Valentimes Day to Miss Chelsea My Favorite Teacher."

"So sweet." I have got to get her out of this room.

"Would you mind to check my box when you go? I need to get my room ready for a sub tomorrow."

"Sure, I can do that." But she doesn't leave. She leans against her desk and keeps talking, "I love it when kids say 'Valentimes.' It's so cute, I almost don't want to correct them. Do you have any plans for tonight?"

Oh my goodness. What's it going to take to get this girl out of her classroom?

"I'm doing something with Kirk."

Chelsea says, "Mmm . . . I'm sure Kirk has something good planned."

Something about her tone strikes me as curious, but I've still got to get her out of here so I can place this note. I affect a nonchalant tone. "Well, I guess I'd better go get my room ready for tomorrow, and you'd better go check that box." I turn to head to the hallway. Maybe she'll follow me.

She grabs my sleeve before I can fully turn around. "Hang on a minute, Melissa."

I look down at my short, blonde friend and notice panic in her eyes. Something clicks in my brain. She's keeping me in here.

"Chelsea?"

She presses her lips together and then whispers to me. "Just stay in here for one more minute."

"What?"

"Don't ask. Just wait a few more seconds."

"Chelsea? What's going on?"

She looks over my shoulder at something behind me. "Okay, you can go work on your classroom now."

Chelsea looks like a mischievous pixie with a sneaky grin and her heart-shaped face cocked to the side and a hand on her hip.

"You little trickster. You knew what I was doing the whole time."

She laughs and holds her hand out to me. "Just give me Jarrett's note. I do need the address to the spa."

Dumbfounded, I hand it to her. Then I turn to walk across the hall to my classroom. My classroom door is closed, and I know I didn't shut it behind me.

"Go on, Melissa."

I nod without looking back at her.

I open the door. The first thing I notice is that the overhead lights are off, and I hear soft music playing from somewhere. Then I see it. The reading corner. There are about a dozen lit candles encircling it, and Kirk is standing in the middle of the bean bags, under the sheer green and yellow colored fabric, standing on the tan rug. He smiles when I look at him.

"Hi Melissa."

I walk to him. "What's going on?" I have an idea, and my heart starts racing.

He takes both of my hands and laces his fingers through them. "Melissa, I don't know how all of this happened. I didn't expect to fall completely in love with a girl from Cool Springs who drove here to tour the mission, and I know you're a blessing from God, because there's no way I deserve someone as kind and smart and hard-working and gorgeous as you." As I realize what's transpiring, my eyes fill with tears. I think about the cute missionary on that hot summer day playing in the water with the kids. Was that when I fell in love with him?

"When I made this reading corner for your classroom months ago, I never dreamed that I'd be doing what I'm about to do in it."

He lets go of my hands and puts a hand in his pocket to take out a ring. He kneels on one knee on the rug and with a shaky hand he holds the ring out to me.

"Melissa, I'm more nervous right now than I've ever been in my life." He takes a deep breath. "I want to spend the rest of my life with you. I want to share a life together. Whether we live in the big, old white house in Diniyoli, or a hut in Africa, or a mansion in a suburb, I want to be there with you. I want to take care of you when you're sick. I want to provide for you financially. I want to share a bed with you every night, and a bathroom sink with you every morning."

I laugh at that, and his eyes shine with tears.

"Melissa, will you marry me?"

*****

The steam rises from my mug of morning coffee as I set it on the small metal table. Forecasters are saying today will be a beautiful day to spend outside, and I agree with them. I lightly push the floor of the porch with my toe and make our new porch swing sway. I look down the long, wide porch and admire my potted flowers spilling out of their pots with shades of pink, white, and yellow. I examine my paint job on the new front door, and I know that I was right to choose red, even though Kirk wanted to paint it black.

I whisper a prayer of praise to the Lord for all of the beautiful things in my life – for a job and a ministry I love, for fun and supportive friends like Devin, Chelsea, Tess, and Janice, for a family who's seen me through it all, and for a husband who fills my days with surprises.

I stand and stretch and look to the sky, taking in the view of the white, puffy clouds against the bright blue backdrop. One of the clouds has three skinny parts that stick straight up, like a trio of glass bottles shaped into a pyramid, stacked and ready to be a target for a pitcher. Another cloud is flat and long with a row of rounded dots bulging up, like a line of buffalo following each other. High above the others is a cloud that has a series of peaks, like a range of sierras watching over all the others. The biggest cloud in the middle of the sky is tall and thin with wispy pieces sticking up and out of the top, like a bride wearing a halo of flowers around her head as she walks through a field of flowers to meet the man of her dreams under the big Oklahoma sky.

Other titles by Martha Fouts:

Does it feel like your life is a chaotic roller coaster of emotions? Maybe you've got too much drama in your life. A drama-free life? Doesn't that sound awesome?

It's God's desire for you to break free from the exhausting drama-filled life and find the peaceful, abundant life He has prepared for you.

This study focuses on the example of Mary the Mother of Jesus, and teaches ten steps you can take to face the trials of life without being overcome by drama.

This book is part workbook, part girl-talk, and part devotional. It's great for small group Bible studies, Sunday School classes, or personal study.

This book is available in e-book and paperback.

54043047R00166

Made in the USA
Charleston, SC
23 March 2016